Corsair

℃

TIM SEVERIN, explorer, film-maker and lecturer, has made many
expeditions, from his crossing of the Atlantic in a medieval leather
boat in *The Brendan Voyage* to, most recently, *In Search of Moby
Dick* and *Seeking Robinson Crusoe*. In writing *Corsair* he has drawn
upon his unique experience as captain of a twenty-oared galley
following the 1,500-mile route of Jason and the Argonauts. He
has won the Thomas Cook Travel Book Award, the Book of
the Sea Award, a Christopher Prize and the literary medal of the
Académie de la Marine. He made his historical fiction debut with
the hugely successful Viking series. *Corsair* is his first Hector Lynch
novel.

Also by Tim Severin

NON-FICTION

The Brendan Voyage
The Sindbad Voyage
The Jason Voyage
The Ulysses Voyage
Crusader
In Search of Genghis Khan
The China Voyage
The Spice Island Voyage
In Search of Moby Dick
Seeking Robinsoe Crusoe

FICTION

VIKING: Odinn's Child
VIKING: Sworn Brother
VIKING: King's Man

TIM SEVERIN

Corsair

PAN BOOKS

First published 2007 by Macmillan

This edition first published 2008 by Pan Books
an imprint of Pan Macmillan Ltd
Pan Macmillan, 20 New Wharf Road, London N1 9RR
Basingstoke and Oxford
Associated companies throughout the world
www.panmacmillan.com

ISBN 978-0-330-44313-5

3 5 7 9 8 6 4 2

A CIP catalogue record for this book is available from
the British Library.

Typeset by SetSystems Ltd, Saffron Walden, Essex
Printed and bound in Great Britain by
Mackays of Chatham plc, Chatham, Kent

Visit *www.panmacmillan.com* to read more about all our books
and to buy them. You will also find features, author interviews and
news of any author events, and you can sign up for e-newsletters
so that you're always first to hear about our new releases.

Corsair

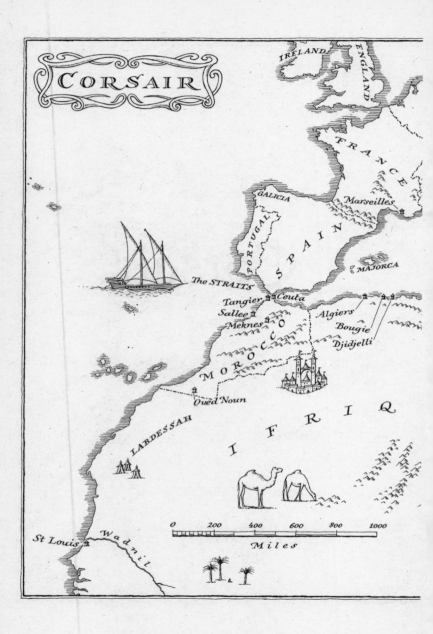

CORSAIR

IRELAND
ENGLAND
FRANCE
GALICIA
Marseilles
PORTUGAL
SPAIN
MAJORCA
The STRAITS
Tangier — Ceuta
Sallee
Meknes — Algiers
Bougie
MOROCCO
Djidjelli
Oued Noun
IFRIQ
LABDESSAH
St Louis — Wadnil

0   200   400   600   800   1000
Miles

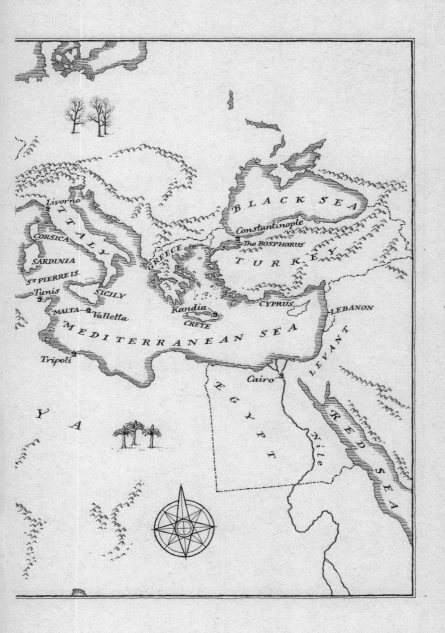

ONE

C

THEY ARRIVED an hour before daybreak, forty men in two boats, cotton rags tied around the shafts to muffle the creak of the oars, and the rowers dipping their blades neatly into the sleek blackness of the sea. The boats were of local design, stolen from a fishing port a week earlier, and if a coast watcher had spotted their approach, the sentinel might have mistaken them for fishermen coming home early from the night's work. Certainly the raiders were confident that their mother ships had been invisible from the cliff tops for they had waited patiently over the horizon, hovering with sails lowered until they had the conditions they wanted: a calm sea and a thin veil of cloud to diffuse the starlight. There was no moon.

The oarsmen eased stroke as the two boats glided into the small cove. They heard the muted surge and backwash of small waves lapping the shingle, then quiet splashes as the bow men jumped out and held the boats steady while the raiders stepped knee-deep into the shallows. The water was warm for this time of year, yet it was far colder than the seas to which they were accustomed. Many of the raiders were barefoot, and as they began their march inland, the callused soles of their feet felt the change from smooth beach pebbles to tussocky grass, then the soft squelch of a boggy stream bed. A smell of rotting vegetable matter came up on the humid summer air. Ahead of them, a nesting marsh bird burst out of the reeds and flew away with a sudden clatter of wings.

Ten minutes of easy climbing along the stream bed brought them to the watershed. From a patch of level ground, they looked down the far slope at their goal. The village was less than half a mile away, a low cluster of dark roofs etched against the broad glimmer of the great bay which thrust far into the contorted and rocky coastline, providing a vast but empty anchorage. There was not a light to be seen, and still there were no warning shouts.

C

THE RAIDERS descended the slope, moving faster now, and were at the outskirts of the village before the first dog barked. 'Who's there?' called a woman's voice from one of the turf-roofed cabins. She spoke in the soft fluid tones of the local speech. 'Go back to sleep, woman,' one of the raiders replied in her own language. There was a short pause as the men stopped and listened. The silence returned, except for the muted growling of the suspicious dog. The intruders moved forward quietly, spreading along the single main street.

At the very centre of the village, in one of the few stone-built houses, Hector Lynch opened his eyes. He lay in the pitch darkness, wondering what had woken him. On calm nights it was sometimes so silent that you could hear the distant boom of waves breaking on the rocks in the aftermath of a heavy swell as the Atlantic gnawed steadily at the granite coast. But this night there was something melancholy and stifling about the lack of sound. It was as if the village had been smothered in its sleep, and was dead. For almost as long as Hector could remember, he and his sister, Elizabeth, had been coming here each summer to study at the Franciscan friary on the island at the harbour mouth. Their mother insisted that he and Elizabeth, his junior by two years, learn Latin and the tenets of her own

Catholic faith from the Grey Friars. Her family were Spanish, shipowners from Galicia, and for generations they had engaged in the wine trade with this remote corner of south-west Ireland where she had met and married her husband. He was of minor Protestant gentry impoverished in the recent civil war and more interested that his children learn practical and domestic skills to help them prosper in the Protestant hierarchy which now ruled the land. The mixed ancestry of their children showed in the sallow skins, dark eyes and jet-black hair which Hector and Elizabeth had inherited from their mother – at fifteen the girl was on the cusp of becoming a real beauty – and in their fluency of languages. They used English when speaking to their father, Spanish with a Galician accent when alone with their mother, and Irish among their summer playmates from the poorer fishing families.

Hector turned on his side and tried to go back to sleep. He hoped that this was the last summer that he and Elizabeth would spend in this isolated backwater. In January their father had died, and after his funeral their mother had hinted to her in-laws that she was thinking of returning to Spain, taking her children with her. Hector had never visited Spain – indeed he had never been farther than the city of Cork – and he had a seventeen-year-old's longing to see more of the world. He nursed a secret and romantic belief that his own name, Lynch, was an omen because the Irish version, O'Loinsigh, meant 'seafarer' or 'wanderer'.

He was thinking about the possibility of a trip to Spain, and what it would be like, when he heard the first pistol shot.

It was the signal for the raiders to begin breaking down doors and wrenching open shutters. Now they made as much noise and racket as possible. They yelled and whooped, banged cudgels against doorposts, kicked over stacks of farm tools. In response every dog in the village began to bark furiously and somewhere a donkey brayed in panic. Inside the cabins the occupants were stupefied by the sudden din. Many slept on beds that were little more than piles of dried bracken covered with blankets on the beaten earth floor, and they were still getting to their feet groggily when the intruders burst in among them. Children clung to their mothers, babies began to wail, and the adults were disoriented and dazed as the raiders began to herd them out of doors. Those who resisted did so from confusion and weariness rather than a sense of defiance. A slap across the face or a well-aimed kick in the backside quickly changed their minds, and they stumbled out to join their neighbours in the street.

The first flush of dawn gave sufficient light for the raiders to make their selection. They spurned those who were bent with age and hard labour or obviously misshapen. A young man with a badly twisted leg was rejected, so too was a halfwit who stood helplessly, his head turning from side to side as he tried to understand the mayhem that surrounded him. Infants were also discarded. One raider casually pulled a baby of less than six months from the mother's arms, and handed the child to the nearest crone as if it was an unwanted parcel. The mother he pushed into the chosen group of able-bodied men, women and their children who had to appear at least five years old if they were to qualify.

But not everyone was caught. There was a flurry as a figure was spotted running away down the road that led inland. A shouted order, and the two raiders who had set off after the fugitive turned back to rejoin their companions. The running man was on his way to fetch help, to alert the local militia, but the invaders knew the village was too isolated for assistance to arrive in time. So they continued their selection with calm efficiency.

Hector scrambled out from his bed and was still pulling on his breeches when the door to his room slammed open. Someone in the passageway held up a lantern so that the light shone full on him. Behind the light he made out the shapes of three men who thrust their way into the room. He caught a brief glimpse of a mustached face as heavily muscled arms reached out towards him. He twisted to one side, trying to evade the grasping hands, but blundered into another man who had circled around behind him. Someone clasped him around his waist, and his nostrils were filled with the smell of sweat and some sort of exotic scent. Hector thrashed urgently from side to side, trying to break free. Then he jerked his head backward, as he'd done when tussling with friends in boyhood games, but viciously this time. He felt a satisfying thump as his skull struck his attacker full in the face. There was a grunt of pain, and the grip relaxed enough for him to twist free. He made a dash for the door, but one of the other men stepped across to block his escape. Once again he was held, this time with a stranglehold around his neck. Choking, he drove his elbow into his assailant's ribs, only to have a hand clamped over his mouth. He bit down fiercely. He heard someone swear, and a growled comment. He realised that the men trying to pin him down were unwilling to harm him, and this gave him hope. There was the bite of cord as someone tried to lash his wrists together, and again he foiled them, slipping his hand away from the loop. He made another dash for the door, only to be tripped this time and he fell sprawling, crashing painfully against the wall. As he tried to get back on his feet, he looked up and saw that the man with the lantern had been standing apart from the fray, holding up the light so that his companions could do their work. At last Hector could get a clear view of his attackers. They were swarthy-skinned and dressed in baggy pantaloons and workaday seamen's coats. The man with the lantern had a long cloth, patterned with red and white checks, wrapped several times around his head. Hector blinked in amazement. It was the first time that he had seen a turban.

A moment later a fourth man walked confidently through the doorway. He was dressed like the others, only more richly, with a brocaded waistcoat over his loose shirt, and his red and blue turban was even bulkier and made of fine cloth. He was a much older man, his white beard neatly trimmed, and he seemed unperturbed by the commotion. In his hand he held a pistol. For a moment Hector thought that he would be shot for resisting so fiercely. But the newcomer only walked across to where Hector was now half-kneeling and, neatly reversing the pistol, brought the butt down on the young man's head.

Just before the crash of pain and the black oblivion that followed, Hector heard the sound that was to haunt him for months to come: the frantic, repeated screams of his sister Elizabeth, calling for his help.

TWO

C

THE HARSH RASP of timber against his cheek brought him back
to his senses. He was propped against some sort of wooden wall,
lying awkwardly, and his face had scraped against the planking
as he slid downwards. A painful lump on his head throbbed,
and his skin was cold and clammy. Worse, it felt as if he was
spinning helplessly in a black void that constantly expanded and
contracted with each beat of his heart. Nauseous, Hector kept
his eyes closed and, from deep down in his stomach, he retched.
He was miserably aware that the real world around him was
swaying and lurching, while close beside his ear was the gurgle
and swirl of moving water.

Hector had only ever been to sea in small fishing boats and
when it was calm so he had never experienced the torment of
acute seasickness. Thus it was several hours before he felt well
enough to take stock of his surroundings. He was in the bowels
of a ship. That much was clear. There was the fetid stench of
bilge water, the discordant creaks and groans of wood on wood,
and the sound of moving water as waves washed against the
hull. The stomach-churning pitch and sway of the vessel was
exaggerated by the fact that barely any light penetrated into the
hold of the vessel. He presumed that it was day time but
whether it was morning or afternoon, or how long he had been

unconscious, he had no idea. Not since he had fallen out of a tree as a boy and landed on his head, had he felt so bruised and battered. He reached up tentatively to touch the lump on his scalp, only to find that his wrists were shackled with iron manacles from which a thick tarred rope led to a ring bolt set in a cross beam. He was tethered in place.

'That's to stop you making trouble or jumping overboard,' said a sly voice close by. Startled, Hector turned to see an old man crouched beside him. He was dirty and balding, and his face with its sunken cheeks and sickly blotched skin wore a pleased expression. Hector concluded that his observer was enjoying the sight of his sufferings. 'Where am I? How long have I been here?' he asked. The residue of vomit in his throat tasted sour. The man cackled and did not reply but scuttled away and laid himself down on the deck boards with exaggerated care, his face turned away from Hector.

Left without an answer Hector carried on taking stock of his surroundings. The hold was some five paces wide and ten paces long, and there was scarcely enough height for an ordinary-sized man to stand upright. In that airless space some thirty people were sitting despondently or slumped on the floorboards. A few had pulled old cargo sacks over themselves as blankets. Others were curled up with their heads buried in their arms. Hector recognised several villagers: the gangling figure of the carpenter and, seated just beside him, a brawny young labourer whom he had sometimes seen setting off from the village to cut peat on the hillside with his slean – a thin bladed spade – on his shoulder. Two men, clearly brothers, were the same fishermen who took it in turn to ferry visitors across to the island friary, and the older man with the gash on his jaw – where someone must have struck him with a club – was the cooper who made the barrels in which the villagers salted down their winter supply of pilchards. They were all still wearing the ragbag of clothes they had put on when they were snatched from their homes, and they looked broken and forlorn. There were also half a dozen children. One of them, perhaps six or seven years old, was whimpering with fear and exhaustion.

But the villagers were not the only occupants of the hold. There were several strangers. In addition to the bedraggled elderly lunatic who had accosted him, there was a small group of men who looked like seamen, and sitting by himself in one corner was a portly man wearing a wig. Judging by his expensive but soiled clothing, he must be a merchant or prosperous shopkeeper. How they all came to be thrown together in these strange and dismal surroundings was something that Hector could not comprehend.

Then, abruptly, he recalled his sister's despairing wail for help and, looking round the hold again, noted that there were no women in the group.

There was the thump of a hammer blow. It came from directly above, the sound magnified in the hollow space. Then a shaft of light struck down into the gloom. Hector squinted upward to where a hatch was being opened. A pair of bare feet and shins appeared as a sailor came down the ladder leading into the hold. The man was dressed in the same garb as those who had attacked him. A sailor's knife dangled from a lanyard around his neck, and he was swarthy and heavily bearded. He carried a large wicker basket which he set down on the floor. Without a word he climbed back up the ladder and closed the hatch. A moment later Hector heard the sound of wedges being driven home. Several of the men who looked like seafarers immediately made their way to the base of the ladder, and began to rummage in the basket.

Hector's tether had been left long enough for him to join them, and he found they were pulling out sheets of thin flat bread which they ripped to pieces and shared out amongst themselves. Beside the basket stood a small tub of water with a wooden scoop. Hector took a sip, spat to wash his mouth out, and then drank deeply. He broke off a piece of the bread and tasted it. It was slightly gritty but wholesome. In the basket were also small fruits which he recognised as a delicacy his mother had occasionally received from her family in Spain. He bit into one and spat out the stone, an olive. Picking out half a dozen of them and another chunk of bread, he retreated to his place by the hull and began to eat, feeling better with every mouthful. Now he realised that he was the only person who had been manacled and tethered. Everyone else in the hold was free to move about.

While his fellow captives fed, Hector picked steadily at the knot in the rope that bound him to the ring bolt. It was some sort of complicated seaman's knot but eventually he managed to work it loose. Holding the tether in a loop so it did not trip him, Hector moved across to talk to the villagers. He was feeling a little awkward. Though he had spent his summers among them, he did not know any of the older men very well. The difference in their backgrounds was too great; the son of a gentleman, however impoverished, had little in common with peasant labourers and fishermen. 'Has anyone seen my sister Elizabeth?' he asked, embarrassed to pose such a question when he knew that each one of the men must have his own immediate troubles. No one answered. He knelt beside the cooper, who had always seemed a sober and level-headed family man, and repeated his question. He noticed that the cooper had been crying. There were streaks where the tears had run down his face and mingled with blood that leaked from the gash in his chin. 'What happened? Where's my sister Elizabeth?' he repeated. The cooper seemed not to understand his question, for he only mumbled: 'God has made a second Taking. To Israel he promised a return from the captivity, yet we are twice punished and left in darkness.'

The man was a devout churchgoer, Hector recalled. Like all of the tradesmen, the cooper was a Protestant and regularly worshipped in the village chapel. It was the poorer sort – the fishermen and the landless peasants – who were Catholic, and they crossed to the island each Sunday to attend Mass with the friars. Hector, with his Protestant father and his Catholic mother, had never given much thought to this arrangement. He had little or no interest in religion, and veered as easily between one faith and the other as switching languages when speaking to his parents. He dimly remembered people talking about 'the Taking', but usually in hushed tones and he had never enquired further, believing it to be none of his business.

Deciding that he would have to take matters into his own hands if he was to find out what was happening, he rose to his feet and walked across to the ladder leading to the hatch. Climbing up, he started to beat rhythmically on the underside of the timber with his wrist fetters. Within moments he heard an angry shout and then the sound of running feet. Once again the hatch was opened, but only a crack, and for a brief instant he caught a glimpse of blue sky with white puffs of cloud before the end of a broad-bladed sword was thrust down to within a few inches of his face. He stood stock-still so as not to provoke the swordsman any further, then slowly tilted back his head so that he could look up and said carefully, first in English and then in Spanish, 'Please can I speak with the captain?' He was gazing past the blade and into the face of the same sailor who had brought the basket of bread. The sailor stared at him for a moment, then called out in a language Hector did not understand. Hector heard a murmured exchange and the hatch was opened wider and a second man, presumably a petty officer, was gesturing for him to climb up.

Clumsy in his manacles and with his tether still looped in his hand, Hector scrambled out of the hatch. After the stuffy darkness of the hold the world was full of light and sunshine, and he breathed deeply, glad to fill his lungs with fresh sea air and feel the breeze against his skin. He was standing on the deck of a fair-sized vessel, and though he was no sailor he could appreciate that the ship was making rapid progress over a sea of such vibrant blue that it almost hurt his eyes. When the vessel heeled slightly to a puff of wind he lost his balance and, recovering, glanced over the ship's side. There, a musket shot away, a second ship was running swiftly on a parallel course, keeping pace with them. From the tip of each of her two masts streamed out long pennants, blood-red in colour, and at her stern flew a large green flag decorated with three silver crescent moons. The petty officer, a short and muscular man, was balancing easily on the sloping deck and waiting for him to speak. 'Please,' Hector said, 'I wish to talk with your captain.' The man's dark brown eyes looked him over. Surprisingly the examination was not hostile, merely professional. Then, reaching forward to take hold of the young man's tether, he led him like a cow to its byre as he strolled towards the stern of the vessel. There, under an awning, Hector saw the same white-bearded man who had struck him down so expertly with the pistol butt. Hector judged him to be in his late fifties, perhaps older, yet he looked trim and fit, and radiated authority. He was comfortably seated on cushions, a dish of fruit lay beside him, and he was exploring his mouth with a silver toothpick. Gravely he watched Hector and his escort approach and listened to what the petty officer had to report. Then, laying aside the toothpick, he said, 'You have courage, young man. You put up a good fight, and now you do not fear what my men might do to you if you anger them.'

'If it pleases your honour . . .' began Hector, and then stopped abruptly. His mouth fell open. He had been about to ask what had happened to Elizabeth, and it had taken several seconds for him to realise that the ship captain had spoken in English. For a moment he thought he had misheard or was imagining. But no, the captain went on in English that was accurate, if a little hesitant, as though he was occasionally searching for the correct phrase. 'Tell me, what were you doing in the village?'

Hector was so astonished that he could barely get his own words out. 'I was a student with the friars on the island. With my sister. How is it . . . ?' he faltered.

'How is it that I speak your language?' the captain finished the question for him. 'Because I am originally from that village myself. Now I am called Hakim Reis, but once I was known as Tom Pierse. Though that is a long time ago now, more than fifty years. God has been kind to me.'

Hector's mind was in turmoil. He could not imagine how this exotic mariner with his foreign dress and outlandish manner could claim to have come from a poor village on Ireland's Atlantic coast. Yet the captain spoke English with the distinctive lilt of the region.

Hakim Reis saw his puzzlement.

'I was just seven years old when I was taken. So too were my mother and father, two brothers and my grandmother. I never saw them again after we were landed,' he said. 'At the time I thought it was the greatest tragedy. Now I know it was God's will and I thank him for it.' He reached down and took a fruit, chewed on it, and then placed the stone back in the dish.

'So I was curious to see what the place is like now. That is why I decided to pay a brief call, and what point would there be in a visit if I did not make a profit from it? I must admit that it is not as I remember, though of course I still knew the hidden landing place and how to approach without being seen. The village is smaller now, or maybe that is how it always seems when one revisits a childhood haunt. Everything has shrunk.'

By now Hector had recovered enough from his surprise to repeat the vital question that was preying on his mind.

'Please,' he tried again, 'I would like to know what has happened to my sister. Her name is Elizabeth.'

'Ah, the good-looking girl who was in the house where we found you. She clawed my men like a wild cat. Such ferocity must be a family trait. She came to no harm, and is safe.'

'Where is she now? Can I see her?'

Hakim Reis wiped his fingers on a napkin. 'No. That is not possible. We always keep the men and women apart. Your sister is aboard the other vessel.'

'When will I see her again?'

'That is in God's hands. We are homeward bound, but at sea one never knows.'

'Then where are you taking us?'

The captain looked mildly surprised. 'I would have thought you would have been informed. Did not the older villagers tell you? There must be some who remembered the last time it happened. But of course they are of a different generation, or perhaps those who were left behind chose to forget.'

'One of the men in the hold spoke to me of "the Taking",' Hector said.

'So that is what they call it. Not a bad name. It was Murat Reis who commanded at the time, a great captain, and his memory is still revered. Foreign-born like myself, a Flamand by origin. Mind you, he did not have my local knowledge and so he was obliged to use a Dungarvan man as his pilot to guide him in.'

Hector recalled that no villager ever mentioned the name of Dungarvan town without spitting, and also some talk of a Dungarvan man being hanged as a traitor. The foreign captain was growing nostalgic. 'When I was a boy I can remember my father forbidding my brothers and me from playing with the dirty children, as they called them. We were told that we would catch foul diseases if we did. He meant the Catholics, of course. In those days the village was remarkable for being home to so many Protestants. Tell me, is that still the case?'

'I believe so, sir. There is a new landlord now, and he has enlarged the chapel. He strongly favours those of the Protestant faith. The Catholics must go for Mass to the friars on the island, and they try to do so without attracting attention.'

'How little changes. The more I hear about the quarrels and rivalries between the Christians, the happier I am that I took the turban.' Noticing Hector's puzzlement, he added, 'Some call it "turning Turk".'

Hector still looked blank.

'I converted to the True Faith preached by the prophet Muhammad, may he be honoured and glorified. It was not such a difficult decision for someone whose memories of home were only of cold and damp, and a place where everyone had to work like a drudge to pay rent to a distant landlord. Of course I did not convert at once, but after serving the man who bought me. He was a kind master.'

At last Hector understood. Maybe the shock of his capture combined with the blow to his head and his fears for Elizabeth had obscured what was now obvious: Hakim Reis was a corsair. He must come from one of the pirate states of Barbary on the coast of North Africa whose ships plagued the Mediterranean and the Atlantic approaches. They intercepted and robbed ships and carried off their crews into slavery. From time to time they also made slave-taking shore raids. Hector wondered how he could have been so slow on the uptake. One evening, several years ago, his father had entertained a local celebrity, the vicar of nearby Mitchelstown, who was renowned for having been held as a slave of the corsairs. Eventually the vicar had been ransomed, and he was much in demand at dinner parties when he would recount his experiences. Hector had been allowed to stay and listen, and he recalled a tall, rather haggard man with a husky voice describing the conditions in the slave pens. Hector struggled to remember his name. There was a joke to it, someone had raised a laugh by referring to a fish being caught by the bay. That was it, the reverend's name was Devereux Spratt, and he was the captive of a foreign potentate called the Bey. Unfortunately the reverend had rather spoilt the pun by announcing primly that the jokester was confused in his geography of the Barbary states. The Bey was the title of the ruler of the state of Tunis, while he had been a prisoner of the ruler of Algiers whose title was Dey.

'I beg you in the name of your Muhammad,' Hector pleaded, 'that when we reach our destination, you will let me speak with my sister.'

'We will be at sea for at least another week.' Hakim Reis gave Hector a shrewd glance, and Hector noticed that the corsair's eyes were pale grey in contrast to the deep tan of his face. 'Will you give me your word that you will make no trouble during that time, now you know that there is a chance you can speak to her?' Hector nodded. 'Good, I will order those fetters to be removed. And do not look so glum. Maybe your life will be blessed, as mine was, and you will rise to command a fine ship. Besides, you will sell for a higher price if you have a happier face.' And to Hector's astonishment he held up the plate of fruit and said, 'Here, take a handful with you. They will remind you that life can be as sweet as you wish to make it.'

The captain spoke briefly to the petty officer, who produced a key and unlocked the manacles. Then he escorted Hector back to the hatchway and he gestured for Hector to go back down into the hold. Once again Hector heard the wedges hammered home.

He had expected his fellow captives to ask him what it was like up on deck. But most of them ignored his return. They were apathetic as though they had accepted their fate. Someone was muttering a prayer for salvation, repeating it over and over again. It was a depressing sound, and in the gloom he could not see who it was. The only person alert to his return was the elderly madman. As Hector settled himself back in his place, he crept up again and hissed, 'Is it to be Algiers or Tunis?'

'I don't know,' Hector answered, taken aback by the accuracy of the old man's question.

'As long as it's not Sallee,' muttered the old man, more to himself than to Hector. 'They say it's the worst place of all. Underground pens where you can drown in liquid shit, and chains so heavy that you can barely walk. They told me I was lucky to be in Algiers.'

'Who are "they" and what do you mean by "lucky"?' Hector asked, wondering what his fellow captive was babbling about.

He was answered with another shifty look. 'Trying to catch me out, are you? Well you won't this time,' the dotard wheezed, and suddenly grabbed at the young man's hand and demanded fiercely, 'What have you got there? Share! Share!' Hector had forgotten about the fruit he had been given. He supposed them to be olives, though they felt more sticky. The old man snatched one away, and thrust it into his mouth. He began to drool. 'Datoli, datoli,' he gloated. Hector tasted one. On his tongue it was the sweetest fruit he had ever known, as if saturated in honey, and there was a hard pip in the centre.

'Have you been in Algiers?' he asked, anxious to glean any information about their fate.

'Of course! Was I not there for five years and more? And then they doubted the tales I had to tell.'

Hector was growing ever more confused by the old man's rambling. 'It's not that I doubt you. Only I know nothing of these matters.'

'I swear to you that I was a beylik slave for all those five years, mostly in the quarries, but sometimes on the harbour wall. Yet I never renounced my faith, oh no, though others did. Even when they beat me, I resisted. What came later was more cruel.'

'What could be worse than slavery? And what's a beylik?'

The old man ignored the question. He was working himself into a frenzy. He grabbed Hector's arm and dug in with his bony fingers. 'After they bought me, they treated me like dung,' he hissed.

'You mean the Algiers people?'

'No. No. The canting hypocrites. After they paid my ransom, they thought I was their thing. They paraded me around, I and a dozen others. We were like monkeys to be stared at. Made us wear our old slave clothes, the red cap and the thin gown, even though it was shivering cold. They had us stand and call out from carts, shake our chains and tell our woes. That is, until they had enough of us. Then they turned us loose without a coin to our names. So I went back to sea, it is the only trade I know, and now I'm taken a second time.' He cackled maniacally and shuffled back to his corner, where he again went through the peculiar pantomime of laying himself down on the hard boards with exaggerated care, then turned his face away.

'Silly old fool. Don't believe a word of his gibberish. He's a charlatan.' The sour comment came from the stout man wearing the wig and the expensive but stained clothes who looked like a merchant. He must have overheard the old man's tale. 'There are plenty of tricksters who go about, claiming they were captives of the Moors and begging for alms. They're fakes.'

'But what did he mean by "paraded around"?' Hector found himself taking an instant dislike to the man.

'It's a technique the redemptorists use. They're the do-gooders who raise money to buy back the slaves from Barbary. After they bring them home, they trundle the wretches around the countryside, putting them on show so that the common people can see what sufferings they have endured, and this encourages them to part with their money to pay for more ransoms.' He gave a knowing look. 'But who's to say where most of the money goes? I am acquainted with a ransom broker myself, a City man who facilitates the meetings with the Jews that act as middle men for the Moors. My friend has done remarkably well, and that's why I tell myself that I won't stay long in Barbary. As soon as I can get word back to my friend, he'll make sure that I'm ransomed early. Then I'll get home to my wife and family.'

'And what happens otherwise?' Hector enquired, careful not to say 'to the rest of us'. The merchant's smug self-interest repelled him.

'Depends what's on offer. If you have money or influence, preferably both, then you won't stay long with the Moors. Those who have neither should be patient. Every nation that calls itself Christian tries to ransom back its citizens sooner or later, provided there are enough funds.'

'How is it that you are here yourself?'

'I'm Josiah Newland, a mercer from London. I was on my way to Ireland when I was taken. Someone in Cork was having money difficulties and obliged to sell off a shipment of linen cheaply. I thought to get there ahead of the competition. So I hired a fishing boat to take me there, but unfortunately it was intercepted by these faithless pirates and they carried off myself and the crew. Those are the crew members over there.' He pointed into the far corner, at the men who had earlier clustered around the basket of bread. 'As you can see, they stick together. They are not at all my type, nor are those base fellows.' He gestured towards the villagers in their miserable huddle. Clearly he thought that Hector was not of their company.

'We were all captured at the same time,' Hector replied, trying to keep his tone neutral. With every word Josiah Newland was revealing himself to be a selfish prig. 'There was a raid on our village.'

The merchant seemed taken aback, though not sympathetic. 'I didn't think that sort of thing happened any longer. There was a time when the corsairs were very bold. They infested our coasts until the King's ships began to patrol more actively. Nowadays those pirates confine their activities to capturing ships at sea, stealing their cargoes and carrying off their crews. Indeed I would not have undertaken my own coasting voyage if His Majesty had not concluded a treaty with the Barbary states. According to the newspapers the Turks promised not to molest English shipping. But then you can never trust the Turks, nor Moors for that matter, they are a treacherous lot. Or perhaps they thought the King of England would not trouble himself unduly about his Irish subjects, for he cares little for Papists.'

Hector did not reply. The mercer was only mimicking the attitude of the King and his ministers in London. To them

Ireland, though a part of the realm, was a troublesome place populated by awkward, difficult and potentially treasonable subjects, particularly if they were followers of the Church of Rome. Hector tried to imagine Newland's reaction if he was to tell him that the corsair captain who held him prisoner was an Irish turncoat who now sailed as a Muslim.

THREE

ℂ

OVER THE NEXT several days Hector, who had an intelligent and enquiring nature, struck up a friendship with one of the seamen who had been captured with Newland. He was a Devon man by the name of Francis Dunton who seemed remarkably unruffled by their abduction. Hector made sure that whenever small groups of prisoners were allowed out of the ship's hold for exercise, he and Dunton were on deck at the same time.

'This ship we're on now,' he asked the sailor diffidently, 'is she anything like the vessels you've sailed yourself?'

Dunton turned to face the young man, and Hector was struck by the similarity between the Devon man and the corsair petty officer who had escorted him to see Hakim Reis. Both men had the same compact, muscular physique, an easy balance on the moving deck, and the same air of calm competence. Dunton's weather-beaten face was tanned to nearly the same colour as the corsair's swarthy complexion. 'No different,' Dunton answered in his slow, gentle accent. 'This here is a sailing ship like any other.'

'Would you be able to sail this ship as well as those who have her now?' Hector asked, impressed by his companion's self-assurance.

The sailor gave a derisive chuckle. 'Better. The man who cuns this ship, gripes her too much.'

'What is "gripes"?'

'Turns her head, her bow that is, too much towards the wind. That slows her down.'

'And to "cun" the ship?'

'That only means to steer her.'

'I wonder if I would ever be able to learn all the sea words, let alone how to manage such a vessel.'

'Seamanship comes natural to some,' answered the sailor in a matter-of-fact tone. 'Those who haven't the knack, can usually learn if they are given enough time. The rare ones are those who can tell a helmsman which way to cun his ship, or can decipher the stars and predict a sure landfall on a foreign shore where he has never been before. That's the man who his mates will want to sail with.'

'You mean a navigator?'

'Correct. Any fool can tell you that we've been heading south since we left the coast of Ireland, and a day ago I'd say we turned more eastward. You can tell that just by looking at the sun, and the fact that each night the air in the hold is getting hotter. I reckon we must have come at least four hundred miles and are close to Africa.'

Hector broached a subject that had been nagging at the back of his mind. 'As a boy I once heard a man speak about being taken as a captive by the corsairs. He told how their prisoners were made to work as slaves in galleys, working the oars. But I don't see any oars.'

'This ship is a sailing vessel, not a galley,' the sailor replied, 'nor even a galleass, which is a word for a ship that has both oars and a sail. A galley would be next to useless out here in the open ocean. Nigh on impossible to row in the waves, and the distances are too great. How would you feed a crew on a voyage of more than a few days? You must trust to the wind when you are far from land. No, this ship suits well enough for her purpose, which is pirating.'

'What about meeting another ship, is there a chance that someone might rescue us?'

'I'd expect we'll sight other ships all right, but whether we'll be rescued is another matter. For one thing, there's our companion over there.' Dunton nodded towards the corsair's sister ship still visible half a mile away. 'Two ships sailing in close company are best avoided in case they're hostile. They can gang up on a stranger. And should we get separated and must sail on our own, then who's to say that this is a corsair ship. If the crew take the trouble to cover those few guns, this vessel could as easy be a merchantman as a pirate. Pull down those pennants and that green flag and run up someone else's colours and she could be Dutch or French or a Brandenburger as much as Turk. That's why ships avoid one another when they meet at sea, just in case of trouble.'

ℂ

THE FOLLOWING AFTERNOON almost proved Dunton wrong. The captives were on deck taking their exercise when a distant sail was sighted from the masthead. Hector noticed Hakim Reis gazing intently in the direction of the approaching vessel before the prisoners were hustled back down into the hold and shut in. Dunton stayed on the lower rungs of the ladder, his head cocked to one side, listening. There was a squeal of ropes running through the wooden blocks. 'Hullo, they're bringing the topsails amain,' he commented. Soon afterwards there was a tramp of feet heading towards the stern. 'And there they go to peak the mizzen. They're heaving to.'

'What does that mean?' asked Hector in a whisper.

'They're stopping the ship, waiting for the other one to catch up,' Dunton explained as Hector felt the motion of the vessel change. Where before the ship had been sailing at a slant, now she was level and pitching up and down gently on the waves.

Dunton sat down against the side of the hold. 'No hurry, younker,' he said. 'It'll be some time before that other sail catches up with us, three or four hours at least.'

'Who do you think it is?'

'No idea,' answered the sailor. 'But my guess is that our captain is a foxy one. He'll pretend he is a friendly vessel, hang out some convenient flag, and wait for the visitor to come close enough, then close and board him. Take him by surprise.'

'Not fire at him?'

'A corsair doesn't use his cannon except in emergency. He doesn't want to damage his prey. Best lay board and board, and seize the other vessel with a rush of men.'

An air of excitement had also brought the other prisoners to life. Even the most depressed villager started to look hopeful of rescue. Newland, the cloth merchant, called enquiringly, 'Friend or foe, sailor?'

Dunton merely shrugged.

It must have been about three hours later – there was no way to mark the passage of time below deck – when suddenly an order was shouted on the deck above, and the prisoners heard the scamper of running feet. 'Hello,' said Dunton. 'Something's not what was expected.'

There were more shouts and then the chanting of a work song, its refrain urgent and forceful. 'They're setting sail again, and in a hurry,' commented the sailor. Within moments the prisoners could again hear the ripple of the waves along the flanks of the ship, and feel the vessel heel to the wind. A flat thud in the distance was followed by two more. 'Cannon!' announced Dunton. More cries on deck, and the answering bang of a cannon from directly above them. The vessel quivered with the recoil. 'God grant that we are not hit. If we sink, we'll never get out of here alive,' muttered Newland the mercer in sudden alarm. Hector glanced at the villagers. Their earlier hopes of being rescued had turned to dismay. Several were on their knees, hands clasped in silent prayer, eyes shut tight. 'What's going on?' he asked the Devon sailor. Dunton was still straining to hear the noises on deck. 'Wish I knew their language. No way of knowing. But my guess is that we're the chase.' Again Hector felt frustrated by his lack of sea lore.

'Does that mean we are in pursuit?'

'No, the chase is the vessel which is pursued.'

'God grant us salvation!' pleaded the cooper. 'Praise the Lord for his Mercy. He who watches over us! Let us pray together for our liberation.' He began to hum a psalm.

'Shut up!' snapped Dunton. 'I'm trying to hear what is going on.'

The cooper ignored him, and his co-religionists in the hold began a dirge which drowned out all but the distant occasional thud of the cannon fire which, as time passed, became fainter and more irregular until, finally, nothing more could be heard.

'Must have outrun them,' grunted Dunton, who had shifted to his favourite position beneath a crack in the deck planking where he could squint out at the sky. 'Or perhaps we lost them in the gathering darkness. It'll be full dark soon.'

The disappointed prisoners settled down for their rest, their stomachs empty, because for the first time in the voyage, no one had appeared at the hatch with their evening ration. 'Let us pray to God that our women and children are safe,' said the cooper, and Hector, who had naturally been silently wondering what might have happened to Elizabeth on the sister ship, found himself praying quietly for her survival as he tried to go to sleep, curled up against a bulkhead. He felt completely helpless as Hakim Reis's ship sailed on towards its unknown destination.

℃

BY NOON the next day the captives had still not been fed, and they were hungrily awaiting the arrival of their usual ration of bread and olives when there was another shattering crash of cannon fire. But this time it was not a single cannon. An entire battery of guns was shooting, and very close by. The ship's armament promptly answered, and the prisoners heard the thud of the gun carriages slamming down with the discharge. The sudden torrent of sound tipped the elderly madman over the edge of sanity. He leapt up from where he had been sleeping, and began to caper and shout nonsense. He hooted and bellowed, and nothing could restrain him. Again came the shocking crash of a battery, and an answering blast from the ship's guns. A strange smell wafted down – the acrid stink of gunpowder.

All at once the hatch was flung open, and not one but five sailors came hurrying down the ladder. But instead of bringing food, they began to shout and point excitedly, urging the captives to go up on deck. Dazed and uncomprehending, the prisoners shuffled forward. Those who stayed were pulled to their feet and thrust forward. Hector found himself following the grimy and naked feet of a villager as he climbed the ladder to the deck, and emerged to see a scene ahead of him never to be forgotten.

Off to one side, less than a hundred yards away, stood a formidable fortress constructed of massive stone blocks on a low and rocky islet. The sides of the fortress were a series of angled surfaces designed to deflect cannonballs. Its parapet bristled with cannon, and from a copper dome, which also served as a lighthouse, rose a tall flagpole from which floated a huge crimson flag. In the centre of the flag was the image of an arm, black on red, brandishing a broad-bladed sword like the weapons wielded by the sailors aboard Hakim Reis's vessel. As Hector watched, white smoke belched from the mouths of the fort's cannon, and a moment later he heard the echoing explosion. He flinched, waiting for the shock of cannonballs tearing into the fabric of the ship. But nothing came. Then he realised that the fort was firing a salute to greet the incoming vessel, even as Hakim Reis's men let off their own guns and gave a great cheer.

But what made him gape was the city which climbed the hill behind the fort. Blinding white in the midday sun, rank upon rank of tightly packed houses extended up the flank of a steep mountain to form a dense triangular mass. The flat roofs of the houses were topped with balconies, their walls pierced with rows of small arched windows. Here and there emerged a turquoise or gilded dome and the spikes of tall spires, and at the very apex of the triangle, far up the slope, was a sprawling complex which Hector took to be a citadel. To the left, outside the city wall and dominating the skyline, loomed another massive castle, its turrets decked out with flagpoles and banners. Orchards and gardens spread across the flanks of the mountains on both sides, and their show of greenery framed the dizzying spectacle of the corsairs' base.

The sound of cheering brought his attention back to the harbour. On the seaward side of the fortress a curtain wall had been built to protect an anchorage. This curtain wall, some thirty feet high and built along the crest of a reef, was also topped with battlements and cannon platforms. The rampart was lined with citizens who had come out to greet them. They were shouting and waving, and a small band of musicians – three drummers and a man with some sort of flute – had struck up a wild skirling tune. Those spectators who were nearest the musicians were clapping in time and a few of them were whirling and dancing with delight.

A shove on his shoulder from one of the crew pushed him into line so that he stood side by side with the other captives at the rail of the ship, facing across to the crowd of onlookers. Hector realised that he and the other prisoners were being put on show. They were the spoils of the corsair's cruise.

A few moments more and their ship was rounding the far end of the harbour wall, with the anchorage opening ahead of them. Moored in the middle of the roadstead were four sailing vessels similar to the one Hakim Reis commanded. But what caught his eye were the dozen vessels deep inside the harbour, their bows tied to the mole itself. Without being told, he knew what they were. Low and sleek and dangerous, they reminded him of the greyhounds his father and his friends had used to course hares in the countryside. He was about to ask Dunton if he was right in thinking they were corsair galleys, when the villager standing beside him said in anguished tones, 'Where's the other ship? The one with our womenfolk and the children?'

Shocked, Hector turned to look. Nowhere could he see the vessel that had accompanied them. She was gone.

FOUR

ℂ

SAMUEL MARTIN, the English consul in Algiers, heard the salvoes of gunfire and walked to the window of his office. From long experience he knew the reason for the commotion. Squinting down into the harbour he recognised Hakim Reis's ship and sighed. The corsair's arrival meant there was work for him, and it was not a task he relished. By inclination and preference Martin was a trader. He would much rather have looked out of his window and seen merchant ships arriving and departing, laden with the honest merchandise from which he had hoped to make his living when he had first arrived in Algiers a decade ago. But it had not turned out that way. Legitimate trade between England and Algiers was on the increase but the Algerines much preferred to make their money by seizing captives for ransom or selling stolen goods, often back to their original owners. Hence the joyous reception being given by the populace to Hakim Reis and his ruffians down at the harbour.

Consul Martin, a small and active man, often wondered if the government in London had any inkling of the complications of being England's representative to a Barbary regency. For a start he never quite knew whom he should be dealing with. Officially the city ruler was the Pasha appointed by the Turkish Sultan in Istanbul. But the Sublime Porte was far away, and ultimately the Pasha was really nothing more than a figurehead. Effective power apparently lay with the Dey and his cabinet of advisers, the divan. But that too was a deception. The Dey was elected by the janissaries, the city's Turkish-born military elite. Known locally as the odjaks, the janissaries were professional warriors, but it was normal that they also followed a second occupation, usually as merchants or landlords. Certainly they devoted more energy to political intrigues than to soldiering. They made and unmade their Deys at an alarming rate, and their favoured method of getting rid of the current officeholder was by assassination. In Consul Martin's time three Deys had been killed, two by poison and one with the garrotte. The Consul was aware that the divan only paid him any attention when it suited them, but he nursed a hope that one day he would be able to influence the current Dey, an elderly odjak, directly through his favourite wife who was reputed to be an Englishwoman. She was a slave girl who had taken the old man's fancy and borne him two children. Unfortunately Martin had yet to meet the lady, and rumour had it that she was as avaricious and corrupt as anyone else in the palace.

The consul sighed again. Had the incoming vessel been a galley returning from a short cruise in the Mediterranean, the prisoners on board were likely to be French or Genoese, Greeks or Spaniards, and therefore not his concern. But Hakim Reis was known to range as far as the English Channel on his man-catching cruises. Recently Martin had helped negotiate a treaty between London and Algiers whereby the Algerines had promised not to molest English ships, or vessels sailing under English passes. But the consul was not sure that Hakim Reis would have honoured the pact. So it was best if His Majesty's consul established just who was on the corsair's roster of captives. And should any of his captives prove to be subjects of the King, then Martin's duty was to find out their identities and what price was expected for them. The best moment to do that was when the prisoners were first landed, before they were distributed among various owners or vanished into any one of the eight bagnios, the slave barracks.

Indoors, the consul liked to wear the loose cotton kaftans and slippers which the Moors of Algiers favoured, and he thought the dress very sensible in the heat. But in public he was expected to dress according to his rank and dignity. So now he called for his manservant, a Hampshire man awaiting the final instalment of an agreed ransom, and told him to lay out his street clothes – a three-piece suit of heavy cloth with a waistcoat and knee breeches, a starched linen shirt with a frilled front and ruffles at the wrist, and a cravat.

Half an hour later, sweating in this turnout, Martin descended to the street. His office and living quarters were in the coolest part of the building, the topmost of the three floors which served as the consulate as well as his residence and place of business. On the way downstairs he passed the rooms where his servants ate and slept, the dormitories occupied by several dozen captives whose ransoms were expected soon or who were part-paid, and finally on the ground floor the storerooms for the commodities he traded – mostly skins and ostrich feathers from the interior. His doorkeeper, a burly and necessary functionary who intercepted unwelcome callers at the house, pulled back the heavy nail-studded door. Martin adjusted his newly brushed periwig and, a little unsteady on the two-inch-high heels of his buckled shoes, he stepped out into the narrow street.

The noise and heat made a double blow. The consulate was situated halfway up the hill of Algiers, and its front door gave directly on to the main street which ran the length of the city, from the docks to the Kasbah at the upper end of the town. Never more than a few yards wide, with high flat-fronted houses on each side, the street was like a sultry ravine. Paved with worn stone slabs, it climbed so steeply that it had to be broken by occasional short flights of steps. The street also served as the main bazaar and emporium of the city, so walking along it meant stepping around stalls and dodging pavement vendors

selling everything from vegetables to metalwork. Asses laden
with panniers plodded up and down the slope, hawkers yelled,
water carriers clattered tin cups against the brass flagons strapped
to their backs. As the consul made his way slowly through the
press of the crowd he wondered, not for the first time, whether
he should retire and return to England. For years he had
suffered the noise and heat of Algiers, and the roguery of its
inhabitants. Yet he told himself once again that it was too soon
to abandon the city. Property prices in England were rising so
fast that he would not be able to afford the country estate on
which he had set his heart.

On the quayside, Martin found the Dey's scribes already
seated at the table where they would enter the new intake of
captives in the city register. Martin knew the chief registrar
slightly and bowed to him, a gesture of politeness which would
do no harm as the Algerines, for all their villainy, valued good
manners. The usual crowd of idlers had assembled to observe
the landing of the prisoners and pass comments on their potential
worth as slaves, while the first boatload of the captives had
already been ferried ashore. Martin noted how bewildered and
frightened the poor wretches looked as they gazed about them
at the strange world into which they were being inducted.
Glumly the consul concluded that the new arrivals were too
fair-skinned to be Italians or Spanish, and he supposed they
must be Dutch or English. The only prisoner taking an intelligent interest in his surroundings was a handsome, black-haired
young man in his late teens. He was looking this way and that,
apparently searching for someone. He seemed agitated. Beyond
him was a short, pudgy man wearing a wig. He was standing
slightly apart from his fellow captives and trying to look as
though he was too superior to be in their company. Martin
wondered if the man knew that his every action was telling his
captors that he was worth a larger ransom.

The consul moved closer to the table. The registrar's
assistant – a Greek slave who, to Martin's knowledge, spoke

at least eight languages – was asking each prisoner the same questions: his name, age, place of origin, and profession. Martin found it difficult to hear their answers over the chatter of the onlookers until, all of a sudden, there was a respectful hush and they turned to look towards the harbour. The captain of the corsair ship was himself coming ashore. The consul was intrigued. To get such a close glimpse of Hakim Reis was unusual. Hakim operated from whichever base suited him so he might as easily have brought his captives to Tunis, Sallee or Tripoli to sell. He was welcome wherever he landed on the coast of Barbary for he was acknowledged to be the most successful corsair captain of them all.

Hakim Reis was dressed in an immaculate white gown edged with gold braid, and a scarlet turban decorated with a large ostrich feather. In his hand he held a light gold-headed ceremonial cane. He came up the landing steps with the brisk tread of a man half his age, though Martin knew the corsair must be at least in his late fifties. The consul watched as the corsair captain approached the registrar and stood beside the desk for a few moments. Martin guessed that he wanted to make his presence felt, so there was no false accounting. At that moment Martin heard someone calling out to him.

'You, sir, you there!' It was the portly man in the wig. He must have recognised the consul by his foreign dress. 'If you please. My name is Josiah Newland. I am a mercer, from London. I need to speak with the King of England's representative at once.'

'I am the English consul.'

'A fortunate encounter, then,' said Newland, puffing slightly in the heat and instantly adopting a self-important tone. 'Would you be so good as to send word by your most competent commission agent that Josiah Newland is taken and wishes to contact Mr Sewell of Change Alley in London, so that matters can be speedily resolved.'

'There is nothing I can do at this time, Mr Newland,' the

consul replied calmly. 'I am here merely as an observer. The Turks have a well-established routine which must be followed. Perhaps later, when the Dey has made his choice, I may be of assistance.'

'The Dey? What has he got to do with it?'

'The Dey, Mr Newland, is the ruler of Algiers and has the right to his penjic or portion. He takes every eighth slave, plus other benefits such as the bare hulls of all captured vessels. Tomorrow or perhaps the day afterwards when he has made his selection, I will see you again.'

'One moment . . .' the mercer was about to continue, but Martin's attention had again been distracted. The registrar's Greek slave wanted a word with him. 'Your honour,' began the slave, 'my master asks me to inform you that most of the captives are from Ireland, one or two are English. He wishes to know whether you will accept their charge.'

'Please tell your master that I will consider the matter, if he would be so good as to provide me with a list of names and other relevant details. I look forward to giving him my reply tomorrow.'

A burst of angry shouts and the sound of blows interrupted him. Farther along the quay, a gang of slaves had been manoeuvring a great block of quarry stone preparatory to fitting it into a gap in the causeway which led to the island fortress. The massive stone had been balanced on a crude sledge with the men harnessed to it like draught horses. The stone had slipped and toppled sideways, and the overseer had lost his temper. Now he was cursing and laying about him with a whip. As the slaves were still fastened to the sledge, they were unable to avoid the lash. They scrabbled and ducked, trying to avoid the blows. It was some minutes before the overseer had vented his anger, and in that time the majority of the men received a thorough thrashing. Martin had witnessed many scenes like it. The great mole at Algiers constantly needed repairs, and its maintenance was the responsibility of the Dey. There was a very good chance that those slaves who were unlucky enough to be taken in his penjic would be assigned to this dangerous and backbreaking chore.

Civilly Martin bowed again to the registrar and started walking back up the hill towards the consulate. He was already considering how best to arrange the fat mercer's ransom. That transaction should not be difficult. The man exuded the self-confidence of someone with access to ready funds, so a well-placed bribe would ensure that Newland was not sent to the bagnios. Instead he would be released into the consul's care for the three or four months that the ransom negotiations would take. The Irish captives were a different matter. If they were Protestants, he could assist them in some small way as he did with their fellow unfortunates who were English or Scots. He could provide them with pocket money which, spread in judicious bribes to their goalers, might ease their life in the bagnio. Later he would reclaim the sum from London.

But if the Irish were Papists, he would be throwing away his own cash. The tight-fisted bureaucrats in London would be sure to query his accounts, and he would never be reimbursed. Sourly he reflected that his own consular salary was three years in arrears. Still, he was in a better position than his colleague and sometime rival, the unfortunate consul for Spain. After four years he was still trying to negotiate the ransom of a Spanish nobleman being held prisoner in the most vile conditions. The captive was a Chevalier of the noble Order of the Knights of St John in Malta, whose ships were fighting an implacable holy war against the Muslims. The Barbary corsairs loathed the Knights, and the feeling was mutual. The Algerines wanted such a huge sum for the Chevalier that there was little prospect of him being released for several more years, if ever. In the meantime the Dey and his divan were stepping up the pressure on the Spanish consul. Recently the Spaniard and his local interpreter had been set upon in the street and beaten up. Now, for fear of their lives, they hardly dared leave their consulate.

Martin tripped on a loose paving stone. The mishap made him uncomfortably aware that his feet, in his fashionable high-heeled shoes, were beginning to swell in the heat. He found himself looking forward to the moment when he could change back into his kaftan and slippers. Setting aside any further thoughts about the corsair's captives, the consul concentrated on the steep climb back up the hill of Algiers.

FIVE

☾

HECTOR STUMBLED THROUGH the next few hours. Numbed
by his sister's disappearance, he barely noticed what was happening as he was inscribed in the register, and he slept badly
in the bleak holding cell where the captives were kept over-
night. Again and again he wondered what might have happened
to Elizabeth and how he might find out. But there was no
opportunity to enquire. At first light he and the other prisoners
were woken and, barefoot and still wearing the soiled clothes in
which they had been captured, they were marched up the hill to
the great building Hector had mistaken for the citadel. In fact it
was the Kasbah, part fort, part palace. In a courtyard the men
were mustered in three lines, and after a short wait the Dey's
head steward appeared. He was accompanied by three men
whom Hector later knew to be two overseers from the public
slave barracks and a Jew who was an experienced slave broker.
The trio walked up and down between the lines, occasionally
stopping to consult with one another or examine a prisoner's
physique. Hector felt like a beast in a cattle market when one of
the overseers reached out to pinch his arm muscles, then prodded
him in the ribs with the butt of a wooden baton. Finally, when
the inspection was complete, the Jew in his black cap and black
gown walked between the lines and tapped four men on the

shoulder. Among them was the strapping young villager whom Hector had formerly seen going out to cut turf. As the four were led away by the guards, Hector heard the crazed grey beard standing beside him mutter under his breath, 'Beylik, poor bastards.'

The old man appeared to be in one of his more lucid moods, for he seemed to remember who Hector was, and announced his own name as Simeon. 'You noticed, didn't you?' he asked the young man. 'They took the strong ones. You were lucky not to be picked. Probably too skinny . . . or too beautiful,' and he laughed coarsely to himself. 'This is Algiers, you know. They keep their pretty boys close to home, not sent off to work as public slaves.'

Hector was feeling light-headed in the heat. 'What's going to happen to us now?' he enquired.

'Off to the badestan, I expect,' explained Simeon.

The badestan proved to be an open square close to the Kasbah's main entrance. Here a large crowd of Algerines had already assembled, and before Hector could understand what was happening, an old man had taken him by his arm in a friendly way, and begun to lead him around the square. It was several steps before Hector realised that he was in the hands of an auctioneer. There was a shouted demand from an onlooker. The old man stopped, then pulled the shirt off Hector's shoulders so that the young man's naked torso was exposed. A few paces further and at another request called from the crowd, the old man produced a thin, whippy cane and, to Hector's shock, slashed it violently across his ankles. Hector leapt in pain. Even before he had landed, the auctioneer had repeated the blow from the other direction, so that Hector was forced to skip and turn in the air. Twice more during the circuit of the square, the cane was used and he was made to jump and spin. Then the auctioneer began to sing out what must have been his salesman's patter, for there were answering calls from the crowd, and Hector guessed that they were making their bids. The bidding reached its climax and the auctioneer was making what seemed to be his last appeal, when a dignified-looking Turk stepped out of the crowd and came across to where Hector was standing. The newcomer was clearly a man of substance. His purple velvet jacket was richly embroidered, and the silver handle of a fine dagger showed above the brocade sash around his waist. On his head was a tall felt hat with jewelled brooch pinned to it. The man said something quietly to the auctioneer who reached up and placed his wiry hand on Hector's jaw. Then he squeezed with a firm downward pull, and Hector involuntarily opened his mouth. The Turk peered into his mouth, seemed satisfied, and murmured something to the auctioneer who immediately led Hector back to his waiting companions.

'I told them my age already,' grumbled Hector to Simeon.

His complaint was met with a gleeful chuckle. 'It was not your age he wanted to know. But the state of your teeth.' The smirking grey beard opened his own mouth and pointed trium-phantly at his own teeth. The few of them that remained were brown and rotten. 'Can't chew with them,' he crowed. 'I'd be no good at all. Even though I've done my time.'

'Where, old man?' asked Hector, growing tired of Simeon's vagueness.

The dotard snickered, 'You'll find out soon enough,' and would say no more.

Hector looked back at the well-dressed man who had bought him. The same purchaser was now interested in the sailor Dunton, and was again talking with the auctioneer even as the guards began shoving all the captives back into line. Those who had not been stripped to the waist now had their shirts or smocks removed. Then the auctioneer walked down the line, followed by an attendant holding a clay pot and a small brush. In front of each man the auctioneer stopped, checked a document he was holding, and then said something to the attendant who stepped forward. He dipped his brush into the pot and made marks on the man's chest in ochre paint. Looking down at the marks as they dried on his skin, Hector supposed they were numbers or letters, but whether they were the bid price or an identity number he did not know.

℃

CAPTAIN OF GALLEYS Turgut Reis had not intended to go to the badestan that morning, but his senior wife had hinted that he get out of the house so that she could have the servants do a more thorough job of cleaning his study. In her subtle way she let it be known that he was spending too much time poring over his musty books and charts, and he would be better off meeting up with his friends for cups of coffee and conversation over a pipe of tobacco. Indeed it was unusual for the Captain of Galleys to be in Algiers in the last week of July at all. Normally he would be at sea on a cruise. But this summer was out of the ordinary as well as stressful. A month earlier his galley, *Izzet Darya*, had sprung a bad leak. When hauled up for repairs, the shipwrights had discovered three or four areas of badly wormed planking that would have to be replaced. The Arsenal at Algiers was chronically short of timber as there were no forests in the neighbourhood, and the owner of the slipway had said he would be obliged to send away for baulks in suitable lengths, maybe as far away as Lebanon. 'Those Shaitan infidels from Malta are running amok,' he warned. 'In previous years I could get deliveries brought by neutral ships. But this year those fanatics have been plundering everything that sails. And even if I can find a freighter, the charges are already exorbitant.' And he had given Turgut a look which clearly told him that it was high time that the Captain of Galleys got himself a new galley, instead of trying to patch up the old one.

But Turgut was fond of *Izzet Darya* and did not want to abandon her. He admitted that the vessel was old-fashioned, hard to manoeuvre and over-ornate. But then he himself was a bit like his ship — old-fashioned and set in his ways. His friends always said that he was living in the past, and that he should keep up with the times. They would cite the case of Hakim Reis. Hakim, they pointed out, had shrewdly switched from a vessel propelled by oars to a sailing ship which had greater range and could stay at sea for weeks at a time. The benefits were obvious from the value of the prizes that Hakim Reis was bringing in, the recent batch of captives for example. But, thought Turgut, Hakim was also blessed with remarkable luck. He was always in the right place at the right time to snap up a prize, while he, Captain of Galleys, might loiter at the crucieri, as unbelievers called the areas where the sea lanes crossed, and not see a sail for days. No, Turgut assured himself, he preferred to stick with tradition, for tradition had elevated him to be Captain of Galleys. That appointment, with all its prestige as the acknowledged head of all the corsair captains of Algiers, was not in the gift of the Dey nor of the divan, nor indeed of the scheming odjaks of Algiers. The corsairs of Algiers had their own guild, the taifa, which came together to nominate a leader, but the Sultan himself had indicated whom they should choose. He had nominated Turgut Reis in recognition of the family's tradition of service in the Sultan's navy, for Turgut's father had commanded a war galley, and his most famous ancestor, his great-uncle Piri Reis, had been admiral of the entire Turkish fleet.

Turgut, when he had received the news, had been both proud and a little anxious. At the time he had been living in the imperial capital and he knew that both his wives would be reluctant to leave. But there was no question of declining the honour. The Sultan's wish was sacrosanct. So Turgut had rented out the family mansion on the shores of the Bosphorus, packed up his belongings, said goodbye to the other courtiers at court, and sailed for Barbary with his family and his entourage aboard the venerable *Izzet Darya*.

Of course they had found Algiers very provincial compared to the sophistication of Constantinople. But he and his family had done their best to adapt. He had deliberately skirted around the local politics and tried to set an example to the other captains, to remind them of the old ways. That is why he still dressed in the courtly style, with full pantaloons hanging low, a resplendent waistcoat and an overmantle, and the tall felt hat, decorated with a brooch that he had received personally from the hands of the Sultan of Sultans, Khan of Khans, Commander of the Faithful and Successor of the Prophet of the Lord of the Universe.

He had not intended to buy any slaves at the badestan until the young dark-haired man caught his eye. The youth had a look about him that said he might one day make an astute scrivano as the locals called their scribes, or, if he had been younger, perhaps even a kocek, though Turgut himself had never much time for clever dancing boys and their attractions. So it was on an impulse that he had bought the dark-haired one, and then, having made one purchase, it had seemed only natural to make a second. He bid for the second slave because the man was so obviously a sailor. Turgut could recognise a mariner of whatever nationality, be he Turk or Syrian, Arab or Russian, and Turgut felt he was able to justify his second purchase more easily. *Izzet Darya* was a rowing galley, but she also carried two enormous triangular sails and she needed capable sail handlers. Moreover, if he was very lucky, the new purchase might even possess shipwright's skills. That would be a bonus. Good timber was not the only shortage in the Arsenal of Algiers. More than half the workmen in the galley yards were foreigners, many of them slaves, and if the new purchase could cut, shape and fit timber, he would be a useful addition to the boatyard. Turgut would rent his slave out for a daily wage or have the cost of his labour deducted from the final bill for the repairs to *Izzet Darya*.

Having made his bids, Turgut followed the captives back to the courtyard of the Dey's palace. Now came the final haggling. It was an auction all over again. Each slave was set up on a block and the bid price, written on the man's chest, was called out. According to custom the Dey had the right to buy the man at that sum if the original bidder did not increase his offer. Turgut noted the frisson of interest among the spectators when a fat pale-skinned man was pushed up on the block. He was too soft and chubby to be a labourer, and the first price at the badestan was already substantial, 800 pieces of eight in the Spanish money or nearly 1,500 Algerian piastres. Turgut wondered if someone had secretly investigated the man's value. In the slave trade you had to know what you were doing, particularly if you thought you were buying someone worth a ransom. Then the bidding became hectic, both sides gambling on just how much money might be squeezed out of the infidel's family and friends. So a common technique when prisoners were first landed was to place among them informers who pretended to be in similar hardship. They befriended the new arrivals and, when they were at their most vulnerable, wormed out personal details – the amount of property they owned at home, the importance of their families, the influence they had with their governments. All was reported back and reflected in the price at the Dey's auction. On this occasion the fat man was clearly English for it was the English consul's dragoman who was defending the original bid, and when the Dey's agent increased the price only by 500 piastres before dropping out, Turgut suspected that the dragoman had already paid a bribe to the Dey to ensure that the fat man was placed in the consul's care.

Turgut had only a token tussle over the final price for the black-haired young man. The captive looked too slight to be much use as a common labourer and, besides, there was a glut of slaves in the city. So the eventual price of 200 piastres was reasonable enough, as was the fee of 250 pieces of eight which he had to pay for the sailor whose name, according to the auction roster, was Dunton. If the latter proved to be a shipwright then, according to Turgut's calculations, he would charge the shipyard 6 pieces of eight per month for his labour.

Turgut was leaving the Kasbah, well satisfied with his purchases, when he came face to face with someone he had been trying to avoid for the past few weeks – the khaznadji, the city treasurer. The encounter was unfortunate because Turgut was severely in arrears with his taxes on the value of the plunder that he had earned when his ship was seaworthy. Not that the Captain of Galleys believed the meeting was accidental, because the khaznadji was flanked by two odjaks wearing their regulation red sashes and yatagans, the ceremonial dagger. The odjaks, as Turgut was all too aware, would be formal witnesses to any conversation.

'I congratulate you, effendi,' murmured the tax collector after the usual compliments and civilities in the name of the Padishah. 'I understand that you have purchased two fine slaves. I wish you well of their employ.'

'I thank you,' answered Turgut. 'I shall put them to useful work in due course.'

'So your ship is to be ready soon?'

The khaznadji knew very well that *Izzet Darya* would be in dock for at least another month, and that as long as his vessel was out of commission, Turgut Reis had no income and a great many expenses, not least of them the mounting costs of the repairs. Being Captain of Galleys was a great honour, but unfortunately it did not carry a stipend. The plundering cruise, the corso, was the only way for him to make a living, just as it was for his crew. Turgut's petty officers and free oarsmen – about half the total – had long ago left to join other galleys. His slave oarsmen came from a contractor, and Turgut had been obliged to terminate the agreement prematurely. Unfortunately the disappointed slave contractor was also the khaznadji.

'Inshallah, my ship will be afloat before long,' Turgut replied smoothly, deciding it was better that he bought himself some time with a gesture of generosity, though he could ill afford one. 'Those two slaves, which you admire, perhaps you would do me the honour of accepting one of them on loan. That would give me pleasure.'

The khaznadji lifted his hand in a small graceful gesture,

acknowledging the gift. He had what he wanted, compensation
for the cancelled hire contract. If the Captain of Galleys went
bankrupt, which would surely happen if his antique galley was
not repaired in time, the slave would automatically become his
property.

Privately the khaznadji despised Turgut. He thought the
man was an old fogey who considered himself superior to the
Algerines and because the captain came from the Seraglio,
the imperial court, he presumed that the young black-haired
slave had been purchased for his sexual gratification. It would
be amusing to humiliate the captain still further by exposing his
handsome young man to abuse.

'You are too kind. I admire your generosity, and indeed it is
a difficult choice. With your permission, I select the dark-haired
one. But it would be improper to retain him for my household,
so I shall place him to the benefit of the city. I will assign him
to the beylik, to do public labour.'

He bowed and moved on, feeling that he had extracted the
best possible outcome from the encounter.

℃

ON HIS WAY back home after the awkward meeting with
the khaznadji, Turgut Reis knew what he would do to restore
his normal good humour. His house was one of the privileges
that came with his rank as Captain of Galleys. A four-storey
mansion, it was positioned on almost the highest point of the
city, with a magnificent view out over the harbour and the sea
beyond. To take full advantage of the location, Turgut had
caused a garden to be created on the flat roof. His servants
had carried up hundreds of baskets of earth and laid out flower-
beds. Sweet-smelling shrubs had been selected and planted, and
a dozen trees rooted in large tubs to shade the spot where
Turgut liked to sit cross-legged, gazing over the view and
listening to the distant sounds of the city spread out below him.
Now, reaching the roof garden, he called for his favourite carpet

to be brought out. It was an Usak in the old-fashioned Anatolian style and made with the Turkish knot. In Turgut's opinion the more recent and popular Seraglio designs with their profusion of tulips and hyacinths and roses were much too showy, though he had to admit that the Persian knotting did give them a softer, more velvety surface. But only the Usak carpet with its pattern of repeated stars was the appropriate setting for his most prized possession – the Kitab-i Bahriye.

He waited patiently while his steward brought up the beautifully carved bookstand, and then the volume itself. Turgut looked down at the cover of the book and allowed himself a few moments of anticipation before he opened it and relished the treasures within. Of course, there were other versions of the Book of Sea Lore as the infidels called it. Indeed the Padishah himself owned the most lavishly illustrated copy in existence, a volume prepared specially for the Sultan of Sultans. But the copy lying before Turgut was unique. It was the original. Prepared 150 years ago by Turgut's forebear, the peerless Piri Reis, the book of maps and charts and its accompanying collection of sailing notes had been passed down in his family for six generations. It was the wellspring from which all other versions had been drawn.

Turgut leaned forward and opened the book at random. He knew every page by memory, yet he never failed to be awed by the vision of the man who had created it. 'God has not granted the possibility of displaying everyone of the afore-mentioned places such as harbours and waters around the shores of the Mediterranean, and the reefs and shoals in the water, in a single map,' he read. 'Therefore experts in this science have drawn up what they call a "chart" with a pair of compasses according to a scale of miles, and it is written directly on a parchment.'

Here was the genius of his ancestor, thought Turgut. The man who wrote those words was much more than the Sultan's High Admiral and a great war leader. He also had the curiosity and penetration to study and learn, and the generosity to donate his knowledge to others.

Gently Turgut untied the silk ribbons of an accompanying folder. It contained a very special map also prepared by Piri, a map of much greater ambition for it summarised what the admiral had been able to find out about the great western ocean beyond the straits which divide Spain and Ifriqya. This map depicted lands far, far out towards the setting sun, places which neither the High Admiral nor the Captain of Galleys had ever visited, but only knew by repute. Piri Reis had spent years sifting and collating information in the writings and log books of infidels as well as Moors in order to assemble this map, the first of its kind in the Padishah's Empire, copied and admired in many lands.

Turgut picked out a typical comment written in the admiral's neat hand, beside a sketch of a weird-looking beast on the west coast of Ifriqya. 'In this country it seems that there are white-haired monsters in this shape, and also six-horned oxen. The Portuguese infidels have written it in their maps.' Turgut sat back and considered. That sentence had been penned a century and a half earlier, yet already the infidels had been showing signs of surpassing the Faithful in their knowledge of the seas and how to navigate them. How had that come to pass? When he looked up into the night sky and searched for the stars that guide mariners at sea, they bore the names that the Faithful had given them, because it was the Moors who had first learned how to use them to find their way at night. Some said the Faithful were obliged to do this because they travelled on the haj across the vast expanses of the desert, and they needed the stars to guide them on their pilgrimage to the sacred places. So Allah in his infinite wisdom had placed the stars in the sky for this purpose. But now it was the infidels who were travelling farthest, and using these same stars to steer by. They were at the fore-front of knowledge. Infidels were designing and building the finest sea-going ships even in the dockyards of Algiers; infidel cartographers drew the best charts; and unbelievers had sailed all the way around the globe.

But Turgut Reis had a secret that he had never revealed to anyone: one day he would, in a splendid gesture, demonstrate that the Faithful still possessed the skills that Allah had bestowed on the followers of the Prophet and, at the same time, burnish his own family tradition. He, Turgut Reis, might never be able to circumnavigate the globe like an infidel, nor explore the farther fringes of the western ocean, but he had the means and the opportunity to expand the Book of Sea Lore that his ancestor had pioneered, and that was just as momentous. That is why, every time he went on the corso, he carried with him his notebooks and brushes, why he made notes of the harbours and anchorages, and drew sketches of the coastlines. The day would come, if Allah willed it, when he would organise all these notes and drawings, and produce a new edition of the Kitab-i Bahriye, updating it to show all the changes that had taken place in the Mediterranean since the days of the High Admiral. It would be his personal homage to the memory of his ancestor.

Belatedly he had come to realise the magnitude of the task ahead of him, and now he worried that its accomplishment was slipping from his grasp. Through God's will he lacked sons who might share in the great design, and with each passing year he felt the burden of his ancestry resting more heavily on his shoulders. In short, he needed a capable assistant to make sense of all his notes, organise his many sketches, and draw fair copies of his maps and charts. Perhaps, Turgut thought to himself, the young man he had bought that day might be just the amanuensis he needed. That, too, might be the gift of Allah.

Turgut bowed his head and closed his eyes. His lips moved in a silent prayer, as he beseeched the Most Merciful, the All-Merciful, that he would be granted a life long enough to fulfil that ambition, and that his eyesight would not fail prematurely.

Suddenly Turgut felt chilly. While he had been daydreaming, the sun had sunk behind the mountains, and the evening was growing cold. He clapped his hands to summon a servant and picked up the Kitab. Cradling it like his own child, he descended the stairs from the roof top, entered his library and replaced the volume in its box of cedar wood. Behind him the servant carried the precious ocean map in its folder, and then stood waiting until his master had laid it safely beneath a coverlet of dark green velvet. As Turgut took one last glance around his library to make sure that everything was in its proper place, he wondered if there was any way that he could retrieve the black-haired boy from the clutches of the khaznadji before the drudgery of being a beylik slave ruined him.

SIX

☾

THE KHAZNADJI was quick to satisfy his grudge. A servant separated Hector from the other captives in the Dey's courtyard, and began to herd him briskly through the narrow city streets. When the bewildered young man asked where he was being taken, his escort only repeated, 'Bagnio! Bagnio!' and urged him to hurry. For a while Hector believed that he was being taken to a bath house to be washed, for he was filthy and dishevelled. But arriving before a grim-looking stone building he swiftly understood that his anticipation was completely misplaced. The building appeared to be a cross between a prison and a barracks, and the stench wafting out of its massive doors, which stood open, made him gag. It was a foul combination of human excrement, cooking smells, soot and unwashed bodies.

After a short delay a bored-looking guard took him in charge, then led him to a side room where a blacksmith fitted an iron ring around his right ankle, hammering down the rivet which held it shut. Next he was led to another anteroom where a barber roughly shaved his head, and then to a clothes store. Here the garments in which he had been captured were taken away and he was issued with a bundle containing a coarse blanket, a smock, and a curious item of dress which he at first took to be a woman's petticoat. Shaped like an open sack, it was sewn across the base, leaving two slits through which he was shown to put his legs so as to make a very baggy pair of pantaloons. He was also given a pair of slippers and a red cap, and another attendant recorded his name in a ledger. Finally he was ushered down the length of a vaulted passageway and thrust out into the open courtyard which formed the centre of the great building. Here he was finally left to himself.

Hector looked around. He was in the largest building he had ever known. The rectangular courtyard was at least fifty paces by thirty, and open to the skies. On either side an arched colonnade ran the full length of the building, its arches supporting a second-floor gallery. From dim recesses between the arches came the sounds of drunken singing and loud voices quarrelling and shouting. To his astonishment a Turkish soldier, undoubtedly the worse for drink, came reeling and staggering out of the shadows and made his way to the gate. He weaved his way past a number of sick or exhausted slaves lying on the ground or sitting propped against the walls. Hector started to walk hesitantly across the open courtyard, clutching his blanket and wondering what he should do next, or where he should go. The whole building seemed unnaturally empty, though it was clearly designed to house at least a couple of thousand inmates. He had walked no more than a few yards when he felt someone's eyes on him. Looking up, he noticed a man leaning out over the balcony from the upper floor, watching him closely. The stranger was a man of middle age, round-headed and with his dark hair cropped close. Half his body remained in shadow, but it was evident that he was powerfully built. Hector paused, and the stranger beckoned to him, then pointed to the corner of the courtyard where a stairway led to the upper floor. Grateful for some guidance, Hector made his way to the staircase and began to climb.

He was met as he emerged on the upper floor and at closer quarters he did not like what he saw. The man was dressed in baggy pantaloons and a loose overmantle and wore the red cap and iron anklet which, Hector now presumed, marked him as a fellow slave. But the man's smile was patently false. 'Benvenuto, benvenuto,' he said, indicating that Hector should follow him. He led Hector a short distance along the balcony, then turned to the right, and Hector found himself in what was evidently some sort of dormitory. Crudely made wooden bunk beds, four tiers high, were packed tightly together, with scarcely room to squeeze between them. There was no window and the only light came through the open doorway. With such little ventilation the room reeked of sweat. All the bunks were empty except for one which contained a lump under a blanket which Hector supposed was either someone asleep or dead.

'Venga, venga,' his guide squeezed his way between the bunks to the back of the room, and was again beckoning to him to follow. Hector saw that the corner of the dormitory had been curtained off by a length of cloth hung from a line. He stepped forward, and the man held aside the curtain so he could pass. As soon as Hector was inside the cubicle, the man dropped the curtain and, from behind, pinioned Hector's arms to his sides. He felt the man's unshaven cheek press against the back of his neck, and hot, fetid breath filled his nostrils. He dropped his blanket and tried to break free, but the stranger's grip was too powerful. 'Calma, calma,' the man was saying, as he wrestled Hector forward until his face was pressed against the wall of the cubicle. Hector felt the man's gut pressing against his back, as he was pinioned in position. A moment later his assailant was pawing at Hector's shirt with one hand, pulling upward, while the other hand was dragging downwards at his loose pantaloons which fell down towards his knees. His attacker was snorting with excitement and lust. Appalled, Hector realised that he was being raped. He thrashed from side to side, trying again to free himself, but it was useless. Every move was anticipated, and Hector was forced harder against the wall. The man was surging now, trying to force himself into Hector, and grunting with effort. Hector felt waves of revulsion.

Abruptly there was a choking grunt, and the pressure pushing him against the wall eased. 'Bastanza!' said a new voice sharply, and there was a gurgling sound. Hector pushed himself clear of the wall and turned to see his assailant clutching at his throat, his thick body arched back, and a third person in the cubicle, half hidden behind his would-be rapist. The newcomer was holding a leather belt which he had looped around the attacker's neck and was now using as a garrotte. 'Bastanza! Bestia!' the newcomer added, pulling the noose tighter so that the cord began to cut off the windpipe. Shaking with shock, Hector pulled up his pantaloons and staggered out of the cubicle, remembering only to scoop up his blanket from the floor.

He blundered past the ranks of bunk beds, and somehow managed to find his way out to the balcony. There he leaned against the balustrade, gasping for air. He felt defiled and frightened. Moments later he sensed someone emerge from the dormitory and stand beside him. 'Are you all right?' It was the voice of his rescuer, and the question was spoken in English. Hector raised his head to look into the face of the man who had saved him. His rescuer was about his own age yet resembled no other man he had seen in his life. His eyes were so dark brown as to appear almost black, and long, straight jet-black hair hung down to his shoulders, framing a narrow face with high cheekbones and a strong nose. His rescuer's skin, Hector was astonished to see, was the colour of peat.

'Malo umbre – a bad man, that one,' explained the newcomer. 'Best you stay out of his way. He's a kaporal and a friend of the aga di baston.'

'Thank you for what you did,' blurted Hector, still shocked.

The man shrugged. 'He cheated me last week. Took my money for a gileffo, and then did nothing. Now he's got a sore throat to remember me by.'

'I'm sorry but I don't understand.'

'A gileffo is what you pay when you want to have the day

off from work. It goes to a kaporal who then arranges with the scrivano that your name is not in the morning roll call.'

He saw that Hector was still too shaken to understand, so abandoned the explanation. 'I am called Dan,' he said, holding out his hand. As he shook hands, Hector noticed that his rescuer had a deep, lilting accent vaguely similar to the way the Devon sailor Dunton spoke.

'I'm Hector, Hector Lynch,' he explained. 'I come from Ireland.'

'I met some Irish when I was a small boy. With them I practised speaking English,' said Dan. 'They had run away from their masters and came to us. We sheltered them, the mesquins. Now I know what it was like for them to be slaves. They told us that they had been sold as punishment for making war in their own country, and sent far from their homes.'

It took Hector several moments to grasp that Dan was speaking about prisoners from Cromwell's campaign in Ireland. He remembered his father telling him how thousands of Irishmen had been shipped to the West Indies and sold off to work as slaves on the plantations. Some of them must have fled their masters.

'You are from the Caribees?' he asked.

'From the Main, the Miskito coast,' replied Dan. 'My people are Miskito, and we have no love for the Spanish who would take our lands. My father, who is a great man among us, sent me on a mission to the King of the English. I was to request that the Miskito become his subjects and, in return, he would supply us with guns to fight off the Spanish. It was my bad fortune to be captured by the Spanish even before I left the Main, and they put me on a ship for Spain to show me off to the people. But their ship was taken by corsairs, and I have finished up here.'

'How long ago was that?'

'I've been here for six months now, and it was lucky for you that I was not at work today. I paid another gileffo to a more honest kaporal, and he arranged it. Here, let me carry your blanket. You need a proper place to put your things.'

Dan led Hector along the balcony, explaining that the bagnio was ruled by a senior Turk known as the guardian bashaw. Under him were his lieutenants, the assistant bashaws, and below them came the kaporals. 'Most of the kaporals are all right provided you pay them a few coins,' Dan stated. 'Not like Emilio who gave you trouble. He blackmails young men. Threatens to have them punished under false charges unless they agree to be his lovers. He and the aga di baston – that's the Turk in charge of beatings – have the same tastes. They both enjoy man love, and there are no women in the bagnio, only men.'

'But Emilio is not a Turkish name,' said Hector.

'The kaporals are not Turks. They are from other countries. Emilio is from some place in Italy, but there are also kaporals from France and Spain, from all over. They are rinigatos, men who have taken the turban, and now have an easier life. You'll find rinigatos everywhere. One has even become the guardian bashaw in another bagnio. A man like Emilio will never go back to Italy. He has too good a time here.'

They had reached another dormitory farther along the balcony. It was arranged in much the same way with tiers of closely packed bunks.

'All the bunks are already taken,' explained Dan, 'but there's enough room to sling a hammock in this space next to my bunk. Tomorrow I'll get hold of some cords and rope. We Miskito use hammocks when we go on hunting trips in the forest so it will be no trouble to make you one. For now you can borrow my straw mattress and sleep on the floor. I'll fix things up with the dormitory kaporal later.'

'I can't thank you enough,' said Hector. 'Everything around here seems so strange and brutal.'

Dan shrugged. 'In my country we are taught to work together when life is hard, and to share what we have. I would offer you some food, but I have nothing left over, and the next rations will not be issued until tomorrow.'

Hector realised that he had not eaten all day and was very hungry.

'The bagnio ration is not much,' Dan added. 'Just a hunk of black bread, and often that is mouldy. You want to stick close to whoever is your gang leader. He'll be given a bowl of vinegar with maybe a few drops of olive oil sprinkled in it. You can dip your bread into the bowl during the meal breaks.'

'Will you be there too?'

'No,' said Dan. 'I live in the bagnio because my master has not enough accommodation for his slaves. He pays a weekly fee to the guardian bashaw to house me. I work as a gardener. I look after my master's masseries outside the city wall, weeding, cultivating, harvesting, all that sort of thing. I go there each morning after roll call. That's where I'll be able to steal the cord for your hammock, from one of his work sheds.'

'So what will I be doing?'

Dan glanced down at Hector's ankle with its iron ring. 'You are a public slave, so you'll do whatever the scrivano assigns you to. It may be in the stone quarries or down at the harbour unloading boats. They'll tell you in the morning.'

'All these words you use, "scrivano", "masserie", and the others, they seem strange yet familiar. What do they mean?'

'That's our bagnio language. A scrivano is a scribe, and a masserie is a garden,' said Dan. 'You must learn the language fast if you are to get by in here. On the work gangs all the commands are given in that tongue – we call it lingua franca, though that seems odd because most of it is Spanish not French. Even the Turks use it when they are speaking with the Moors who don't understand Turkish. There are so many different peoples held in the bagnio, all with their own languages, that we must have a way of understanding one another.'

'My mother was from Spain,' said Hector, 'and she taught me and my sister to speak her language.'

'Then you are fortunate,' commented Dan. 'Some prisoners seem never to learn to speak the lingua franca – the moskovits, for example, who come from the northern lands. They are always apart, and I feel doubly sorry for them because there is never any chance that they will be free. No one in their own country sends money to pay for their release. Some other countries send priests with chests of coin to purchase the liberty of their countrymen. The French do that, and the Spanish also. But their priests often quarrel.'

'What about the English? Do they buy back their people?'

'I don't know for sure. There's a rumour that this will happen soon, when the King in London has enough money to spend on his subjects. If that happens I will continue my journey and bring greetings to the King of England from the Miskito.'

Hector could no longer hold back the question that had been tormenting him since he landed.

'Dan, you said that there are only men in the bagnio. What happens to women who are captured by the corsairs? Where do they go?'

The Miskito heard the anguish in Hector's voice.

'Why do you ask? Do you know a woman who was captured? Your wife, perhaps?'

'My sister, Elizabeth. She was taken at the same time as myself, but placed on another ship, and she did not arrive here in Algiers.'

'Is Elizabeth beautiful?'

'My sister's friends used to say that Elizabeth was bathed in May dew when she was a baby. Where I come from the young women go out at dawn on the first day of May to gather the morning dew and wash their faces with it. They believe the dew makes them beautiful for the coming year.'

'If she is as lovely as you say,' answered Dan, 'then you need have no fears about her safety. The Turks treat their women captives very differently from the men. They never expose the women in public, and they treat them with respect.

But they are still prisoners, and if they come from rich or powerful families, the Turks will demand a great ransom for their release.'

'And what if a woman does not have a rich family?' Hector asked quietly.

'Then a good-looking woman will find a place in her owner's household. Maybe she will be a servant or – and this has happened – she even marries her captor.' Dan paused. He was wondering how to explain gently that it was far more likely that Elizabeth would become her master's concubine when a sudden sound of catcalls and jeers came up from the courtyard. 'Come. The work gangs are returning. There's more to know if you are to survive in the bagnio.'

The two men returned to the balcony, and Hector looked down into the courtyard to see crowds of slaves pouring into the compound. All of them wore the red slave cap, and most looked gaunt and emaciated. One group was powdered with chalky dust which, Dan explained, showed that they had returned from a day working in the stone quarries. Others had streaks of dried mud on their arms and faces as they had been cleaning out the city sewers. A few slaves headed straight for the arcades, several climbed the stairways towards their dormitories but the majority loitered in the courtyard, gossiping or filling in time. Packs of cards and dice appeared as half a dozen gambling sessions began.

'Where do they get their money?' he asked Dan as a group of card players began tossing small coins into the centre of their circle. 'They don't get paid wages, do they?'

Dan laughed. 'No. They steal.' He pointed out a man whose face, even from that distance, looked badly mutilated. 'That one is the king of the thieves. He's a Sicilian. He was caught several times by the Turks, and thrashed. But it did not deter him. Finally the aga di baston lopped off his nose and ears as punishment. But that still had no effect. He simply can't leave off stealing. It's his nature, and now the Turks treat his thievery as a joke.'

More and more slaves were entering the courtyard, which was slowly filling up with men. Without warning a brawl broke out between two groups. There were shouts and curses. Punches were thrown, and two men were down on the ground, mauling one another.

'Remember what I said, about the moskovits,' observed Dan. 'They are the ones with the heavy beards and matted hair. The darker-skinned slaves they are fighting look like they are Spaniards. It's not enough that we are all slaves of the Muslims, but we have to quarrel among ourselves about who worships the Christ god properly. The Spaniards and Italians insult the Greeks, the Greeks spit on the moskovits, and all of them mock – what do you call it – the Puritana.'

'The Puritans. I know what you mean. The Puritana, as you call them, are those who enslaved the Irish you met at home,' commented Hector. 'In my country, too, there are bitter quarrels between those who call themselves Protestant and those who respect the Pope in Rome.'

Dan shook his head, perplexed. 'I have never been able to understand why the Christians manage to have so many quarrels and hatreds among themselves. We Miskito all believe in the same gods and spirits, whether they are of the sun or rain or hurricane or in the sea. Slavery to us is natural. We ourselves hunt slaves, taking them from the weaker tribes around us. But we make them slaves only to do our work and because it gives prestige to their owners, not because we hate their religion.'

The fighting in the courtyard had attracted the attention of the Turkish guards from the gate. They came running into the courtyard and began to break up the fight using whips and cudgels to separate the contestants. The Russians and their opponents drew apart, still looking sullen, but they offered no resistance to the intervention of the guards.

'Whatever happens,' advised Dan, 'whether you are kicked or whipped, or punched in the face by a Turk, you must never strike back. I could pull that unnatural beast Emilio off you because he is foreign-born. But if he had been a true Turk, my certain punishment would be death. Never hit or insult our Turkish masters, that is one rule which everyone respects. Even if the Turk is drunk.'

'But how can that be? I thought that the Mussulmen are forbidden to take alcohol.'

'I'll show you something,' answered Dan, and led him towards the stairway.

They descended to the courtyard and Hector followed the Miskito into one of the side rooms in the arcade. It was a tavern, and doing a thriving business. The place was crowded with slaves, drinking and carousing, the smoke from their clay pipes creating a thick fug that made Hector's eyes water.

'Where does he get the alcohol?' he whispered to Dan, nodding towards the landlord behind his counter at the back of the room. 'He buys it from the merchant ships who come to trade in Algiers, or from the corsair captains who capture it as part of their booty. Then he resells it, often to the Turks themselves because the city authorities turn a blind eye to their own people who come into the bagnio for a drink, provided they don't make an exhibition of themselves.'

Hector noticed a small group of Turks standing close to the counter who were obviously the worse for drink. 'Look behind them,' said Dan, lowering his voice. 'Those big men over there, they're paid by the landlord to keep an eye on the Turks. If any Turk gets drunk and it looks as if he will make trouble, one of those fellows will quietly escort him out of the bagnio. The landlord cannot afford a disturbance. If there is a fight, the guardian bashaw has the power to shut his tavern and order him to be beaten, even though the landlord is giving him a cut of the profits.'

'You mean to say that customers of the tavern can just walk in and out of the bagnio?'

'Yes, until an hour or so after dusk. That is when the gates are locked shut.' Dan cocked his head to one side. 'Listen, you hear that shouting? It's the beylik foreman. He's calling out what the jobs will be tomorrow. It's time we went back up to the dormitory. If it's your first day at work, you'll need all the rest you can get.'

As they climbed back up the staircase Hector asked why the slaves did not attempt to escape if the gates were left open.

'Where would they go?' Dan replied. 'If they run inland, the Moors of the countryside will catch them and bring them back to the city and receive a reward. If they get as far as the mountains, they will be eaten by wild animals. Should they reach the desert beyond the mountains they will get lost and die of thirst.'

'Couldn't they steal a ship?'

'The Turks have thought of that, too. When a galley comes into port after a corso, the first thing they do is order the galley slaves to dump all the oars overboard into the harbour. Then the oars are towed ashore and placed in a secure warehouse. A few slaves have managed to escape by swimming out to visiting merchant ships and stowing away. But the ship captains take good care to search their own vessels before they leave Algiers. If the Turks find an escaped slave aboard a visiting ship, they'll seize the vessel and put it up for sale. The captain and his crew are lucky if they are not enslaved as well.'

They had reached their dormitory, and Hector stretched out on the lumpy straw palliasse Dan had lent him. He lay there, listening to the sounds of the other slaves settling to their rest, the creaking of the bunks, the grumbles and mutterings, the coughs and spitting as men cleared quarry dust from their lungs and mouths, and the gradual chorus of snores. He felt the nagging, hard pressure of the iron ring around his ankle, and after everything he had learned that day he wondered if he would ever find out what had happened to Elizabeth.

SEVEN

☾

'WAKE UP YOU DOGS! Rise you foul unbelievers! Wake and get to work!' Hoarse shouts from the courtyard of the bagnio roused Hector the next morning. The man in the lowest bunk close to him groaned. Then he farted loudly and deliberately so that Hector supposed it was his customary sardonic way of greeting the new day. Holding his breath, Hector got to his feet. 'Time to get going.' It was Dan's voice. The Miskito was already out of his bunk and folding his blanket. 'Get down to the courtyard and listen for your name in the roll call. Then follow what the others do. Try to stay in the background. I'll see you this evening.'

It was barely light, and Hector heard a thin wailing call, then another and another, the sound hanging in the air over the high walls of the bagnio as he descended the stairway to the courtyard. He had heard that cry five times a day since he had been landed at Algiers. It was the adhan, the Muslim call to prayer. At the foot of the stairway he almost tripped over an old man already down on his knees, touching his forehead to the ground. The iron ring around his ankle showed that he was a fellow slave and Hector presumed he was a convert to Islam. When the old man rose stiffly, Hector took the chance to enquire, 'The end of that call, the part which goes something

66

like as-saltu kairun min an-naum, what does that mean?' 'It means "prayer is better than sleep", the old man muttered grumpily, and shuffled off to join the throng of slaves gathering around the entrance to the passageway which led to the gates of the bagnio.

Hector followed and, peering over the heads of the crowd, saw the red-capped figure of a scrivano standing on a stone block, a paper in his hand. He was gabbling out names at a tremendous pace, speaking so fast that it was difficult to catch what he was saying though it was clear that he was directing the men to their day's tasks. Finally Hector heard his name called out, and managed to identify that he had been assigned to a gang of about fifty men forming up under the supervision of an overseer equipped with a short staff. Among them he recognised the Sicilian master thief with the chopped-off nose and ears. Hector looked carefully but he could see none of the men who had been taken prisoner with him in Ireland. He could only imagine they had all been placed in other bagnios. Mindful of Dan's advice, he mingled with his group, trying not to attract attention as they headed down the passageway towards the bagnio gates. No one spoke.

They walked for more than an hour. First through the city, then out of the landward gate and, after a long slow uphill trudge, to a place where the hill had been cut open in a long scar, the pale rock showing raw in the morning light. Only then did Hector understand that he had been assigned to quarry work. A scatter of tools lay where they had been abandoned the day before – sledgehammers, wedges, crowbars, shovels and coils of rope. All the equipment was battered and poorly maintained. Hector paused, wondering what was expected of him. Immediately the overseer was yelling at him, 'Aia! Subito!', and pointing towards a sledgehammer with a splintered handle. As the sun rose higher and the day grew hotter, he found himself working in partnership with a gaunt, silent Russian. Their task was to gouge a line of holes in the rock face, each hole about a yard from the previous one. They took it in turns, one man swinging the sledgehammer, the other holding a metal spike which served as the rock chisel. Very quickly Hector's arms and shoulders were aching from the weight of the hammer, and his hands were swollen and bruised from his grip on the spike though he took care to wrap his fingers in a rag. They had prepared four holes and were starting on a fifth when something changed. The nearby workmen had stopped work. The sounds of hammering and chipping had ceased, and suddenly the quarry was silent. Hector put aside the iron spike, stretched, and flexed his hand to ease the cramp. Abruptly the Russian said his first words in hours – 'Boum! Boum! Boum!' – flung aside the sledgehammer and took to his heels. Hector hesitated only for a moment, then started to follow. He had taken only a few strides when there was a deep, heavy explosion and the ground beneath his feet heaved. A blast of air pushed him forward and he fell face down, landing painfully on rubble. A moment later shards of rock and pebbles began to fall from the sky, pattering all around him. One or two struck him painfully on his back as he wrapped his arms around his head to protect himself.

Shaken and half deafened, he got to his feet. A wide section of the rock face close to where they had been working now lay tumbled down in great slabs at the foot of the cliff. The other slaves thought his narrow escape was a great joke, and were hooting and laughing. The Sicilian was making a weird braying and snorting sound as he guffawed, the air gushing out of his ruined nose. Hector understood that they had known about the impending blast, and deliberately chosen not to warn him. He smiled ruefully at them, rubbed his bruises and silently cursed them for their uncouth sense of humour. He blamed himself for failing to realise that the holes were for gunpowder charges that would split the rock. 'Subito! Subito!' the overseer was shouting again angrily and gesticulating that the slaves were to get back to their places. Hector turned and was about to pick up the sledgehammer when there was a second explosion, smaller this time and farther along the rock face. A cloud of dust spurted out, and several chunks of rock hurtled through the air. One fragment, the size of an orange, struck a man who had been walking forward to check the newly exposed rock face. There was a grunt of pain as the man staggered back, clutching his right arm.

This time there was no laughter. The other slaves looked on nervously. 'Subito! Subito!' bellowed the overseer. He rushed forward, this time striking the slaves with his goad, driving them back to work. Hector, still dizzy from the earlier blast, failed to move. The overseer caught sight of him and waved at him to go to the assistance of the stricken man. Hector went forward and put an arm around the victim, who was gritting his teeth with pain and cursing in English. 'Shit powder. Shitting cheap powder.' Hector helped him to where he could sit down on a coil of rope. The man bent forward in pain, still clutching his shoulder and swearing. He did not wear a slave's iron ring on his ankle, and was better dressed than the men from the bagnio.

'Is there anything I can do?' offered Hector. The man shook his head angrily.

'Should have known better than to trust that muck,' he said and kicked angrily at a nearby keg. Hector saw that it was marked with a triple x in red paint. 'Cheap bastards. Should learn to make their own powder,' continued the injured man.

'What happened?' asked Hector.

'Late blast,' came the short reply. 'Should have all gone off at once, but this powder is useless. The Turks must have bought it off some swindling trader who knew it was unfit.'

Hector supposed that the injured man was some sort of technician in charge of the blasting. The man kicked at the keg again, and it rolled on one side. It had the letters d, m, n scratched across the base.

'Those letters on the base. Maybe they are short for "damno"

— Latin for "condemned",' Hector volunteered. The technician looked at him.

'A smart-arse are you? But you're probably right. Here, go off and check the other kegs stored under that tarpaulin over there before this happens again.'

Hector did as he was told and came back to report that two out of the eight kegs stacked there also had the code scratched on them. The technician spat. 'I'll get the overseer to assign you as my assistant. I'm going to be useless with this damaged arm for the next few weeks, and the quarrying never stops.'

℃

THAT EVENING Hector arrived in the bagnio so exhausted that he could barely put one foot in front of the other. He was also half-starved. As anticipated, the only meal of the day had been an issue of coarse bread, delivered mid-morning by two elderly slaves wheeling a barrow. To quench their thirst the slaves only had water from an open cask, filthy with a film of quarry dust floating on the surface. 'Here eat some of this,' offered Dan when they met up in a corner of the courtyard. He unwrapped a bundle and Hector saw that it contained a melon, some beans and several squashes. Hector accepted the offer gratefully.

'I usually manage to sneak away a few vegetables from my gardening at the end of the day,' said Dan. 'My master probably knows that this is happening, but he doesn't make a fuss. He appreciates it is as a cheap way of feeding his slaves to keep up their strength, and that we'll work better if we have a share in the crop. Anything extra that I don't eat myself, I sell in the bagnio.'

'Is that how you obtain the money for the gileffo?' asked Hector.

'Yes, everyone in the bagnio tries to have some sort of extra income. I sell my vegetables in the evening; others do odd jobs. In this place we have shoemakers, cutlers, barbers, tailors, all sorts. The lucky ones manage to get themselves jobs in the city, working for Turks or Moors, either full-time or on Friday, which is our day off. It's the ones who don't have a trade who suffer. They're work animals, nothing more.'

Hector told him about the accident at the quarry. 'The technician who was hurt, he was English yet he wasn't wearing a slave ring nor a red hat. How does that come about?'

'He'll be one of the skilled men to whom the Turks give their liberty in exchange for using their skills,' suggested Dan. 'Or he might be a volunteer, someone who's come to Algiers to find work. The Turks don't insist they convert, just so long as they do their jobs. Some of them have nice houses and even have their own servants. There's a master shipwright in the Arsenal, a Venetian, who is so much in demand that he's paid more by the Turks than when he worked at the Venice shipyards.'

'The technician wants me to assist him until his arm has healed,' said Hector. 'He seems a decent fellow.'

'Then if I were you, I'd make myself as useful as possible to that powder man,' advised Dan without hesitation. 'It will mean that you have to spend less time swinging a sledgehammer or crawling through the sewers with the city work gang. Just make sure you learn the usanza.'

'What's that?' Hector asked. He bit hungrily into a piece of raw squash.

'It means custom or habit in the lingua franca. My own people the Miskito have something similar. Our elders who guide us – we call them the old men council – tell us how it was in the old days and they insist we follow the ancient customs.'

He broke off another piece of squash and handed it to Hector.

'It is the same here in the bagnio. The rules and regulations have built up over time and you learn them by watching others or following their example. If you break these rules, the Turks will tell you that it is against usanza and therefore a fantasia.

That means it is unacceptable conduct – and you will be punished. The system suits our masters. The Turks want everything to remain as it is, with them in control. So Jew must remain Jew, Moor must stay Moor, and there is no mixing between different peoples. The Turks go so far as to refuse to let any native-born Algerine become an odjak. Even the son of a Turk and a local woman is forbidden from joining the janissaries. To become an odjak you must either be a Turk from the homelands or a rinigato, a Christian who has converted.'

'I find it strange,' said Hector, 'that foreign slaves are given an opportunity denied to the local people.'

Dan shrugged. 'Many slaves do take the turban. It is said that there are only three ways of getting out of the bagnio: by ransom, by turning Turk, or by dying from the plague.'

EIGHT

C

Consul Martin was finding mercer Newland a bore. He was beginning to wish that his dragoman had not been so adroit with his bribe to the Dey's office. The tubby English business-man had been released into consular care on the very same day as the slave sale, and for more than a month Consul Martin had been enduring Newland's tedious company while waiting to hear back from London about his ransom. The consul had given the cloth merchant a room in his house, and it was only common courtesy to invite him to dinner from time to time. Unfortunately the mercer had no interesting conversation to offer and held very entrenched opinions, so the invitations, which had originally been once or twice a week, had now lapsed. Consul Martin, however, made an exception when he finally got news that an official government delegation was on its way from London to Algiers to deal with the hostage question. Martin presumed that whoever was raising money in London for Newland's ransom would take the opportunity of sending the payment with the government delegation.

'One hopes that the delegation from London will have a fair wind for their voyage here, Mr Newland,' said the consul, rolling a small pellet of bread between his fingers. It was the last morsel of a flat loaf of particularly delicious local bread. When on his own, the consul adopted the Turkish style of eating, reclining on cushions on the floor. But when he had Christian guests, he kept a more normal service with table and chairs. However, he drew the line at serving hearty meals of roast meat and potatoes. He and his guest had just eaten a delicious lamb kebab and homous. 'The weather in the Mediterranean is very unpredictable. So there's no way of knowing exactly when the envoy will arrive.'

'Have the terms of my release been finally agreed, do you know?' asked the mercer bluntly.

'That I can't say. The envoy is on government business and his official duty is to arrange the ransom of ordinary English captives, not men of substance like yourself.' The consul watched Newland preen himself at the compliment. 'But it is to be expected that your own principal – I think you said it was Mr Sewell of Change Alley – will take advantage of this delegation to conclude the matter of your own release. If all goes well, you should be travelling back with the envoy himself.'

The mercer adopted his usual self-important tone. 'I hope that the negotiations over the ordinary captives, as you call them, will not delay matters.'

'That is difficult to predict. Unfortunately there is a history of the Algerines demanding high ransoms, and the envoy arriving with insufficient funds to meet them. Inevitably a period of offer and counter-offer follows until a final arrangement is agreed.'

'Could you not point out to the Dey and his bandits that I, and the others, should never have been taken prisoner in the first place; that our kidnap broke the terms of the treaty between our countries? You should insist.'

Inwardly the consul grimaced. The thought of insisting on anything with the Dey and the odjaks was counterproductive as well as dangerous. 'The Algerines enjoy bartering,' he commented blandly. 'They feel cheated if there are not some negotiations.'

'Then the bartering should be done by men who are used to

it, to men of affairs,' Newland asserted. 'We would get a better outcome.'

'I'm sure that the local intermediary who acted on your behalf, the Jew Yaakov, was very skilled in his negotiations,' reassured Martin.

'But the treaty, the treaty. The Algerines cannot be allowed to get away with ignoring their treaty obligations.'

The consul thought to himself that Newland, if he had not been so self-opinionated, should know by now that the Dey and the divan made and broke agreements as it suited them. He wondered if he should point out to Newland that many a merchant would vary or break a trade agreement if he could do so without being sued and it was to his advantage. Yet Newland was expecting the Algerines to behave differently when, in fact, their slave-taking was merely a matter of business. In the end the consul decided not to provoke the mercer.

'The fact is, Mr Newland, that when you and those unfortunate Irish were taken prisoner by the corsair Hakim Reis, the treaty was temporarily set aside. The Dey had announced in council that it was being suspended because too many ships were sailing under English passes to which they were not entitled, and that the English were abusing the terms of the treaty by selling their passes to foreign shipowners.'

'So that rascal Hakim Reis was within his rights to take us?'

'Technically, yes. The Dey and the divan had made their decision to abrogate the treaty some weeks earlier. They informed me that a state of war between our nations was being resumed, and I sent word to London to that effect. But there was no public announcement until the same week you were captured.'

'News travels quickly in this part of the world if that corsair scoundrel was so well informed.'

'Hakim Reis is an unusually successful and acute corsair, Mr Newland. He seems always alert to the most immediate opportunity. It was your misfortune to be in his path.'

'And how long did this state of war continue?' persisted Newland. The tone of his question indicated that he thought Martin was making excuses, and that he had failed to insist that the Dey met his obligations.

'For less than two months,' answered the consul, making an effort to keep even-tempered. 'Last week I was summoned to the Dey's palace and told that the treaty would be restored, on the orders of the Sublime Porte. That is an excuse the Dey uses often. He says one thing, then reverses his position, claiming that he has been overruled by the Sultan. But it does mean that the envoy from London will be warmly received and there is every likelihood that your own release is imminent.'

And not a moment too soon, he thought to himself.

ℂ

THE INJURED mining technician was the first to tell Hector about the rumour of a delegation from London. The two of them were at the quarry, weighing and mixing measures of gunpowder for a new set of blasting charges. The technician, Josias Buckley, seemed strangely unexcited by the news. 'Aren't you looking forward to going home?' Hector asked, puzzled.

'No, I won't be going home as you call it,' Buckley replied as he gently transferred another spoonful of the black powder from a barrel into a canvas pouch. 'I'll be staying here. This is where I've made my life.'

Hector looked at Buckley in astonishment. During his weeks as his assistant, he had grown to respect the man for his skill and the careful, patient way in which he had guided him in the art of handling explosives.

'What about your family? Won't they be missing you?' Hector asked. He was thinking back, as he so often did, to what might have happened to Elizabeth.

'I have no family left,' replied Buckley quietly. 'My wife and I never had children, and she was working at the mill when there was an accident. That was back at home in England, near two years ago now. She and a dozen others were blown to pieces. There was not even enough left of her to give her a proper burial, poor soul. Afterwards I decided I would seek my fortune here in Barbary. I imagined there would be a demand for gunpowder men like myself so I came here of my own free will. The beylik pays me a wage, and I share a house with others like myself, ordinary men who came here to find a new home. The Turks do not demand we change to their religion.'

They finished preparing the gunpowder and were carrying the mix over to the rock face where the work gangs had drilled out the holes ready to receive the charges. Hector noticed how the labourers moved away nervously as they approached. At the first of the holes, Buckley began to pour in the gunpowder. 'Two pounds' weight is about right,' he said to Hector. 'Make sure the powder is packed evenly. No lumps. Here pass me a length of fuse, will you?'

With the powder and fuse in place, he took a conical wooden plug from the sack which Hector had carried for him and, pressing it into the hole, began to tap it into place, the pointed end upward. The first time Hector had seen this done, he had dreaded an accident. But Buckley had reassured him that gunpowder would only ignite with a spark or fire, not from the blow of a hammer. 'Now, lad,' he said, once the plug was driven tight, 'fill the rest of the hole with earth and chippings and tamp everything down so that it is nice and snug. But not too tight so that the fuse chokes off and doesn't burn through.'

They moved on to the next hole in the rock to repeat the process, and Hector took his chance to ask, 'Where was the mill where you worked before?'

'In the county of Surrey where my family had lived for generations. Years ago we used to make up small quantities of gunpowder in our own house until the government regulations came in. Then the big mills took over, and the monopolists had their chance. The small family producers could not compete, so we went to work in the mill. Of course we got jobs straight away as we knew the trade so well. My father and grandfather and his father had all been petremen, as far back as anyone could remember.'

He saw Hector was looking bemused.

'Petremen,' he repeated, 'that's what they called the men who went round the country looking for saltpetre. They had authority to go into hen houses, barnyards, farm middens and take whatever scrapings they could find. Without saltpetre – and a lot of it – there's no gunpowder.'

'Sounds like Latin,' said Hector. 'Sal-petrae would mean "salt of stones", so how come you found it in a hen house?'

'There you go again. You're too smart for your own good, what with all that education,' answered Buckley, poking a wooden rod into the next drill hole to make sure that it was not clogged. 'You find saltpetre wherever stale piss or dung has had time to ripen. Don't ask me how. It's said that the best piss for saltpetre comes out of a drunken bishop.'

He chuckled. 'The petremen would gather up the ordure and carry it back to their homes where they could boil and strain and purify it. Slow work. It takes nearly a hundred pounds of scrapings to make a half pound of petre, and that's the main ingredient for gunpowder – seventy-five parts of petre to ten parts of brimstone and fifteen parts of charcoal, and you should use willow charcoal if you can get it.'

He laid the rod aside and reached out for the bag of tools and materials that Hector was carrying.

'Now everything's different. The gunpowder mills bring in their saltpetre from India. And there's no more grinding by hand, which used to take hours and hours. It's all done by machines. Big stamping machines. And of course the people who are employed don't have the old knowledge, and so accidents happen. A wild spark, and the whole lot goes up. So my wife dies, and both my cousins.'

He paused to cut off another length of fuse cord, and laid it carefully into the next hole before pouring in the correct measure of powder.

'When I first came here,' he went on, 'I had dreams of setting up my own gunpowder mill and supplying good powder to the Turks. In my family there was a story that in the days of Queen Bess we got our petre from Barbary and it was made into the cannon powder that stopped the Great Armada. So I thought I would find petre here in Algiers, and add brimstone from Sicily because everyone knows that you find yellow brimstone near volcanoes. But as it turned out, I never found the petre and the Sicilian brimstone was poor stuff, full of impurities. So I had to go round the local pigeon lofts, just like my great-grandfather, and collect up the droppings. In the end it wasn't worth it. I could make serpentine but not the corned powder that the Turks wanted for their cannon and muskets.'

'I don't know the difference,' Hector said deferentially. He felt that if he was to work safely with Buckley, he should learn everything that the technician was willing to tell him.

'There's a world of difference. Serpentine is what we made at home, basic gunpowder if you like. It's all right if you keep it dry and mix it well. But it's unreliable. It was a charge of serpentine, exploding late, which near cost me my right arm the other day. Corned powder is mill-made, and shaken through sieves so it is graded nice and regular. Small grains for muskets and pistols, larger grains for the big guns. There's no one making corned powder in all the lands of the Grand Turk, as far as I know. Certainly not here in Algiers. Anyone who managed to do so, would command his own price.'

'Talking about price,' Hector ventured, 'if it's true that there's someone coming from London to buy back captives, what sort of price will he be paying?'

Buckley gave the young man a sympathetic glance. 'Whatever his budget allows. And then only if he is an honest man.

There are a lot of sticky fingers when it comes to handling ransoms.'

Ⓒ

WORK AT THE quarry finished an hour before sunset, and as soon as he was free to do so, Hector hurried back to the bagnio, eager to find Dan. He was looking forward to telling him about the expected envoy from London and that they were soon to be ransomed. From his first day in the bagnio when Dan had rescued him from the lecherous kaporal, Hector had found himself increasingly grateful to his fellow captive. The Miskito had continued to share with him the vegetables he stole from his gardening, and had coached the young Irishman in the ways of the bagnio. Without that knowledge Hector doubted he would have survived.

Hector could not see his friend in the bagnio courtyard, so he went up to their dormitory to see if perhaps Dan had gone there. But without success. Wondering what had detained Dan, Hector was halfway back down the stairway when he noticed two Turkish guards enter the courtyard through the arched passage leading to the main gate. They were carrying a prisoner between them. Hector stopped short. The man hanging between the two guards was Dan, and his legs were trailing limply on the ground. Hector knew at once what had happened. He raced down the stair and across the courtyard, arriving just at the moment the two guards dropped their burden and Dan collapsed on the ground, face down. 'Dan!' he cried anxiously, 'try to get up on your knees, and put one arm over my shoulder. I'll lift you.'

Hearing Hector's voice, Dan raised his head and gave a grimace of pain. 'Usanza and fantasia,' he muttered. 'I forgot my own advice.' Then, his face contorted with the effort, the Miskito half-rose and clung to his friend so that Hector was able to assist him slowly and carefully up to the dormitory where he laid Dan gently on his bunk.

The normally phlegmatic Miskito groaned as he stretched out his legs.

'Was it bad?' asked Hector.

'Forty blows. But it could have been worse. Might have been fifty or more. The aga di baston was that pervert, Emilio's friend. He laid on specially hard for what I did to his crony.'

'How did it happen?'

'It was stupid of me. I was working in the masserie when a Turkish guard discovered a local woman hiding in the bushes nearby. I had seen her several times before, and knew she used to meet up with one of the other gardeners from time to time. He's a Spanish slave and sells stolen vegetables cheaply to her as she's a poor woman and has little money to spare. But the guard thought she was having a love affair with one of the gardeners, and began to beat her. I intervened as the Spaniard wasn't nearby. This made the guard think that I was the lover, and he began beating me too. The commotion brought other guards, and I was taken back down to the bagnio. They clamped my ankles in a wooden yoke which the two guards held up so my shoulders were on the ground and my feet in the air. Then the aga di baston laid on. I was lucky he was beating only the soles of my feet with his staff, for if he had hit me in the ribs I think he would have smashed them. Still, I'm probably luckier than the wretched woman. She'll be severely punished for consorting with a slave.'

'Lie still while I get some salve for your feet from that French prisoner who was an apothecary. He'll sell me some ointment,' said Hector. Dan winced as he reached inside his shirt and produced a purse dangling around his neck. 'Here take the money from this,' he offered. 'Don't let him cheat you.'

'What about tomorrow?' Hector was worried. 'It will be days before you can walk again, and you need rest.'

'Fix it with our friendly kaporal. Give him the remainder of the money. Make it a big enough gileffo so that I am excused work for the next week or so.'

'Leave it to me,' said Hector. 'At least I've some news to cheer you up. Someone's coming from London with money to purchase the release of all English slaves. Maybe when he hears that you were captured by the corsairs when you were on your way to London with a message for the King of England from the Miskito people, he will pay for your release as well so you can complete your mission.'

Dan grinned weakly. 'Your news, my friend, helps dull the pain more than any ointment. If I had to stay here, I don't think that I could face another dose of the bastinado.'

©

CONSUL MARTIN was a humane and sensitive man so normally he disliked visiting the bagnios. Quite apart from their stench and squalor, the slave barracks depressed him because they made him feel a fraud. His standing instructions from London were to be polite and friendly when meeting with his fellow countrymen held prisoner. But he was also told that he was to avoid being drawn into any discussions about possible release. If pressed, he was to discourage any speculation on the subject.

In the consul's opinion that turned him into a hypocrite.

So he was in an altogether more optimistic mood on the morning he accompanied Mr Abercrombie, the newly arrived English envoy, to interview the prisoners. At last there was a chance to redeem these unfortunate wretches, some of whom had been waiting five or six years for release back to their own country. Nor did the cheerless demeanour of the envoy – the 'commissioner' as he preferred to style himself – dampen the consul's good spirits.

Abercrombie was exactly the sort of person that Martin had expected. He had the manner of a long-serving bookkeeper, and the lugubrious expression on his narrow face was enhanced by a long upper lip and a voice that was lifeless and flat. The commissioner had arrived three days earlier aboard a 40-gun English warship now anchored in the harbour, and his present task was to visit the various bagnios where English prisoners were being held. There the envoy would audit the true value of each slave, for it had been agreed with the Dey that whoever owned the slave was to receive a ransom equal to the sum the slave had originally fetched at auction. Naturally the commissioner made it plain that he mistrusted the accuracy of the sums that the Dey's secretary had written down for him.

Abercrombie had also told the consul that he intended to check the identities of the captives on the Dey's list because it was not unknown for impostors to pretend to be dead or missing prisoners in the hopes of obtaining their freedom. In addition, Abercrombie saw it as his duty to make sure that the captives were in good health. It would be a waste of funds, he primly reminded Martin, to ransom an invalid who would then die on the way home.

The audit was well into its second day by the time that Martin and the commissioner, accompanied by their dragoman, arrived at the bagnio where Hector and Dan were being held. According to the official list there were no more than half a dozen English prisoners in the bagnio, and it was clear to Martin that Abercrombie was eager to finish up quickly. A lieutenant of janissaries met them at the gate. After apologising for the Guardian Pasha's absence, he informed his visitors that all the English prisoners were assembled and ready for their interviews. He then ushered them into the interview room where Martin found the vekil hardj, the Dey's under-treasurer, already waiting. With him was the Greek slave whom Martin remembered as the interpreter who assisted when new captives were landed in the port. Martin also noted that the interviews were to be held in the same room where new prisoners had their iron anklets fitted. A number of these chains and anklets had been left on display. Wryly he surmised that these manacles were a deliberate encouragement for the commissioner to pay generously for the prisoners' release.

The half-dozen cases were soon dealt with, and Abercrombie

was gathering up his documents and about to take his leave when the Greek, on a quiet suggestion from the vekil hardj, spoke up.

'Your Excellency, my master asks if you will be interviewing the other slaves today, or do you wish to return tomorrow?'

The commissioner kept his dour expression. Turning to Martin, he asked, 'What other prisoners? I hope this is not just an attempt to extract additional funds. We have already exceeded our budget as it is. According to the register, there are no other English captives in this slave barracks.'

Martin looked questioningly at the interpreter.

'The people landed by Hakim Reis,' the Greek murmured. 'Their status, you will recall, is undetermined.'

The commissioner was waiting for Martin to explain. 'What is all this about?' he enquired acidly.

'Hakim Reis is a well-known corsair,' began Martin.

'I know, I know,' interrupted Abercrombie. 'He was the man who took the mercer, Newland. His London agent has been pestering the ministry for weeks, and I have brought with me the first instalment of the money for his ransom. This matter need not detain us.'

'There were other prisoners taken by Hakim,' the consul explained. 'I put their names on a separate register and sent a copy to London.'

Abercrombie searched among his papers. 'I have no record of this,' he said peevishly.

'Should we not interview them while we are here?' suggested Martin.

'Very well. But let us not waste any more time.'

The Greek nodded to the guard waiting at the door, and he ushered in a man whom Martin instantly recognised. It was the intelligent-looking youth who had caught his attention on the dock. He was leaner and more tanned, but there was no mistaking his black hair and his alert expression.

'Your name?' snapped the commissioner, obviously impatient with the additional interview.

'Lynch, sir. Hector Lynch.'

'Your place of birth?'

'The county of Cork, sir.'

'That's in Ireland is it not?'

'Yes, sir.'

Abercrombie looked down at the paper on the table before him. 'I do not see your name on this inventory. Your parents and family? Have they made any attempt to contact the authorities in London?'

'My father is dead, sir. And my mother may not know what happened to me. She could have moved back to live with her own people.'

The commissioner raised his head and regarded the young man with mistrust. 'Her own people? Who are they?'

'Her family are from Spain.

'From Spain?' Suspicion had crept into the commissioner's voice. 'She is a Papist?'

'Yes, sir. My mother is of the Catholic faith, my father was Protestant.'

Abercrombie pursed his lips. It was obvious to Consul Martin that the English envoy was now hostile to the young man. His line of questioning soon confirmed his antagonism.

'Your deceased father, was he born in Ireland?'

'He was, sir.'

'And had his family lived there for several generations?'

'That is right.'

Commissioner Abercrombie gave a small dry cough. 'Then I regret, Mr Lynch, that your case falls outside my remit. The treaty between His Majesty's government and the authorities in Algiers regarding the redemption of prisoners, covers only those of His Majesty's subjects born or living in England, Scotland and Wales. There is no mention of Ireland in the text. It would therefore be improper of me to approve disbursement of funds outside the terms of my authority.'

Consul Martin saw a look of disbelief cross the young Irishman's face, followed by one of stubbornness. Lynch remained standing in front of the desk. The commissioner mistook his attitude for incomprehension.

'It means, Mr Lynch, that I am unable to authorise payment from the funds at my disposal in order to effect your release or that of others of his Majesty's Irish subjects. Doubtless that matter can be considered on my return to London. I shall draw attention to this omission, and it is to be hoped that the Council will amend the relevant clauses within the treaty. Until then the matter is out of my hands.'

Martin had been expecting the young Irishman to react with disappointment, even anger. But to his surprise the young man only glanced down at the Dey's list and asked, 'With your honour's permission, are there any women captives on your list?'

Irritably, the commissioner turned the sheet of paper face down and replied, 'That is none of your affair.'

'I ask because my sister, Elizabeth, was also taken captive at the same time as myself, and I have had no news of what has happened to her.'

Consul Martin, seeing that the commissioner was not going to answer the question, intervened. 'We have interviewed all the women prisoners currently in Algiers. There are only five of them, and all their ransom values have been agreed. There was no mention of any Elizabeth.' Only then did the consul see the light of hope fade from the young Irishman's eyes.

'That will be all, Mr Lynch. You may go,' said the commissioner curtly.

'I have a favour to ask,' said the young man. He was still standing his ground.

'You try my patience,' said Abercrombie. He was getting angry.

But the Irishman was not to be put off. 'There is a prisoner here in the bagnio who was taken by the Algerines while travelling to London with a message for the King. In all conscience, he should be considered for ransom. He is waiting outside.'

'This is as presumptuous as it is preposterous . . .' began Abercrombie, his voice sour with disbelief. And again the consul thought he should intervene.

'Where is he from, this message bearer?' he asked.

'From the Caribees, sir.'

Consul Martin glanced at the commissioner. Like everyone else engaged in commerce, he knew that the political influence of the West Indian merchants in London was very strong. Anything to do with the Caribees was a matter to be handled carefully. The commissioner clearly had the same reaction so Martin decided that it was best to be prudent. 'On your way out, please be so good as to tell this person to come in.'

As the young Irishman turned and walked towards the door, the consul found himself wondering if perhaps the authorities in London had been right all along, and that it was kinder never to encourage a prisoner's hopes, even for a moment. Martin tried to imagine how he himself would react if he had been repudiated so brusquely by the country he had expected to protect him. He very much doubted that he would have mustered the same dignity and self-restraint shown by the young man as he left the room. The consul hoped that the next interview would not turn out to be equally as shameful.

℃

HECTOR LOITERED in the bagnio courtyard as he waited for his friend to emerge from his interview. Deliberately he ignored the black disappointment of his own interrogation as he wondered how Dan was faring.

It was no more than five minutes before his friend reappeared, his expression unreadable. 'The man in the dark clothes did not believe me,' said Dan tonelessly. 'He asked to see a copy of my message for the King. I answered that the Miskito have no writing. We speak our messages, even the most important ones.'

'What did he say to that?' asked Hector.

'He told me that he needed proper evidence, something written on paper, that I was telling the truth. The man sitting beside him was more friendly. He said that he had heard of my people, the Miskito, and that they had helped the English. He even suggested to his companion that because the Miskito asked to be considered as subjects of the King, then my name might be added to the list of those who would be ransomed.'

'And the other man did not agree?'

'He answered that he would apply the same rules as he had followed in your case, and that, in addition, the treaty with Algiers only concerned English subjects taken from ships flying the English flag. I had already told him that the corsairs had taken me out of a Spanish ship, so it seems I could not be included on the ransom list.'

Hector looked down at the worn paving slabs of the courtyard. For the very first time in his captivity he despaired. He was crushed by the thought of spending year after year in the bagnio.

'I'm sorry, Dan,' he said. 'I'm really sorry. It seems that there is nothing we can do to get out of here. We'll stay until we rot. No one is going to lift a finger to help us.'

But to his surprise, Dan answered calmly, 'Then we ourselves will lift a finger.'

Hector looked at his friend in puzzlement. 'What do you mean?'

'I mean that we will turn Turk. It doesn't take much. All you have to do is raise a finger to the sky in the presence of two witnesses who are good Muslims, and acknowledge that Allah is the true God and Muhammad is his prophet. That's all there is to it . . . and of course you have to be cut.'

'Cut?'

'Yes, someone with a knife trims back the skin on your manhood, as a sign that you have converted.'

Despite himself, Hector looked queasy.

'Well, why not?' Dan went on. 'Once you have become a rinigato – become a Muslim – you have a much better chance of finding proper work that takes you out of the bagnio, and it is forbidden to send you to serve in the galleys. You may think that life is hard when working in the quarries, but it is nothing compared to being chained alongside three or four other prisoners and hauling on the handle of a 30-foot-long oar. It's late summer now, and soon all the galleys are coming back to harbour. But come the spring, every able-bodied man in the bagnio risks being sent to the oar benches.'

Hector thought for a moment. 'Is there no other way to get out of here? How about the gunpowder man? He's at liberty and he remains a Christian.'

Dan shook his head. 'No. The gunpowder man came to Algiers of his own free will. He can stay a Christian. It's not the same for us. That's the usanza.'

'Aren't you worried about becoming a Mussulman?'

Dan shrugged. 'As I told you, the Miskito believe in many gods and spirits. And so do the Turks, though they say there is only one God. My master who owns the masserie is a Mussulman but he still believes in what he calls djinns and efrit, the wicked spirits who might snatch him away or do him harm. So I can acknowledge Allah as the one God and still believe in the spirits whom my people have always respected.'

'Dan, it's easier for you to take this step than it is for me. My mother, if I ever see her again, will be heartbroken.'

'Maybe your mother would understand. Hector, listen to me. If you want to search for your sister, you have to get out of the bagnio. There's nothing you can do to find her or help her while you are confined here. If you become a rinigato, at least you can make enquiries among those who have taken the turban.

Maybe they have heard what happened to her. Besides, if you are worried about turning Turk, you can always wear a cross secretly. That's what some of the other rinigatos do, because they are afraid that their own God will ignore them after they die.'

'All right,' announced Hector. He had come to his decision. At times Dan seemed so much more level-headed, more confident than himself, even though there was little difference in their ages. 'I'll go through with this, but only if you do the same.'

'Of course,' said Dan. 'We are in this together.'

NINE

C

TWO MEN STOOD in the late evening sunshine watching the English third-rate weigh anchor and then work clear of the Algiers mole.

Down by the harbour Consul Martin was feeling homesick, regretting that he had declined the invitation to accompany Abercrombie back to England. Martin had excused himself, saying that he had pressing commercial matters to attend to in Algiers, but the truth was that he did not relish spending the six-week voyage in close company with the glum commissioner and Newland the self-conceited mercer. The final details of Newland's ransom had been settled smoothly. Abercrombie had brought with him a down payment of ten per cent of the sum the Algerines demanded for the mercer's release. Newland's business associates in London had advanced the cash, and a professional ransom broker in Naples was standing surety for the rest. The balance was to be transferred when the cloth merchant reached home safely. The speed of this commercial transaction had underscored the cumbersome progress of the government redemption plan which had eventually allowed only three dozen English captives to depart. Not one of the Irish had been redeemed. The commissioner had made it clear, after the unsatisfactory interview with Hector Lynch, that he did not wish to encounter any more of the young man's countrymen. So Martin had given up trying to locate them in the bagnios.

No one would ever hear of these unfortunates again, the consul thought to himself as he turned to walk back up the hill to his residence, his despondency only tempered by relief that he was finally rid of the tiresome Newland.

The other figure watching the warship stand out to sea also felt mildly relieved. When Captain of Galleys Turgut Reis had heard that the English prisoners in Algiers were to be ransomed, he had bribed the Dey's secretary to remove the name of the English sailor-slave, Dunton, from his list. Dunton had proved to be a clever boat builder, and Turgut calculated that Dunton was worth much more than his purchase price if he continued to work in the Arsenal, particularly as the shipmaster there had finally found sufficiently lengthy timber to repair *Izzet Darya*. Turgut was all too aware that he had to have his galley ready for the start of the new cruising season in three months' time if he was to escape from his financial difficulties. Anything which speeded up her repairs was a priority, particularly the services of a skilled shipwright.

Looking down from his roof garden, Turgut was glad that his little stratagem had succeeded. He even took pen and paper to draw a rough sketch of the departing English third rate for future reference. It was quite possible that one day *Izzet Darya* might encounter the vessel during a corso, and previously the captain had found it difficult to tell whether the sailing ships of the unbelievers were fitted out for peace or war. To his eye they all had much the same lines and sail plans whether they were carrying rich cargoes or a broadside of cannon. How unlike his beloved *Izzet Darya*, he thought to himself. No one could mistake the galley's long, menacing hull for a plump trading vessel. *Izzet* was a platform for fighting men, not a tub filled with merchandise. He held up the completed sketch for the ink to dry in the faint breeze, and once again he reassured himself that he had been right not to switch to using a sailing vessel for the corso. There was something discreditable about the way those tall ships fought from a distance, gun to gun. Their opponents were no more than tiny figures in the distance. Far better to do battle honourably, hand to hand, and look your adversary in the eye. That was his personal usanza.

A discreet cough broke into the captain's thoughts. A servant had appeared on the roof garden, carrying a note. It had just been handed in, the man said, by a slave from the bagnio. Unfolding the paper, Turgut saw that the penmanship was neat and regular, the letters well formed as if prepared by a professional letter writer. Turgut's long experience in reading foreign charts meant that he was familiar with the crabbed script of the unbelievers, and he found no difficulty in deciphering the sentences written in the lingua franca. The author of the note stated that he wished to profess his belief in Allah and humbly asked the reis to give his consent to a ceremony of conversion. For a moment Turgut was puzzled. Then he recalled that a slave had to have his master's permission before adopting Islam. Turgut frowned. The note was unsigned. He wondered which of his slaves wanted to convert to the True Faith. Turgut presumed that the messenger had taken advantage of the rest period at sunset when the bagnio gates still stood open, and run up the hill to make the delivery. 'Where is the man who brought this?' he asked.

'He is waiting in the street,' the servant replied.

'Send him up,' he said. 'I'll hear what he has to say.'

A few moments later, the messenger appeared, and Turgut saw it was the young man whom he had loaned to the city treasurer.

'Who is responsible for this?' he asked, holding up the paper.

'I am, effendi. I wish to become a Mussulman.'

'And who wrote it for you?'

'No one, effendi. I wrote it myself.'

Turgut thought back to the day he had purchased the young man at auction. He remembered wondering even then whether the alert-looking young man might one day be a useful addition to his household, useful for his brains rather than his brawn. Had it not been for the malevolence of that greedy city treasurer he would have already found a more suitable use for this literate youngster. It occurred to Turgut that now he had a way to outwit the khaznadji. He would approve the young man's conversion, and then inform the treasurer that the young man would soon be a good Muslim and therefore should live in a household where the Faith was respected. That should shame the khaznadji into returning the slave to Turgut's custody.

'I am pleased that you have decided to say the shahadah. You have my consent,' Turgut said. 'You must remind me of your name so that I may inform the Guardian Pasha and arrange for the ceremony to take place here in this house. I will provide the witnesses.'

'My name is Hector Lynch, effendi.' Hector gave the reis a frank look. 'Would his excellency be so benevolent as to sponsor the same ceremony for my friend also? He too wishes to profess the Faith.'

Turgut was about to turn down the request when Hector went on, 'My friend has no fellow countrymen in the bagnio. He is a stranger from a distant land, far to the west across the ocean sea.'

Turgut stroked his beard, his curiosity aroused. An image from his ancestor's map came to mind — the chart of the western ocean, its far shore decorated with pictures of curious-looking animals and cryptic descriptions. Perhaps here was an opportunity to unravel some of these mysteries.

'I will talk with him. Return with him at this time tomorrow, and I will decide.'

ℂ

THE FOLLOWING EVENING Hector brought Dan to the captain's mansion, both men wearing their cleanest clothes. After a short wait, they were shown up to Turgut's library. It was an airy, spacious room, its ceiling painted with interlocking geometrical patterns of red, green and black, cabinets and shelves lining the walls. They stood respectfully in front of the captain, who regarded them gravely.

'Peace be upon you,' he began.

'And upon you also be peace,' they chorused dutifully.

'Your companion tells me that you also wish to say the shahadah. Is that so?' the captain asked Dan.

'Your excellency, that is correct.'

'Have you told this to your master?'

'Not yet, sir.' Dan paused. 'If your excellency would be so generous as to buy me, the cost would be reasonable.'

'And why is that?'

'I was recently in trouble. But it was a mistake.'

'Whether you were in trouble justly or unjustly does not concern me. It is more important that you are useful to me,' said Turgut. He pointed to his bookstand. His ancestor's map of the western ocean was on display. 'Look there, and tell me if you see anything which you recognise.'

Dan stared at the map and, after a short interval, shook his head. 'No, your excellency. There is nothing. If it please your excellency, I do not know how to read.'

'You don't recognise any of those little pictures and drawings?'

Dan again shook his head, and Turgut was disappointed.

'Well at least you are honest. Can you think of any reason why I should buy you?' he asked.

Dan was at a loss, and there was an awkward silence until Hector spoke up.

'Effendi, my friend is highly skilled with ropes and rope-work,' he said. 'He would be very useful in the Arsenal.'

Turgut turned his gaze on Hector, his brown eyes troubled. So even the slaves in the bagnio, he thought to himself, knew about his desperate need to get *Izzet Darya* ready for the corso. It was humiliating, yet he had to admire the quick wits of the young man.

'Very well,' he agreed. 'I shall discuss the matter with your master. If he quotes a satisfactory price, then I may decide on the purchase and you will be informed.'

As Dan and Hector hurried back down the hill to the bagnio, Dan asked, 'Your idea that I was a rope worker, and could help in the Arsenal. What made you think of it?'

'My first day in the bagnio,' said Hector. 'There was no spare bed in the dormitory and you offered to make me a hammock. You said that the Miskito made them when they went out on hunting trips, so it seemed logical that you could handle ropes, make knots and all that sort of thing.'

☾

WITH THE GRUDGING agreement of the khaznadji, Hector was removed from beylik duties and reassigned to live and work in Turgut's household. He arrived there on a chilly winter morning, his meagre belongings wrapped in a blanket. The steward, himself a French slave, showed him to the room at the rear of the building which he would share with the other staff. 'You'll find the captain is a fair master,' the steward confided as they skirted the mansion's central courtyard with its trellises of flowers and vines and a large fountain splashing in the centre. 'He's a bit behind the times in his ideas as he's spent most of his time away in Constantinople in the Sultan's court. But if you serve him faithfully, he'll look after you well.'

'What about his family. Are they here?' asked Hector.

'Both his wives are,' said the Frenchman. 'But you won't see much of them. The reis keeps an old-fashioned establishment, and the women's quarters are separate. They occupy most of the second floor. You'll find a guard on duty at the door, so you're not likely to blunder in on them. As for children, the reis has none. It's his great regret. I'll introduce you to the other servants later, but right now you are due to start your first day's work. The captain is already with his books and charts. You're to help in his library.'

The reis glanced up from the parchment he was reading as Hector was shown in and, after greeting him courteously, waved towards an untidy pile of papers on a low table and said, 'Tell me what you make of them.'

Hector knew he was being set some sort of test. He began to sift carefully through the documents. Within moments he had identified them as pages torn from ships' logbooks. Most were in Spanish, but some were written in French or Italian, while others were in Dutch. A few were in languages he did not know but he could guess their content because shipmasters of every nationality seemed to be concerned with the same topics – wind, weather, landfalls, customs dues and lading. He said as much to Turgut, who seemed well satisfied with his answer.

'Good. Next I want you to check whether they contain any useful information, the sort of details that could be included in a map or written into a guidebook to instruct pilots.'

It took Hector the rest of the day to sort through the paperwork. He set aside those pages which were useless, and classified the remainder according to the areas they described. 'I've made a list of all the ports mentioned, and assigned a colour to each port,' he reported to Turgut. 'I've attached the appropriate coloured thread to every page where that port is mentioned.'

Turgut walked over to a large cedar wood chest in one corner of the room and lifted the lid. 'In here I keep the notes and observations which I have compiled during half a lifetime of voyaging. They are in no sort of order. I will want you to find a way of checking the information contained in them against the details in the ships' logs, and then work out which is more likely to be correct. To do that, you will first have to learn to read my writing, which is often untidy as it was done on shipboard, and the script is Ottoman.'

'I will do my best, effendi,' offered Hector. 'In the bagnio a Syrian Christian, who was taken prisoner in the Levant, showed me a little of the Arab way of writing. With practice, I should be able to carry out your wishes.'

'Excellent!' said Turgut, whose enthusiasm to update the Kitab-i Bahriye was increasing with every task he loaded on his new scrivano. 'I will arrange a tutor for you, a learned man of my acquaintance. He will give you some lessons in the formal elements of our calligraphy, and it would do no harm if you also began to acquire some Turkish from him as well. Lingua franca is all very well for basic communication, but there will be times when it is necessary to discuss the finer points of navigation and map preparation. This library is where you will work every day from now on, except Friday of course. I will give instructions to my steward that your midday meals are to be brought up here. That way you will not waste time.'

℃

IN THE DAYS that followed, Hector discovered he enjoyed the tasks set for him. He relished the challenge of deciphering faded or incomplete notes scribbled down by unknown shipmasters, then arranging the snippets of information into a coherent form which – the Captain told him – one day might take on the shape of a map or chart. He learned to read his master's writing, even though the captain had the disconcerting habit of using both the flamboyant diwani script of the court and more ordinary workaday lettering in the same sentence. Within a fortnight Hector also understood enough spoken Turkish to follow the captain as his master worried his way through the jumble of information accumulated in his archives over the years. At random Turgut would select a document from the chest and read it out, often hesitating as he tried to remember what exactly he had meant to record so many years ago. It was Hector's job to correlate that information with the material he had already extracted from the logbooks of the shipmasters. As the days passed and Hector showed more and more of his ability, Turgut Reis gradually slipped into the habit of treating him more like a talented nephew than a possession he had bought at auction.

℃

ONE MORNING Hector was alone in the captain's library, poring over the salt-stained pages of a Dutch sea captain's logbook, when his attention was distracted by a glint of light reflecting from a bright object on one of the cabinet shelves. Feeling in need of a break from his work, he strolled over to investigate. A shaft of sunlight was shining on a thin brass disc about as broad as the palm of his hand and inscribed with Arabic writing. There were four similar discs, one of which was cut away with a series of strangely shaped holes. It was obvious that the discs had been made to fit neatly into the face of a circular instrument made of heavy brass lying beside them on the shelf. He was standing in front of the cabinet wondering about the device, when Turgut Reis entered the room behind him and said, 'That was given to me by my father's father, peace be upon him. After you become a Muslim, you may one day be glad to own such an instrument yourself. Here, let me show you why.'

Picking up the instrument, Turgut brought it up to his eye. Hector saw that attached to the back of the device was a small brass bar with a peephole at each end. This bar could be turned on a pivot. 'You hold it like this,' said the captain, squinting through the peepholes as he moved the bar gently, 'and take a sight on the star you have selected. It is like taking aim with a musket. The alidade, which is the name we give this bar, measures for you the angle to the horizon.'

He turned the instrument over, and showed Hector the numerical tables inscribed on the back.

'If you have fitted the correct discs you can read off the time when the sun will rise and set wherever in the world you are, which stars and constellations will be in the night sky overhead, and the times they will rise and fall. That way you will know the qibla, the true direction of the kaaba in Mecca, and so you will be able to say your prayers in the right direction and at the right times.'

'A sailor on the ship that brought me to Algiers could tell which direction we were travelling and about how far we had come by looking at the night sky,' murmured Hector. 'He said there was much more to be learned from the stars.'

'He spoke the truth,' answered Turgut, 'and, by Allah's will, it is the people of the True Faith who enriched our understanding of the marvels of the firmament. Let me show you something else.'

He went to another cabinet and lifted out what looked like a round paper lantern, and rotated it carefully in his hands. 'See what is written on the surface.' On closer inspection, Hector saw that the lantern was made of parchment stretched on a fine mesh of copper wire. The surface bore dozens of pictures. He recognised a bear, the figures of several men, a creature which was part goat and part fish, another in the shape of a crab. It took a moment for him to realise that they were the signs of the zodiac and the constellations.

'It is a map of the heavens,' said the captain. 'I bought it many years ago from a merchant who was selling curios. The Sultan himself owns many such items – they are called celestial globes by those who study such things – and the Sultan's are far more substantial. One is an immense ball of pure marble carved to show the forty-eight constellations and more than one thousand and twenty-five stars. But this one, though humble, is important to me. Look closely.'

Hector examined the figures on the globe. Each picture was drawn to enclose a group of stars. But it seemed to him that the stars were so scattered and irregular that it took a great deal of imagination to see how they defined the figure. But the captain was speaking again, his voice animated.

'The salesman told me that one of the great scholars of the north – I believe he was a Dutchman – drew this star map more than a hundred years ago. It encompassed everything he knew about the heavens, all that he had learned from his reading and his years of study. The moment I saw it, I knew I had to buy it. Because I noted that when the Dutchman came to write down the names of the buruj, the constellations, he used the language and writing of the men whose wisdom he had acquired — the language of the holy Qur'an. See, here he has written Al Asad Buruj for the constellation shaped like a lion; and here is Al Akrab Buruj, the insect with a deadly sting in its curved tail.'

Now Hector understood his master's enthusiasm for the globe. It was true that instead of writing out the names of the constellations in Latin or his native tongue, the Dutch map maker of the stars had inscribed the names in Arabic. 'And here! And here . . . and here!' Turgut was pointing to the names of individual stars also marked on the globe. 'Note the names he has given them: Rigel, which means "the foot" in the language of true believers; Altair is "the flyer", and this star here, Alderbaran, signifies "the follower" because it appears to pursue that cluster of six stars in the constellation we call Ath-Thawr, the Bull.'

A memory stirred in Hector's mind . . . of a market day back in Ireland when his mother had taken him and his sister into a fortuneteller's booth. He had been no more than six or seven, but still remembered the shabby brown drape which served as a door. It had been spangled with stars and zodiacal signs.

'Using this star map and the brass instrument with the discs you showed me, can someone predict the future?' he asked.

Turgut hesitated before replying. 'The instrument and the globe, used together, can be used to calculate the position of the stars at the moment of a person's birth, and from that information it may be possible to foretell an individual's destiny. But great care is needed. The Prophet, peace be upon him, cautions us, "Behold what is in the heaven and earth! But revelations and warnings avail not folk who will not perceive."'

He replaced the globe carefully in the cabinet and, turning back towards Hector, added gravely, 'It is wiser to use these things for the true path of observance, even as the pilgrims of the haj rely on the stars to direct their paths across the trackless deserts and the seas.'

TEN

℃

'HE'S A VERY DECENT MAN,' Hector told Dan when the two friends next met at the bagnio on their Friday rest day. 'His steward told me that the captain never orders any of his servants to do any job that he would not be prepared to do himself. He said that Turks of the ruling class believe that the only people fit to rule, are those who have themselves served. The captain comes from one of the best families in Constantinople, yet he started off as a lad scrubbing slime off anchor cables as they were winched aboard the galleys. When he grew strong enough, he had to spend six months on the oar bench.'

'My master is reluctant to sell me to your captain, even if I want to turn Turk,' said Dan. 'Since my bastinadoing, I've been given only the most unpleasant tasks in the masserie. My master seeks to add to that punishment.'

Hector looked around the bagnio's grim courtyard and recalled his unpleasant experience with the lecherous kaporal. He had never seen his friend so glum.

'If only there was some way you too could help out in the library,' he said, 'then you too would be transferred to live in the captain's house.'

'A library job is not likely when I don't know how to read or write,' Dan pointed out. 'That page he wanted me to examine meant nothing. Just a lot of black lines and some pretty pictures poorly drawn. I could have done better myself.'

Hector looked at his friend questioningly. 'What do you mean, "done better"?'

'Those pictures of trees and fish were all very clumsy, and someone had tried to draw a bird you call a parrot. But it was not like any parrot I had ever seen. Wrong shape and the colours were all odd. That's why I told the captain that I couldn't recognise anything. Maybe I should have said there was a badly drawn parrot.'

'You mean you could have produced a better picture of it.'

'Yes.'

'Then show me,' said Hector, suddenly excited. He went to where one of the bagnio letter writers was squatting against the wall, waiting for clients. He paid for a sheet of paper and the loan of pen and ink and thrust them into Dan's hand. 'Draw me a parrot,' he demanded.

Dan looked dubiously at the materials. The pen was cut from a goose quill, and the nib was frayed and blunt. The paper was dirty and slightly crumpled. 'I wouldn't be much good with these,' he said.

'Why not?'

'I paint and draw on skin, not paper.'

'You mean on vellum made from sheepskin, like the monks who taught me in Ireland.'

'No. I make my pictures on human skin.'

For a moment Hector looked dismayed, thinking that his friend was about to reveal that the Miskito flayed human corpses to obtain their skins. But Dan's next words reassured him.

'I paint on living people. It is something that I learned as a youngster. There's a jungle tribe who live inland from the Miskito coast and go around half naked, with their skins painted with pictures of birds and trees and flowers. When I was a boy the Miskito council sent me to them as some sort of hostage, while one of their youths came to live in my family. Their women folk are the artists. They spend hour after hour painting coloured pictures on the skins of their men. They think it makes the men look handsome and attractive. If the work is cleverly done, the pictures seem to come alive because they move as the muscles ripple. Because I was a stranger from outside the tribe, they indulged me and showed me how to make the paints and brushes.'

'You had to make your own brushes?'

'It's not difficult. You cut a twig from a certain type of bush, chew the end until it is soft, and use that as the brush.'

'And what about the paints?'

'We mixed coloured earth or the powder of certain stones gathered in the river beds, and coloured sap from jungle plants. There was scarcely a colour that we couldn't create. Blues and reds were easy, yellow more difficult. For a special occasion like a feast or a wedding, the women would first paint their men with the pictures. Then they puffed grains of shiny sand over them while the paint was still wet, so that their men folk glittered.'

Hector looked at his friend in astonishment. 'Show me what you can do. Though we won't find any coloured earth or jungle plants in the bagnio.'

In response, Dan approached a huckster selling cooked meats from a brazier, and asked him for a small nub of charcoal. Returning to Hector, he took from him the sheet of paper and, laying it flat on the ground, smoothed it out. He made four or five swift strokes with the charcoal, and then held it up for Hector to see.

On the page was the unmistakable image of a seagull, swerving in mid flight.

'Will that do?' Dan asked.

Awestruck, Hector took the sheet of paper. 'Do! Even if I had all the time in the world, and the best materials, I could never have drawn something like that.'

'I'd prefer to be an artist than a gardener,' said Dan.

'Dan, if I can get you a supply of paper, and some pens of the sort we use here, do you think you can teach yourself how to draw and colour with them? You would have to learn how to make the sort of pictures you saw on that map, only better, much better.'

'Making pictures comes more easily when you do not know how to read or write,' the Miskito answered confidently.

Every Friday in the month that followed, Hector coached Dan in the art of illustrating maps and charts. He prepared a list of the subjects – mountains, ships, fish, wind roses – and made rough sketches to show Dan how they should look. Once, after much soul-searching, he stole a loose page from a disintegrating collection of charts held in the captain's library, and brought it to the bagnio to show his friend, replacing the page next day.

Finally, when he was satisfied that Dan had mastered the use of paper and ink, Hector was able to return from the bagnio to the captain's mansion carrying what he believed would be Dan's salvation.

℃

WHEN TURGUT entered his library the following morning, Hector was ready with his demonstration. 'With your permission, effendi,' he said, 'I would like to show you a drawing.'

Turgut looked at him enquiringly. 'A drawing? Something you have found among the logbooks?'

'No, effendi, it is this,' and Hector pulled from his sleeve a sheet of paper on which was Dan's most recent effort with pen and coloured ink. It was a picture of Algiers seen from the sea. All the salient features were there: the harbour mole and the lighthouse, the city walls, the Dey's castle on the summit and the gardens at either side.

Turgut recognised it at once. 'And you made this yourself?'

'No, effendi. It was drawn by the slave who is my friend. The one whose home is across the western ocean.'

Turgut was quick on the uptake. 'I take it that you are

suggesting he is qualified to help in the library, that his skill could be valuable in preparing a new version of the Kitab-i Bahriye.'

'That is so, your excellency.'

Turgut thought for a moment and then said quietly, 'Friendship has its obligations. I will increase my offer of his purchase price with his master. As soon as that is settled, your friend can begin work as a draughtsman and illustrator and come to live in this house. That also will be an auspicious time for both of you to celebrate your adoption of the True Faith. In the meantime you should be thinking about your new names.'

℃

'I HOPE THE ABDAL has a steady hand and a sharp razor,' said Dan on the morning that he and Hector were due to profess Islam. The two friends were at Turgut's mansion preparing for the ceremony the captain had called their sunnet. They had already paid a visit to one of Algiers' public bath houses and were putting on new white cotton gowns.

'Judging by the number of slaves from the bagnio who converted to Islam, the abdal must have plenty of practice in removing that piece of skin,' said Hector, trying to sound more confident than he was feeling. 'I'll be glad when it's over. It will put an end to all the jokes about being too sore to walk straight.'

'... or make love again,' added Dan.

'I wouldn't know,' confessed Hector. 'I've never been with a woman properly. Just had one or two encounters with village girls, but always brief and they never meant anything.'

'Then you've got something to look forward to, though you don't earn enough to visit the bordellos that the odjaks use. They aren't allowed to marry until they've reached senior rank and until then must live in men-only barracks. No wonder they appreciate good-looking young men.'

Hector ignored his friend's banter as he looked into a mirror to adjust his red slave cap which he had been told he should wear during the ceremony. 'Have you decided what you will be called in future?' he asked.

'I'll be Suleiman Miskita – Suleiman the Miskito. What about you?'

'The captain suggested that I become Hassan Irlanda – Hassan from Ireland. He's offered to act as my sponsor even though I really don't need one.'

'Turgut Reis has really taken a liking to you, hasn't he?'

'No more jokes, Dan,' said Hector seriously. 'I think it is because he doesn't have any family of his own.'

'Well then, let's not keep him waiting.'

Together the two friends made their way to the mansion's central courtyard where a small group of the other servants were waiting for them. Spread on the ground was a large carpet, on which stood jugs of flavoured drinks and trays of food – a first course of sheep's head and feet served with fried eggplant and cucumbers in yoghurt, followed by a sweet course of pears and apricots, grape paste and halva flavoured with almonds. Hector's tutor in calligraphy had already arrived and Hector caught a glimpse of the abdal, the specialist who would perform the circumcision, as he disappeared into a side room with his bag of surgical tools.

Moments later the captain himself appeared, resplendent in a dark red jacket over his embroidered shirt, full pantaloons, and a maroon turban with matching silk sash. With him were two of his friends, both elderly men with grave expressions and full white beards. They were to witness the act of profession. The captain was in an expansive mood. 'Peace be upon you,' he said genially to the assembled company. 'This is an important day for my household. Today you are my guests and I want you all to enjoy yourselves, so take your places and we will eat together.'

He seated himself at one end of the carpet and invited his two colleagues to sit beside him with the abdal next to them.

Dan and Hector were to be seated directly opposite. When his guests had eaten their fill and the trays had been cleared away, Turgut called for everyone's attention. 'My friends,' he said, 'the ceremony for the taking of the right path is always an occasion for celebration. When there is sunnet for the sons of the Sultan, the festivities last for fifteen days and nights. A thousand plates of rice and fifteen roast oxen are despatched daily to the people of the city, there are fireworks and parades, and the harbour is a mass of coloured lights attached to the masts of the assembled vessels. Today may seem very humble by comparison, but nevertheless it is equally a time of rejoicing, and the proper ritual must be observed.' Rising to his feet, the captain then beckoned to Dan to come forward. The Miskito stepped into the centre of the carpet and stood facing his master. Turgut asked him formally, 'Is it your wish to acknowledge the true Faith?'

'It is, effendi.'

'Then raise your finger, and pronounce the shahadah loudly and clearly so that all may hear.'

Obediently Dan did as he was told, and recited the words, 'There is no god but God and Muhammad is the Messenger of God.'

Turgut turned to his valet standing in the background, and nodded. The valet came forward with a pair of scissors. Removing Dan's red cap, he threw it on the ground and then deftly clipped away the Miskito's long hair leaving only a central top knot. Next the valet clapped his hands, and his assistant brought forward a length of tan-coloured muslin which the valet carefully wound around the Miskito's head as a turban. When the valet was satisfied, he stepped back and Turgut announced in a loud voice, 'From now on you will be known as Suleiman the Miskito. In the words of the holy Qur'an, "He who rejects false deities and believes in Allah has grasped a firm handhold which will never break." '

To murmurs of approval from the audience, the valet then escorted Dan away to the side room, even as the abdal quietly left his place and followed.

Next it was Hector's turn. Rising to his feet, he stepped into the centre of the carpet, and at the captain's prompting held up his index finger and repeated the words of the shahadah, as Dan had done. After his red cap had been removed and his head shaved, he too was given a turban, though this time it was a more expensive length of fine white cotton shot through with gold threads. Then, Turgut stepped forward and placed in his open palm a little container, the size and shape of a pill jar, fashioned of brass. As Turgut pressed a catch on the side, the lid sprang open revealing a little compass, its needle quivering gently. Engraved on the inner side of the open lid were lines of Arabic writing. 'Here are inscribed the names of the cities and countries of the known world,' said Turgut, 'and should you ever find yourself in such places, consult the needle to learn the qibla that you may worship towards the pillars of Islam.' Then, to everyone's surprise, he leaned forward and gave Hector a formal embrace. As he did so, he whispered in his ear, 'Don't be afraid. It happens at once, and is a wonderful thing as Allah has wished. Praise be to God.' Then he stepped back, as his valet led away Hector for his circumcision.

To his alarm Hector could not see Dan anywhere when he was ushered into the side room where the abdal stood waiting beside a low bed. The only other furniture in the room was a sturdy stool. 'Do not be afraid,' said the abdal. 'Your friend is recovering next door, and will soon rejoin the celebrations. The pain is quickly over. You may lie on the bed or be seated on the stool, whichever you prefer. Osman, the valet here, will remain to bear witness.'

'I prefer the stool,' said Hector, his voice unsteady.

'As did your friend. Pull up your gown, and sit down then, with your legs spread apart.'

Hector did as he was instructed, and the abdal reached

forward and took the young man's penis in one hand and gently teased forward the foreskin. Next, as Hector peered down anxiously, the abdal was holding in his free hand an instrument which Hector first thought was a set of dividers of the type he himself used when measuring distances across a map. But these dividers were made of wood, each limb flat-sided. Hector broke out in a cold sweat as he realised it was a clamp. Expertly the abdal closed the clamp upon the foreskin, nipping it tightly so that it could not retract. Hector shut his eyes and clenched his fists so that the nails dug deep into the palms of his hands. He sucked in air and held his breath, while hearing the soft mutter of a voice saying, 'Allâhu akbarre'. Then came an agonising spike of pain which made him gasp, and a shocking moment later the warm spurt of blood striking the inside of his thigh. Even as he quivered with the pain, he sensed the blessed pressure of some sort of poultice or bandage being pressed to his wounded manhood.

ELEVEN

☾

'GLORY OF THE SEA', *Izzet Darya* lay becalmed. The green banner of Algiers with its spangles of silver and gold crescents hung limp from its staff, and the sea around her hull had an oily sheen. The passing of an occasional swell was so faint as to be noticed only in the slight flexing of her monstrous main spar made from three lengths of straight pine lashed together like a great fishing rod. The spar and its furled sail weighed more than four tons, and the Captain of Galleys had ordered them to be lowered in order to ease the strain on the galley's single mast with its enormous block and tackle. When a breeze did come, it would take thirty strong men hauling in unison on the massive six-inch halyard to raise the spar back aloft. Then the lightest and most agile members of the crew would have to shin up and let loose the bindings so that the single enormous sail fell open and sent the galley slicing through the water. But for now there was not a breath of wind. *Izzet Darya* was motionless, silent except for the steady thump of her pumps and the gush and trickle of bilge water falling back into the sea, for the galley's elderly hull was incurably leaky, and only steady pumping kept her light and manoeuvrable. Turgut Reis was resting his oarsmen because *Izzet Darya* was where he wanted her to be, lurking at a cruciero, a crossroads of shipping lanes. Three leagues east

was the island of St Pierre where Turgut's men had recently
taken on fresh water from a friendly population, and past this
point came merchant traffic rounding Sardinia's southern cape
on their paths between Marseilles, Leghorn, Sicily and the straits.
So the corsair galley waited, as dangerous as an ageing pike
poised in ambush among the reeds.

From his position on the aft deck Hector looked down
the length of the venerable galley. In the flat light of dawn the
vessel appeared even narrower and longer than usual. Her beam
was only sixteen feet, less than a tenth of the distance to her bows
where he could make out the squat black shape of her single
bow chaser, an iron cannon pointing forward into the dense mist
which blanked out the horizon. Earlier Turgut had confided to
him that *Izzet* had once mounted three fine bow chasers of
bronze made by skilled Hungarian gun founders, but he had
been obliged to sell the more expensive guns to pay his dockyard
bills and outfit his ship and get to sea. A single catwalk ran all
the way down the spine of the galley. Here on most corsair
ships the overseers patrolled, keeping an eye on the slaves and
lashing them to their work if they shirked. But on *Izzet Darya*
there was no need for such discipline because most of her
oarsmen, now relaxing on the benches, were volunteers. In that
matter, at least, Turgut had been fortunate. He had announced
his impending departure for the corso in early March, and just
two weeks later buba, the plague, had struck the city. To
Algerines the plague was a commonplace, lurking unseen and
occasionally emerging to decimate the closely packed population. But buba was a summer affliction and rarely felt so early.
It had taken the city unawares. After several of the more
important citizens had died, there had been a rush to escape the
scourge. Scores of men had volunteered for *Izzet Darya*'s crew
though Turgut was promising no wage, only a share in the
plunder.

So now 160 men were packed aboard, not counting the
squad of forty janissaries under their aga who were the ship's

chief fighting force, and already the food rations were scrimped. Hector knew the precise details because he had come aboard as the captain's scrivano, charged with keeping track of how many sacks of grain and dried fruit, jars of oil and vinegar remained. *Izzet* had sailed from Algiers with supplies for less than a month at sea because this was all that Turgut could afford, and now, three weeks into the cruise, the men were grumbling about the meagre helpings of couscous, which was their staple diet. The last full meal they had enjoyed was after the marabout, the holy man, had led the prayers for success on the corso. Eight sheep had been ritually slaughtered when *Izzet*'s well-greased hull had been eased down the slipway, coloured bunting fluttering from her rigging. The blood and guts from the dead sheep were thrown into the sea as a sacrifice, but the flesh reserved for the crew's meal once the galley had made its ceremonial exit from Algiers harbour, the onlookers on the ramparts shouting their good wishes, and the crew saluting the tomb of Sidi Ketaka on the hill, without whose help no corsair crew could hope for success.

But their achievement had been indifferent despite the sacrifice. Off the coast of Majorca the galley had intercepted a dozen vessels, mostly small tartans and poleacres. Each time the galley had forced the stranger to heave to, then lowered a boat and sent across a team for the visita, the inspection to check the vessel's nationality and lading. Whenever the vessel proved to be Christian, it had been Hector's job to scrutinise the ship's papers while the anxious captain hovered beside him, pleading that he was an honest trader and carrying only protected goods. Several captains had produced passports issued under the terms of a treaty between their own government and the Dey in Algiers promising protection from seizure of vessel and cargo. Disappointingly, these claims had proved to be true, and Turgut had honoured the passes, allowing the captures to go free. Only two vessels had turned out to be genuine prizes, and even then their cargoes were wretched enough – bundles of firewood, bales of unworked goat hair, and some millet and cheese which had been added to *Izzet*'s dwindling stores. A minor consolation had been the discovery of some sacks of coffee beans, probably destined for some Moorish sheikh.

Hector stepped around the hooped canopy which sheltered the spot where Turgut and the aga of the janissaries spread their sleeping mats at nightfall. It still felt odd not to have the weight of his slave ring on his right ankle. The previous day Turgut had insisted that the ring be struck off. 'I am still your master, but now that you have adopted the Faith I have no wish to treat you as a chattel,' he had announced. 'From now on you should regard yourself as a member of my household, and a valued one at that. As the Prophet, peace be upon him, told us, "Your slaves are your brothers and Allah has put them under your command. So whoever has a brother under his command should feed him of what he eats and dress him of what he wears." '

Aboard the galley the captain was following the Prophet's advice. Like all his crew Turgut went barefoot and wore simple working clothes, a cotton gown or long shirt over a pair of drawers. Hector was grateful for the loose fit of the baggy garments because he was still conscious of his circumcision. His penis had healed during the two weeks' convalescence allowed after circumcision, but it was still inclined to occasional discomfort in the heat.

A sailor clambered up the companionway that led from the oar deck, and as he came level with Hector, there was something familiar about his face. A moment later Hector placed him. It was the English sailor Dunton with whom he had shared the hold on Hakim Reis's vessel. 'I had not expected to see you again,' he said.

Dunton checked in his stride and for an instant did not recognise the young Irishman. 'It's the lad from Ireland, isn't it,' he then exclaimed. 'You've changed. You look older and more grown up.' He glanced down at Hector's bare leg. 'Also it seems you've taken the turban.'

Belatedly Hector noted that Dunton was still wearing a slave ring on his ankle though he had discarded the red slave cap and, like everyone else, wore a nondescript cloth wrapped around his head. 'Yes, I converted,' Hector said simply.

'Can't say I blame you,' observed Dunton, not the least surprised. 'But how come you are on the aft deck with the officers? You've not become a garzon have you?'

'No, I'm the captain's scrivano,' said Hector. A garzon was lingua franca for the young men who sometimes shipped aboard as companions and bedmates for the officers and senior odjaks. 'I also help the captain in his chart-making.'

Dunton looked impressed. 'Always took you for a clever one,' he said. 'What's that you've got hanging round your neck?'

'It's my qibla finder,' said Hector. 'It shows me the direction in which to pray.'

'Mind if I have a look,' observed Dunton. He had opened the little case and saw the compass needle. 'Handy enough aboard a ship which turns every which way.'

'What about you? What have you been doing these past nine months?'

Dunton shrugged. 'Much the same as what I would have been doing at home if I had been stuck on shore for the entire winter,' he answered. 'I was put to work in the Arsenal, doing shipwright's work. I helped get this old tub back afloat. She's a right old-timer. Half her joints are shaky and she's long past her best days. Wouldn't wonder if this turns out to be her last voyage.'

He spat expertly over the side.

'I'm not sure I'd have joined her crew if I had been given the choice. But my master is the same captain, as you call him, and he was very keen to have me aboard because there's a shortage of good seamen. Plenty of volunteers to pull on an oar, but not many who know how to get the best out of a ship under sail. In all but name I'm the caravana, the foreman in charge of sail handling. Officially the caravana is a Turk, but he knows sod all about the job, and leaves it to me to organise the tasks. If this cruise goes well, I might even come back with a bit of cash to buy my freedom and then settle down in Algiers. I like the climate and the pay is very good if you've got shipwright's skills.

'But I thought that all the English prisoners had been ransomed last autumn and gone home?'

'Seems I was left off the list,' said Dunton. 'And we won't see another delegation from London for several years. I hear that the English consul died of the plague, and he's not been replaced as yet. So, my best hope is prize money from this corso. Then there'll be nothing to stop me from bringing my wife and children out to join me.'

'You mean you'll share in the plunder?'

'That's usanza. Even the humblest galley oarsman gets a cut of the prize money, and it doesn't matter if he is a slave. It's just a single share, and in theory he's meant to hand it over to his master. But if your master likes you, you get to keep it. By all accounts the captain is a decent old stick, and would let you hang on to what you earn if you serve him well.'

Dunton glanced up at the banner which was still hanging slack. 'I'd better get going. This mist won't last all day. I need to tighten those wooldings on the main spar while I have the chance. It's nice to get the chance to talk English for a change too.'

'So you haven't met my friend Dan? He speaks English.'

'No, who's he?'

Hector pointed to the foredeck where Dan was talking to one of the odjaks. 'That man there.'

'The foreign-looking one with dark skin? I took him to be an usif, a blackamoor slave. How come he's so friendly with the odjaks?'

'He's a musketeer,' Hector told him. 'He made quite an impression on them.'

℃

IT HAD HAPPENED on the afternoon before *Izzet Darya* set sail from Algiers. The captain had told Hector that he would take him aboard as his scrivano, but he had made it clear that there was no place for Dan aboard the galley. Naturally Hector asked the captain to change his mind, only to be reminded that an illiterate artist would just be an extra mouth to feed. So Hector had resigned himself to being parted from his friend when Dan arrived at the dockside on an errand for Turgut's steward. He had been told to bring Turgut's prayer mat and some extra clothes out to the anchored galley, and by chance had hitched a ride with a boatload of odjaks coming aboard with their bedrolls and weapons. As the odjaks climbed on to the galley, one of the janissaries had handed his musket to Dan to hold. Dan had taken the weapon and, glancing at the firing mechanism, commented that it was out of alignment. 'Are you armuriero, a gunsmith?' the janissary had asked. 'No, but I am a marksman, and this is a fine weapon,' Dan had answered. Flattered, the janissary had asked Dan if he would like to try out the musket for himself, and the two of them had gone to the galley's bow where Dan had loaded the musket and, under the watchful eye of the odjak, took aim at a mark, a dead cat floating in the water. He sank the carcass with his shot. The janissary had been so impressed that he had called on his fellow soldiers to watch another demonstration of Dan's marksmanship, and when he again hit his target – a clump of floating weed – they had applauded. By now the aga of the janissaries had strolled over to observe what was going on, and when Dan missed his third shot by only a narrow margin, the aga had enquired where he had learned to shoot so accurately. 'Among my people,' Dan had replied proudly. 'That's why we are called the Miskito. Outsiders believe that our name is taken from the flying insects which infest our coast, but that is wrong. The Spanish call us Miskito because we are the only native people in those lands who have learned how to use guns against them. So they call us the musket people.' 'If you are prepared to fight the infidel, then you should assist us,' was the aga's comment, 'we always need good marksmen, and those who can help repair our guns.' The aga's authority in matters of warfare was equal to the powers exercised by the captain himself, so Dan had found himself co-opted as an auxiliary with the odjaks, and – to Hector's delight – the Miskito had joined the corso.

℃

NIMBLY Dunton swung himself up on the mainspar, straddled it, and began attending to a frayed rope binding when, abruptly, he raised his head and looked out into the mist. 'Hello!' he said softly, 'Something's coming our way.' Other crewmembers had heard the noise too, and there were calls for the pumping crew to cease work for a moment. In the silence that followed, a rhythmic heavy splash and groan could be heard. Quite where the noise came from was difficult to tell, but it was approaching. On the foredeck, the janissaries who had been smoking and talking put down their long pipes and took up their muskets, and quietly prepared the primings. Turgut, alerted by the sudden tension aboard, walked to the starboard rail and cocked his head to one side listening. 'Galleot or maybe brigantine under oars,' he said.

Dunton dropped down softly on the deck beside Hector. 'Friend or foe?' he murmured. 'The Religion doesn't normally operate in this area, though they've got eight large galleys in their fleet, about the same size as *Izzet*, which would give us a run for our money.'

'The Religion? Who are they?' whispered Hector.

'The Knights of the Order of St John of Jerusalem. A bunch of nobles who act like pirates when it suits them, and from the best families in Europe. Claim they are fighting for the Cross.

Hate Barbary corsairs. They operate out of Malta. One of their petty officers was a slave shipwright alongside me in the Arsenal.' Dunton stopped talking as the aga scowled at him, demanding silence as he also listened, trying to locate the direction of the approaching ship.

Several minutes passed, and it became clear that the unknown vessel was moving at a leisurely pace. The splashes of the oars were slow and unhurried, the sound increasing only gradually. *Izzet*'s own rowers settled in their places and dipped the blades of their thirty-foot-long sweeps quietly into the sea, awaiting orders. Some were looking expectantly towards Turgut on the stern deck, others half-turned, trying to peer out into the mist. Abruptly, through the mist, came a cry, 'Sieme! Sieme!' Dunton mouthed, 'Together! Together!' and made a rowing gesture. Moments later, a dark patch in the mist became the unmistakable shape of an oared vessel, and there was a startled shout, 'Aia! What ship?' '*Izzet Darya*! In the Name of Allah,' roared back Turgut. The advancing galley had stopped rowing, but her momentum carried her forward so that she could be clearly seen as a brigantine, an oared vessel about half the size of *Izzet Darya*. 'Merhaba, welcome! From what port?' called Turgut. 'From Djidjelli. Corsan!' The tension aboard *Izzet Darya* relaxed. 'Fellow corsairs from Barbary,' explained Dunton. 'Hunting the same patch of sea.'

Hector's knowledge of Turkish was good enough to follow the shouted conversation between Turgut and the captain of the newcomer. The brigantine had been on the corso for less than a week, and had managed to intercept three infidel vessels, two Spanish and the third French. None of the prizes were very valuable, but the captain of the French ship had curried favour with his captors by telling the corsairs that he had sighted a large merchantman, of unknown nationality, hull down on the horizon and apparently heading towards Leghorn. In pursuit of this potential prize the brigantine had ventured north hoping to intercept the vessel which would now be delayed by the calm. 'Have you seen any of those shaitans from Malta?' called Turgut.

'No, nothing. It's too early in the season for them. They like to lie in bed with their harlots,' came the reply.

'Will we join forces then?' enquired Turgut.

'D'accordo!' came back the reply. 'One hand makes nothing, two hands make a sound.'

Turgut smiled into his beard at the Turkish proverb as he called back, 'We wait until the mist lifts, then spread out but stay in sight of one another, and cruise northward.'

'Agreed! And may Allah go with us.'

'Our luck has changed!' said Turgut cheerfully, coming back across the deck. 'Let the storemen issue a double ration so we may eat our fill, and be ready for what fortune brings.' Dunton went forward to rejoin his shipmates and, as Dan took his meals with the odjaks, who had their own achtchi or camp cook, Hector found himself seated on the aft deck with the captain and his officers as they ate a simple meal of falafel and bread. From time to time the captain glanced across at the brigantine which lay hove-to half a musket shot away. He continued to be in a good mood.

'Allah has been kind to us,' he said to Hector. 'Having a second ship means we can sweep a wider swathe of sea in search of prizes. And should we find only small coasters, the brigantine is fast enough to catch them easily. It will save us from having to lower our ship's boats, and that means fewer visitas for you.'

'The brigantine comes from Djidjelli,' Hector observed. 'Already you have a drawing of their harbour in your files, but if you wish I could go across and interview their captain and update the information.'

'Maybe later,' answered Turgut. 'Less than four years ago I was in their port, not a good harbour, shallow and exposed but adequate if you want to take on supplies. The ruler of Djidjelli acknowledges the Dey as his overlord, and we leave him to his own devices. Just so that he does not interfere with our corsos.

The same is true of Bougie a short distance down the coast. Let us hope that his information about the rich merchant ship turns out to be correct.'

'Your excellency, if we do find and capture this ship how would we divide the spoils? The brigantine brought the news, so does her crew have first choice?'

'A shrewd question, and the answer is that together we return to Algiers, with our prize. In Algiers the division is made by a court of arbitration composed of senior reis who decide on matters of precedence, acts of valour in the fight and so forth.'

'And do they also decide who receives the prisoners as their reward?'

'Of course. Often the value of the prisoners exceeds the value of the captured hull.'

'And if we capture women, for example, where would they be held?'

Turgut looked at Hector searchingly. 'Do you have a special reason to ask that question, and is that why you volunteered to visit the brigantine?'

'Forgive me for asking, effendi. When I was taken by the corsair Hakim Reis, my sister was also captured. She was placed on one ship, while I was kept on another. Since that time I have not seen her. I wish to learn what might have happened to her, and where she is now.'

'Tell me the details, as best as you remember them.'

Hector recounted the story of his capture and when he finished his account, Turgut paused to take a sip of coffee before replying, 'I did not meet Hakim Reis after that venture when he raided Ireland. He was always lucky on the corso, quick to pick up prizes and welcome in any port to sell them. It would be normal for him to keep the women captives apart from their menfolk. I would do the same myself. The men are less likely to make trouble if they see their women could be punished. But I would have expected Hakim Reis and his escorting vessel to have entered their final harbour together and disposed of the

booty in the same market place. That makes the final division
of the profits easier as I have explained. I can only suppose that
something happened to separate Hakim Reis from his raiding
consort. You mentioned some sort of exchange of gunfire.'

'And where might the other ship have gone?' asked Hector.
'Could it have gone to Djidjelli or to Bougie? Is that where I
should look for my sister?'

'If you volunteered to visit the brigantine in order to ask if
anyone knew about her, then I'm afraid your enquiry would
have been futile. Had the women captives been sold in Djidjelli,
or Bougie for that matter, the news would have reached Algiers
which is not so far away. No, I think your sister was taken
farther afield.' Seeing the disappointment in Hector's face, he
added, 'You must not be too hard on yourself. Consider your
own captivity. You must admit, it has not turned out to be so
disastrous. Here you are aboard a fine ship and one of Muhammad's people. Hakim Reis was right when he told you that, with
luck, you could yourself rise to command. For all you know,
your sister might be much happier than you fear.'

'It is difficult to think with such optimism, effendi. I still feel
responsible for her well-being.'

'Hassan Irlanda,' said Turgut kindly. 'In Turkey we have a
saying – "patience is the key to Paradise." We must all accept
the fate that Allah decrees. Keep up your search for your sister,
but pursue it in the knowledge that it may never reach a con-
clusion. Rest assured that your sister will have been treated well.
She would have been classified as murtafa'at; that is, first class.
Wherever your sister was brought ashore for sale, everything
about her would have been recorded by the amina, the woman
inspector who examined her. Even as a conscientious jeweller
notes the qualities of a special gem, her good points, the nu'ut,
and her defects, the uyub, will have been written down. Somewhere that record and description of your sister still survives.
Find it and you will be on the trail of your sister. Or find
someone who sailed with Hakim Reis on that corso or, better

still, find Hakim Reis himself. Then ask why the vessels were separated and where the missing ship would have gone.'

Hector finished his meal in silence, turning over in his mind Turgut's advice and, still troubled, was on the point of asking again whether he could visit the brigantine to enquire if anyone had heard of Elizabeth, when there was an order for the oarsmen to stand to their sweeps. Dunton reappeared on the aft deck. 'The pilot must think the mist is due to lift soon,' he said as he checked the preventer ropes which secured the great spar. 'Or maybe he's worried how far we've drifted in the mist. Strange currents around here, according to the store keeper's assistant. He's a local man from Sardinia and used to fish these waters before he was captured by the Turks, and became a rinigato like yourself. Tells me that the current can be strong enough to set a ship ten or fifteen miles in a day.'

A series of calls and commands was heard along the catwalk as *Izzet Darya* slowly got under way, the same shouts repeated from the accompanying brigantine, whose sweeps also began to rise and fall ponderously as the two ships nosed their way forward. Occasionally Dunton looked up at the mast top where the captain's insignia, a long red and gold pennant, dangled listlessly. 'A sea fret like this normally lies close to the water, like a blanket,' he said to Hector. 'On a tall ship, you can send someone to the mast head as lookout, and often he'll be sitting up there in the bright sunshine with a blue sky above his head. Yet when he looks down past his feet, he can scarcely see the deck for the vapour. Ahha! There's a patch of blue now.'

Hector followed his gaze, and indeed the mist was thinning. A glimpse of blue sky had appeared, and on the aft deck around him the daylight seemed to be growing brighter. 'Shan't be long now before we are clear of this,' observed Dunton confidently. 'Then it'll be time for the brigantine to stand clear and take up her cruising station.'

But that manoeuvre was not needed. Half an hour later the two corsair vessels rowed their way out of the mist. In a few oar strokes they passed from the close damp haze and emerged into a bright open world with a sparkling calm sea of intense blue. Looking astern, Hector saw that the edge of the mist was like a sheer grey wall, yet scarcely higher than a ship's mast. A sudden exclamation from the galley's pilot made him swing round again.

'Alhamdullilah,' the pilot burst out, pointing ahead. There, no more than five miles away, was a ship. She was utterly becalmed. Hector had never seen a craft as large or ponderous. Like Hakim Reis's corsair ship which had raided Ireland, the vessel was an outright sailing vessel. Her three tall masts were rigged with great square sails which, at that moment, hung slack and empty and useless. Amidships her lowest point was twice the height of the low-slung galleys, and the stern of the vessel rose far above the sea in a series of decks that formed a wooden castle. Even at that distance it was possible to make out a massive ornamental lantern, twice the height of a man, which crowned the tall stern. The gilding on the lantern glinted in the sunlight.

'God's Blood!' muttered Dunton beside him. 'That's a royal ship, I wouldn't wonder. Can't make out her flags, but she could be Spanish or Dutch maybe. She'll be a tough nut to crack.'

A hurried council was already forming up on the stern deck of *Izzet Darya*. The captain, his chief officer, the pilot and the aga of the janissaries clustered in a group, and Hector could overhear snatches of their conversation. The pilot was urging caution, warning that the strange ship was too powerful to attack. The aga of the janissaries, stroking his mustache and striking an attitude, retorted that if the pilot could bring the galley close enough for his soldiers to board, his janissaries would soon clear the foreigner's decks. The galley's chief officer, a grizzled Turk, said nothing but waited patiently for the captain to speak, and all the while the oarsmen kept up their steady beat, moving the great galley forward.

Turgut Reis gazed thoughtfully at the sailing ship. This was not a vessel he had seen before, though it did have a certain similarity to the warship that had brought the English ransom agent to Algiers. He wished he had brought his sketch of that ship with him, even though this ship was much larger and, as yet, showed no flag. If only he had that sketch, it might help him decide whether the stranger was a warship or some rich merchant vessel. He looked again at the distant vessel. She was no more than four miles away now, and still helpless and becalmed. The captain thought about his ill luck on the corso so far, the debts that awaited him when he returned to Algiers, and that he had only a few days' supplies left before he would have to return to base. He thought, too, about the damage to his reputation if it was said that he had shirked a fight with a large infidel ship. He knew his pilot was a cautious man who would always advise care, just as he knew that the aga was certain to demand a direct attack and boast of the courage and the fighting spirit of his odjaks. The captain did not doubt that at close quarters the weight of numbers and the terrifying charge of the janissaries would win the day. But first he had to get *Izzet Darya* close enough to board the stranger.

'They're lowering their boats!' It was his chief officer who spoke, excitement in his voice. Turgut squinted into the distance. Yes, it was true. There was activity on the stranger's deck. They must have been shocked by the menacing sight of two corsair galleys emerging as if by magic from the mist, and heading towards them. Figures on deck were hurriedly lowering boats into the water, and a large boat which had been towed astern was being hauled closer so that oarsmen could scramble aboard. 'They're abandoning ship!' said a voice. Turgut wondered if this could be true. Often the crew of a vessel attacked by corsairs would leave their ship and flee for safety in their small boats. They would head for the nearest coast where they would run ashore and hide rather than be taken captive. But the Sardinian coast was too far for the small rowing boats to outrun the brigantine. 'No,' said another voice, 'they're trying to tow their ship out of trouble.' That was more likely. The ship's longboat and its tenders were moving to the bow of the becalmed stranger, and hawsers were being lowered to them. Maybe they were hoping to outpace their pursuit until darkness covered their escape.

The captain made up his mind. 'Allah concealed us from our enemy until the time was ripe! Now we attack!' he called out. Turning, he gestured to the accompanying brigantine that both ships were to advance at full speed and close with their prey from directly astern. Seeing this, the oarsmen in the waist of *Izzet Darya* began to cheer a rippling 'Ya Allah! Ya Allah! Ya Allah!' as they laid on their oars and began to increase the tempo of their stroke.

Hector felt the galley's motion increase beneath his bare feet, and looked to the bow platform where Dan was checking the muskets of the janissaries. Dan glanced up and waved. Beside him Dunton said quietly, 'Well here we go! The captain's not the sort of person to run away from a battle. Let's hope he's not about to catch a Tartar.'

'What do you mean?' asked Hector.

Dunton was staring intently at the sailing ship. 'Seems to me,' he said softly, 'that she could be built for war. That big stern castle and the heavy bulwarks on the bow are the marks of a fighting ship. Still, if the calm stays with us, it shouldn't matter too much. Right now, her main deck cannon – if she's got them – are nigh-on useless. If we attack from directly astern, they can't be brought to bear. She'll have only one or two stern chasers, so she's vulnerable.'

The words were scarcely out of his mouth when there was the sound of a cannon shot, and a puff of smoke from the ship's towering stern. A moment later, a cannonball skipped across the surface of the sea, sent up a trail of white splashes, then plunged into the sea, half a mile ahead of the approaching corsairs.

'Levarim! Levarim! Lay on your oars! Lay on your oars!' yelled the overseers on the catwalk. But there was little need for their exhortations. The oarsmen of *Izzet Darya* were already at full stretch, eager to close with their prey and earn the plunder they craved. Only in the bow, where there were three or four benches of slaves who had been placed aboard by their Algerine masters, was it necessary for the overseers to ply the courbash. 'Strongly! Strongly! My children,' Hector heard Turgut say under his breath, and he wondered if the captain had the same worry as Dunton that the aged galley was heading for a mistaken target.

Again the thud of a cannon, and the splash of a cannonball, this time closer to the galley. 'Good shooting,' commented Dunton. 'Those are not amateur gunners.'

'Why don't we fire back?' enquired Hector.

'No point,' came the reply. 'Our iron gun hasn't the range, and besides it will hamper the oarsmen if we have to load and train the weapon. We'll just have to take our medicine for the next few minutes. Run the gauntlet of those stern chasers until we are close enough to open fire ourselves. Better yet, get alongside and board her.'

℃

'FORTSA! FORTSA! Row Hard! Row Hard!' the galley's overseers were cheering on their men, and *Izzet Darya* surged forward, steadily closing the gap.

A double thud as, one after the other, the two stern chasers of the sailing ship fired at the approaching corsairs. This time a cannonball threw up a burst of spray which drenched the portside oarsmen.

A closer explosion as *Izzet Darya*'s own gun answered. Hector felt the galley tremble beneath his feet. But the shot fell short.

'Watch out! She's coming round!' cried Dunton. Hector looked forward over the heads of the straining oarsmen. Where before the sailing ship had presented her tall stern to the galleys, now he could begin to see along her quarter as slowly she began to turn. Out to one side he saw her boats. Their crews were rowing frantically, the towlines taut. 'They're pulling her to bring her into position so she can use her main armament,' said Dunton. He sounded worried. *Izzet Darya*'s pilot had seen the danger, and called out to the helmsmen to try to stay directly astern of their prey.

Another twenty oar strokes, as 160 men in teams of five strained at each huge oar handle, and then their opponent began to open fire with her main deck guns. There was no broadside, just an irregular series of loud reports as each gunner found he could bring the advancing corsair vessels into his sights. Dunton was counting, 'five . . . six . . . seven.' He paused as the cannon shots ceased. 'Thank Christ for that!' he muttered. 'Seven, maybe eight cannon a side. She's an armed merchant-man. We should be able to cope with that.' His sigh of relief was cut short as another cannon fired, then another, and another. Looking ahead, Hector saw that the sailing ship was almost entirely obscured in a great cloud of gun smoke billowing around her. 'Oh shit!' blurted Dunton. 'Twenty guns a side, maybe more. She's a ship of war, a fourth-rate at least.'

There was a bellow of rage from the aga. The Turk was staring off to the side, at the accompanying corsair brigantine. One entire side of the brigantine's oars had stopped, the blades poised level with the sea. For a moment Hector thought that perhaps a cannonball had struck and damaged the ship. But then in a sudden moment of silence he distinctly heard the cry, 'Siya! Siya! Back! Back!' and the oars began to move again, but this time in reverse. Inexorably, the brigantine began to turn, swinging away from *Izzet Darya* in a tight arc, as the smaller ship altered course, away from the fight. 'Cowards! May you rot in hell!' The aga was brick red with anger, roaring and raging as the brigantine completed her turn. She was fleeing from the scene, abandoning the attack, and putting as much distance as possible between herself and the cannon fire. 'Seems they were counting cannon shots as well,' said Dunton bitterly.

Turgut Reis stepped forward to the rail that divided the stern deck from the lines of benches where his crew were still labouring their oars. Many of the rowers were beginning to show signs of exhaustion, others were wild-eyed with fear. 'My children!' he called out. 'We press on! Now there is all the more plunder for us. Allah will protect us! Soon we will be alongside. Fifty gold pieces to the first man who climbs aboard.'

There was a rattle of musket fire from the bow platform. Hector saw that the janissaries had begun shooting, aiming forward over the low breastwork that surrounded the bow platform. He wondered whether their target was really within range or whether the odjaks were firing their muskets to vent their frustration. He could not see Dan.

Suddenly there was an appalling crash and the galley quivered from stem to stern. A cannonball had struck the vessel, but for a moment Hector could not identify any damage. Then he saw the gaping hole on the port side, where the shot had torn away the outrigger support for the forward oars. He heard screams of pain and fear, then remembered that this was where the slave oarsmen had been placed, chained to the oar benches. *Izzet Darya*'s iron cannon fired, and a neat round hole suddenly appeared in one of the stranger's limp sails.

'They're firing too high, stupid bastards,' said Dunton. 'We can't take much more of this. We've got to get closer.'

Another crash, and this time the cannonball cut a bloody path through the rowers on the starboard oar benches. The rhythm of the oar strokes faltered. Hector felt the galley slow down. 'Avanti! Avanti! Forward! Forward!' yelled the overseers, and this time they were lashing even the volunteer oarsmen. Hector could detect that the crew was very close to panic. 'Ya Allah! Ya Allah! Ya Allah!' The rowers tried to take up the cadence of their work again, but the galley was partially crippled. Hector was reminded of a many-legged insect which struggles onward even when a third of its legs has been torn away. He looked forward, trying to see what was happening to Dan, and could not see his friend. Astonishingly, he saw that the janissaries were utterly unperturbed. He witnessed one of the odjaks set down his musket, calmly relight his long pipe, then pick up the musket again before taking aim.

'Bloody hell!' Dunton gasped, dismay in his voice. Hector looked round, trying to see what had alarmed the sailor. The enemy ship was less than a couple of hundred yards away now, every detail clearly visible. In a few moments *Izzet Darya* could close the gap, and then her boarding party would get in action. Soon the fight must be over.

Then he knew what had unnerved Dunton. The long pennant which hung from the stranger's masthead was stirring. Hector could make out its colours, red and white. And the gun smoke which had shrouded the tall hull was drifting clear in wisps. The calm had ended, and a light breeze had sprung up. Even as he watched, Hector saw the great sails begin to flap and lift as they filled with the wind, and slowly the sailing ship began to move through the water. Even as the crippled corsair galley desperately tried to close the gap, the great ship began inexorably to slide out of reach.

'Fortsa! Fortsa!' The overseers were in a frenzy, demanding a final effort from the oarsmen. But the oarsmen were nearly collapsing. Hector, his nostrils filled with the smell of gunpowder, heard their sobs of exhaustion and effort. Several of the men were merely going through the motions of rowing, trying to keep time with their comrades. Here and there Hector saw a rower give up the effort, and slump to the deck.

Another crash, and this time a cannonball smashed a bloody track through the oar benches, body parts flying into the air. The fervour and discipline of the oarsmen began to disintegrate, as more and more of them realised that their efforts were useless.

Izzet Darya could not catch the sailing vessel. Several teams of oarsmen stopped rowing, releasing their grip on the oars and sitting down on the benches, their bare chests heaving as they gasped for breath. The motion of the corsair galley slowed to a crawl as their prey steadily drew farther and farther away.

Dunton was shouting at one of the Turkish petty officers. Hector guessed the Turk was the caravana in charge of sail handling. 'Leva! Leva!' Dunton was bawling, waving his arms frantically. 'Hoist sail! Hoist sail!' But there was no response. The Turk seemed at a loss, unable to act. It was the captain himself who responded. Moving to a position where the oarsmen could see him clearly, he called out, 'Well done, my children! You have given of your best. Now is the time to make best use of the wind that comes also from Allah. We will become falcons!' He had raised his right arm in a gesture of encouragement when, shockingly, he was struck by a hail of metal. One moment he was standing on the aft deck, and the next instant his body had been flung backward and he was just a lifeless heap on the deck, his white gown like a rumpled shroud. Nor had his officers escaped unscathed. The pilot was clutching at his face, blood seeping between his fingers, and the aga was staring down, numbed, at a mangled foot. 'Oh Lord be our Protector!' groaned Dunton. 'Perrier guns. They're going to finish us off.'

Hector tore his gaze away from the sight of the dead reis and looked towards the big sailing ship. The crew were brailing up the sails, slowing their vessel now that she was at a safe distance from the crippled galley and could manoeuvre. Even as he watched he saw activity on the high stern deck. Men were clustering around the light swivel cannon mounted along the rail, the perrier guns which could send hails of small shot and sweep a deck clear of men.

'Leva! Leva!' Again Dunton was roaring and gesticulating. He leapt up on to the main spar and frantically began unlacing the sail ties. Farther forward, the braver and more experienced sailors on the crew were hastily uncoiling the main halyard where it had been stowed, and laying it out along the catwalk.

Those overseers still on their feet began to push and shove men into position where they could begin to raise the sail. A tall, thin Algerine with a wild look in his eye began to chant a work song, and incredibly some sense of order and discipline returned as perhaps a score of those not wounded began to haul on the great rope and the massive mainyard slowly began to rise.

The spar was dangling some ten feet in the air when there came another crash of cannon, the loudest yet. This time it was not the irregular thump and report of individual guns, but the ragged roar of a broadside. At point blank range the warship's gunners could not miss. The broadside struck the stationary galley amidships, and broke her back. Men and oars were flung into the water. The bow and stern both tilted upward as the mid section of the venerable hull began to sink under water. The sea rushed in on the benches and Hector heard the desperate screams of the slave rowers still chained to their benches and unable to escape. The stern deck slanted under his feet, and sick at heart he watched Turgut's corpse slip down and come to rest against the rail, itself already half under water.

Shocked and dazed, he grasped at a splintered post. Then, as the stern section began to roll over, he was washed into the sea.

As he came back to the surface, he realised that something had changed. The sounds of firing had nearly stopped, though the air was still thick with gun smoke. He coughed and choked. Something nudged against his shoulder, and he clutched at it blindly. He found he was grasping the canopy from the galley's stern deck. Air had been trapped within the cloth so that it had risen to the surface, and was bobbing, half submerged. Steadying himself with one hand on the makeshift raft, Hector looked around.

The captain's bloody death had distracted him from thinking about Dan's fate, but now he scanned the mess of flotsam and wreckage, trying to spot his friend. The bow section of the galley was almost gone below the surface, and he saw only the heads of a few strangers nearby. Dan had disappeared. Closer to hand he glimpsed a face that was familiar. Thirty yards away was Dunton. He was clinging to a small piece of floating wood which was insufficient to keep him afloat. Every few seconds Dunton would submerge, coming back to the surface with panic in his face. 'Here! Here! Swim over here!' Hector called out. Dunton heard him, and twisted round to face him. Again he half-disappeared and was spitting water as he came back to the surface. 'I can't!' he gasped. 'I cannot swim!'

Hector had learned to swim during his summers on the Irish coast and now he slid into the water and struck out for the English sailor. 'Here, hang on to me,' he gasped as he reached Dunton. 'I'll tow you back.'

Dunton was floundering desperately. 'It won't work. That slave ring on my ankle pulls me down.'

'Come on!' snarled Hector. 'Hold on round my neck. You can do it!'

With a sudden lunge Dunton abandoned the sinking flotsam and grabbed on to his rescuer. Hector clenched his teeth and began to swim, trying to regain the raft. The effort was enormous. However hard he swam, he was making little headway. Dunton was a dead weight on his back, pulling him down. Hector took great mouthfuls of air and knew that his strength would soon ebb away. He swallowed a mouthful of seawater, gagged, and for a moment he thought that he too would drown. Squeezing his eyelids shut to clear his eyes of the salt water he looked ahead, trying to judge how far he had come. He was still not halfway to the makeshift raft. 'I said you could not make it,' whispered Dunton behind his ear, and then – miraculously – the sailor's grip relaxed and Hector found himself swimming free. He glanced over his shoulder and had a last glimpse of Dunton as he slipped under the water.

Even without the English sailor on his back, Hector was at his last gasp when finally he reached out and touched the floating canopy. Pulling himself up on its slippery wet surface, he lay there panting. Dimly he was aware of other survivors from the disaster who approached the raft. Once or twice he felt the canopy shift beneath him as they too heaved themselves on to its surface. He lay with his eyes closed, utterly spent and still in shock from seeing the captain meet his death. The captain had bought him in the same way as a farmer buys a promising colt at auction, yet Hector could only remember Turgut's kindness, his compassion, and the words of encouragement when his protégé had faced his sunnet – 'Don't be afraid. It happens at once, and is a wonderful thing as Allah has wished. Praise be to God.' Hector hoped that the same was true for the manner of Turgut's death.

Abruptly a hand was seizing the collar of his loose shirt, and he found himself dragged off the canopy, then hauled bruisingly over the edge of a small boat, and dumped into its bilges. A voice said in English, 'We've got another of the bastards.' Someone knelt on him painfully and tied his wrists behind his back. A short while later he was pulled to his feet and then half lifted and half thrown up the side of a ship where he found himself on a steady, dry deck. Swaying with exhaustion, he kept his eyes down and watched the salt water trickle out of his clothes and make a wavering line across the planks. He felt wretched.

'Ti! Moristo? Mauro? Turco?' a voice was asking aggressively. Someone was trying to establish his nationality, speaking in rusty lingua franca and standing so close that he could smell the interrogator's foul breath. But Hector felt too tired to answer. 'He's not wearing an ankle ring. Must have been one of the crew,' claimed another voice gruffly. Someone was fingering the qibla still hanging from its thong around his neck. 'Look at this,' said the first voice. 'He's an Allah worshipper all right. Saw this when I was in the bagnio at Tunis.'

Hector raised his head and found himself looking into the hostile face of a common sailor. A jagged scar running from the corner of his mouth to his right ear gave him a brutish look. Behind him stood a short, badly shaved man wearing a wig and dressed in clothing which had once been of fine quality but was now shabby and stained with grease spots. Hector took him to be a ship's officer.

'My name is Hector Lynch,' he said, addressing the officer. 'I am from Ireland.'

'A Papist turned Mussulman, that's droll!' mocked the officer. 'A bucket that has dipped twice into the sink of iniquity.'

'My father was a Protestant,' began Hector wearily, but his reply was cut short by the officer's retort. 'You're a renegade and turncoat, whatever stripe of faith you were before. To be serving with Barbary pirates means you deserve to hang. But as you are worth more alive than dead, you will be kept in chains until we reach port. Then you will wish you had gone to the bottom of the sea along with your thieving friends.'

Hector was about to ask the ship's destination when the sound of a hammer on iron distracted him. A little distance behind the officer, the ship's blacksmith was striking off the ankle ring of a starved-looking galley slave who must have been rescued from the wreck of *Izzet Darya*. Standing next in line, awaiting his turn and dressed only in a loincloth, was Dan. The Miskito, Hector recalled, had been wearing his slave ring when he had joined the corso, and Turgut Reis had not ordered it to be removed. Clearly the warship's crew had mistaken Dan for a slave they had liberated from the corsairs. Deliberately Hector forced himself to look away. Any sign that he knew Dan would betray his friend.

'Take the renegade and put him with his fellow blackguards!' ordered the officer, and Hector found himself pushed across the deck to join a group of bedraggled survivors from the galley; among them were several odjaks. As he stood waiting to be led away to the prison hold, Hector heard a cheer go up. The starved-looking man had been freed from his slave ring, and several of the warship's crew were gathering round to slap him on the back and congratulate him on his liberty. As Hector watched, Dan stepped forward impassively and placed his foot on the blacksmith's anvil. A few sharp blows and the blacksmith had knocked out the rivets from the ring, and again a cheer went up. But this time, the congratulations were cut short as the starved-looking man suddenly turned and, snatching at Dan's loincloth, whipped it away so that the Miskito stood naked. Pointing at Dan's circumcised penis, his accuser screamed, 'Rinigato! Rinigato!' and gave a vindictive whoop of triumph.

TWELVE

C

CHEVALIER ADRIEN CHABRILLAN, Knight Grand Cross of
the Order of St Stephen, was thoroughly satisfied with his day's
purchase. Through his agent, Jedediah Crespino of the well-
known Tuscan banking family, he had just acquired thirty prime
slaves for galley service. The slaves had appeared on the Livorno
market unexpectedly and Jedediah had snapped them up. An
English warship, the *Portland*, had sunk a large Algerine corsair
off Sardinia, and pulled a number of her crew from the water.
Naturally the *Portland*'s captain wanted to profit from his victory
so he had landed his captives at what was the biggest slave
market in the Christian Mediterranean, with the possible exception of Malta. Tall and aristocratic, Chevalier Chabrillan was
a familiar figure in Livorno. Always immaculately dressed in the
red uniform of the Order, he had a reputation as something of
a dandy. Indeed observers had been known to remark that
such a renowned galley captain had no need to take so much
trouble with his appearance, always powdering his cheeks and
parading the latest fashion in periwigs and buckled shoes. His
celebrity as a warrior for the Faith, they said, was already sufficient to make him stand out. Chabrillan, they agreed, was a true
heir to the days when the Duke of Florence had been able to
send two dozen galleys under the flag of St Stephen to confound

the Turk. And when the Grand Magistry had announced that it could no longer afford to equip and man such a large fleet, the Chevalier had offered to meet the costs of keeping his own vessel in commission, and had obtained permission to cruise in company with the vessels of the Order of St John of Malta. So his frequent appearances in Livorno were usually to buy and sell slaves or to negotiate the disposal of prizes.

Livorno was ideal for such transactions. Declared a free port by the Duke of Tuscany less than a decade earlier, it was now a thieves' kitchen on a grand scale. On the waterfront and in the counting houses it was quietly acknowledged that the transactions of men like Chabrillan were best not investigated too closely. Ostensibly the galleys of the Orders were licensed only to cruise the sea in search of vessels belonging to 'our enemies of our Holy Catholic Faith', as Grand Master Cotoner in Valletta put it. Such vessels could be seized and sold, together with their crews and cargoes. And should a Christian ship be found to be carrying Muslim-owned goods, then the Order's captain could impound only the goods but must release the vessel. Often, however, both goods and ship were confiscated, and on occasion the Christian crew themselves were held for ransom or even sold as slaves.

In such delicate traffic Livorno relied on its Jewish population. There were nearly three thousand of them, and they had been granted exceptional privileges. Here a Jew could own property, wear a sword at any hour, employ Christian servants and did not have to wear the Jewish badge. They also operated a complex network of commerce with their co-religionists in Tunis, Malta and Algiers. It was for this reason that Chevalier Chabrillan valued his connection with Jedediah Crespino so highly.

ℭ

'ONE HUNDRED SCUDI a head, a most satisfactory price if I may say so, though the English captain did insist that he was paid at once and in silver,' observed the Jewish banker. He and Chabrillan had met in the Crespino's private apartments at the end of the day's business. Jedediah lived in great style even though his office was only a minor outpost of the Crespino mercantile empire. He ran his business from a building overlooking the docks, and the first-floor room in which the two men now sat was sumptuously furnished with heavy brocades, fine furniture, rich rugs and a brilliant display of coral ornaments — a sign of the commerce in trinkets and religious artefacts which had been the mainstay of the Crespino fortune in the early days. 'Will you be selling on the slaves or keeping them for yourself?' the banker continued.

Chabrillan turned back from the window where he had been admiring the fine bronze statute put up on the waterfront to honour the memory of Grand Duke Ferdinand. It was most appropriate, he had been thinking, that the Duke's statue was supported by the figures of four Turkish slaves in chains. 'No, I want this batch shipped to Marseilles,' he said. The Jew nodded appreciatively. 'Ah yes, I hear that King Louis plans to expand his galley fleet.'

'He intends to develop the most powerful naval force in the Mediterranean, and his royal Galley Corps needs oarsmen wherever they can be got. The French are running out of convicts to put to the benches, and I have been commissioned to act as their purchasing agent for foreign slaves. My budget is impressive.'

Crespino regarded the tall aristocrat with interest. He wondered why Chabrillan, who was known for his piety and his fierce hatred of the Muslims, should now seek to serve the Sun King, Louis XIV of France, whose antipathy to the Turks was not so consistent. The answer was not long in coming.

'I have accepted a captaincy in Louis's Galley Corps which was offered to me. I will devote most of my time to it. I believe the Corps will soon become an essential ally in the Everlasting War.'

The Everlasting War, the Jew thought to himself, was madness. A mutual destruction pact between the Christians and the Muslims, it had been going on for centuries, and if men like Chabrillan had anything to do with it, would go on forever. Meanwhile, of course, the Crespinos in Livorno, the Cohens in Algiers, and his particular acquaintance Lazzaro dell'Arbori in Malta did very well out of arranging ransoms, negotiating prisoner exchanges, disposing of plunder, bartering slaves, and a host of discreet commercial transactions.

'Are you not afraid that Louis and his galleys might become so powerful that one day they will surpass the Order of St John in the Mediterranean?'

Chabrillan shrugged. 'Most of the Knights of St John are themselves French. They serve the Order and the Pope, but they retain allegiance also to France.'

'A fine balancing act.'

'No less than yours.'

The Jew inclined his head. 'If you wish, I can also arrange the delivery of the slaves to the royal galley base at Marseilles.'

'Yes. Please do that. I need the men there as soon as possible. In Marseilles they will be assessed and distributed among the French galleys so it would be helpful if you could provide me with their individual details, ahead of time, so that I can pre-select the best ones and have them added to the crew of my own vessel when it joins Louis's fleet.'

'Then I will arrange for the slaves to be forwarded to Marseilles in two lots. If you can arrange for the selected slaves to be identified, they will be sent – after some delay – in a second consignment. By the time they arrive in Marseilles someone will be ready to allocate them to your ship.'

'One more thing,' the Chevalier added. 'When you are preparing the paperwork, you might value the slaves at one hundred and thirty scudi per head. The French will pay the extra money without question, and I would be obliged if you would forward the surplus to Malta for the benefit of the Order of St John. Grand Master Cotoner needs all the available funds so he can proceed with his improvements to the fortifications of Valletta. Once that work has been completed, La Religion shall have the finest harbour in the Mediterranean.'

So this was what the Christians meant when they spoke about robbing Peter to pay Paul, the Jewish banker thought. Chabrillan was living up to his reputation as a fanatic who stopped at nothing to prosecute the Eternal War. Little wonder that he was known as 'the Lion of La Religion' and his galley, *St Gerassimus*, flew Chabrillan's personal banner, which displayed the Five Wounds of Christ. The Jew had heard extravagant stories about Chabrillan: that he had accomplished more caravans, as the marauding cruises against the Infidel were called, than any Knight whether of St John or St Stephen, and that he had played a heroic part in the valiant defence of Crete against the Turk. There, it was said, he had been taken prisoner by the Muslims and tortured. Perhaps this accounted for his hatred of Muslims.

In all his experience Jedediah Crespino had never encountered a man so fiercely zealous for his faith.

℃

'I'M AMAZED that you did not sink and drown,' Hector said to Dan. 'That iron ring around your ankle should have pulled you under.'

Dan laughed. 'Every Miskito has to be a strong swimmer. The Miskito coast is a place of swamps and backwaters. In the rainy season the rivers flood and everything is submerged. So we build our houses on stilts and sometimes we must swim to reach the places where we keep our boats. And when we go to the sea for fishing we think nothing of it if our canoes, which are no more than hollow logs, capsize and tip us into the water. Every Miskito child learns how to turn the canoe the right way up, then climb aboard and bale it out. So when the galley sank it was easy for me to reach the nearest piece of floating timber and scramble up on it. I was there only a short time before the sailors from the warship came in their small boat and collected me.'

'I'm sorry that you were identified as a renegade, Dan. I feel responsible because I encouraged you to become a Muslim.'

'Hector. If you think back, it was me who first suggested that we take the turban. Now, as a result, we find ourselves both back in a situation which seems much like the one we sought to escape. Perhaps together we can again find a way out of it.'

Hector found it difficult to share his friend's optimism this time. The two of them were shackled hand and foot, then attached to a length of iron chain linking them to a third captive, a taciturn and luxuriantly mustached odjak from *Izzet Darya*. The janissary's name, Hector had learned, was Irgun. Well over six feet tall and big-boned, he rarely smiled and had an unshakeable calm manner. Standing nearby were four more odjaks, all prisoners taken from the sea by *Portland*, and similarly chained together in a group. They were waiting at the head of a gangplank and about to disembark from the merchant ship that had brought them from Livorno. 'That's Marseilles up ahead,' a sailor had said to Hector as the ship made her landfall. 'Richest port in all of France. Full of whorehouses and taverns. Not that you'll enjoy them. You're the King's property now.'

Hector had no idea what the sailor was talking about, for they had caught only a brief glimpse of the man who had paid for them, a Jewish commission agent who had come aboard the English warship in Livorno and spent some hours closeted with the captain in his cabin. The next morning they had been taken ashore and placed in a noxious cell where they were then held for three weeks, being fed on scraps, before being shipped out again.

Gazing about him, Hector could see evidence of Marseilles's prosperity. On two sides the basin was overlooked by fine buildings, five or six stories high and roofed with slate. Part warehouses, part offices, their tall fronts glowed yellow in the afternoon sun. To the west, behind him, two powerful forts guarded the entrance to the harbour whose waters were furrowed by an armada of wherries, skiffs, palangriers, tartans and lighters, being rowed or sailed about their errands. At the foot of the gangplank, the wharf was bustling with activity. Dockers were piling up bales and crates, rolling huge barrels and manhandling enormous brown earthenware storage jars, cursing and cajoling as they loaded the goods on to donkeys and ox carts. Stray dogs ran here and there. Porters staggered past, bent-kneed under the burdens hoisted on their shoulder poles; and, ignoring the chaos, little gatherings of merchants and store clerks, traders and dealers were busy gossiping or bargaining with one another. 'Allez! Allez!' a shout came from behind him. A grey-haired man in a leather waistcoat had come aboard clutching some papers, and was now ordering the prisoners to go ashore.

It was awkward to negotiate the slope of the gangplank without snagging their chains, but, once on land, Hector and his companions shuffled in the direction the man in the waistcoat indicated – towards an enormous building which dominated the south-eastern corner of the waterfront. Its walls were painted blue and decorated with yellow motifs which Hector recognised as the fleur-de-lis, the symbol of the French king. Another huge yellow fleur-de-lis surmounted the great dome which rose from the interior of the building. Smells of pitch and tar, of raw timber and hot metal, and the sounds of hammering and sawing told Hector that they were approaching a vast Arsenal and shipyard.

'Allez! Allez!' Their drover was shouting at them to go around the building and approach it on the landward side. As they turned the corner, Hector saw ahead a sight he would never forget. Coming down the busy street which led from the heart of the city was a column of about fifty men. They were dirty and dishevelled, with long matted hair and unkempt beards.

Most were dressed in rags, and some wore broken boots or clogs while the rest were barefoot. They moved slowly as if exhausted. All of them wore metal collars, and from each collar a light chain joined each man to a central heavier chain, so that the entire column was linked together as a single unit which made a mournful clanking sound as it limped forward. At the head of the column rode an overseer mounted on a bay horse, and on each side were more mounted men, clearly guards, equipped with bullwhips. Three or four carts brought up the rear of the column and – to Hector's astonishment – several desperate-looking women were keeping pace, occasionally darting into the column to speak to one or other of the chained gang.

'Halte-là!' The leather waistcoat shouted at Hector and his companions to stand where they were and allow the column to pass in front of them. As Hector and Dan looked on, a double gate in the Arsenal's yellow outer wall swung open to receive the long, sad file. Led by the mounted officer, the column began to be swallowed up, though the women were prevented from entering. Uniformed sentries blocked them from going any further. The women beseeched and begged, but the soldiers firmly held their muskets crosswise as a barrier, holding them back. One tearful woman fell to the ground, keening in anguish.

'Allez! Allez!' The leather waistcoat was bawling urgently at his charges to move forward and enter the Arsenal before the gates were shut and barred. Once inside they found themselves in a large open parade ground where the prisoners of the column were standing meekly. Guards were removing the iron neck collars, and then dividing the prisoners into small batches. As each batch formed up, it was escorted to what looked like the main administration building and taken inside. Several minutes would pass, and then a guard appeared and shepherded away another batch of prisoners. Eventually all the prisoners had been removed, and the square was empty except for Hector, Dan and the odjaks. Their escort in the leather waistcoat had walked away, ignoring them. Moments later a guard came to the open door and beckoned to Hector, Dan and Irgun.

They were directed into a large whitewashed room where bent over a table was some sort of official dressed in an ill-fitting black coat with tarnished silver buttons. His pen was poised over a ledger. 'Nom?' he enquired curtly, without even raising his head which, Hector observed, was flecked with specks of dandruff. Clearly the official was a receiving clerk and had mistaken them for another batch of prisoners from the column. Grateful to the friars who had taught him French Hector replied, 'Lynch, Hector.'

The clerk scratched down the information in the ledger. 'The crime of which you are condemned?'

'No crime,' said Hector.

Angrily, the clerk looked up and saw the three prisoners from *Izzet Darya* standing in front of him. 'Where are you from?' he demanded. 'You are not with the chain.'

'We are from the galley *Izzet Darya*.'

At the mention of the galley, Hector thought he saw a glimmer of recognition in the official's eyes. 'And your name?' he asked Dan. The Miskito understood what was wanted, and answered simply 'Dan'. Again the pen scratched across the surface of the ledger. Next it was the turn of the odjak but he did not answer, and stood silent and staring down at his interrogator from his great height. 'He does not comprehend,' Hector intervened.

'Then you tell me what he is called.'

'His name is Irgun.'

'Any documents to confirm your identities?' the clerk said irritably.

'No.'

'Then I shall put you all down as Turks. That will be all,' and he began to fill in a column he had left blank in the ledger.

'Guards! Uncouple that big Turk and put him with his fellows where he belongs. Take the other two away, take off the linking chain, and keep them separate from the rest. Tomorrow they will be assigned to their duties. And if there are any more Turks outside, you can conduct them to their cells without bothering me with the details.'

The guards led Hector and Dan down a long corridor, across a courtyard, and through a series of doors which were unlocked and then relocked, and finally left them in a cell some twenty feet by twenty feet. It was unfurnished except for a layer of damp straw, two benches and a bucket that was evidently being used as a latrine. Stretched out on one of the benches was a tough-looking man with close-cropped dark hair who sat up as the cell door slammed behind them and regarded them with distaste.

'How come they put you in with me?' He spoke French with a strong accent. At some time his nose had been badly broken.

'What's that?'

'You're Turks.'

'No. I'm from Ireland, and Dan here is from the Caribees.'

The broken-nose man hawked and spat in the straw. 'Then how come he's wearing a leg ring? Anyhow Turks, Moors, slaves — doesn't matter which. They all mean the same thing if you're condemned to the oar. And if you're Irish, how come you're here?'

'We were in the bagnio in Algiers, and converted. Now we're treated as renegades.'

'You're lucky they didn't hang you the instant they caught you. That's King Louis's usual way of dealing with renegades. They must be in too much need of oarsmen to give you the long drop.'

'Who are they?'

'The King's Galley Corps. I've been here before, and that's

why they're keeping me apart from the others. To stop me tipping them off about what's to come and how they can dodge the worst.'

'What others?'

The man nodded towards a small barred window, set high in the wall. Hector stepped up on the bench, took a grip on the bars and hauled himself up so he could look out. He was staring down into a large hall, as bare and bleak as his own cell. Seated or lying on its straw were the crowd of disconsolate prisoners who had just arrived with the chain column.

'I was with that lot on the stroll from Paris,' explained the fellow prisoner disdainfully as Hector lowered himself back down. 'Took us nearly a month, and more than half a dozen died on the way. The argousins...' Seeing that Hector did not know who he meant, he explained, 'The argousins are the convict-warders. They weren't any worse than usual, but that thieving bastard of a comite who was in charge had done the usual corrupt deal with the victuallers. We were served half rations, and nearly starved.'

'If you're not a slave, what are you here for?'

The man laughed without mirth, and turned his face to one side, exposing his cheek. 'See here.' Beneath the grime Hector could just make out the letters GAL marked in the skin. 'Know what that means?'

'I can guess,' Hector answered.

'That's how I was branded three years ago. I was a galerien, a convict galley oarsman. But I was too slippery for them, and managed to get myself a pardon. Paid a clever lawyer to say that there had been a case of mistaken identity and there were plenty of other vagabonds and rogues called Jacques Bourdon – and they had taken up the wrong one. But it took him so long to get my case heard that I had already been marked for galley service by the time my pardon came through. And the lawyer had cost me all the money I had, so I had to go back to my old trade when I returned to Paris. That was the only way to stay alive.'

'Your old trade?'

Jacques Bourdon shot out his right hand, and for a moment Hector thought the convict was going to hit him. But Bourdon only raised his thumb. Burned into the soft flesh between thumb and forefinger was the letter V. 'Don't often see someone with two brands, do you?' he boasted. 'That one stands for voleur. I'm a thief, and a good one too. Started by nicking things when I was a youngster, and didn't get properly caught until I was in my teens when I stole a pair of candlesticks from a church. That's how I got my first brand. But I wouldn't do anything so obvious as church robbing now. I pick pockets and locks. It's less risky, and I wouldn't have been caught the second time if a jealous rat had not informed on me.'

'What about all those others?' asked Hector. 'What have they done that they find themselves here?'

'I didn't bother to ask. But you can be sure that they're the usual riff-raff. There'll be swindlers and murderers and thieves like me. Some won't have paid their debts, and others have committed perjury. Probably some smugglers, too. Rascals caught moving contraband tobacco or avoiding the salt tax. Then there are the deserters from the army. Like you, they're lucky not to have been hung or shot. And naturally every last one of them will swear that they are innocent of the crimes for which they have been found guilty and sent here. A few might even be telling the truth.'

Hector was silent. It seemed to him that this prison was the sink of injustice. Then he said, 'But surely, if you were able to get a pardon, the innocent ones could do the same.'

The pickpocket regarded him sardonically. 'Yes, if they have enough money hidden away or someone on the outside who can help. But once inside here, the chances of getting out are almost nil. Deserters and renegades like yourself are condemned for life, and even if by some miracle their cases come up for review, the Galley Corps has often lost track of its own oarsmen and can't locate them.'

Hector recalled the clerk who had just written down their details in the ledger. 'But surely it's all recorded in the official files.'

Bourdon laughed outright. 'The clerks couldn't care less whether their book entries are correct. Half the time they know they are being told lies, and so they scribble down what pleases them. If a man gives a false name, that's accepted. And if he lies about the reason why he is sent to the galleys, then that's all right too. And if the entrant stays silent before the clerk, or he's too frightened and confused to answer why he's been condemned, or he doesn't even know the charge against him, do you know what the clerks write down then? They note down that he has been condemned to the galleys and add "without saying why". Goodbye to any hope of redemption.'

'I find that difficult to believe.' Hector's spirits were sinking even further. 'Everyone knows why they are here, or at least has some idea of the reason?'

'Listen to me, Irishman,' said the pickpocket, seizing Hector by the arm. 'There were people who walked with me all the way from Paris who had not the least inkling why they were in chains. Maybe an unknown enemy had reported them to the authorities. All it takes is an accusation planted in the right quarters and accompanied by a juicy bribe. Then there's a show trial at which you have to prove your innocence when you are already presumed to be guilty. And heaven help you if you are a Protestant and you are answering to a Catholic judge. Being a Protestant is getting dangerous in France.'

THIRTEEN

C

NEXT MORNING Hector awoke from a fitful sleep to hear his name being shouted aloud. A guard was banging on the open cell door and calling out that he and Dan were to make themselves ready for an interview with the commissaire of the Arsenal. As he got to his feet, Hector was surprised to hear Bourdon call out impudently, 'What about me?' In answer, the guard opened the door, walked across the room and struck him hard across the mouth. Undeterred, the pickpocket asked, 'So who's the commissaire now? Another of Brodart's friends?' The guard scowled as he turned on his heel and the pickpocket called out to his retreating back, 'Whoever it is, tell him that Jacques Bourdon's a man with whom he can do a little business!'

'What did you do that for?' Hector asked. 'It only made him angry.'

The pickpocket shot Hector a quizzical glance. 'I don't suppose you even know who Brodart is,' he said.

Hector shook his head.

'Jean Brodart is our lord and master. He's Intendant of Galleys and chief administrator of the Galley Corps, appointed by Minister Colbert himself. He's also one of the most corrupt men in the kingdom. Brodart and his cronies are skimming every livre that King Louis pays out for his precious Galley Corps. They're up to every trick, whether putting non-existent workers on the payroll, demanding kickbacks from suppliers, selling off surplus stores, writing up fraudulent bills of lading. Believe me, compared to the Intendant and his gang, the swindlers and fraudsters on the chain were innocent lambs. Wait and see, my message will get through. Brodart's underlings can't resist even the smallest crumb.'

When the guard returned half an hour later it was to escort Hector and Dan back to the administration building and up a staircase to the first floor until they arrived before a door guarded by a sentry in a blue uniform with white crossbelts. Their escort knocked, and they were shown into a large room lit by tall windows which gave a view across the city.

'I understand you are latecomers with the consignment from Livorno,' began the commissaire, who had been standing look-ing out towards the distant roof tops. Commissaire Batiste was a pear-shaped man, badly shaved, and with several expensive rings glittering on his puffy fingers. 'I have a note here saying that you are to be assigned to the galley *St Gerassimus*. That is very irregular, particularly because the *St Gerassimus* has not yet joined the fleet, though she is expected shortly. Do you have any idea why you are singled out for special treatment?'

'No, sir,' Hector answered. 'No one has told us anything.'

'The Arsenal is going to need every able-bodied man that can be found so I have decided that you will be held here pending the arrival of the *St Gerassimus*, and put to work. Later her captain can explain matters more fully.' He scribbled some-thing on a piece of paper and, turning towards the guard, said, 'They are to be enrolled under premier comite Gasnier. Go and find Gasnier, wherever he is, and deliver them in person, and get his signature on this paper as a receipt. And tell the comite that he's to train them to be productive.'

They returned to the ground floor and, escorted by the guard, began to make their way through the Arsenal, searching for the comite. The place was an immense, sprawling maze of warehouses, magazines, depots and armouries, so their quest took them first to an iron foundry where anchors and chains and metal fittings were being forged, then to a vast draughty shed where sails were spread on the floor or hung from beams to be cut and sewn. Next was a ropewalk in which teams of men were twisting huge ropes and cables, then several wood-working galleries where mast makers and carpenters were shaving and straightening spars and oars, and finally a melting shop where half-naked labourers toiled over the huge pots that bubbled with boiling pitch and tar. Finally they reached a series of long, low, barn-like structures. The smell of rotting seaweed and the sight of ships' masts protruding over the perimeter wall told Hector that this side of the Arsenal bordered directly on the harbour. Their escort took them through a side door and, all at once, they were looking down on the skeleton of a galley which lay in dry dock. Two dozen men armed with mallets were swarming over the vessel, busily knocking her to pieces. 'Comite Gasnier!' the guard called out over the din of the hammers. A paunchy bald man, dressed in scuffed work clothes, was standing at the edge of the dry dock, supervising the work. He waited for a moment, to satisfy himself about some detail, then came over to speak to them.

'New recruits for you, comite,' said the escort respectfully. 'The commissaire says that you are to make something useful out of them.'

Gasnier looked at Hector and Dan thoughtfully. Hector had the impression of a solid, sensible man. The comite's calm gaze took in their manacles. 'Right then, leave them with me,' he answered, then turned back to his duties, leaving the two prisoners standing where they were.

It was almost another hour before Gasnier paid them a second glance when, after shouting something to an underling who seemed to be his foreman, he came over to the two prisoners and announced, 'I don't want to know what you did to get yourselves here, only what you can do for me in the future. First let me say that if you behave yourselves, I'll treat you fair. But if you give any trouble, you'll discover what a hard man I can be. This is the moment for you to tell me what you think you are good at. Speak up!'

Hector stumbled over his words as he answered. 'I was a clerk on a galley for a few weeks,' he said. 'And my friend here was with the musketeers.'

'A musketeer, eh?' The comite looked at Dan. 'He doesn't speak French, does he?'

'No, sir.'

'Well, that's no harm. He doesn't need to speak the language if he's got clever hands. Can he mend guns?'

'I believe so, sir.'

'What about you? A clerk, you say.'

'Yes sir. I was responsible for keeping track of stores.'

'Any good at it?'

'My master seemed satisfied.'

'Well if you're going to be a storekeeper here, you need to keep an extra sharp lookout. All sorts of things go missing. See that galley down there?' the comite nodded towards the dry dock where the men were keeping up an incessant thumping and banging with their mallets. 'Notice anything unusual?'

Hector stared down at the workers. The men were busily breaking down the galley, carrying away the timbers and setting them on one side in neat piles. Most of the workers were wearing what seemed to be a prison uniform of a parti-coloured jacket of dark red and brown worn over heavy canvas trousers. The legs of the trousers were also in different colours, one brown and one buff. All of the men wore bonnet-like caps, but some were dark blue and others were scarlet. He guessed that these marked a different status between the prisoners, and was about to comment when he noticed something else. The planks, frames and beams that were being stacked up were freshly cut.

The workers were taking to bits a galley that had never been put to sea. He said as much to the comite.

'That's right,' confirmed Gasnier. 'That's what they're doing,' but he did not explain further. He only beckoned to an assistant and instructed him to take Dan to the armoury and leave him there in charge of the chief armourer for assessment as a gunsmith. Then, addressing Hector again, he said, 'You report to the head storekeeper. He'll tell you what to do. You'll find him in the main depot over by the sail loft.'

©

THAT EVENING Hector and Dan met when work at the Arsenal finished for the day and they were shown to their dormitory.

'I never imagined there were so many muskets in all the world,' Dan told his friend. 'There are ten thousand of them stored in the Arsenal — four galleries lined with rack after rack of guns, and they all have to be checked and cleaned and repaired as necessary. I'm to be one of forty gunsmiths employed in that task.'

'Will you be able to manage?' Hector asked.

The Miskito nodded confidently. 'I passed my test. The head armourer handed me a musket and used sign language to ask me what was wrong with it. I pointed to a dangerous crack in the barrel which would burst one day, and I mimed the sort of injury the explosion would do to the man who fired it. He would lose an eye or be scarred for life.'

Dan stretched luxuriously, extending his arms above his head.

'As soon as I passed my test, an armourer removed my wrist and ankle chains and only left the ankle ring in place. He told me that I will be handling gunpowder from time to time, and the less metal I have about me, the less chance there is of a spark setting off an explosion.'

'Wish the head storekeeper would do the same for me,'

commented Hector. 'Wrist fetters are a real handicap when it comes to handling a pen.'

He was about to continue when a voice behind him said, 'I told you that the commissaire would snap up the least crumb.' Hector turned to see Jacques Bourdon standing in the doorway, a smug look on his branded face. 'It only goes to prove the old saying that appetite comes with eating,' the pickpocket added as he sauntered into the room.

'You mean you managed to bribe the commissaire?'

'It didn't take much, just two small silver coins.'

'And where did you get the money?'

'And wouldn't I have been stupid not to make a few advance arrangements when I heard I was to be taken south from Paris with the chain? I sent my lass on ahead to Marseilles with the cash from my last robbery. I couldn't hide it on me because I knew those swine of argousins would strip and rob us on the way down here. So she was waiting at the Arsenal gate for one last embrace and it was the sweetest kiss she ever gave me. A mouthful of silver.'

The pickpocket sat down on a bench. 'It seems I've also managed to get myself assigned to that missing galley of yours. What's her name? *St Gerassimus*, though who was Gerassimus, or what he did to deserve his sainthood, I've no idea. But the rumour is that the galley's to receive the pick of the new Turkish slaves in from Livorno, and that's good news. Turks make the best oarsmen, as anyone in the Galley Corps will tell you, and if your fate is to be a galley oarsman there's no better place on the bench than alongside a great big strapping Turk. Which reminds me,' the pickpocket nodded towards Dan, 'you said your friend here isn't a Turk, then why's he wearing that ring, and no chains?'

'He's working in the armoury,' Hector explained. 'It's to avoid accidents.'

Bourdon appeared unconvinced. 'Tell him not to get any

fancy ideas about running away, now that his legs are free. He looks enough of a foreigner, with that long ugly face and brown skin, to be mistaken for a Turk.

Thinking back, Hector recalled that few of the men he had seen dismantling the galley had been wearing chains.

'That's how you'll recognise the Turks among the other galley men,' Bourdon continued, 'Turks don't wear leg chains or even wrist fetters when on shore.' He leaned back against the wall, clearly pleased to be showing off his superior knowledge. 'They only wear an ankle ring. The authorities know that the Turks will very seldom try to escape, because where would they go? They would find it very hard to get aboard any ship to take them home, and here in France who would take them in? So there's no point in keeping them chained up, except on a galley at sea for fear they mutiny and take over the vessel. And even a mutiny is unlikely. The funny thing about the Turks is that they'll settle down to whatever job is given them. They'll work as hard on a Christian galley as on one of their own religion, and often you'll get better treatment from the Turk on the galley bench beside you than from your Christian neighbour at your other elbow.'

'Surely a Turk will try to escape if an easy opportunity presents itself,' said Hector doubtfully.

'If that happens, the good people of Marseilles enjoy a spot of fun,' answered Bourdon. 'There's a fat reward to anyone who brings him in to the authorities, so the local folk organise search groups and pass the word to be on the lookout for a foreign-looking cove. When they locate their quarry, they chase him, just like running down a hare or stag.'

'And when they catch him?'

'They bring him back to the argousin-major, and collect their reward.'

'And the Turk?'

'He doesn't run away a second time. His ears and nose are

cut off, and from that moment onward he is kept chained to the bench, and not allowed to go ashore.'

℃

HECTOR HAD BEEN only a fortnight in his job as a storekeeper's assistant when he came to appreciate the truth of Bourdon's claim that the management of the Arsenal was riddled with graft. He was standing at the iron-bound gates of the powder magazine, making a tally of the gunpowder kegs arriving from an inbound galley, when he noted something strange. There was a strict rule in the Galley Corps that whenever a vessel returned to port she sent ahead her ship's boat loaded with all her kegs of powder. These were placed in the Arsenal's thick-walled powder magazine for safe storage because some years earlier a fully armed galley had blown up in harbour, either by accident or sabotage, and there had been heavy loss of life. Hector had issued gunpowder to the same galley just two days previously, and now he observed that while the number of barrels he received back was the same as had been given out, several of the markings on the kegs were different. Since his days in the stone quarry of Algiers he had made a habit of noting down the different markings on the kegs, and when he checked with the head storekeeper his suspicions deepened. 'Our gunpowder comes from all over France,' the storekeeper told him blandly. 'It depends on the contractors. They're all small producers because there are no large gunpowder factories, and naturally each maker has his own marks. Just write down the number of barrels returned, and leave the list with me.'

When Hector mentioned the incident to Bourdon that evening, the pickpocket rolled his eyes in mock surprise. 'What do you expect? The commissaire who organises the purchases of supplies for the Corps will have lined his own pocket when he placed the original powder contracts, and naturally the head storekeeper takes a cut when the materials are delivered into store. So he looks the other way when the captains and quarter-masters on the galleys have a bite at the same cherry.'

'But how do they do it?' asked Hector.

The pickpocket shrugged. 'I have no idea, but you can be sure that if there's a way of turning a quiet profit, someone will have found it. My guess is that the galley captains are selling the better quality powder to the Marseilles merchants, and replacing it with low-grade, cheaper material. But it's not your job to say anything. You don't exist as far as France is concerned. You are a non-person. Even if you reported your suspicions to someone like comite Gasnier who has the reputation of being incorruptible, and he brought the matter before the authorities, you could not serve as a witness. Once you've been committed to the oar, you are legally a dead man. If I were you, I'd try to work out how the fraud is being done, and then keep that knowledge to yourself until you can use it to your own advantage. But be very careful! The people who run this place take good care that King Louis stays so besotted with his precious Galley Corps that he doesn't ask awkward questions. They wouldn't look kindly upon anyone who might upset their cosy schemes.'

ℂ

JUST HOW FAR the Intendant and his staff would go to impress the King became clear when the head storekeeper summoned Hector to his office the very next afternoon.

'I am selecting you for special duty. The Intendant has informed every department that next Thursday the Arsenal is to demonstrate its skill and efficiency in the Royal Presence by building, launching and equipping a new war galley in just thirty-six hours.'

Hector was too astonished to reply.

'Of course it's nothing more than a stunt,' the storekeeper sniffed. 'But that's what Intendant Brodart has ordered us to do, so we have to put up with it. The Intendant boasted to the King and to the minister that the Arsenal is capable of such a feat. Premier comite Gasnier has known about it for weeks. Now it's official.'

'With respect, sir, do you think it can be done?' Hector asked carefully. 'I thought that a galley took at least a year to build, maybe twice as long. And the timbers have to be kept until they are seasoned, and that takes at least a couple of years.'

The head storekeeper regarded the young Irishman suspiciously. 'Who told you that?' he asked.

Too late Hector realised that much of the timber he had seen in the Arsenal was green, although according to the official records it had been kept in store for years. The head storekeeper, he concluded, was well aware of the fraud.

'I don't know,' he said vaguely. 'Maybe that's something that the boat builders do at home and I picked it up there.'

'The royal Galley Corps uses only the finest hand-picked timber,' his superior said quietly, and with a slight edge of menace in his voice continued, 'Anyhow we will not be issuing timber for this new galley from stores. Everything has been prepared, as you would have noticed if you had kept your wits about you.'

The remark reminded Hector of comite Gasnier's comment when he had first seen him at the dry dock.

'You mean the new galley which will be built in the presence of the King, has been built before?'

'You have sharp eyes,' admitted the storekeeper. 'Gasnier's dry dock gangs have been practising for weeks. Pulling apart a galley, then putting her back together again. Not the whole vessel, of course, just the more awkward sections. This time it will be the real thing, and I'm loaning you to Gasnier as a tallyman. Your task will be to keep track of the materials, ensuring a smooth flow. The royal demonstration is scheduled to start at dawn next Thursday and the galley must be ready to put to sea, fully armed and crewed, by noon on Friday.'

☾

AS IT TURNED OUT, the King, who was known for his capricious decisions, cancelled his visit to the Arsenal at the last moment. But Intendant Brodart decided that the demonstration would go ahead, knowing that reports of its outcome would reach the court. Long before daylight on the appointed day Hector reported for duty at the dry dock. There he found some five hundred carpenters assembling on the edge of the dry dock, which was empty except for the 160-foot keel of the galley lying ready on its chocks. In the flickering light of banks of torches the carpenters were being divided into squads of fifty, each led by a senior shipwright and a foreman. Nearby were marshalled two companies of nailers, and behind them again a hundred caulkers were preparing their caulking irons and pots of tallow and tar. Each man was already wearing a cap whose colour told him on which particular section of the vessel he would work. Hector's responsibility was to a gang of porters, forty men, standing by to carry the ready-cut timbers from stacks on each side of the dry dock. He was to make sure they picked up the right pieces in the correct order, and took them to the proper sector the moment they were needed.

'Listen to me, men,' bellowed comite Gasnier. He was using a speaking trumpet and standing on a scaffolding where he could look down on the entire dry dock and direct the progress of the building. 'You're doing a job that you've done over and over again in the past. So just follow the orders you get from your foremen and supervisors and think about nothing else.' He paused while an assistant repeated his words in Turkish. Looking around, Hector realised that at least every fourth man in the building teams was a Turk. Among them he thought he recognised the hulking figure of Irgun, the odjak from *Izzet*

Darya. 'It is vital not to get in one another's way,' Gasnier went on. 'Do your job as fast as possible, step back and let the next man get on with his work. Above all, there will be no talking or shouting. You are to work in silence and use hand signals. Anyone caught talking will receive ten lashes. Only supervisors and master shipwrights may speak, and then only in a quiet voice. All other instructions will be given by whistles, and there will be a drum beat every hour, on the hour, so that you can keep track of time. Now stand by for the signal to begin.'

The start whistle blew. The porters seized the first dozen frames and carried them at a run down the ladders into the dry dock. The shipwrights hoisted them into position and began to peg them into place. By the time the first frames were secure, the porters were already arriving with the next frames in the sequence. Hector had to admit that the skill and discipline of the workforce was astonishing. In less than half an hour every frame was fitted in its proper place, a task that would normally have taken fifteen days to complete. Then, without pausing, the carpenters turned to the task of laying in the deck beams and then the planks, bending and clinching the timber so adroitly that by noon the entire hull was finished, and the carpenters were kneeling on the upper parts, urgently pegging down the deck boards. Below them the teams of caulkers were hammering oakum into the seams. By then, the cacophony of hammering and sawing had risen to such a deafening crescendo that Gasnier's rule against talking was unnecessary, for no one could have heard themselves speak. Only at dusk, when most of the wood-working was done, did the noise begin to subside as the carpenters withdrew, leaving the painters and carvers and gilders to add their decorative touches by the light of torches. By midnight the caulkers had begun to check their work, pumping water into the hull, then looking for leaks and plugging them before draining out the vessel, and applying a final underwater coat of tar. Even as the master caulker reported to Gasnier that the hull was watertight, his workmen were scrambling out of the dry dock to avoid the rising water, for the sluice gates had been opened and the dock was flooding. A priest came aboard to bless the vessel and was still saying his prayers as the galley was warped out into the harbour and alongside the quay.

By now Hector's job was done, and no one paid him any attention as he stood, bleary-eyed and exhausted, watching the riggers step the masts and spars. 'Just short of nine o'clock,' said someone in the crowd beside him, as Dan's colleagues from the armoury manhandled on to the fore deck the galley's main armament, a 36-pound cannon and two smaller artillery pieces. The Arsenal's porters were in a human chain, loading and stowing the galley's ballast, munitions, oars and sea-going gear. There came the tramp of feet and the clank and rattle of iron. Along the quay marched five companies of galley men, fifty men in each company, all in new multi-coloured prison garb and their chains newly blackened. Reaching the galley, they halted. Their argousins blew a short blast on their whistles, and the oarsmen turned and ran up the gangplanks where they dispersed to their benches and then quietly sat while the argousins chained them to their seats.

Now, for the first time in thirty-six hours, Hector saw Gasnier relax and give a quiet smile of approval. The galley's captain and officers, resplendent in their best uniforms, went aboard, and a lad unfurled the standard of the royal Galley Corps, the golden fleur-de-lis on a red field. A trumpet sounded, and the galley pushed off from the quayside. More blasts from the argousins' whistles and the oarsmen laid in place their 38-feet-long sweeps, rose to their feet, and stood ready, hands on the oar grips. A drum began to beat and the oarsmen took up a steady deep-throated chant as the great oars began to move to the rhythm, dipping into the dirty harbour water, propelling the galley away from the dock. 'Brodart promised His Majesty that the galley would be ready for sea trials before noon on the second day,' said the same voice, 'and he's kept his word.'

Hector raised his arm to shade his eyes as he watched the

newborn galley heading towards the harbour entrance. It was a beautiful sunlit morning, with scarcely a breath of wind, and another galley was inward-bound, entering between the guardian forts. As the two galleys passed, they saluted one another, dipping their ensigns as they passed. Hector saw that the arriving galley flew a flag whose badge was a red fork-tailed cross on a white field. 'St Stephen's Cross,' said the longshoreman. 'That must be our new recruit. That's the *St Gerassimus*.'

FOURTEEN

𝕮

'WELCOME, CHEVALIER, your visit to the Arsenal is indeed an honour.' Commissaire Batiste had a fulsome greeting for Adrien Chabrillan as the Knight of St Stephen was shown into his office. 'Intendant Brodart asks me to present his sincere apologies that he cannot be here in person. He has had to leave on an urgent matter – an audience with His Majesty.' The commissaire looked pleased with himself. 'We launched a new galley yesterday, after building her in less than thirty-six hours, a most prodigious feat, don't you agree? His Majesty wishes to hear the details from the Intendant himself.'

'I saw the new galley,' commented Chabrillan dryly. He suspected that Brodart, far from going to answer the King's questions, was headed to court to make sure that as many people as possible knew about the successful demonstration.

'Remarkable, truly remarkable,' the commissaire added immodestly. He crossed to a table where a scale model of the galley was on prominent display. 'One of our galeriens, a jeweller who got a little too free with his clients' possessions, took more than eighteen months to produce this model. Yet our Arsenal craftsmen managed to build the full-sized vessel, 185 feet long and 22 feet beam at the waterline, in little more than a day. And no skimping on the materials either, finest Provençal oak for the knees and planks. Tough stuff to work. An exceptional achievement.'

He looked at his visitor, expecting a gesture of approval, and was unprepared for Chabrillan's chilly response. 'A galley is only as good as her crew, and I've come to you for more men. *St Gerassimus* had a brush with a Turkish brigantine on the way here. Nothing conclusive as the Turk fled, but I lost five banks of oarsmen from a lucky shot, and my galley was already under-strength. A tenth of my regular oarsmen were bonnevoles, volunteers, and they are accustomed to work for plunder not pay. Many of them have chosen not to enter the service of the King. I trust you will be able to make up the shortfall.'

'These extra oarsmen you seek, would they be in addition to the Turks and demi-Turks who arrived from Livorno six weeks ago and are waiting to join your vessel?'

Chabrillan looked down his nose at the commissaire, not bothering to conceal his disdain. 'Of course. Though I have no idea what you mean by a demi-Turk.'

'A private joke of mine. A circumcised renegade,' the commissaire explained. 'There are two of them in the Livorno batch, a young Irishman who has proved useful as a storekeeper, and his foreign companion works as a gunsmith. They have received no training for the oar and may not be as strong as the Turks. But perhaps they would be adequate.'

'If they are renegades then all the more reason that they serve aboard my vessel,' Chabrillan replied. 'On the *St Gerassimus* we pride ourselves on the number of backsliders who have been made to see the error of their ways. I understand that you received a chain from Bordeaux recently.'

The Chevalier was altogether too nosy, the commissaire thought, as he regarded the tall, dandified figure before him. Chabrillan had been ashore for only a few hours, yet already he had been making enquiries about the facilities available to him now that *St Gerassimus* was part of the royal Galley Corps. The commissaire disliked meddlesome galley captains. They were a distraction from the serious day-to-day business of profiteering from the operations of the Arsenal. Batiste was from a mercantile background and held his lucrative post because he was a first cousin to Intendant Brodart, and he mistrusted those commanders who were aristocrats and put on airs.

'Yes, yes. A chain did arrive, about eighty felons, mostly tax evaders and vagrants. Several may not be suitable material for the oar . . .' he began, but Chabrillan cut him short. 'I'll be the judge of that. When can I inspect them?'

The commissaire hesitated. It was nearly noon, and he was looking forward to a leisurely lunch with a trio of echevins, aldermen of Marseilles. They were finalising a plan to acquire a parcel of land adjacent to the Arsenal, so that next year the King could be informed that the galley base needed more space and, after a suitable interval, that a site had been found which was good value. The transaction ought to net a fourfold profit for the syndicate. 'Regretfully, I have pressing duties for the rest of the day, but if you would be willing to inspect the prisoners in the company of the receiving clerk, that can be arranged at your convenience.'

'Without delay, if you please,' retorted Chabrillan.

The commissaire summoned an aide and ordered him to escort Chabrillan to the holding cells where the convicts of the chain from Bordeaux were waiting their assessment.

'And while the Chevalier is examining the convicts,' the commissaire added, 'you are to arrange for the Turks from Livorno and the two renegades to be made ready for galley service and delivered to the *St Gerassimus*, also that pickpocket, what's his name – Bourdain or something like that.' Turning to Chabrillan, he enquired, 'Who should my man ask for at the quayside? He will need a receipt.'

'He can deliver the oarsmen to my premier comite, Piecourt. He has full authority in these matters. Piecourt will also see to the necessary training of the men while I am away. As soon as

I have selected the extra men I need, I set out for my estates in Savoy. In the meantime *St Gerassimus* needs maintenance work and I trust you will have this done promptly now that you have told me how fast your workmen can perform. When I return, I expect to find my vessel fully seaworthy again and her complement properly trained.'

'The Arsenal will make every endeavour to meet your requirements, Chevalier,' the commissaire assured his guest, though inwardly Batiste was already scheming how he could rid himself of the troublesome Chevalier. On his desk was an instruction from the Minister of the Marine. It ordered the Galley Corps to conduct trials to establish whether a new artillery invention, an exploding shell, was suitable for use at sea. He decided to recommend to his superior, Intendant Brodart, that the most suitable vessel for the test was *St Gerassimus*. The sea trials would keep the Chevalier of St Stephen busy, and if they went disastrously wrong might even blow him to smithereens.

Chabrillan stalked out of the commissaire's office with the merest hint of a polite farewell, then made his way to where the receiving clerk was already waiting, his black coat hastily brushed in an attempt to smarten his appearance.

Chabrillan nodded at the clerk as he strode into the large gloomy hall where the chain prisoners were being held. 'Have the prisoners paraded in a line,' he ordered crisply. Slowly the newly arrived convicts shuffled into position, urged on by casual blows and curses from their goalers.

'Now have them strip.'

Awkwardly, for many of them were hampered by their fetters, the prisoners removed their tattered and lice-ridden clothing, and dropped the garments to the stone floor.

'Over against the opposite wall,' Chabrillan commanded. The prisoners, trying to conceal their nakedness with their hands, shuffled across the room and stood, shivering, to face their examiner. Chabrillan walked along the line, looking into their faces and glancing at their bodies. 'This one, and him, and this one,' he announced, selecting the strongest and fittest, until he had picked out a dozen men. 'Make a note of their names, have them dressed properly and sent to my ship,' he instructed the receiving clerk, 'and now let me see your ledgers.'

Meekly the clerk brought the Chevalier to his office, and showed him the list of names he had entered for the newly arrived chain. Chabrillan ran his eye down the columns, picking out those he had selected. He found he had chosen three army deserters, a poacher, a perjurer, and two sturdy beggars.

'What about these?' He pointed out the entries for five men against whose names the clerk had written, 'without saying why'.

'Just as it says, sir. They were unable to tell me why they had been sent to the galleys.'

Chabrillan fixed the clerk with a questioning stare. 'So why do you think they were condemned to the oar?'

The clerk shifted uneasily. 'It's hard to say, sir,' he answered after a short pause. 'My guess is that they are Protestants, those who call themselves the Reformed. They have made problems for those of the Apostolic and Roman faith.'

'Excellent. The Reformed make reliable oarsmen. They are serious and honest men compared to the usual felons and rogues who are condemned to the oar. I shall be glad to have them aboard,' and without another word, Adrien Chabrillan left.

©

'HECTOR, did you find out anything more about where your sister might be?' asked Dan as he wriggled his shoulders inside the red and black woollen prison jacket he had just received from the Arsenal stores. Clothes issued to prisoners came in just two sizes, small and large, and the Miskito's jacket was too tight on him. It was a warm afternoon in early summer and the two friends, together with Bourdon the pickpocket and a dozen Turks taken captive from the *Izzet Darya*, were being led along the Marseilles quay by an elderly warder whose relaxed manner indicated that he did not believe they would try to escape.

'I asked everyone I could for information about where the Barbary corsairs land and sell their captives, but I didn't learn anything more than I already knew. She could have been landed in any one of half a dozen ports,' Hector answered. He too was uncomfortable in his new clothes. In Algiers he had grown used to loose-fitting Moorish clothing and, working in the Arsenal, he and Dan had continued to wear the garments they had been wearing when captured. Now his legs felt constrained by the stiff canvas trousers issued by the Arsenal stores. The trousers fastened with buttons down the outer seams so that they could be put on over leg chains while his other new garments – two long shirts, two smocks in addition to a jacket, and a heavy hooded cloak of ox wool – could all be put on over his head. He had also been issued with a stout leather belt, which was there not just to hold up his trousers. It was fitted with a heavy metal hook over which he could loop his leg chain while he was at work so that leg irons did not hamper him. 'I wrote a letter to an old friend of my father's, a clergyman in Ireland who had been a prisoner of the Moors. I asked him if he had heard anything. But when I tried to send the letter, I was told that prisoners in the Arsenal were forbidden from communicating with the outside world. I had enclosed a note for my mother in case she is still living in Ireland, though I suspect she has moved back to Spain to live with her own people. Maybe she has heard directly from my sister. It's impossible to know. Life as a convict galerien in the Arsenal is as cut off from the outside world as being a slave in the Algiers bagnio.'

'Maybe that will change now that we're being transferred to a galley,' Dan tried to cheer up his friend.

'I doubt it. Look over there,' Hector nodded towards the far side of the docks. 'Aren't those the masts and spars of galleys? At least ten, I would say. All neatly lined up side by side.'

'Which one's ours?'

'Can't tell from this distance. But I heard that she's hired to the royal Galley Corps by her commander who's a Knight of one of the Orders. It's being said that he is a fire-eater and his premier comite is a cold-hearted tyrant.'

'Maybe someone aboard her can give you the information you're looking for,' Dan responded. As usual he was quick to point out the best possible outcome. 'Don't the Knights take their galley slaves and convicts from wherever they can get them?'

'That's true. I've not given up hope of tracing Elizabeth. The thought of finding her helps to keep me going. I sometimes wonder why you never get discouraged.'

Dan gave his companion a steady look. 'I have often thought about my homeland and the mission I was given by my people, but when that sour-faced man from London came to Algiers to ransom the English prisoners and he refused to help me, I realised the world is a much larger and more complicated place than the Miskito imagine. Now I'm resigned to the fact that I am unlikely ever to deliver the council's message to the King of England. Yet I feel that my travels may turn out to be for my people's benefit. Something tells me that I will surely get back home. When I do, I intend to bring something worthwhile with me.'

The prisoners had turned the corner of the harbour basin, and were approaching what looked like a busy pedlars' market. The wharf was covered with open-sided stands and booths which served as shops and stalls. As the convicts threaded their way between the booths, Hector saw men repairing shoes and doing metalwork, butchers and barbers, tailors, a man making hats, and stallholders selling every conceivable item from haberdashery to pots and pans. For some odd reason nearly every stall had dozens of pairs of knitted socks for sale, which hung up like strings of onions. Looking more closely, Hector realised that every one of the stall holders was a galerien.

'Same old junk,' Bourdon spoke up. 'I wouldn't be surprised

if some of those goods were on sale when I was last here.' The pickpocket was staring hard into the face of a man standing by a barrow on which lay a strange mixture of items – a pair of scissors, several fine handkerchiefs, some carved buttons, a snuff box, and various small articles which Hector could not immediately identify. 'Some of the vendors are no different either.'

Hector saw the stallholder's right eyelid flicker very slightly as he winked at Bourdon.

'Who is he?' he whispered to Bourdon.

'A thief like myself,' came back the quiet reply. 'I would say that he also fences stolen goods on the side, though it looks as if trade is a bit thin at the moment.'

'But how . . .' began Hector. They had paused while the Arsenal warder stopped to examine some lace on sale in one of the stalls.

'These baraques?' said Bourdon. 'They're run by the comites of the galleys. The port officials rent the stalls to the comites from the galleys, and the comites then put their galeriens into the booths to staff them. If the galerien has a useful skill, a carpenter or lacemaker for instance, he conducts his trade from the baraque, and the townsfolk come there for his services. Any money he earns is handed over to the comite. If he's lucky, the comite may let him keep a bit of it for himself. But if the galerien doesn't have a trade, then he has to learn to make himself useful in some other ways. That's why you see so many knitted socks. The comites hand out wool and knitting needles to their most useless galeriens, and they have to take up knitting. Naturally the comites claim that by keeping the galeriens busy in port they are less likely to make trouble. But of course the main reason is that the comites earn a nice living from their charges.'

He gave Hector a nudge. 'Look. Over there. That's someone who's either so clumsy or so stubborn that he cannot earn his comite any money, at least not yet.' Hector saw a man dressed in a galerien's parti-coloured uniform. He was wearing leg irons and cradling a cannonball in his arms. 'His premier comite will make him carry that cannonball around until he learns something that'll earn a bit of money,' Bourdon explained.

Their easy-going guard had finished at the lacemaker's stall and was strolling towards the far end of the quay. There he turned aside and pushed his way between two booths to bring his charges before what Hector thought for a fleeting moment was a fairground tent of blue and white striped canvas. It took a second glance to establish that the tent was a great canopy which covered the full length of a 26-bench war galley of the first class.

A halberdier stood on sentry duty at the foot of the gangplank. Dressed entirely in scarlet and white, from the red stocking cap on his head to his spotless red breeches with a contrasting white belt and coat lapels, he came smartly to attention, and bawled out at the top of his voice – 'Pass the word for the premier comite!' From somewhere inside the huge tent the call was repeated, and Hector heard the summons passing down the length of the galley. Then came a pause filled with the incessant background noise of the shoppers at the baraques, the mewling of the gulls, and the distant shouts of watermen. Finally, after a delay of about five minutes while Hector and the other prisoners waited patiently on the quay, a man appeared at the head of the gangplank and stood there, quietly surveying them. Dangling from a cord around his neck was a silver whistle which glinted in the sun.

Hector was taken by surprise. He had expected a rough brute of a man, violent and coarse. But the man who now stood looking them over had the appearance of a mild-mannered shopkeeper. He was of medium height and dressed in sober dark clothing. He would have passed unnoticed on the street except for his skin, which was uncommonly pale, and the fact that his close-cropped hair was a light sand colour. He did not wear a wig. 'That will be all, warder. You may leave the prisoners with me and return to your work,' the comite spoke quietly, barely raising his voice, yet every word carried clearly. His duty done, the elderly guard strolled off. But the comite made no move. He stayed at the head of the gangplank, gazing down on the prisoners, judging them. 'You are joining the galley *St Gerassimus*, and from now on you belong to her,' he announced. 'My name is Piecourt, and I am the premier comite, so you also belong to me. Serve the vessel well and you will become proud of her. Serve her badly, and you will regret the day you were born.' He spoke in French with an Italian accent. Then, to Hector's surprise, he repeated his warning, this time in fluent Turkish. Hector felt the odjaks around him stir uneasily. A moment later, Piecourt was repeating his caution a third time, using lingua franca. Aware of the impression he had made, the premier comite of the *St Gerassimus* reached for the silver whistle hanging around his neck and held it up for them to see. 'From now on the only language that matters to you is the language of this whistle, because this whistle is my voice. Everything you do will be controlled by it. You will soon be like dogs, the best-trained dogs. Obedient dogs are fed and cared for; disobedient dogs are whipped. Remember that.'

Without turning, Piecourt called back over his shoulder – 'Rowing master Yakup! New recruits for the oar. Introduce them to their benches.'

This time the creature who emerged from beneath the canvas awning was what Hector had anticipated, a broad-set, squat, dark-skinned man with a shaven head, enormously developed shoulder muscles, naked to the waist and wearing a pair of loose drawers. Also he sported a luxuriant mustache. Branded on his forehead was an eight-pointed cross. Hector deduced that *St Gerassimus*'s rowing master was a Christianised Turk, a renegade who had scarred on himself the symbol of the Knights.

'Get in line, tallest to the rear!' Yakup demanded, padding barefoot down the gangplank. Bourdon hesitated for a moment and opened his mouth to speak. Immediately the rowing master casually cuffed the pickpocket on the side of the head. The blow seemed lightweight, but the Frenchman gave a gasp and nearly fell. 'You heard what the comite said, no chattering.' Confused as to what they were meant to do, the prisoners milled around until they were in some sort of order. Hector, smaller than most of the prisoners, found himself near the head of the little column which followed the rowing master up the gangplank and on to the *St Gerassimus*.

His first impression was that the galley was identical to Turgut Reis's *Izzet Darya*, but then he realised that *St Gerassimus* was less ornate, more workmanlike. The blue and white canopy was held above head level on posts and under it three or four dozen of her crew were hard at work. Some were scrubbing and cleaning the woodwork, others were industriously splicing and mending ropes, and one squad had formed a human chain to empty one of the vessel's stores, handing up boxes and bales through a hatch and stacking them neatly amidships. Hector followed the rowing master almost halfway up the central gangway, heading towards the galley's bows, before he identified what was unusual. There were upwards of sixty men aboard, yet there was no sound of human voices. The men were working in total silence. Whenever one of them looked up from his chores to glance at the new arrivals, he took only the quickest glance before hurriedly looking back down again at his work. The quiet aboard *St Gerassimus* was eerie.

Yakup came level with the last half-dozen oar benches, halted, and turned to face the prisoners. As they advanced towards him in single file along the narrow gangway, the rowing master pointed to one side or the other, indicating to which bench each prisoner should go. Hector stepped down from the gangway to his bench and, looking back, saw that his new overseer was distributing the prisoners in balanced groups, so that each rowing bench had at a mix of large and small oarsmen, old and young. The last man assigned to each bench was an odjak. 'Tomorrow you begin to learn. Now you clean,' grunted the rowing master. He pulled up the plank which covered the gangway. Beneath was a cavity which served as a locker. From it Yakup extracted a long-handled deck brush and an iron scraper which he tossed to the prisoners. 'Clean!' Hector noticed the padded leather covering on the bench where he stood was stained. It appeared to be dried blood. The bulwark next to him was newly patched. Someone had made a temporary repair where, by the look of it, a cannonball or a hail of grapeshot had damaged the vessel.

'Pretend to be busy!' hissed Bourdon out of the side of his mouth. The pickpocket had been assigned to a place on the bench beside Hector. 'This is worse than I thought.'

'What do you mean?' whispered Hector, keeping his head down so that the rowing master could not see his lips move.

'This is a ship of fanatics,' answered Bourdon. 'No booze, no rest, plenty of lash.'

For the rest of the afternoon Hector and the other prisoners worked in silence, scrubbing and cleaning the area around the benches they had been assigned. When they finished, they replaced the brushes, scrapers and swabs into the locker under the gangway, and stowed their spare clothing in the same space. Yakup, who had been hovering on the gangway, suddenly jumped down among them. Bending down he picked up a length of heavy chain lying under the oar bench. One end of the chain was fastened to a beam, and now he threaded the loose end through the leg irons of each man, tethering them to their place. Finally he secured the end to a metal hoop with a heavy padlock. They were chained in place. Pointing to the central gangway he said '*Coursier!*' Next he slapped the padded seat of the oar bench with his hand and growled '*Banc, banc trois!*' Placing his foot on a removable board raised about a foot off the deck, he declared '*Banquette!*' Using this board as a step, he braced his other foot on a wooden bar attached to the oar bench in front, which he called the '*contre pedagne*'. He mimicked rising up with both hands extended as if holding an oar, then falling back with all his weight. 'Vogue! Tomorrow vogue!'

The sound of singing interrupted the demonstration. Hector turned to see a column of galeriens shuffling along the gangway. All of them wore leg irons, and the chains between their ankles were looped and held up on their large metal belt hooks. They were singing a hymn as they advanced, and they must have been the galley's regular oarsmen for they made their way straight to their allocated benches and sat down, five men to a bench. The leader of each group then leaned down and picked up the deck chain by their feet, passed it through their ankle fetters and meekly held up the loose end so that an argousin could come forward and attach a padlock. Only then did the galerians end their hymn, and wait silently.

A whistle sounded. At the far end of the galley, a figure appeared on the stern deck. It was Piecourt again. 'A galerien has uttered execrable blasphemies against the Virgin Mary and all the saints in Paradise,' he said. His soft voice contained a tone of menace which Hector found unsettling. Piecourt descended the short ladder down from the stern deck, and walked along the gangway until he was about a third of the way down the vessel. Turning towards the port side he ordered, 'Quarterol, strip. Vogue avant administer punishment. Black bastinado.' Hector watched as the fourth man along the nearest oar bench stood up and began to peel off his shirt. The man's hands were shaking. An argousin released the padlock on the bench chain so that the half-naked galerien could clamber up on the gangway. There he lay down, face to the deck. His arms and legs were seized and held firm by the oarsmen on the nearest benches so that he was stretched out, spreadeagle across the walkway. Slowly the largest oarsman from his bench climbed up and stood over his prostrate companion. Piecourt handed him a length of tarred rope. Then Piecourt stepped back and waited. The man hefted the rope in his hands. Hector could see that the rope flexed but did not curl. The dried tar, he concluded, must make it almost as stiff as a wooden stave. 'Strike!' ordered Piecourt. The oarsman took an upward swing with the rope and brought it down on the victim's back with all his strength. From where he sat Hector could see the red slash where the blow had cut the flesh. 'Strike again!' snapped Piecourt, expressionless. Only after twenty strokes and the victim appeared to have fainted, did the premier comite stop the punishment. 'Send for the barber surgeon. Vinegar and salt. Then put him in the cable locker till he heals.'

'Doesn't want the poor bastard to get gangrene and die,' muttered Bourdon. 'They never waste a trained oarsman.'

Hector had been feeling sick to his stomach. 'Does that happen often?' he enquired quietly.

'Depends on the premier comite,' Bourdon told him. 'Don't let it put you off your food. That should be next.'

Another whistle sounded, and this time it signalled the distribution of the evening meal. A small kitchen had been set up on the port side, where the eighteenth bench had been removed. There three galeriens were tending a large cauldron of soup. This broth was now ladled into small buckets and carried along the coursier by trusted galeriens, who slopped the broth into wooden bowls held up by the chained prisoners. Another trusty followed, handing out fist-sized loaves of bread. When the food arrived at Bench Three where Hector waited, he noticed that the big odjak seated nearest to the gangway received a larger portion. Beside him Bourdon whispered, 'Don't complain. The vogue avant always gets a larger helping than the others. It's to keep up his strength. You'll not begrudge it, I can promise you that. The vogue avant is the key man on the rowing team.' The pickpocket bit into his bread. 'At least the food's good aboard this ship. Something to be thankful for.'

Hector looked doubtfully into the wooden bowl he had been handed. It contained a small portion of oily bean soup. It smelled fermented. 'It can be worse than this?' he enquired. Bourdon nodded, his mouth full. 'Bastard contractors provide the Galley Corps with rotten provisions, and the comites serve short measure on the daily rations because they want their galeriens to spend any money they earn in buying extra stores and grog from the comite's shop. This meal is full measure and decent grub.'

Hector's guts churned at the smell of the soup, and he realised he needed to relieve himself. 'How do I get to a latrine?' he demanded.

'Over there,' Bourdon nodded towards the outer rail of the galley. 'Stick your arse over the side and let go.'

Miserably Hector crawled over his companions as each man on his oar bench shifted so that he could slide his leg chain along the central tether until he had enough slack to reach the edge of the galley. Life in the bagnios of Algiers had never been as vile and degrading as this, he thought, as he defecated over the side of the galley.

He was crawling back into his place in the middle of the bench, when there was another call on the whistle, followed by a subdued muttering among the galeriens. It must have been the signal that gave them permission to talk among themselves. Immediately Bourdon leaned forward, tapped the galerien in front of him on the shoulder, and asked where he came from. When the man replied 'Paris', the two of them began to speak together, keeping their voices low and talking so rapidly in city slang that Hector was barely able to follow their conversation though it was obvious that Bourdon was asking questions. Only when the pickpocket eventually sat back straight on the bench beside him was he able to enquire, 'What did you find out?'

Bourdon looked thoughtful. 'That man's a forcat, a convict. Says he ran away to sea as a youngster, got into various scrapes and finished up on a merchant ship sailing out of Lebanon. He signed on thinking that the owner of the vessel was a Christian Greek but when the ship was intercepted by a Maltese galley of the Order of St John and searched, it turned out that the real owner was a Turk and they were carrying cargo for an Egyptian Pasha. He was taken off the merchant ship, brought back to Malta as a prisoner and tried in the Order's court. The judges found him guilty as a traitor to his country and to his faith, and condemned him to the oar for life. They even put a slave price on him to reward the crew who had captured him. Apparently the owner of *St Gerassimus* bought him – paid for him right on the courtroom steps – and he's been on the galley for the past three years. He doesn't expect ever to get off it unless by death or illness.'

'So he's as badly off as we are,' commented Hector.

Bourdon still looked pensive. 'And that's what puzzles me. He says that nearly all the oarsmen on the *St Gerassimus* are renegades captured or bought from many different countries, plus a number of Turks. Hardly anyone is serving out a set number of years at the oar. They are all lifers, and the last of the volunteer oarsmen left the galley at Malta. He thinks that the galley's owner wants a permanent crew so that the *St Gerassimus* becomes the crack galley in the fleet. Our friend claims that the galley is already the best-managed and best-disciplined vessel in the Mediterranean. It seems odd, but he was almost proud of being aboard.'

The comite's whistle shrilled yet again, and the galèrien who had been talking with Bourdon called, 'Five-minute warning. Better get yourselves ready for the night. Take a leak and spread out your cloaks. The nights can be chilly. No more talking as soon as the lights are out.'

Looking down the galley, Hector saw some oarsmen were assembling small platforms perched on short poles about three feet high. Moments later they had erected little canopies over the platforms so that there were half a dozen smaller tents within the great awning. 'What are those for?' he asked. 'That's where the comites and the senior argousins sleep,' answered the galerien. 'Floating above our heads like in the clouds. Those oarsmen beneath their beds have the "reserved seats". They wait as servants on the comites, and eat scraps from their food.'

'What about us? Where do we sleep?' Hector wondered looking around.

'Just where you sit,' came the answer. 'Take it in turns to stretch out on the banc, or down on the deck. There won't be room for all five of you, so a couple of you will have to sleep kneeling, with your head on the bench.'

'There doesn't seem enough room.'

'It's luxury now,' the galerien assured him. 'Just wait until you have to share your bench with the handle of your oar.'

Belatedly Hector realised that he had not yet seen any oars on the *St Gerassimus*. He was wondering where they might be when the whistle blew again and a total silence fell on the galley.

℃

NEXT MORNING he discovered what had happened to the galley's sweeps. After a meagre breakfast of water and bread the crew of the galley were marched off the *St Gerassimus* and along the quay to where two small vessels were lying. They were galliots, half-sized galleys used by the Corps as training ships. Neatly laid out on their benches were long oars with scarlet and white blades and shafts. Hector recognised the livery of the *St Gerassimus*. 'Crew to divide,' bellowed the rowing master who had accompanied them. 'Benches one to twelve on the first galliot; benches thirteen to twenty-six in the second vessel.' Hector and his companions found their way to the forward benches and were shackled in place when Yakup, armed with a bullwhip, appeared on the gangway above them. 'You with the GAL on your cheek,' he said, pointing at Bourdon, 'show them what to do.' Bourdon gripped the wooden handgrip pegged to the side of the massive oar shaft which was thick as a man's thigh. He placed his right foot on the edge of the bench in front of him. 'Now take a stroke!' Bourdon struggled to push the loom of the sweep away from him, rose up as if climbing a stair, then fell back with all his weight, tugging on the handgrip. The huge oar did not stir. 'Again!' ordered the rowing master. He flicked the bullwhip's lash across Bourdon's shoulders. The pickpocket gritted his teeth and repeated his effort, still the oar did not budge. 'Now you!' barked the rowing master, pointing at Hector. Hector took hold of the adjacent handgrips and copied Bourdon's movements. Very slightly the oar handle moved. 'And you!' This time it was Dan who joined the effort, and ponderously the massive sweep began to shift. 'And you!' The fourth man on the oar bench added his weight, but it was only when the burly odjak, seated farthest inboard, helped the other oarsmen that the heavy sweep began to rise and fall in a ponderous movement. 'Enough!' barked the rowing master, turning his attention to the next bench of novice oarsmen. As soon as Yakup was out of earshot, Bourdon hissed, 'Once the galley starts moving, watch out for the oar handle behind us. It'll knock our brains out. Here we go!'

The rowing master had finished his instructions and now gave a signal to a comite standing on the poop deck. The comite brought a whistle to his lips and gave a single blast. Every one of the oarsmen swayed forward, still seated on his bench, arms extended, pushing the oar handles in a low arc ahead of them. The whistle sounded again, and the oarsmen stood up all together, raising their hands so that the blades of the oars dipped into the sea. A fourth blast, and the oarsmen flung themselves backward, dragging the blades through the water as they fell back on the leather-padded benches. Scarcely had they regained their seats than the whistle was signalling them to repeat the movement, and a drummer alongside the comite struck the first beat of a slow steady tempo as the galliot gathered way.

'Get the rhythm, get the rhythm,' grunted Bourdon beside Hector. 'It's not strength which matters, it's the rhythm.' He gave a gasp as the rowing master's whip slashed across his shoulders. 'No talking,' came the harsh command.

The training galley lumbered forward, heading towards the harbour mouth, and Hector could see the other galliot keeping pace. Then they had passed the guardian forts, and all at once were in choppy water. It became difficult to control the massive sweep as the galliot began to roll in the waves. Seawater splashed across Hector's feet making him aware of how low the vessel lay in the water. On the oar directly behind him the inexperienced crew lost their balance. He heard a yell. Something made him duck, and the heavy handle of the loose sweep passed over his head, its oarsmen having lost their grip. The next moment the blade had tangled with its neighbour, and the massive handle swung back through a short arc and he heard a crunch as it struck an oarsman on the chest, cracking his ribs.

A burst of swearing, and the rowing master was running down the coursier towards them, his face twisted in anger, as the galliot faltered. 'Row, you dogs! Row!' he shouted, hitting out with his whip while the unfortunates on the oar handle tried to get back on their feet and bring their sweep back into action. Their injured companion lay crumpled under the bench. In one swift movement the rowing master jumped from the gangway and kicked the injured man under the rowing bench like a bundle of rags where he would not impede his fellows. A moment later he was back up on the coursier shouting at the crew to increase the pace.

For the next three weeks, Hector, Dan and the other new recruits to *St Gerassimus* learned their trade at the oar. It was a cruel apprenticeship. They rowed until their backs and shoulders ached. Their hands blistered, and when the blisters burst, the skin peeled away leaving the flesh raw and bleeding. The soles of their naked feet were bruised by the constant pressure against the banquette and bench in front of them. Night after night they came back to the *St Gerassimus* to eat the same unpalatable ration of bean soup and bread, and then fell into an exhausted sleep, only to be roused at dawn by the comite's insistent whistle. However, as the days passed, their muscles strengthened and grew accustomed to the strain; thick calluses developed on their hands and the soles of their feet, and they achieved the knack of setting an even rhythm and obeying the steady pounding of the drum. Before long they could recognise each call on the comite's whistle, so that they stopped and started, increased or lowered the speed of their strokes, or reversed direction of their blades as fluently as if they were a single machine. And with the improvement in their skill, Hector found that he and his companions on bench three were developing a conceit. At first it was a matter of winning races against their colleagues in the other training galliot. Then, after the Arsenal dockyard workers had finished their repairs on *St Gerassimus* and the galley could put to sea, it became a demonstration of their superiority over the other galleys in the fleet.

They never saw their captain. In his absence Piecourt ran the galley, adjusting the performance of *St Gerassimus* with a care that reminded Hector of a harpist he had once seen tuning his instrument. Piecourt and the rowing master shifted oarsmen from one bench to another, varying their weights and strength until they had achieved the best performance. Hector, Dan and Bourdon were regulars on the third bench, with the big odjak Irgun as their vogue avant, but it took some time to find the best quinterol, the fifth oarsman who sat farthest outboard. Then, one day, Piecourt put beside them a man whose nose and ears had been crudely sliced away. When Hector quietly asked the newcomer his name, there was no reply only a snuffling sound through the cratered nostrils. When Hector repeated the question, the unhappy man turned his ravaged face towards him and opened his mouth. The tongue was missing, torn out. Even Bourdon, the hardened pickpocket, was shocked.

The mute leaned forward and with his fingernail slowly scratched some signs on the oar handle, then sat back.

Hector stared at the marks. They meant nothing to him at first, but then the memory came back to him of lessons with the monks in Ireland. They had taught him the rudiments of Greek, and the letters made by the mute were Greek. They spelled out 'Karp'.

'Your name is Karp?'

The mute nodded. Then cupping a hand on each side of his

head, he stared straight at Hector. 'You can hear, but you cannot speak?'

Again the nod, and Karp sketched out a cross in the Greek style, the four arms of equal length.

'You are a Christian? Then why are you here?'

Laboriously Karp tried to explain but Hector could only piece together occasional scraps of his story. Karp's homeland was somewhere to the east and ruled by the Turks, but how he came to be a slave on the *St Gerassimus* was not clear. Nor could Hector unravel the reason for Karp's mutilation. He could only presume that it was punishment for trying to escape or, perhaps like the Sicilian thief in the bagnio of Algiers, he was an inveterate criminal.

At dusk when the comite's whistle blew and Hector knelt down and placed his head on the rowing bench to begin his rest, he fell asleep listening to Karp's breath rushing in and out of the wreckage of his face.

©

CHEVALIER ADRIEN CHABRILLAN returned to his ship for the Festival of the Galleys. Piecourt had prepared for the great day with his usual meticulous attention. The great blue and white awning had been taken down and stowed, and the crew had washed and scrubbed the deck planking until it gleamed. The dockyard's painters and gilders had been busy, primping and beautifying the galley's carved decorations. The sailmakers had sewn and fitted new canopies and tilts for the poop deck, using roll after roll of velvet and brocade and given the added touch of gold fringes. The spars and rigging of *St Gerassimus* were hung with bright flags and banners, some showing the fleur-de-lis of France but many more with the cross of St Stephen. The halberdiers of the guard were in their best uniforms.

The Chevalier came aboard at noon with his guests, a cluster of well-born gentlemen, several wealthy merchants and their ladies, and all were dressed splendidly for the great occasion.

They paused to admire the wonderful spectacle of the fleet: galley after galley neatly moored, flags and pennants rippling in the light breeze, their gaily painted oars fixed at an upward angle so they seemed like the wings of birds. Then they sat down to a splendid meal at tables arranged on the poop deck and covered with white linen. All the while, there was no sight nor sound of a single oarsman aboard the galley. *St Gerassimus*'s benches stretched away empty, leather padding gleaming with polish, as the Chevalier's guests savoured their way through the seven courses of their repast. Only when they were toying with dessert – served with a sweet wine from Savoy – did Piecourt, who had been standing in the background, step forward and blow a single long blast on his whistle.

Hector, Dan and two hundred other galeriens had spent the past four hours crouched in the narrow space between the benches. Piecourt had promised thirty lashes of the black bastinado to any man who spoilt his surprise for the captain's guests. Hearing the whistle, Dan and his companions took a deep breath and, as one man, exclaimed 'Hau!' At the same time they stretched up their right arms, fingers extended, in the air. The Chevalier's guests startled by the sound which seemed to come from the belly of the vessel, looked up to see a forest of fingers appear above the benches. 'Hau!' repeated the hidden oarsmen as they extended their left arms, and the number of fingers suddenly doubled. 'Hau! Hau!' and they raised first one arm and then the other. 'Hau!' This time the galeriens lay down on the deck boards and waved their right legs above the benches, then their left. The guests looked on, amazed. Now the oarsmen sat up. All together, they suddenly raised their heads above the galley benches. Each man was wearing his red prison cap issued by the Arsenal, so that the effect was as if a field had suddenly sprouted a sea of red flowers. So it went on. More than two hundred oarsmen performed the routines that Piecourt had made them rehearse for days, standing up, sitting down, taking off their shirts, opening their mouths, coughing in unison, bowing to their audience, removing their caps, putting them on again, until finally they all stood, half naked and facing their audience. Then they gave the chamade, rattling their chains in a sustained clattering roar until Piecourt gave a final sharp blast on his whistle and every galerien abruptly stopped, dropped his arms to his side, and stood silently to attention, staring straight ahead.

The distinguished guests broke into spontaneous applause.

FIFTEEN

☾

A MILE FROM WHERE *St Gerassimus* floated on an indigo blue sea, the first slopes of the Barbary mountains rose behind the close-packed buildings of a small Moorish town where a river drained from a cleft in the mountains. In front of the town a dozen or so feluccas and caiques lay at anchor in the roadstead, their decks deserted. The foreshore too was empty except for the rowing boats abandoned by the sailors who had fled their vessels the moment that *St Gerassimus* had appeared over the horizon. The arrival of the galley had taken them by surprise. In the past the town's walls had proved stout enough to resist all but a prolonged attack, and the place was too insignificant to reward a major assault by any enemy. So the attention of a first-class war galley caused some puzzlement among the citizens though there was no great concern as they watched the new-comer hover quietly in front of the town, her oars occasionally moving as she maintained her station. The more observant of the townsfolk did, however, note something a little unusual about their visitor. The galley was not floating level. She was down by the bow.

On board *St Gerassimus*, premier comite Piecourt too was anxious — but for other reasons. The morning after the Festival of Galleys the Chevalier had summoned Piecourt and the sous comites to tell them that the galley was to put to sea within the week. During the banquet Commissaire Batiste had informed the Chevalier that the galley was to proceed to the Barbary coast, there to test the newest artillery weapon in the Corps Arsenal. The order came from Minister Colbert himself, and was to be obeyed with all despatch. Details of the armament were kept secret, and it was not until Piecourt saw the monstrous device floated out to his galley on a pontoon that he feared the result. The weapon was grotesque: a short, black cannon that reminded him of a gargantuan beer pot sitting on a heavy wooden sledge. What this monstrosity weighed he had no idea, but it had required a triple tackle to hoist the gun on to his galley's foredeck, the rambade. As the monster was lowered into position he distinctly felt the galley tilt forward. He had removed the ship's other guns, and shifted ballast further aft. He had also ordered the galley's main anchor, normally kept in the bows, to be stowed below deck nearer the stern. Yet even when this was done, *St Gerassimus* still felt unwieldy, and the squat black mass on her foredeck appeared to him like an ugly wart.

But worse was to come. On the morning *St Gerassimus* left Marseilles harbour, she hove to outside the pier head so that the Arsenal's gunpowder barge could come alongside to offload the test ammunition for the cannon — a hundred hollow cast iron globes filled with explosive and half as many kegs of a fine-grade gunpowder as propellant. The gunpowder was stowed in the galley's magazine but the bombs, as the technician who accompanied the shipment called the heavy spherical projectiles, had to be kept separate. Some were already primed and fused and coated in sticky tar. Apparently they were to be sprinkled with gunpowder immediately before they were inserted into the gun's gaping mouth. In theory the gun then shot the bomb high in the air, the tar-and-gunpowder coating ignited and, as the bomb blazed through the sky, the weapon lit its own fuse. When the device dropped into the target, it cleared any defences and smashed through any obstacle before exploding with massive damage. What happened if the fuse caught fire too soon and the bomb burst prematurely inside the cannon did not bear thinking about. *St Gerassimus*'s mission was to test the reliability of the weapon.

'Do you think the gun will work with the new bombs?' Hector had asked Dan as they sat in the warm sunshine, chained to their oar bench and waiting for orders as the galley drifted on the glassy calm.

'I don't know,' answered the Miskito. 'I heard about it when I was in the armoury in the Arsenal, but never saw it for myself. The gun was kept in the artillery park.'

'Yet the technician recognised you when he came aboard.'

'He visited the gunsmiths a couple of times while I was working with them, to ask if we could improve one of the new designs of fuse. It's a plunger which is screwed into the bomb casing. When the bomb lands on target, the plunger is meant to drive inwards, striking sparks from a flint and igniting the powder inside the bomb, just like a musket. He didn't know much about boats as far as I could tell. He's more a technical man.'

'You would have thought they would have picked someone with better sea legs. He was seasick all the way here from Marseilles,' said Hector. He looked over his shoulder for at least the twentieth time, to gaze at the coast of Africa.

'Apparently a galley makes an ideal platform for his mortar – that's his name for the launching gun – because the weapon is so heavy and awkward to move about on land,' Dan continued. 'But a ship can take the gun wherever it is wanted, and a galley can aim the mortar accurately by manoeuvring so that the gun is exactly at the right range and angle to throw its bombs on target—'

His explanation was cut short by Piecourt's voice. 'You there! Get up on the rambade! The gunner wants you.' The premier comite was on the coursier, pointing at Dan. 'Secure your oar, and take your companions with you.' He bent down to unlock the padlock to the bench chain and allow the men to slip clear, but when Karp and the vogue avant Irgun made as if to move, Piecourt raised his whip threateningly. 'Stay where you are!' he ordered.

Dan led Hector and Bourdon on to the wooden platform of the rambade. The technician was fussing over the mortar. It sat on its massive sled, pegged and chained to the deck. Nearby a large tray held several bombs, a tub of fuse cord, and a number of fuses to be tested. At a safe distance, lashed against the rail, were some small kegs of gunpowder.

'The first job is to check the bombs and their contents,' said the technician, a small worried-looking man with badly bitten fingernails. It seemed he was also to act as gunner. 'Any of you know about gunpowder?'

Bourdon gave a sardonic laugh. 'Only how to make this mark,' he said, pointing at the letters GAL branded on his cheek. 'That's how they make the brand permanent. They rub in gunpowder as soon as the hot iron is lifted.'

'I've worked in a quarry,' Hector interjected. 'I'll show him.'

'Good. The gunpowder must be kept separate at all times. Even empty barrels can contain fine particles which may explode,' warned the gunner, then turned towards Dan. 'I need you to make sure that the correct charge is loaded into the mortar's chamber, and that the firing fuse is properly inserted in the bomb, and in working order. You'll find all the tools you need in that canvas bag over there.'

As Dan prepared the mortar, Hector and Bourdon checked over the bombs. They removed each bomb's wooden plug, mixed and poured in more gunpowder through a funnel, made sure the powder settled evenly in the hollow sphere, and finally tamped home the plug again. It reminded Hector of the days when he was setting blasting powder into the rocks of the Algiers quarry. Careful to observe the gunner's safety instructions they returned the empty barrels to their place against the rail. The sailors and the galley's gun crew normally stationed on the rambade had made themselves scarce. Even Piecourt was standing far enough away to avoid the worst effects of an accident.

'I'm ready to try a ranging shot,' called out the technician. 'Line up the vessel, if you please. The bow must point straight at the target.'

Piecourt squinted ahead at the town, then blew a series of calls on his whistle. Obediently the oarsmen dipped their blades into the sea, the starboard side pulling ahead, while their companions backed water. The galley slowly swivelled. A sharp blast on the whistle and the oarsmen maintained the galley in position. Glancing astern, Hector saw that the officers of *St Gerassimus* had all gathered on the poop deck. They were too distant for him to recognise individuals and he wondered which was the captain, the celebrated Chevalier who was said to be such an implacable adversary of the Muslims. Even when Chabrillan had hosted his celebration of the Festival of Galleys, the galeriens had been forbidden to look directly at the Chevalier and his guests. To do so, the oarsmen had been warned, would be treated as insolence and punished with the lash.

His thoughts were interrupted by a deep coughing thud, a large cloud of dense black smoke, and the galley shuddering along her entire length. Beneath his feet Hector felt the bow of the galley suddenly dip into the sea as the massive recoil of the mortar thrust downward. A ripple spread out from her hull as if a giant rock had been dropped into the water.

The bomb could be seen high in the air, a black spot trailing smoke and flame as it raced upwards, hurtling towards the shore. Then it arched over and dropped back towards earth, only to splash harmlessly into the shallows, a hundred yards short of the town wall. There was no explosion.

'Bring the vessel in closer, please,' asked the gunner.

Again Piecourt's whistle blew. The galeriens took a dozen strokes, then paused. The galley glided nearer to the thin line of surf.

Another bomb was loaded, and this time when it was fired, the projectile landed halfway up the beach and there was a muffled explosion.

'Closer yet, please,' asked the gunner. 'Bring the galley nearer to the target area.'

'There may be shallows here,' Piecourt warned. 'I'll not risk the ship. If we come much closer, it may bring us in range of the town's own cannon. They could have a few great guns, and be holding fire, so as not to waste powder. Just one shot could do us a lot of damage.'

'I cannot increase the angle of the mortar,' complained the artilleryman. 'It's already set at forty-five degrees for maximum range. I can only add to the propelling charge, and that might burst the barrel.' He gave Dan a worried look. 'Get your friend from the quarry to help you measure accurately. We don't want any mistakes.'

All through the afternoon Dan, Hector and Bourdon worked on the rambade. They checked and primed the bombs, loaded them into the gun's maw, cleaned out the mortar's chamber after each shot and cleared the touch hole, helped the artilleryman to recharge the mortar and set the fuse, then to fire the weapon once the oarsmen had placed the galley in position. Bomb after bomb was sent towards the town, sometimes dropping short, occasionally veering off course and falling wide. One detonated in mid-air with a premature explosion that sent fragments of the metal casing pattering into the sea, an accident that drew a frightened intake of breath from the artilleryman. With practice, they learned just how much powder was needed to propel the bombs to reach their target, and just how much coating of powder was needed so that the missiles exploded on impact. The plunger fuses were soon abandoned for they usually failed to work. By the time the sun was setting, every bomb they fired was landing on target, and they could see the dust spurt up when they hit.

But there was no apparent effect on the town. The place

remained silent and still. No one emerged from the gates, nor was anyone seen on the battlements. No one fled into the hills. No fires broke out. It was as if the place was abandoned and uninhabited. Only a thickening of the dust haze above the buildings hinted at the destruction that must have taken place. By the time the light faded nearly all the bombs in the ammunition store had been fired away, and there was a tone of disappointment in the gunner's voice as he called a halt to his bombardment.

Piecourt ordered the oarsmen to row a safer distance offshore and there the *St Gerassimus* dropped anchor.

Black with powder smoke and half deaf, Hector and his two companions returned to their oar bench and were shackled in place. 'We did more damage to the galley than the town, I think,' said Hector quietly.

'What do you mean?' asked Dan.

'The rambade shuddered badly every time the mortar fired. It was worse after we increased the charge in the mortar's chamber. The deck planks started to lift. By evening the beams under them also were loose. When Bourdon and I went aft to fetch more powder from the magazine, the water in the bilge was rising faster than usual. I'm surprised that no one else noticed.'

'Perhaps they did and they kept their mouths shut. The officers were all too far away, and the rest of the petty officers are too frightened of Piecourt to interfere. He seemed to enjoy bombarding the town. He's someone who relishes other people's discomfort even if it's only at a distance. I doubt that the townsfolk enjoyed their day.'

'I wouldn't be surprised if the galley was being shaken to pieces,' said Hector. 'I've seen a galley built and know how fragile the joints are. Once the main fastenings give way, there's little to stop the vessel falling apart.'

'What would you say are our chances of surviving in that town,' muttered Bourdon. He was shaking his head from side to side, still trying to clear his hearing, and staring towards the distant land.

'I expect they would hang us from the walls after the damage we've been inflicting.'

'Not if they knew we had been forced to our work.'

'And how would you get there?'

'I'd go for a swim right now if it wasn't so far,' said Bourdon with a wink and shook his sleeve. One of the gunner's work tools dropped into his hand. It was the thin spike used for cleaning out the touch hole of the mortar. 'Never seen a better picklock. I lifted it from his tool bag when he was packing up, and he'll not miss it until the morning. I could have us loose in no time at all.' He folded his fingers over the implement, and when he opened his hand again, the tool had disappeared as if by magic. 'Told you I was a good pickpocket,' he said, a confident grin on his branded face.

Piecourt's whistle blew the signal for the galeriens to take their rest, but Hector found it difficult to go to sleep. He lay there, thinking whether it would be madness to take up Bourdon's suggestion of an escape and – as always – whether he would ever be able to track down Elizabeth. He shifted uncomfortably on the wooden deck and looked up at the sky and noted that the stars had vanished. The heavens had clouded over. From time to time he heard the tread of Piecourt or one of the sous comites walking the coursier as they carried out their night patrol, and he heard the call of the sailor on watch on the rambade, reporting all was well. As the hours passed, Hector became aware of a gradual change in the motion of the anchored galley as she tugged at her cable. *St Gerassimus* was beginning to pitch and roll. The noise of the waves increased. Pressing his ear against the deck planking Hector was sure that the sound of the bilge water swirling back and forth was louder. He sensed a general discomfort spreading among the galeriens as they slept or dozed all around him. Little by little he became aware of men waking up, and he heard the sound of retching as those with weak stomachs began to succumb to seasickness. He sat up and listened. The voice of the wind was definitely louder. A large swell passed under the galley and made her lurch. He heard raised voices. They came from the foredeck, and almost immediately there was the sound of Piecourt's whistle. It was the order to man the sweeps. He struggled to his feet and sat down on the bench, his ankle chain tugging painfully. Fumbling in the darkness, he joined his companions in freeing the handle of the great sweep from its lashings, and sat ready to take a stroke. It would not be easy. Now *St Gerassimus* was rolling heavily in the waves, and with each minute the motion of the galley was growing wilder. Piecourt's whistle sounded again. Hector and the other oarsmen took a long steady stroke, then another, and tried to set a rhythm. There were shouts from the foredeck, and he heard the command for the rambade crew to hoist anchor. In reply there were yells and curses, and a surge of water passed across his naked feet. He detected a note of alarm, even panic.

The galley was definitely in some sort of trouble. Hector tried to make sense of the sailors' shouts. Farther aft a sous comite was shouting. He was ordering three benches of galeriens to set aside their oars and man the pumps. The anchor must have been raised, for he felt the galley slew sideways, and there was a sudden tremor as she fell aslant the waves. Hector and his bench mates nearly lost their footing as the galley canted over so far that they were unable to reach the water with their blades, but rowed in the air. A moment later the galley had tilted in the opposite direction, and their blades were buried so deep it was impossible to work them. The chaos increased. In the darkness men missed their strokes, slipped and fell. Piecourt's insistent whistle cut through the darkness, again and again, but it was useless. Rowing was impossible.

The wind strengthened further. It was keening in the rigging, a thin, nagging screech. *St Gerassimus* rolled helplessly. Someone shouted out an order to hoist sail, but was immediately countermanded by another voice which said that this was too dangerous, that the main spar would tear the mast out of its step. Sailors ran aimlessly up and down the coursier, until a petty officer roared angrily at them.

Gradually the sky grew lighter, bringing a cold, grey dawn and a vista of angry waves racing down from the north. The galley was in real distress. Designed for calm waters, she was unable to hold up against the force of the sea. She was drifting helplessly, no longer controlled by her crew. Hector looked downwind. The galley was perhaps two miles away from land, though he did not recognise the coast. The gale must have driven her sideways during darkness. He saw a bleak expanse of bare mountain, a narrow beach, and the sea thrashing into foam on a coral shelf that reached out from the shore towards them.

'Let go the bow anchor again!' bellowed Piecourt. 'And bring the main anchor up on deck and made ready. Fetch up the main cable!'

A seaman on the rambade leaned out over the sea, knife in hand, and cut free the lashings which held the smaller bow anchor in place so that it plunged into the sea. Half a dozen of his mates ran back along the coursier and opened the hatch leading to the aft hold where the main anchor had been stowed. Two more men squeezed down into the cable locker in the bows where the galley's main hawser was kept only to reappear a moment later, wild-eyed with fear. 'She's sprung her bow planks,' their leader shouted. 'She's taking water fast!' Hardly had the words been uttered than the men who had gone aft also re-emerged on deck. 'There's four feet of water in the bilge,' someone cried. 'We'll never be able to get the main anchor up.'

Piecourt reacted coolly. 'Get back down in the cable locker,' he snapped. 'Find that main cable and bring it up.' The frightened sailors obeyed, and returned, dragging the end of the six-inch main hawser. 'Now fasten it to that bitch of a mortar, and fasten it well,' the comite told them, 'and bring levers and a sledgehammer.' His men did as they were ordered, and soon the mortar was trussed up in a nest of rope. 'Now break the gun free! Smash the bolts and planks if need be,' urged Piecourt, 'then dump the cannon overboard!' Working in grim silence the men attacked the fastenings that held the mortar in place. It took them nearly twenty minutes to loosen the gun so that they could take advantage of a sudden tilting of the deck and slide the monstrous cannon and its carriage overboard. It disappeared into the sea with a hollow, plunging sound that could be heard even over the roar of the gale. The hawser ran out, then slowed as the mortar struck the sea bed. The sailors secured the hawser, and the galley felt the drag of the monstrous cannon so she slowly turned her bow towards the waves and hung there, no longer drifting helplessly down on to the coast.

Hector had to admire Piecourt's composure. The premier comite eased himself into the cable locker to see the extent of the leak for himself, then calmly made his way along the coursier to the poop deck where Hector saw him confer with the ship's officers. Next, Piecourt beckoned to the foredeck crew who also went aft and began to unship the galley's rowing boats from their cradles above the oar benches. The galley heaved and wallowed but eventually the two boats were hoisted out and lowered into the water where they rose and fell, bumping wildly against the galley's side. It was when the sailors and several of the warders, the argousins, climbed into the boats, and were joined by the artillery man and the officers from the poop deck, that Hector realised they were abandoning ship.

The other galeriens realised it too. A low moan arose from the oar benches interspersed with angry shouts. Piecourt spoke quietly to the remaining warders who loaded their muskets and stood to face the oar benches. The two boats, filled with men, pushed off and began to pull for the shore. Their course was downwind, and within minutes the men were scrambling out of the boats and splashing up on land while the oarsmen turned and began to row back out to the galley. Their return trip was slower, and by the time they reached the *St Gerassimus*, the water which had been around Hector's ankles was now up to his knees. Whatever injury the galley had suffered, she was sinking fast

The boats made two more trips to the beach and soon there was no one left on the poop deck except Piecourt, the rowing master and half a dozen armed argousins. Just before midmorning the galley was awash, the sea lapping the tops of the oar benches, and the galeriens were frantic. They swore and pleaded, raged and wept, tugged at their chains. Piecourt gazed at them pale-eyed and utterly implacable. 'May you rot in hell,' one of the oarsmen shouted. 'No,' called the premier comite. It was the first word he had spoken directly to the benches. 'It is you, you infidels and heretics, who will suffer torments. I shall not even think of you.' He lifted from his belt the ring of the heavy keys for the padlocks on the oar benches, held it up for all to see, and deliberately tossed it into the waves. Then he turned, stepped into the boat and gestured at his men to row for shore.

Spray from a wave crest wetted the back of Hector's neck. In front of him was a piteous sight – the heads and naked torsos of two hundred galeriens glistening above the waves as they stood on their benches and tried to escape the rising water. Flotsam, odd lengths of timber, a galerien's cloak half filled with air so it floated, all drifted past him. Beside him, Bourdon blurted, 'I dared not move while those swine argousins were watching. I'd have been shot. Let me have some slack on that chain so I can try to get at the padlock.' Irgun, the big Turk, reached sideways, seized the padlock where it was attached to the coursier and held it steady. The galley was so low in the water now that every wave submerged the padlock, and sea water gushed out of the keyhole as it reappeared. Bourdon lay prone across his companions and began to feel inside the padlock with the tip of the spike. He choked as a wave crest filled his mouth, then closed his eyes as if asleep as he concentrated on feeling for the levers within the lock. Twice the spike slipped out, and once the point stabbed into Irgun's fist. The big Turk did not flinch. Finally Bourdon withdrew the tool, bent the thin tip at a right angle, then plunged it deeper and gave it a twist. The padlock popped open.

'Well done!' blurted Hector, the pressure on his ankle chain suddenly relieved. He took a deep breath and bent forward, head underwater. He groped for the heavy bench chain, pulling it clear of his leg irons. To his right he felt Karp do the same. Coughing and spluttering all five men scrambled up on to the coursier whose top was already being lapped by the waves. 'Help us!' screamed an oarsman from a neighbouring bench. Bourdon turned and handed him the spike. 'You'll have to help yourself,' he shouted back. 'There's too little time.'

Hector looked around him. Amidships the galley was entirely underwater. Only the poop deck and the rambade were above the waves. The rambade was only a few paces away. Hitching up his leg chain to his belt hook, he shuffled on to it.

'What do we do now?' asked Bourdon, looking at the distant shore. 'It's too far to swim. Our leg irons will drag us down. They'll be the death of us.'

'Not if you do as I show you.' It was Dan who spoke. He crossed to where the empty gunpowder kegs were still lashed in place. Selecting a barrel, he unbuckled his heavy galerien belt, wrapped it around the keg, and cinched it tight. 'Hold the barrel in your arms, sideways like this, and jump overboard. When you're in the water, make sure you get the centre link of your leg chain on to the belt's hook. Then push down with both feet. It'll be like riding in stirrups. The barrel should take your weight. Don't try to swim, just concentrate on staying upright, clutching the barrel, and the wind and waves will carry you ashore.'

With that, he jumped into the sea, holding the barrel against his chest.

Hector watched his friend come back to the surface, the keg in his arms dipping this way and that, spinning and turning in the water so that one moment Dan was on the surface, the next he was beneath the sea. But soon Dan had found his balance and could be seen leaning forward across the keg, with his face far enough out of the water so that he could breathe. The barrel gyrated slowly as it drifted towards the shore. 'Come on. Hurry!' he shouted back at his companions, and one after another they leaped into the sea.

☾

IRGUN DID NOT reach the shore. Perhaps he was too heavy to be supported by an empty keg or it filled with water and sank, or he failed to secure his leg chain on the belt hook. But Hector, Bourdon and Karp drifted into the shallows where Dan was waiting to assist them on to land. 'What made you think of that?' asked Hector. He was shaking with exhaustion as he sat down on the beach to rest. 'Our canoes at home,' said the Miskito. 'I told you how we turn them the right way up after they capsize. But it's not always possible. So if the wind and waves are right, a sensible fisherman just hangs on and waits until he is blown ashore. That's if the sharks don't take him.'

'I've never seen a shark. If there are any in this region, they'll soon be feasting on those poor wretches,' said Hector. He was looking back towards the galley. All that was now visible of the *St Gerassimus* was a section of the outrigger which had once supported her great sweeps and the blades of several oars pointing to the sky like enormous spines. The galley must have capsized while he and the others were coming ashore. That way, he thought to himself, the galeriens chained on board would have drowned more quickly than if the vessel had settled on an even keel. He had scarcely known any of them, yet a sense of great weariness and gloom oppressed him.

A touch on his arm abruptly brought him back to his surroundings. Karp was pointing up the beach and making an alarmed snuffling sound. A man was walking towards them. For a moment Hector thought he might be another survivor from the wreck, because he was wearing what looked like a galerien's long hooded cloak. But the stranger's garment was loose and grey, not brown. Then he saw other men, similarly dressed, cautiously making their way down the rocky hillside behind the beach.

'Greetings,' Hector called out, getting to his feet and forcing a weary smile. He spoke first in lingua franca, then in Turkish, but received no answer.

The group of strangers, about a dozen men, came closer, and stopped a few yards away. They were Moorish-looking but with paler skins. Most kept up the hoods of their cloaks, but those who did not, had shaven heads except for a long lock of hair which hung down the back of their scalps. They wore thin fillets of leather across their foreheads. Only a few carried old-fashioned muskets. They stared at Hector and his companions.

'Greetings,' he tried again. 'Can you help us, please?'

One of the strangers said something to his companions in a language Hector did not understand.

Then, to Hector's surprise, Dan intervened. He spoke slowly and haltingly, choosing his words carefully. The man who seemed to be the leader of the group replied and the two of them exchanged a few sentences.

'Who are they?' Hector asked his friend. 'And what is that language you are speaking?'

'They call themselves amazigh, "the free people",' Dan replied. 'Several of the gardeners who worked with me in the gardens of Algiers spoke the same language, or something very similar. I can't understand everything they say, but they are from a village in the hills. Apparently they saw the galley in difficulties and came down to the beach to investigate if there was anything to salvage. They were frightened of the armed men who came ashore earlier in the boats so they kept out of sight.'

'That must have been Piecourt with the ship's officers and the other sailors.'

'Apparently they went off along the beach, and turned

inland. The amazigh said that they won't get far. Their clan chief lives in that direction and they'll fall into his hands.'

'So what about us?'

'They've recognised that we are slaves from the galley, and I've told them that you and I are Muslims. If they're like my workmates at the masseries, they're also followers of the Prophet.'

'What about Bourdon and Karp?'

'I didn't say anything about them. The amazigh seem friendly enough. They're taking us to their village. Once we're there, they'll get the village blacksmith to remove our leg irons.'

The climb through the foothills was almost more than the four castaways could manage. The land rose steeply, one rocky slope succeeding another, the narrow footpath twisting and turning its way along dried-up watercourses and then up screes of fallen rock. Occasionally they passed clumps of pine trees, and beside the track Hector noted plants he remembered from his days in Algiers – wild lavender, purple thyme and white rock roses. Eventually, when the sea was far below them, their guides led them into a small settlement made up of single-storey houses, their walls of unmortared stones. In the centre of the village a mountain spring had been diverted through wooden pipes to splash into a stone trough placed in the shade of a venerable cedar tree. Here the village blacksmith knocked out the rivets that closed the ankle rings on the visitors' legs, demanding no payment except that he keep the metal for himself, and the village headman asked Dan to go with him the following day to meet with the clan's council of elders. They would decide what was to be done with the castaways. In the meantime they were his guests.

Dan and the headman left long before daybreak, and Hector and Karp waited all morning for his return, seated in the village square and watching Bourdon entertain the village children with sleight of hand, making pigeon eggs and other small objects appear and disappear. Trying to remember what he had learned from Turgut Reis's maps and charts, Hector broke off a twig and was drawing in the dust so that he could work out where *St Gerassimus* had sunk. He had made a rough outline of the Mediterranean when, unexpectedly, Karp took the twig from his hand and scratched a mark to the north of Constantinople, then pointed to his chest

'Is that where you come from, Karp?' Hector asked. His companion nodded, then clumsily drew some letters in the dust. Hector managed to puzzle them out.

'You are a Bulgar?' he asked. Again Karp nodded, and held out his hands, the wrists close together. 'You were taken prisoner?' Again the nod. 'Where was that?' Karp looked down at the map in the dust and, hesitantly, placed his finger at its eastern end. 'In the Holy Land?' This time Karp shook his head, and drew some more letters in the dust. They read 'Kan—'. Hector stopped him. 'You were taken prisoner at Kandia?'

Turgut Reis had told him all about the siege and fall of Kandia. It was a famous victory for the Turks. As a galley commander Turgut had witnessed the final capitulation of the city to the forces of the Sultan. It had taken the Turks fourteen years of siege to bring Kandia to its knees, and they had allowed the defenders, Venetians and their allies, to leave after handing over the keys of the city.

'But the Christians were given free passage out of the city, were they not?' Hector commented. In response, Karp opened his mouth, pointed to the mangled root of his missing tongue, and made an angry gurgling noise as he shook his head.

'The Turks tore out your tongue?' Now Karp was really agitated. He shook his head furiously from side to side. 'If it was not the Turks, then who did that you?' asked Hector gently. He hoped to calm the Bulgar. To his astonishment, Karp got to his feet, drew a cross in the dust, and deliberately stamped down on it.

The sound of distant musket shots prevented further questions.

There was a flurry of consternation in the village. The women and children rushed inside their houses to hide. The menfolk grabbed up their guns and ran to take up position to cover the approaches to the village. But when the volley of musket shots was repeated, it must have been some sort of announcement because the men relaxed and began to gather in the square, looking expectantly towards the path that led up from the coast. After a little while Hector was relieved to see Dan appear. He was accompanied by the headman and a distinguished-looking elder whom Hector guessed must be the clan chief. But what caught Hector's attention was the armed escort following on their heels – a dozen fierce-looking Negroes carrying spears and muskets. With them was a white man dressed in a long gown of red satin decorated with lines of pink silk ribbons tied in bows. His rapier hung from a wide baldrick of red brocade, and he was wearing a wide-brimmed hat embellished with a white ostrich plume.

This flamboyant apparition strode towards Hector and his companions and announced formally, 'In the name of the Emperor, I summon you to attend on His Majesty, Moulay Ismail.' To Hector's stupefaction this command was delivered in Spanish.

℃

'HIS NAME IS Luis Diaz and he's an officer in the army of the Sultan of Morocco,' explained Dan some time later when the two friends had a chance to talk together privately. 'The amazigh are tributaries of the Sultan, and Diaz and the soldiers were on a tax-collecting mission among them when he heard about the wreck of the galley. He wanted to interview the survivors about the bombs dropped on the town. He showed up while the amazigh council of elders were still discussing what to do with the other survivors from the *St Gerassimus* whom they had picked up.'

'News travels fast,' observed Hector.

'The mortar bombardment was a sensation. Everyone's talking about a wonder weapon.'

'And did Diaz learn anything?'

'Piecourt is in charge of the survivors, and is claiming to know nothing about the mortar. He said that the *St Gerassimus*'s commander and all the ship's senior officers had taken the two small boats in order to go along the coast and try to reach a friendly port to fetch help, and the bomb technician had gone with him. There was not enough room in the boats to carry all the survivors so the premier comite had been left in charge of the land party.'

'I wonder where the boats were heading.'

'Piecourt didn't say. He and the rowing master were there with a dozen sailors and several petty officers, some of whom I didn't recognise. They weren't at all pleased to see Diaz. They had already asked me if I could persuade the amazigh to send word to Algiers, to the Jewish ransom brokers there, about their plight. Piecourt even offered me a reward if I could arrange this.'

'Well, all that's changed now. I have the impression that the amazigh will do whatever the Sultan or Emperor, however he styles himself, wants.'

'No doubt about it. They made no objection when Diaz told them that he was taking charge of survivors from the galley. He said they were his prisoners from now on, and he would be sending them to the imperial capital at Meknes to be questioned.'

'And does that include us?'

'I expect we will be better treated. The amazigh informed Diaz that we had been slaves aboard the galley. Apparently convicted criminals and runaway slaves from other countries are given their freedom once they reach the Emperor's territory, provided they can make themselves useful.' Dan hesitated. 'Hector, there's something else you should know, though you may not like what you hear.'

'What's that?' asked Hector.

'The Emperor accepts tax from the amazigh not just in cash but in kind. If the amazigh cannot pay in cash or goods, they sometimes offer their young women for the Sultan's harem. They pick out the girls with the palest complexions. The Sultan has a special liking for women with fair skins. He also buys them from the corsairs. In Meknes you may be able to trace what has happened to your sister.'

SIXTEEN

'I PICKED UP the hat and gown from the rubble of one of the forts outside Tangier, though the feather was sadly mangled,' said Luis Diaz, preening himself in his colourful costume. 'One of the English officers must have dropped them when the garrison ran back inside the main defences after blowing up the fort. I was with the Emperor's siege army at the time. Moulay is determined to capture Tangier from the King of England and add it to his dominions.'

'This Emperor Moulay, what's he like?' asked Hector. In the two weeks he had been in the Spaniard's company, Luis had proved to be an amiable escort, friendly and always ready to talk as they travelled into the interior on their way to Meknes, the imperial capital. Until now Hector had tactfully avoided asking how the Spaniard came to be serving a foreign emperor in Barbary.

'Moulay Ismail is shrewd and utterly ruthless,' answered Diaz frankly. 'He's the most unpredictable and dangerous man you would ever wish to meet, a despot who treats everyone as his personal slave. Oh yes, and he loves animals.' He gave Hector a mischievous glance. 'It's just that some of his animals expect to be fed. Last time I was in the palace, Moulay was watching the senior comptroller of his treasury trying to avoid several hungry lions. Moulay suspected the comptroller of false accounting so he had the man lowered into the lion pit in the palace menagerie. The Emperor was sitting up on the edge of the lion pit, looking down as the animals stalked their prey, and he was enjoying every minute of the show. The wretched financier ran around for a good ten minutes, whimpering and pleading for his life, before the lions finally pounced.'

'Was the man genuinely guilty?'

Diaz shrugged. 'Who knows. The Emperor didn't care, and he had other things to think about. The lions were still excited. One of them leaped up and tried to pull the Emperor off the wall. If Moulay hadn't been wearing a mail shirt as he always does, he would have been dragged down into the pit as well. But the lion's claws didn't get a grip.'

'Why on earth do you serve a man like that?'

The Spaniard grimaced. 'I've not much choice. An unfortunate matter of a death at Ceuta where I was serving as a soldier. Someone was killed in a brawl over a woman. I thought it best to leave the city and offer my services elsewhere. Besides, I'm in good company. Men from almost every nation serve Moulay – two of his doctors are French; his field artillery is operated by Hollanders and Italians; there's a clever gardener from England who does the royal parks, and so many Spanish are enlisted in his cavalry or as musketeers that we have formed a mess of our own. You'll meet some of them when we reach Meknes which should be tomorrow, or perhaps the next day, if this cursed mud and rain doesn't slow us down too much.'

Hector and his companions were riding mules commandeered from the amazigh, while Ruis was mounted on a handsome cavalry horse of a breed native to the region. Somewhere far behind them Piecourt and the group of captives from the galley were on foot, herded along by the black soldiers. Hector did not feel sorry for the premier comite and his people though it had been cold and wet for most of the journey.

Luis Diaz swerved his horse to avoid a particularly treacherous-looking puddle. 'When we get to Meknes, I'll bring you to see the Emperor. He'll reward me if I've done the right thing in fetching you to his presence. But if you anger him and he gets irritated, I'll suffer. So listen carefully to what I have to say. First of all, take note of what Moulay is wearing. If he is wearing green, that's all right because that's his holy colour and Moulay prides himself on being a direct descendant of the Prophet and a good Mussulman. He always has a copy of the Qur'an carried in front of him, prays five times a day, observes the month of fasting, all that sort of thing. So if his clothes are green, he's likely to be in a good mood.'

The Spaniard adjusted his plumed hat to a more rakish angle before continuing.

'But if Moulay is wearing yellow, be very, very careful in what you say. That's his killing colour. On the days he dresses in yellow, he tends to have people executed or mutilated. Of course I'll try to avoid your meeting him on a yellow day, but it may be too late by the time we get an appointment. But whatever colour he is wearing, you must always treat him with the greatest deference. Fall down on your face before him, answer his questions honestly and clearly, and above all, don't go so near to him that you touch him. The last time that happened, the unfortunate man had his arm instantly sliced off with a scimitar by one of the Black Guards. And watch out for changes in the emperor's complexion. Though his skin is tawny, you can tell his mood by the reddish tinge that spreads right across his face when he is getting angry. If that happens, stand clear. Something terrible is going to happen.'

Hector decided this was the moment to ask the question that had been troubling him ever since Dan had told him about the Emperor's harem. 'Are there any women in the palace?' he asked. 'And is there any way of making contact with them?'

Diaz gave a yelp of sarcastic laughter. 'You are looking to get yourself treated with something nastier than being thrown to the lions, like being stretched out on a rack and sawn in two parts, from the crutch upwards. That was the fate of the last person who meddled with the Emperor's women. Of course there are women in the palace. Moulay's harem is the largest in the known world, several hundred women according to rumour, and he considers himself a great stallion. He rarely lies with the same woman twice. One of the French doctors told me that in the space of three months no less than forty sons were born to Moulay in the harem. The palace grounds swarm with his children, and a pestilential pack of brats they are. Completely out of control as no one can lay a hand on them.'

Though shaken, Hector persisted. 'Is it true that he prefers light-skinned women?'

Again, the sarcastic bark of laughter. 'The Light of the Earth, as he is called, prefers virgins of whatever colour. But he's not choosy. If someone's wife takes his fancy, then he'll make the necessary arrangements, for he pretends he follows the Qur'an in all things . . .'

Seeing Hector had not understood, the Spaniard went on, 'The Qur'an forbids adultery, so the Emperor makes sure that the woman becomes a widow.'

'The man sounds like an ogre.'

'Oh, he certainly is,' answered the officer blithely, and spurred his mount forward.

℃

MEKNES CAME IN SIGHT the following afternoon, and the travellers paused to take in the view. The city was built on a spur of land overlooking the river Fakran, which flowed across their path on its way towards the Atlantic. The valley floor was intensively cultivated, the greenery of the fields and orchards rising up the slope to lap against the suburbs of the imperial capital. The nearest houses were unexceptional, low buildings in the natural colours of the mud and clay from which they were built, their roofs of tile or thatch. Behind them stood the city proper, a great number of more substantial houses huddled together in a dense mass with the domes and spires of mosques rising above the congestion. There was no sign of a city rampart. Instead, to the left from where the travellers stood, a great boundary wall reached to encompass what was almost a second city. This wall, painted white, was four stories high and seemed to go on for ever, curving away out of sight. Hector judged that it was perhaps three miles long, and beyond it he glimpsed the tops of pavilions and towers, turrets clad in shining green tiles, the domes of mosques, some of them gilded, and a series of edifices in blue and white whose functions he could not guess. Clearly the whole enormous conglomeration was some sort of gigantic, sprawling palace. Beside him Bourdon let out an exclamation. 'That place makes even King Louis seem restrained!' Luis Diaz looked across at him enquiringly, and the pickpocket added, 'I mean the King's new palace at Versailles. His builders had just made a start on it when I was last in Paris, so I went to have a look. It was vast, yet it was nothing compared to this. What manner of king could command such an undertaking?'

'Not a king, but an emperor,' corrected the Spaniard, 'and the work never ends. Moulay wants his palace to extend from here to the sea, that's more than eighty miles.'

'He's mad!' muttered Bourdon.

'Perhaps so. But that's no consolation to the poor wretches who are building it. Squads of men are perpetually working on the wall. They are either heightening it or lengthening it, or painting it, or repairing it because sections of it are always cracking and crumbling or falling down. And inside the enclosure it is even worse. The Emperor is forever ordering some new building or other. Then he tears down one after only six months or wants it changed. It is mayhem. But come, you will see for yourself,' and he rode forward down the hill.

Hector could not keep his eyes off the palace enclosure as he rode forward. Perhaps this was where his sister was to be found, he wondered. As he approached, he began to hear a curious sound. At first it was only the barking of dogs. He had never heard such a cacophony of howling and baying in all his life. It was as if the entire city was populated by the animals. Noticing his puzzlement Luis Diaz commented, 'You'll get used to that din. The city is plagued by dogs, most of them are strays and curs. They run in packs and eat the rubbish. Yet no one seems to do anything about it. Maybe because the Emperor is fond of animals, and the citizens fear his anger if they cull them.'

'It's not just the barking of the dogs,' Hector answered, 'it's that other sound, the thumping in the background.'

'Like I said, the building work is constant in Meknes, and nearly everything is made out of hardened clay. What you are hearing is the sound of that clay being pounded into position. Look over there, and you'll see what I mean.'

They were passing along the face of the palace wall, close enough to see the work in progress. At the foot of the wall a gang of about forty men was standing over great wooden troughs and using shovels and heavy bars to mix what looked like a thick pinkish-yellow dough. Other men were then carrying buckets and baskets of the stuff up crude ladders propped against the wall. Reaching the top of the wall they tipped the mixture out in front of a third team standing on the summit. These men were creating the strange thumping noise by pounding down on the mix in unison, using great wooden mallets to beat it into shape between heavy wooden planks and adding to the height of the rampart. The scene reminded Hector of a colony of ants working to fortify their nest. Looking more closely, he noted that all the labourers were white men. They were dressed in ragged clothes, bare-headed and without shoes. They seemed half-starved and desperate. He realised they were slaves.

Diaz led them into the city itself, guiding them along narrow lanes ankle-deep in mud. A number of the passers-by wore the grey hooded cloaks of the amazigh, but the majority were Moors or Arabs in brightly coloured jackets sewn with decorative buttons and wearing red caps. Their loose linen drawers reached down to mid calf, leaving their feet bare, a sensible arrangement given the condition of the muddy streets, though some of the wealthier ones teetered along on thick-soled cork slippers trying to steer clear of the muck. Against the damp and chill, most were swathed in a fine white blanket wrapped around the body, leaving only the right arm bare. They showed little interest in Hector and his friends, and even Karp with his damaged face attracted scarcely a second glance, which left Hector wondering if such mutilation was perhaps another of the imperial punishments.

'This is where I live,' announced Diaz as they reached an unprepossessing building that looked more like a cattle byre than a dwelling and, after tying up their mounts, pushed open the door. Inside, the place was no more attractive, a large room poorly furnished with a couple of tables and some plain chairs and benches. Several doors apparently led off to bedchambers, and there must have been a kitchen somewhere to the rear as Hector could smell cooking. He also noticed that the roof leaked in one corner.

'It's not much, I know,' said Diaz, 'but this is what the Emperor assigned to his Spanish officers. We were told to evict the Jew who owns the place here and, believe it or not, the Jew now has to pay rent to Moulay for letting us live here. I know it makes no sense. But you'll find that is the rule here in Meknes. Everything is back to front.'

A trio of white men, dressed in vaguely military costume, were sitting at one of the tables, playing cards and drinking from earthenware mugs. 'Let me introduce you to my fellow officers,' said Diaz. 'This is Roberto, Carlos and Lopez. Like myself, they are all cavalrymen. A couple of musketeers from Castille are also billeted here, but right now they are away on campaign. The Emperor has an army in the south, putting down a local rebellion among the mountain people, and they've been sent to help out. You can use their room until they return.'

He clapped his hands and shouted out for food to be brought. Somewhere to the rear of the building a voice answered him.

Over a meal of grey, stringy boiled mutton and couscous Diaz explained to his countrymen that he had brought the castaways to Meknes after hearing about the great mortar. 'A wise decision,' said the man called Roberto as he idly shuffled the pack of cards. 'If Moulay had learned about the gun, and that you were nearby and failed to act, he'd have had you tossed.' He turned towards the visitors. 'Being tossed, for your information, does not mean being thrown out of the imperial army. It means just what it says. Being thrown up in the air, and you'll be lucky to escape with your life when it is done by the Black Guard. They are very skilled at it. The Emperor gives the nod, and those devils step forward and grab you, one at each limb. Then they fling you up in the air, and stand back. It's a fine art and they have it to perfection. They calculate how you will fly up in the air, how far you go, and whether you turn or spin.' He gave a sardonic chuckle. 'A bit like judging the way the bomb flies out from that big gun Luis just told us about. When you get tossed, the Black Guard stand back and let you crash back on the ground. They can arrange it so you fall on your face, or your back, or your side. Whatever they choose. It is up to them whether you are stunned or merely bruised, or break a leg or an arm. Then if the Emperor commands, they'll do it several times so you are suitably battered. Or if he wants you dead, they can make sure that you land on your head at just the right angle to break your neck. It helps, of course, when they do this over a marble floor.' He began to deal out the cards to his companions. 'For a moment when you first came in,' he added, looking at Dan, 'I thought you might be a member of the Black Guard, and that gave me a fright, I must admit.'

'Those tax collectors with you were they Black Guardsmen?' Bourdon asked Diaz.

'Not exactly, though one day they might become that,' he answered. 'Blacks are the backbone of the Emperor's army. Some are recruited from the tribes. But the majority are bred to the service. They are the sons of soldiers who have served previous rulers, and are brought up to a military life. They are trained to be tough, live in special camps, exercise in fighting with sword and spear, and are shown how to handle a musket.'

Here one of the Spaniards interrupted. 'Not that they use guns very much. The weapons they are given are shoddy rubbish, and likely to blow up in your face. And the powder is no better. Half the time it doesn't explode. The Emperor's infantry often finish up using their muskets as clubs. Still, don't let me interrupt our friend's yarn.'

Diaz waved his hand dismissively. 'You may have noticed that my escort of tax collectors was lightly dressed even though we were in the mountains. That's part of their training. They are issued only with a thin cotton shift and no footwear, not even a turban. After five years' instruction they are considered to be fit for duty. Later, if they distinguish themselves in battle, they may advance to the elite company which protects the Emperor's person. Then they're Black Guards, and utterly loyal to Moulay. He has them drilled like mastiffs, vicious and ready to attack anyone.' He stretched his legs to ease his riding muscles. 'But enough of that. It's time to return my horse to the imperial stables, and we might as well drop off the mules there too. You'll see for yourself that Moulay's cavalry get better equipment than his foot soldiers.'

Remounted, Diaz took Hector and his companions back through the muddy city streets to a great gateway in the outer wall of the royal enclosure. Its enormous doors of worked bronze stood open and, as they passed under the archway, Luis said, 'We buried a wolf's head here last year when this gate was used for the first time. The Emperor killed the wolf – it was from his menagerie – with a scimitar. Then he told us to bury the head in the centre of the gateway, while he himself interred the body outside in the main road. I suppose it's meant to bring good luck.' He turned his horse to the left as soon as they were inside the gate, explaining that it was wiser to avoid the centre of the palace compound. 'You never know where you might run into Moulay,' he warned. 'He roams the palace with his escort, poking and prying into every corner. If he comes upon a work gang putting up a building, he's been known to take off his outer robes, strip down to his shirt and seize a shovel, then work alongside them in some sort of frenzy. Equally, if he is in a bad mood and thinks someone is slacking, he'll send in the Black Guard with cudgels and have the labourers thrashed on the spot.'

They rode for some distance when, at the far side of the compound, they entered on a broad, well-made roadway carried on a series of arches across a shallow valley. 'I always feel a little more relaxed when I reach this point,' admitted Diaz. 'There's less chance of meeting Moulay out here. The only time he's likely to come this way is if he's taken it into his head to go on an outing with some of his harem. He has them put up on mules and donkeys, and he rides at the head of the procession like some sort of peacock. His eunuch guards fan out ahead to clear away any onlookers, using whips and swords. But everyone who has any sense has already made himself scarce. Should you be unlucky enough to be trapped with nowhere to run, the best course is to bolt behind a bush and fall flat, with your face to the ground and hoping you are not noticed.'

The Spaniard gestured towards the ground beneath his horse's hooves. 'Moulay boasts that his horses regularly walk over the heads of his Christian captives. There are twenty-four arches to this causeway, and all but the central one have been closed off to make a row of cells. That's where his Christian prisoners are lodged. We are actually riding over the slave pens.'

'Dan and I have spent time in the bagnios of Algiers,' Hector told him. 'So we know what it's like to be a slave.'

'So how did you get out? Did you convert?'

'Yes, we both turned Turk. It seemed the only escape.'

Luis nodded his understanding. 'Not much different from my deserting my post in Ceuta, and joining the Emperor's army. The trouble is that there's little chance of going back. I doubt I would be accepted again into the service of Spain and so I had better make the rest of my life here, or perhaps I will find my way out to the Americas where my history would not be discovered, and even if it was, no one would pay much attention.' He pointed ahead to a series of long, low buildings arranged in parallel lines. 'There are the imperial stables now. To a cavalryman they rate as the eighth wonder of the world.'

In the next hour Hector understood the Spaniard's enthusiasm. The stables of the royal palace were awe-inspiring. There were three miles of barn-like buildings, and an army of ostlers and grooms was hard at work, cleaning and watering, sweeping up the horses' droppings, and trundling barrow loads of manure out to the gently steaming middens. 'There are never less than a thousand horses stabled here, with one groom for every five animals so the place is kept spotlessly clean,' Diaz announced. He was relishing his self-appointed task as a guide and clearly was someone who was prepared to talk for hours about horses and their care. They were his passion. 'Note the drains of running water which run the length of each stable so the horse piss is carried away. You will notice also that there are no mangers. The local custom is to feed the horses with chopped hay and sweet herbs strewn on the ground, and use nose bags for their barley. Those outhouses over there are filled with enough fodder for at least six months.'

He marched to the end of one stable block and threw open the door to a vast harness room where saddles and bridles hung in neat lines. A little farther on was an armoury with rack after rack of sabres and muskets which reminded Dan of what he had seen at the Marseilles Arsenal. But the Spaniard saved his greatest surprise to the last. He led his companions to a smaller stable, set apart from the others, and more substantially built. Nodding to an attendant, he led Hector and his friends inside where they found themselves looking at two dozen horses kept in open stalls. The animals turned their heads to gaze at the men, and one of them whickered softly. 'Look under them,' said Diaz. Peering in, Hector saw that each animal, instead of standing on sawdust or straw, was standing on a fine Turkish carpet. 'These horses are revered,' explained Diaz. 'They eat only hand-sifted grain and fresh green stuff. No one but the Emperor himself may ride them, and he does that very rarely. Instead they are led at the head of parades, all decked out in rich trappings of silk and brocade, wearing harnesses made of tooled leather inlaid with precious stones, silver and gold thread woven into their manes and tails. An attendant, preferably a Christian slave, follows close behind to catch their droppings in a bucket, while another groom immediately lifts up their tails to wipe them.'

'Why all this for a bunch of ageing nags?' demanded Bourdon sceptically.

'Because these horses have made the journey to Mecca,' answered Diaz, 'and don't scoff. If you are ever in real trouble with the Emperor, your best chance is to throw yourself between the feet of a sacred horse when the Emperor rides by, and claim the Emperor's benevolence. That way you at least stand a chance of having your request granted.'

℃

IT WAS ANOTHER two days before a palace messenger showed up at the Spaniards' billet with a summons. Diaz was ordered to appear before the Emperor with the survivors from the galley and they were to explain the workings of the great cannon. 'I told you that Moulay is keen to capture Tangier,' the Spaniard said gleefully to Hector and the others as they hurried towards the palace. 'Normally one has to wait weeks for an audience with Moulay.'

'But none of us – Dan, Bourdon, Karp nor I – know much about the mortar,' Hector objected. 'All we did was prepare the bombs, load them, and clean the weapon.'

'But you must have noted the shape and size of the gun, the thickness of its barrel, the design of its chamber, the way the bombs were prepared. Put all those details together and there should be enough information for Moulay's master gun founder to make a copy. And if he is able to make a replica, we will all be richly rewarded.'

Despite Diaz's confidence, Hector was full of misgivings as the Spaniard led them through the wolf's-head gate. The weather had improved, and it was a warm, bright morning. They walked along a series of avenues in the palace grounds. Now and then Diaz had to stop to get his bearings, apologising that so much building work had been done since his last audience with Moulay five months earlier that he was in danger of losing his way. 'The messenger said that we were to meet the Emperor by the place where he keeps his cats,' he explained.

'You mean at the lion pit? That doesn't sound very encouraging,' commented Bourdon dryly.

'No, no, his cats. The Emperor is very fond of cats. There are more than forty of them, all sorts of colours and types, from tabbies to pure white. The Emperor collects cats. He is sent the most remarkable ones from all over his kingdom, and also from foreign countries. He has cats with eyes of different colours, long-furred cats, cats that love to swim, cats with no tails. He keeps them in a special enclosure and they are trained to come to him when he calls.'

They passed through a bewildering array of pavilions, arcades and courtyards, many of them embellished with marble fountains and reflecting pools. They skirted around a sunken garden planted with cypress trees and surrounded by balustrades of jasper, and then made a detour around a handsome colonnaded building which Diaz warned was the residence of two of the Emperor's principal wives. Everywhere was a profusion of inlay work, cut-stone tracery and delicate stucco, and when Diaz risked taking a short cut down a long corridor leading through a reception hall, Hector marvelled at the painted plaster ceiling overhead and the thousands of small tiles, red and green and white, which had been laid to make a chequerwork pavement. Very occasionally he glimpsed a servant who quickly darted away out of sight, so this entire, remarkable assemblage of buildings and open spaces gave the impression of being deserted.

Finally they came upon a small group of courtiers standing beside yet another sunken garden. It was crossed by a causeway covered with trellised vines so that it formed a long leafy tunnel. Judging by the nervous expressions on the faces of the courtiers, who were all dressed in rich Moorish costume, they too were awaiting the arrival of the Emperor. Hector glanced into the netted enclosure behind them, and saw it was home to a variety of cats who were sunning themselves, sleeping or prowling the perimeter of their cage.

The largest and most magnificent of the cats, a spotted creature the size of a small leopard, alerted them to the approach of the Emperor. Long before the humans could detect anything unusual, the animal suddenly sat up and gazed with its huge, yellow eyes down the leafy tunnel. Then the big cat yawned luxuriously, curving its pink tongue, rose to its feet and padded over towards the edge of the enclosure where it sat down again and gazed fixedly towards the causeway. The cluster of courtiers stirred with apprehension, adjusting their robes, shifting from one foot to another, making small coughing sounds as they cleared their throats.

'Here he comes now,' Diaz whispered in Hector's ear. 'Get ready to fall down flat on your face.' Hector waited, standing long enough to see a bizarre cortège approaching down the trellised causeway. It was led by two immensely tall black soldiers in white gowns and holding muskets. Behind them came half a dozen veiled women wearing a harness over their flowing garments. The traces of their harness led back to a wickerwork chariot on four wheels which they were pulling along at a slow walk. On each side of the chariot marched more members of the Black Guard, and to the rear a footman was holding a yellow and green umbrella over a man riding in the chariot. The latter was wearing a huge white turban, at least a yard in circumference, and even at that distance there was the flash of the jewelled brooch pinned to the cloth. Hector obediently prostrated himself in the dust after he had noted thankfully that the Emperor, for it had to be Moulay riding in the chariot, was wearing green.

'Bono! Bono!' a deep voice said some moments later, and he sensed that the chariot had stopped and the Emperor had got out and was speaking over the backs of the courtiers. Still no one on the ground stirred. 'Allah ibarak fi amrik sidi! God bless thy Power!' the courtiers around him chorused, their faces still pressed to the dust. 'You may rise,' announced the Emperor, and Hector heard the courtiers getting to their feet. As he followed their example, he looked out of the corner of his eye and noted that all the Moors were standing meekly, still staring at the ground. Only when the formal ritual of blessing and response in the name of the Prophet had been completed did they raise their eyes and look upon the potentate they addressed as Light of the Earth.

Moulay Ismail was thinner than Hector had expected. He was a man of medium height with a very black skin. His face, beneath the huge turban, was gaunt, and he had a pronounced hook nose which contrasted with a full-lipped and sensuous mouth. His beard jutted forward and had been dyed light ginger, as had his bushy eyebrows. His dark eyes were expressionless as he surveyed his submissive courtiers, and the Black Guards of his escort watched them suspiciously. The umbrella holder had moved forward so he was now standing directly behind the Emperor and twirling the umbrella constantly. The women had retreated demurely into the background. 'Admiral!' Moulay demanded sharply. 'Where are the men who can tell me about the ship gun?' He spoke in Arabic, and Hector understood the gist of the question. One of the courtiers, a distinguished-looking Moor in a dark brown robe trimmed with black and silver braid, gestured towards Diaz and his companions, then bowed deeply. Moulay said something which Hector did not catch, and then the courtier, whom Hector took to be the commander of Moulay's navy, began to translate in heavily accented Spanish.

'His Majesty the Light and Sun of the Earth wishes to know about the big gun carried on a foreign vessel. We hear reports that a city has no defence against such a weapon.'

Hector felt a nudge. Diaz, standing beside him, wanted him to answer. Hector swallowed hard, and then took the risk he had been calculating from the moment he had seen the Emperor. He replied in Turkish, speaking directly to the Emperor.

'Your Majesty, the gun is called a mortar. It fires shells called bombs filled with gunpowder that explode on reaching the target. They travel up into the air from the gun and drop from the sky.'

Moulay turned his head to look directly at him, and the black eyes were like coals. Hector felt a shiver of anxiety, but kept his gaze fixed on the great jewel in the Emperor's turban.

'Where did you learn to speak Turkish so well?' Moulay asked.

'In Algiers, Your Majesty.'

'And what country are you from?'

'From a country called Ireland, Your Majesty.'

For a moment Moulay paused, as if considering a rebuke. Then he said curtly, 'You have told me nothing that I do not know already.'

'The principle of the gun has been known for many years, Your Majesty,' Hector went on. 'But only now is it possible to make bombs which are so destructive.'

'Are they strong enough to knock down city walls?' asked Moulay.

'I believe so, Your Majesty. If they strike at the right point.'

'Good, then I want to have such guns and bombs, many of them, in my army. That must be arranged.' The Emperor obviously considered the subject closed because he turned his attention towards one of the courtiers.

'But Your Majesty . . .' began Hector when he felt another nudge in his back, much more urgent this time.

It was too late, Moulay had swivelled back to face him, and Hector saw a faint red flush beginning to spread in the Emperor's cheeks. It was clear that Moulay was not accustomed to being interrupted.

'What is it!' he enquired sharply.

'There are others from the ship who may know more about the gun,' Hector ventured. 'Those who were in charge of the vessel. They are now your prisoners.'

Moulay looked towards his Admiral, and raised his eyebrows questioningly. 'That is correct, Your Magnificence,' the courtier confirmed smoothly. 'They will arrive here soon, a party of petty officers and sailors. They are on foot.'

An amused smile twisted the sensuous mouth.

'I take it that you were a slave on the galley,' Moulay said, addressing Hector again. 'So I appoint you to be the examiner of these infidels. You will interrogate them about the gun and its bombs, and pass on that information to my gunfounder. And when you have done that, you can help my Jews assess the amount of ransom we will demand from the King of France for the return of the captives. I am told that the ship flew the flag of France.'

'I have a favour to ask, Your Majesty.' For a second time Hector interrupted the Emperor, and he heard a low moan of dismay from Diaz beside him. He also detected two small white patches beginning to appear beside the Emperor's nostrils. They too, he had been warned, was a sign that the Emperor was losing his temper. But he pressed on, 'I beseech Your Majesty to help me in finding my sister. She was taken by corsairs and must be somewhere in Barbary. Her name is Elizabeth . . .'

Around him Hector felt the courtiers draw back in alarm as if to distance themselves from such insulting disrespect to their overlord. Two of the Black Guards, sensing the fraught atmosphere, moved forward threateningly. Unexpectedly, Moulay laughed. It was a laugh of incredulity tinged with cruelty. 'You expect me to help you find your sister? What a creature she must be! Lovelier than a houri in Paradise, and her brother among the most impudent of men.' Moulay paused to make a strange clucking sound. 'Why should I care about a stranger's sister when I have eighty-three brothers and half-brothers and I cannot even count the number of my own sisters. However, you are a brave man. If you deliver a wall-destroying gun to me, a kale-kob, this will be your reward: I will order the release of your sister should you find she is a captive in my realm. I will do this in honour of Allah's Apostle, peace be upon him, for he released the sister of his mortal enemy Aidiy ibn Hatim, when she was his captive. And by this act he won the allegiance of Aidiy ibn Hatim who thereafter became his treasured companion.' Again the Emperor made the strange clucking sound, and this time Hector, who had fallen silent, realised that Moulay was summoning one of his cats. There was a scrabbling sound as a magnificent white cat, with a bushy tail and a coat like fluffed silk, clambered up the sides of its enclosure and leaped to the ground. Tail straight in the air, the animal ran across the ground and leaped up into Moulay's arms who began to cradle and pet it as he repeated, 'Remember! I want a kale-kob, a castle smasher!'

SEVENTEEN

C

'I THOUGHT YOU WERE going to get your neck broken,' grumbled Diaz as he hurried Hector and the others away. 'Moulay is not usually so forbearing. He's like those cats of his. You never know what he is thinking and which way he will jump. He'll toy with a victim for hours before pouncing. Then it's all over in a moment.'

They were returning through the palace compound by a route that took them towards an area of large, square buildings with the appearance of storehouses and depositories. 'I think you were saved by the fact that you come from Ireland. I dare say Moulay's met very few people from that country, and when you appeared in front of him to answer about this miraculous new gun and said you were Irish, he must have thought that fate had taken a hand. His master gun founder is an Irishman. He's been casting cannon or repairing Moulay's artillery for years, and he's very popular with those of us who like to celebrate now and then, because he's allowed to keep large stocks of alcohol. He claims it's an essential ingredient for his craft. Ah! There he is, the small man in the leather apron just coming out of the foundry.'

Hector saw a stooped, white-haired figure emerge from the nearest of the buildings, wipe his face with a cloth, then stand in the open, fanning himself. His clothes were soaked with sweat.

'Greetings Sean,' called Diaz. 'I've got some helpers for you. By order of the Emperor himself.'

The gun founder looked at them placidly. Hector judged him to be about sixty years old. Beneath his shock of white hair he had clear grey eyes in a face permanently discoloured with ingrained grime, and his hands and bare forearms were marked with dozens of small burns and scars. The gun founder coughed to clear his throat, spat carefully and wiped his face again before replying.

'Help's always welcome,' he said, looking Hector and his companions over. Hector noted that his voice, like all his movements, was calm and unhurried. His Spanish was slow and deliberate. 'What are they meant to do?'

'Explain to you about some sort of new artillery the Emperor wants copied,' said Diaz cheerfully. 'This is Hector. He's a countryman of yours.'

'Is he indeed?' responded the old man and, addressing Hector, said, 'I'm Sean Allen from Meath though it's a long time since I was there. And yourself?'

'Hector Lynch from Cork County, and these are my friends: Dan is from the Caribbees, Jacques Bourdon from Paris, and Karp is a Bulgar, though he's a mute.'

The gun founder shot Karp an amused glance and said, 'He's a silent bugger, so?' No one understood the quip and he added, 'Buggers or bugres, that's what you call someone who's awkward. It's on account of so many Bulgars being trouble-makers. Something to do with their religion. They are said to be extreme heretics. Not that I care.'

He paused to wipe his brow again.

'I saw enough bigotry back home when I was at the siege of Limerick with Cromwell's son-in-law, Ireton. I minded and mended his cannon for him, and what he did to those who led the resistance sickened me and I left poor unhappy Ireland.

Since then I've served the Sultan in Istanbul, the Bey of Tunis, and now the Emperor of Morocco. They all need guns and will employ those who have the knowledge to make them. Now tell me about this artillery I'm supposed to copy. What's so special about it?'

'I don't know the technical details,' Hector answered, 'but it's a short, fat gun which shot flaming bombs in the air and they fell into a town and exploded.'

'Nothing new there,' said the gun founder, now mopping the back of his neck with the cloth. 'Mortars have been used for years. Ireton had four of them when we besieged Limerick, and a Hungarian built a truly enormous one for the Grand Turk when he besieged Constantinople and that was two centuries ago. I saw his great mortar on display in the city. It was so big that it shot stone cannonballs that weighed five hundred pounds. Mind you, it must have taken the stonemasons a month of Sundays to chip and shape each cannonball so it fitted right. Not exactly a rapid rate of fire.'

'The gun we saw used ready-made hollow shells of metal fitted with different sorts of fuses. Some worked, others didn't. The gun was mounted on a galley, and that's why we are here. It shook the galley to pieces.' Hector stopped talking, conscious that he had said something which had caught the gun founder's attention.

'A mortar carried on a ship. That's different altogether,' Allen said thoughtfully. 'Some clown failed to compensate for the recoil. It would need a different sort of carriage from the usual one for land guns, something that would allow the downward thrust to be converted to a sideways motion. I heard that a Dutchman – Coehorn I think is his name – has come up with an improved mortar, perhaps that is what was being used on board that ship.' He was half talking to himself, imagining the practical problems of his new commission from the Emperor, and Diaz had to interrupt him. 'Sean, I've got to get back to my own billet. I'll leave your new helpers with you. I presume you can find space for the extra members of your team.'

'Yes, of course,' said the gun founder absent-mindedly, 'I'll see that they are looked after.'

Allen turned towards the building behind him, and pulled open the door. His visitors quailed at the blast of heat though the gun founder seemed to be oblivious to the temperature as he led Hector and the others inside. 'This is the foundry itself,' he explained, as they stepped around a mass of glowing metal in a pit. 'We had a pour a few hours ago and are waiting for the metal to cool down. It's nothing special, just a small brass culverin. The Emperor likes to boast that he has a full-sized gun foundry, but in fact we haven't the facilities to make anything much bigger than this. Most of our work is repairing damaged cannon or casting round shot and grape for his field artillery. A ten-pound ball is heavy enough to knock down the mud walls of the forts that the tribes build for themselves in the interior. But a true siege cannon, like the weapon you are talking about, is another matter altogether.'

He had reached the far end of the foundry, and passing through a double door and then across the narrow lane he brought his visitors into an even larger building. It was an arms depot. Here were rack upon rack of sabres and muskets, trays of pistols, bundles of pikes and an array of blunderbusses. Clusters of bandoliers hung on pegs, and disposed here and there on the floor were heaps of body armour, corselets, greaves, and helmets of many different styles and in varying condition. 'The Emperor hates to have any war material thrown away,' confided the gun founder. 'Half of this stuff is so antiquated as to be useless, like that arquebus over there. But when Moulay comes on an inspection he'll suddenly ask to see some piece of equipment which he remembers from months earlier, and there's all hell to pay if it can't be produced immediately. You there!' He called out to a lad who was replacing an old-fashioned

Spanish helmet in a chest. 'Don't put it in like that. Wrap it first in paper so it keeps its gleam.' Hector noted that the gun founder had spoken in English. 'Does everyone in the foundry use English?' he asked. 'I should hope so,' answered the Irishman. 'I've got a score of youngsters working here for me, and every one of them is English. It's another quirk of Moulay's. Every time his people capture an English youngster, the lad is assigned to work with me in the Arsenal. My guess is that Moulay thinks the English make the best gun founders and gunsmiths.'

'And do they?' Hector enquired.

'Depends who you speak to. The French gun foundries at Liège are among the most advanced in the world, and the Spaniards would claim that they make the finest musket locks. The Italians write well about the theory of gunnery; while the Dutch are great innovators. And from what I witnessed in the Grand Seignor's foundry outside Istanbul, I can assure you that the Turkish topcus as they call their gun founders are no slouches.'

They entered a room, clearly Allen's office, which was partitioned off from the rest of the armoury. Looking around, Hector noticed a shelf of books and pamphlets on the art of gun founding and the manufacture of powder and rockets. Sean Allen carefully closed the door of the study behind them, opened a cupboard and took out a large green glass flask and several glasses. 'One of the privileges of my post,' he explained, as he removed the stopper from the flask and began to pour. 'It's a blessing that the making of incendiaries can require spirits of alcohol. Take the repair of spoilt gunpowder, its restoration as you might call it. We get a great quantity of bad gunpowder brought to us. Either it got wet while on campaign with the Emperor's army, or maybe it was captured out of some foreign ship and we find that it got damp from lying in a ship's hold for too long. The Emperor is very pleased to receive such tribute, but unless the gunpowder is repaired it is useless. So what do we do?'

The gun founder took a gulp from his glass, walked over to the bookshelf, and took down a volume. It was written in Latin and entitled *The Great Art of Artillery*. Clearly Allen was an educated man.

'It's all written up here,' continued the gunsmith. 'We make up an elixir of two parts brandy with one measure each of white wine vinegar and purified saltpetre, and add half measures of oils of sulphur and samphire. Then we sprinkle the elixir over the damaged powder and put it out in the sun to dry. When the powder is completely dried out we package it again in barrels, and place it in dry store. Then it's as good as new.' He closed the book with a snap and took another mouthful of his drink. 'Of course there's always brandy left over, and it's amazing what a thirst a man works up when he is in the heat of a gun foundry.'

Noticing that Hector had barely touched his glass of brandy he went on, 'Drink up! Surely you're not an abstainer. That would be a disappointment, what with your coming from the old country.'

'No,' replied Hector, 'Dan and I did profess Islam when we were slaves in Algiers but that was under duress. And anyhow we saw plenty of Turks who came to drink in the bagnio's taverns. Neither of us care much for religion.'

'Very understandable. Half the captives here in Morocco take up Islam just to make life more bearable. It's mostly the fanatics who refuse.' The gun founder produced paper and pen from his desk. 'Now, give me a description of the mortar that you saw on the galley.'

'Maybe it will be easier if Dan draws a picture of it for you,' suggested Hector. 'He's good with pen and ink.'

'All right, then,' answered Allen, handing the pen to the Miskito and he watched as Dan quickly sketched out the mortar and its sledge. 'Ah! I see the fault. The gun carriage was wrong. If it had been designed so that the mortar rolled back when it was fired, and was not pinned in place, it would not have shattered the foredeck. Perhaps a rocker or a curved slope to absorb the recoil would have done the trick.' Taking back the pen from Dan, he quickly drew an improved gun carriage. 'That's one problem likely solved,' he said, 'but that's not what the Emperor wants. He's after those exploding bombs, and as noisy and spectacular as possible. Can you tell me anything about them?'

'They were about twelve inches in diameter and a perfect globe,' answered Hector, 'except for the hole where they were filled and fused. At that point there was a collar like the neck of your brandy flask though much shorter. The globes were already packed with gunpowder when they were loaded on the galley, but if one of them needed topping up, we poured in more gunpowder through the hole, then plugged it with one of the fuses.' He went on to describe the different fuses that were tested, and finally added, 'The bombs had small handles on each side of the fuse so when Karp and I were loading them into the mortar, we could get a grip to lift them. Each bomb must have weighed maybe forty pounds.'

Allen looked pensive. 'I imagine the hollow globes were cast, and not made from wrought iron. Cast iron bursts with more destructive power, throwing smaller shards of metal and doing more damage. But the thickness of the wall of the globe has to be just right, and the gunpowder inside calculated nicely, as well as being of the highest quality.' He sighed, 'And that is going to be my main problem here. Getting hold of the right powder to make the bombs. As I said, much of the stuff we hold in stock here is repaired powder, and that would never do.'

'I worked in a quarry once, in Algiers,' ventured Hector, 'and I remember how the ordinary corned powder was unreliable. The powder we used on the galley to top up the bombs, as well as for the charges inside the mortar, was fine-grained and very black.'

'Would you recognise it again if you saw it?' asked Allen.

'I think so.'

'Then come with me,' said the gun founder. 'You others can stay here and pour yourselves some more drinks. We won't be long.'

Allen took Hector to a low, squat, windowless building, half sunk in the ground and made with immensely thick walls of stone. Unlocking a heavy wooden door, he led the young Irishman inside the gunpowder magazine. It was two-thirds empty, with perhaps a hundred barrels and kegs of gunpowder set out on the earth floor.

Allen crossed to the farthest corner where a single small keg stood by itself. Tipping it on its side, he rolled it nearer to the daylight from the open door, and removed the plug. He poured a small quantity of its gunpowder into the palm of his hand and held it out for Hector to see. 'Is that the sort of stuff you used on the galley's mortar?' he asked.

Hector looked at the little heap of black grains. 'Yes, or something very like it.'

'Thought so. That's French powder. Best-quality pistol powder, hard to find,' he grunted. He replaced the bung, rolled the keg back into its place, and ushered Hector out of the magazine. As Allen carefully locked the door behind him, Hector asked, 'Will you be able to get more of that powder? Enough for the bombs?'

'We can't make that quality here and my supplier is, you might say, irregular,' Allen replied. He gave a hiccup, and Hector realised that the gun founder was slightly tipsy. 'He's a corsair who calls in at Sallee. Mostly he operates in the Atlantic, off the Spanish coast or as far north as the Channel. Sallee is convenient for him whenever he has interesting goods to sell. He's a countryman of ours who took the turban as you did, though rather more seriously. Name of Hakim Reis.'

Hector felt his spine tingle.

'Hakim Reis.' he repeated. 'He's the corsair who took me captive.'

'Don't hold that against him. Man-catching is a good slice of his profession, and he's a decent enough sort.'

Hector tried to keep his voice steady. 'Will there be any chance of meeting him?'

Allen gave him a shrewd look. 'Not thinking of taking revenge, are you? I wouldn't recommend it.'

'No, no. I just wanted to ask him some questions. When do you think Hakim Reis will next be here?'

'Impossible to say. He comes and goes as it suits him. He might show up next week, next month or perhaps never again if he's been sunk at sea or died of the plague. But one thing about him is that if war is declared, he seems to be early on the scene, and the first to come into port with the spoils.'

Hector thought furiously as he tried to find another thread that might lead him to locating Hakim Reis. 'That powder he sells to the Emperor. Where does he get it?'

'I'd say he has good contacts on the Spanish coast. There are plenty of small bays and inlets where you can meet up with people willing to sell war material to the highest bidder, and never mind where the guns and powder finish up.'

'But you said that was French-made gunpowder. How would he obtain that?'

'Gunpowder's a valuable commodity. It could have changed hands several times, passed from smuggler to smuggler until it reaches someone like Hakim Reis who has a ready market for it.'

'And you have no idea who any of these smugglers might be, and whether they know where to find him?'

The gun founder looked at Hector searchingly. 'Why so keen to meet Hakim Reis?'

'He may be able to help me locate a member of my family —

my sister. She was also taken captive, and I've heard nothing of her since. I promised myself I would find her.'

Allen pondered for a moment, and when he spoke his tone was sympathetic. 'I wish I could help you. I've known Hakim since the early days when he used to come in with shoddy muskets to sell. I did ask him on one occasion whether he could get me a further delivery of best powder, and he said he'd consult with someone he called Tisonne, or maybe he said Tison, I can't remember exactly. But he never mentioned the name again, and I've never heard of it, not in these parts anyhow. And if Tisonne or Tison is a professional smuggler, it could be his cover name, not his real one. Then he'll be even more difficult to locate than Hakim himself.'

Hector and the gun founder had arrived back in the armoury where they found Dan examining a musket from the display. 'What do you think of it?' asked Allen.

'This is exactly the sort of gun we have at home among my people. I hadn't expected to find one here. The weapon must be at least fifty years old. It still uses the old-fashioned matchlock,' observed the Miskito.

'Indeed it does. Have you worked with guns?'

'Back home, and for a brief period in the workshops of King Louis's Galley Corps in Marseilles.'

The gun founder gave a grunt of satisfaction. 'You've just talked yourself into a job. Rather than helping me concoct exploding bombs, it will be more use if you could supervise these English lads here in the armoury. Show them how to repair the older weapons. Your French friend and the silent bugger can help you. Meanwhile Hector can assist me in providing Moulay with his castle smasher.'

'Perhaps I could start by interviewing the other survivors from the galley,' suggested Hector. 'They should reach Meknes in the next few days, and I could ask them for more information. They might cooperate if they think it will help obtain their early release. Moulay has already appointed me as the go-between to arrange their ransom.'

'That's just the sort of quirky idea that would entertain the Emperor,' Allen agreed. 'Our friend Diaz will be able to tell us when the prisoners from the galley arrive and where they will be held. He stops by here most evenings as he and his cronies are fond of my brandy.'

C

IN THE END it was several more days before Diaz reported that comite Piecourt and the other captives from the *St Gerassimus* had arrived in Meknes. They had been added to the palace labour force, and were being held in the cells built into the arches under the causeway leading to the royal stables. The following evening when all slaves would have returned from their work, Hector set off to find his former masters. Walking along the line of twenty-four arches, he caught sight of the unmistakable figure of Yakup, the rowing master. The renegade Turk was squatting against one of the stone pillars supporting the roadway above. He was stripped to the waist and had tilted his head back against the stonework. The distinctive fork-tailed cross branded on his forehead was clearly visible. As Hector approached, two men emerged from the archway, deep in conversation. One was a tall, ascetic-looking figure and Hector did not recognise him. The other had a pale skin and close-cropped sandy hair. It was Piecourt. Both were dressed in the loose tunic and cotton pantaloons worn by slaves. 'Good evening, comite, I would like a word with you,' said Hector quietly. Startled, Piecourt broke off his conversation and swung round towards him. As he did so, the slanting rays of the evening sun fell square on his companion's face and Hector saw that his otherwise handsome features were marred by a scattering of small dark blue spots spread across his right cheek from just below his eye to the jaw line. 'Who are you?' asked Piecourt. A moment later the light of recognition dawned in his eyes. 'You are from the galley, aren't you? Middle oarsman, bench three, port side.'

'That's correct, comite,' said Hector. 'But I am now in the employment of the gun founder to His Majesty Moulay Ismail.'

Piecourt's mouth twisted in a sardonic smile. 'Come to think of it, we've already met your bench companion, the brown man. He interviewed us when we were first captured. So more than one of my dogs have survived. What do you want?'

'I need to interview the technician who looked after the mortar on *St Gerassimus*, also her captain and anyone else who can provide information about the gun.'

Piecourt was expressionless. 'Then you will be disappointed. The technician and the captain are not here. After the galley foundered, the captain took the two ship's boats and headed west along the coast, to seek help. The technician went with him.'

'Is there anyone who could provide me with any information about the gun? It would help your case. The Emperor is disposed to look kindly on anyone who is cooperative.'

'That is not enough reason for me or anyone else to help the infidel. On the contrary, you would be doing yourself a great favour, if you would send word to Algiers, to Iphrahim Cohen the Jewish ransom broker. Once he learns that we are being held here, he will arrange our release. As I already told your brown friend, you could earn yourself a handsome reward. Later you and your friends from bench three might even receive a royal pardon from His Majesty King Louis. I have friends who can arrange such things.'

'It is too late for that, Piecourt. Moulay Ismail has already given orders for your ransom. I am to advise and consult with his own ransom broker, here in Meknes.'

The comite still seemed unperturbed. 'We are not worth very much. There are only myself and the sous comites and a number of common sailors. The officers left in the boats. I repeat: the sooner you get word to Algiers, the more you will benefit.'

There was something about Piecourt's manner which made Hector suspicious. The comite was hiding something.

'I'll take a moment to look around your cell,' he said.

Piecourt shrugged. 'You don't need my permission.'

Stepping inside the cell, Hector was immediately brought back to his days in the Algiers bagnio. The far end of the archway had been blocked off with a wall of bricks, and the near entrance could be closed at night with double doors. The result was a narrow, high room where the only light and air came in through two small windows high up in the far wall. Looking about him, Hector was impressed with the cleanliness of the cell. The occupants were keeping it swept and there was no sign of rubbish. Everything was neatly in its place. It was evident that discipline among the occupants was very good. For their sleeping arrangements the Frenchmen had rigged up a series of bunks from lengths of timber and matting. Due to the height of the cell, these bunks extended upwards for four tiers, and the topmost could only be reached by climbing a ladder. Several of the beds were now occupied by men relaxing after their day's work, while a group of another half a dozen were playing cards on a home-made table placed on the ground between the tiers. Among the card players were two sous comites who had been subordinate to Piecourt, and a sail handler who had worked on the rambade. They glanced at Hector incuriously before returning to their game. It occurred to him that the ship's officers and freemen had known no more about galeriens toiling in the waist of the vessel than the latter had known about the occupants of the poop deck. And Piecourt had been right, there was no sign of the technician who could have answered questions about the mortar and its bombs.

As he left the cell, Hector saw that Piecourt had now deliberately placed himself so he could ignore his visitor. He was seated next to the rowing master and also leaning back against the pillar of the arch. The two of them had their eyes closed as they basked in the sun waiting for the time when the prisoners had to return to their cells and be locked in for the night. Their colleague with the speckled cheek was nowhere to be seen.

Walking back through the gathering darkness, Hector was troubled. There was something he had failed to notice during his visit to the prisoners. Piecourt had been too cool, too composed. It was almost as if, by his nonchalant indifference, he was trying to distract Hector's attention.

He voiced his disquiet to Dan the following day. They were in the armoury where the Miskito was carefully examining the long barrel of an old-fashioned musket. At a work bench nearby Jacques Bourdon was dismantling the weapon's obsolete firing mechanism. 'Piecourt's hiding something,' said Hector, 'or at least he was not telling me the truth.'

'Hardly surprising,' Dan replied. 'In the bagnio, if you remember, it was wise to say as little as possible to strangers or anyone in authority in case you got yourself or a friend into trouble.'

'But this was more than that. Piecourt deliberately discouraged any conversation with me. I have a suspicion that he knows one of the prisoners can supply information about the mortar but didn't want me to identify who the man is.'

'And you are sure the technician wasn't there?'

'Definitely. I had a good look round and couldn't see him anywhere, though I did recognise one of the men who normally worked on the rambade.'

'I doubt that the sailor would know very much,' said Dan. He was holding the musket barrel up to the light so he could squint down inside the barrel. 'If you remember, the regular rambade crew was terrified that the mortar would burst, or a bomb explode while still on deck. So they kept well clear when the gun was being tested.' He picked up a small file and scraped at a rust mark on the musket barrel, then put the musket barrel on one side, and called out to Bourdon, 'No need to fix that lock, Jacques. This gun's so rotten that it would blow up the face of the man who used it. Get one of the lads to give it a polish and put it back in the rack so it looks good on display if Moulay comes round on an inspection. But make sure that it doesn't get issued for active service. I'm condemning it.'

'That's one of the guns I got from Hakim Reis, back in the old days,' commented Allen. The gun founder had just come out of his office on his way to the foundry where the new brass culverin was being chipped out of its mould. 'Those muskets were made specially for the export market. Shoddy, cheap stuff.' Turning to Hector, he asked whether he had come back with any more information about the galley mortar. When Hector admitted that he suspected the French comite of the *St Gerassimus* was holding something back, Allen suggested a new approach. 'Why don't you go to speak with Joseph Maimaran, Moulay's ransom agent? He's very clever. See if he can devise a way of putting some pressure on the comite to make him talk. I know Joseph quite well as I obtain all my brandy and spirits from the Jews because they have the monopoly on distillation. I'll send one of the English lads with you, and he'll bring you to Maimaran's house. It's in the Jewish quarter, of course, so you'll need to explain your business to the guards at the gate.'

℃

THE MELLAH, the Jewish quarter, lay deep within a maze of narrow streets to the rear of the palace compound, and the young lad who guided Hector took gruesome delight in explaining that its name meant 'the place of salt' because Jewish butchers were obliged to pickle the heads of traitors before the heads were nailed up on the city gates. The youth also managed to get himself lost, and it was only by following a stranger dressed in a Jew's black skull cap and cloak who was walking bare foot – the boy explained that the Jews had to go shoeless by Moulay's order – that they finally came to the gateway in the wall enclosing the Jewish enclave. Here Hector and his guide were allowed to pass after handing over a small bribe.

Joseph Maimaran's house lay at the end of a narrow alley and had a modest unpainted door set so deep in the surrounding wall that it was easily overlooked. The humble appearance of the building was as unassuming as its owner who greeted his visitor warily. Maimaran was at least sixty years old, and possessed one of the saddest faces Hector had ever seen. There were deep shadows under his doleful eyes, and the small mouth beneath the prominent nose was permanently downturned and despondent. Hector had to remind himself that Joseph Maimaran, according to Allen, was one of the richest men in Morocco. His wealth had helped bring Moulay to power and he was acknowledged leader of the Jewish community. This meant he had to tread a delicate path. Often, when Moulay needed money, Maimaran was expected to extract it from his fellow Jews, and he could not ask for the return of any loan to the Emperor. If he did so, he risked suffering at the hands of the Black Guard.

'I've come about the prisoners from the French galley *St Gerassimus*,' Hector began carefully. 'The Emperor gave instructions that I was to assist you in setting the amount of their ransom.'

'So I believe,' answered Maimaran, who made it his business to stay closely informed about the Emperor's latest whim.

'He also wants to acquire a siege gun similar to one on the galley, and for that I need information from the prisoners.'

'And have you had any success?'

'Not yet. I was wondering whether it would be possible to reduce the amount of their ransom if they cooperated in the matter of the gun.'

'It is a proposition fraught with risk,' commented the Jew. As he observed the young Irishman in front of him, Maimaran wondered if the young man knew just how angry and violent

Moulay would be if he learned that he had been denied a full ransom.

'Sean Allen thought you might be able to suggest another way forward.'

Maimaran pretended to give the matter some thought. But he had already decided he would prevaricate. He spread out his hands in a gesture of helplessness. 'At this stage I don't know what to propose. I know too little about the case. It would be helpful to have some more information about the French prisoners, any details that would help me calculate their ransom.'

Hector looked disappointed. 'Would there be any advantage in getting in touch with other ransom brokers? The leader of the prisoners is a man called Piecourt. He has twice asked that someone send word of their capture to Algiers. Apparently there is someone there – an Iphrahim Cohen – who can arrange their speedy release.'

This time Maimaran's hesitation was genuine. Hector's suggestion was a surprise. Of course, Maimaran knew that the leading ransom brokers in Algiers were the Cohen family. He had dealt with them in the past, though in matters of trade, not as ransom brokers. Again the Jew was cautious. 'Did this man Piecourt give any reason why this Iphrahim Cohen should be told?'

'No. He only asked that someone contact him.'

'An interesting idea . . .' It was odd, Maimaran reflected, that a comite of the French Galley Corps should know the identities of the leading ransom agents in Algiers. 'Again, it seems that we need to be better informed about the Frenchmen. One of my assistants will visit them. He will assess their ransom value – he is an expert in these matters – and report back to me. In the meantime I suggest you also try to learn more about them. You said that is the Emperor's wish: that you act as the go-between.'

With that remark, Maimaran shifted the responsibility back to Hector and brought the interview to an end.

CORSAIR

Luis Diaz was waiting in Sean Allen's office when Hector got back there, and the grin on the Spaniard's face contrasted with the gun founder's tone of exasperation. 'One moment the Emperor wants a castle smasher,' Allen was saying, 'and the next instant he sends word that there's to be a fantasia. That means we'll have to waste some of our small stock of pistol powder so there will be even less for bomb experiments.'

Hector was startled. 'Is the Emperor going to have someone blown from the mouth of a cannon?'

Diaz laughed aloud. 'Whatever makes you think that?'

'In the bagnio of Algiers our Turkish guards accused us of a fantasia if we did or said something insolent or disobedient.'

'This is a different sort of fantasia, thank god,' the gun founder reassured him. 'One which delights our horse-mad friend here. It involves a lot of over-excited cavalrymen charging around on their horses and firing guns in the air. It's spectacular and very profligate as it uses up a great deal of gunpowder. It is aptly known as Laab al-Barud or Powder Play.'

Luis Diaz's grin only broadened. 'Sean, don't be so grumpy. Our young friend deserves a day out from this smoky hellhole. I'll take him and his companions along to see the show. In the meantime you might be so good as to issue me with half a keg of good pistol powder so I can bring it to the royal stables without further delay. The fantasia is scheduled for today, after the evening prayer. There's no time to waste in gossiping.'

Diaz's good humour continued as he left the Arsenal with Hector and his companions, closely followed by a servant leading a mule loaded with the precious powder. 'A fantasia is really something special. You'll never have seen anything like it before. Two or three hundred first-class riders mounted on some of the very best horseflesh in the world.'

They came to the causeway where it crossed over the prison cells, and Diaz advised them to wait there: 'This is the best place to see the show. It'll take at least a couple of hours for the riders to get ready, so you can spend the time catching up with your former shipmates from the galley. As it's Sunday, they'll be having the day off. But leave someone up here to keep yourself a good spot as it'll soon get crowded.'

Leaving Dan to hold their place, Hector went down into the shallow gully with Karp and Bourdon and headed towards the arch where the crew of *St Gerassimus* were lodged. He was intent on cross-examining Piecourt, but as they reached the Frenchman's cell, a surly-looking inmate told him that the comite was absent, and so too was the rowing master. Nor would anyone tell him where they had gone. Hector was left with the impression that the crew members of the *St Gerassimus* had been told to be as unresponsive and obstructive as possible if he returned with any questions. Only when Bourdon met up with some of his countrymen who failed to recognise him was the pickpocket able to learn that the comite and the rowing master were at mass. 'Apparently there's a clandestine chapel in the last archway. It's been set up secretly by two Franciscan priests who came to Meknes to negotiate some prisoner releases. Moulay has been keeping the priests waiting for months, quibbling about the size of the ransom. In the meantime they conduct secret masses for the faithful. The comite and a couple of the other men from the galley are there now.'

'Karp, would you mind coming with me into the chapel and having a look round?' Hector asked. 'I have a feeling that it might be dangerous for me to go in there by myself. Jacques, perhaps you can stay outside and keep watch. Warn us if you think that we might get ourselves trapped inside.'

The three men made their way to the furthest archway. It was much smaller than the others, and had been closed off with a wooden doorway. Quietly Hector pushed the door open and slipped inside with Karp at his heels.

It took a moment for their eyes to adjust to the almost total dark. A service was in progress. The chapel was tiny, so cramped that it could hold no more than a score of worshippers. All of them were crushed together and on their knees as they faced a portable altar set up against the far wall. In front of the altar a priest was also kneeling, his hands clasped in prayer. There was no window to the tiny room, and the only light came from a single candle placed on the altar which illuminated a cross made from woven straw pinned against the far wall. In the dense gloom Hector could not identify the individual figures of the worshippers. They all appeared to be dressed in slaves' clothing though he thought he recognised the broad shoulders of the rowing master. Deep in their prayers, none of the congregation turned their heads as they murmured their responses to their priest's invocation.

As unobtrusively as possible, Hector sank down to his knees. Beside him he felt Karp do the same. The chapel was so crowded that he found it difficult to avoid the bare feet of the man directly ahead of him. Hector kept his head bent forward, wondering at the intense devotion of the worshippers. The chapel was airless and the smell of the close-packed bodies filled his nostrils. He admired the courage of the priest who would risk holding such a mass, and the ardent devotion of his flock.

Slowly he became aware that Karp beside him was beginning to shake. At first it was a slight quivering, but then it became a pronounced movement, an uncontrollable tremor that shook the man's body. For a moment Hector wondered if Karp was about to have a fit. When he glanced sideways he saw that the Bulgar's eyes were wide open. He was staring in horror at the ground in front of him, as if witnessing something terrible. Hector tried to make out what was frightening his companion. In the half-light all he could see were the feet of the man kneeling directly in front of Karp. Looking closely he saw that on the sole of each foot was a brand. Someone had burned the sign of the cross deep into the flesh, leaving a hard scar.

Fearful that Karp would draw attention to their presence, Hector reached out and grasped the Bulgar's arm reassuringly. Karp turned his anguished face towards him, and Hector gestured that they should leave. Quietly rising to his feet and still keeping his hold on Karp, Hector eased open the chapel door and the two men stepped outside into the daylight. Looking into Karp's face, Hector saw that the Bulgar had tears in his eyes. He was still shaking.

'What is it, Karp? What's the matter?' Hector asked gently. The Bulgar was making incoherent strangled sounds, though whether they were from terror or rage it was difficult to say. Something warned Hector that it would be wiser if he and the Bulgar were not seen near the chapel.

'We had better move away,' Hector went on. 'It's safer.'

Bourdon joined them and the Bulgar began to calm down, but his chest was still heaving and he was making unhappy guttural sounds. Suddenly he leaned down and pulled off the sandal he was wearing. Holding up his foot, he sketched the sign of the cross on the sole, then pointed into his ruined mouth and made a fierce gurgling sound. 'The man with the branded foot is something to do with your tongue being torn out, is that it?' Hector asked. Karp nodded vehemently. Squatting down he drew in the dust the outline of a ship, a galley. Next he marked a flag with a cross and, pointing down towards the ground, uttered a deep anguished roar. 'He's from the galley? From our galley?' Karp nodded. 'Karp, we'll sit down quietly when we get back to the foundry. There Dan can help us with pen and paper and you can tell us precisely what it is that you want us to know.'

At this point there was a shout. It was Dan leaning over the edge of the causeway and beckoning to them. 'Come on up,' he called, 'the fantasia is about to start. Hurry!' Hector, Bourdon and Karp made their way up to the crest of the causeway to find that a crowd of spectators had assembled. Most were courtiers from Moulay's entourage, but there were also a number of foreigners, including the three Spanish cavalrymen they had last seen at Diaz's billet. Everyone was jostling together and looking towards the royal stables. Hector placed himself near the edge of the crowd where he could look down and also watch the entrance to the secret chapel. Soon he saw figures appear. The Mass must have finished, and the celebrants were leaving. They emerged in twos and threes, and hurried away quietly. Hector guessed that the priest must have instructed them to remain as inconspicuous as possible. He saw the rowing master, his squat figure unmistakable even though he was in the deep shadow cast by the setting sun. Close behind the rowing master came Piecourt. Once again he was accompanied by the same tall figure of the man he had been with when Hector had visited the cell. Then, finally, he saw the figure of the priest holding to his chest a box which must be the folding altar.

Behind him there was an excited murmur and Hector turned to see that the crowd was now gazing intently down the broad road which led towards the royal stables. In the distance was movement, a low cloud of dust. He strained his eyes and the dust cloud resolved itself into a line of horsemen advancing across a broad front towards the causeway at a slow walk. As the riders drew closer, he began to distinguish that they were all dressed in white robes which flowed and billowed around them. Soon he heard the low rumble of many hooves, hundreds of them, and he realised that there were many more horsemen behind the first squadron. Rank after rank of riders were coming forward. Suddenly, as if on a single command, the front troop of horses passed straight from a walk into a full gallop. They were heading directly towards the spectators as if determined to ride them down. Their riders began to whoop and yell, standing in their stirrups and waving muskets. Some were throwing their weapons up in the air and catching them as they continued their headlong rush. Hector felt his heart pounding as the ground trembled under the hooves of their charge. The horsemen were much closer now. He could see the magnificent accoutrements of their mounts – deep saddles covered with brocade, bridles and reins of tooled leather stamped with gold, velvet saddle blankets edged with silver and gold fringes and tassels, broad breast bands worked with filigree. He heard the cries of the riders urging their animals to gallop even faster. Involuntarily he flinched back expecting the onrushing horsemen to crash into the crowd. Suddenly one of the riders, an older man riding to one side, gave a signal. As one, the front rank of the horsemen swung their muskets forward, holding them two-handed across their bodies so the muzzles pointed over their horses' ears and fired their guns. There was a single, ear-splitting salvo, and the air was filled with puffs of smoke torn through by the arcing sparks of the burning wads. In the same instant, the front rank of riders had reined their horses to a halt, so that the horses heaved back on their haunches only yards from the onlookers. A touch on the reins, and the animals spun on the same spot and went tearing away, with the robes of the riders flapping out behind them and their exultant cries ringing in the ears of the crowd.

Again and again, troop after troop, the riders charged down in the fantasia, fired their guns, wheeled around, and raced away only to regroup and charge down again. As Hector got over his surprise, he began to recognise the pattern in their movements. There were ten squadrons of riders, each performing their manoeuvres at the full gallop, perhaps a thousand horses in total. Each squadron was distinguished by its own particular feature – the colour of the bridles, the size and colour of their horses. One squadron in particular was more magnificent than all the rest. It was composed mostly of horses that were the palest cream in colour. Their tails and manes had been allowed to grow almost to the ground so that they streamed out spectacularly as they galloped, and their discipline was perfect. In that pale squadron three horses stood out. Two were jet black and the third was a handsome pale grey covered with black spots. Each time this squadron charged forward, these three horses were always a few paces ahead of the rest, and they were controlled by a single horseman. The animals were superbly schooled for they stayed close together at a full gallop and allowed their rider to leap from saddle to saddle, occasionally throwing up his musket and catching it again. And it was always this same rider who, as he came careering up to the crowd in advance of his squadron, was the one who gave the command to fire the guns. On the third occasion that this squadron, now like ghostly riders in the near-darkness, completed the fantasia, their leader came to a halt so close to Hector that flecks of foam from his horse's mouth – it was the speckled grey – flew out and landed on his face. At that moment Hector recognised the rider was Moulay Ismail.

EIGHTEEN

☾

JOSEPH MAIMARAN's hooded eyes regarded Hector with the same caution shown on the young man's previous visit to his house only twenty-four hours earlier.

'I am sorry to disturb you again,' Hector began awkwardly, still standing at the half-open door, 'but there have been important developments since we last spoke. They concern the French prisoners.'

Maimaran could see that his visitor was agitated. Hector had arrived alone in the Mellah and his manner was hesitant, yet eager. Without a word he led the young man along a narrow corridor to the plainly furnished back room where he normally discussed business with his commercial clients. Waving Hector towards a chair, he sat down at a small table, folded his hands and asked, 'Have you been able to learn more about that great gun?'

'No. Sean Allen thinks that it will be very difficult, if not impossible, to satisfy the Emperor's request.'

'That is disappointing. His Majesty, as you must be aware, expects a prompt and successful response to all his demands. If you fail to supply him with a great gun, then perhaps you should make sure that Moulay receives a considerable sum for the ransom of the prisoners. It could save you and your friends from the unpleasant consequences which often result from Moulay's displeasure.'

'That's why I came to talk to you again.' Hector's careful tone put Maimaran on his guard. He waited for Hector to continue. 'It's about the prisoners themselves. Do you know very much about them?'

'Only what my assistant reported. He interviewed them this morning. He tells me that they are of the middle or lower rank, and none of them are likely to have rich families who would pay large sums for their release. So we will have to apply to their master, the Galley Corps of France, for their redemption. My assessment is that the French will offer a prisoner exchange – captive Muslim oarsmen for the Frenchmen – rather than any cash. Unfortunately, in the past the French have bartered one Muslim oarsman for every four of their nationals in these circumstances. They say that our rowers are three or four times more durable than their own nationals.'

Hector took a deep breath before stating, 'One of the prisoners is a fraud. I believe that Moulay Ismail can obtain a very great ransom for him.'

Maimaran felt a sense of disappointment. He had been curious about the Irishman's suppressed excitement. Now he feared he was about to hear an all too familiar story. Maimaran had been arranging prisoner ransoms for many years and was thoroughly experienced in the twists and turns of the process. Of course the captives lied. They had good reason to fake their identities and pretend that they were not who they seemed to be. Those who came from poor backgrounds tried to get better treatment from their captors by claiming they had wealthy families who could pay for their release. Others who came from rich families pleaded poverty so that their ransoms would be set cheaply. Very occasionally a master even changed places with a loyal servant. The master was then allowed to return home in the role of a negotiator to arrange a ransom for his 'master'. But on getting to his own land, he revealed the deception knowing that the captors would release the servant as being of little value. But these ruses were so well known to men like Maimaran that they seldom worked any longer.

Hector sensed the Jew's scepticism. 'Please hear me out. If the Emperor discovers that a captive of such high value has slipped through his fingers, both of us will suffer.'

Maimaran bridled at the warning. Such implied threats often came from those who sought to profit from his disadvantaged status as a Jew.

'What do you think is the real value of our French prisoners?' he enquired, smoothing his black robe, then placing both hands palm down on the table in front of him.

Hector chose his words carefully. 'Have you heard of a man known as "The Lion of La Religion"?'

'Naturally. His reputation has reached us though he operates, if I recall, in the farther end of the Mediterranean.'

'What do you know of him?'

'That he is a Knight of Malta and a most virulent and implacable enemy of Islam. He is perhaps the most notorious of all the knights of the Order of St John. He has become a figure of hatred for the followers of Muhammad. They both fear and loathe him.'

'I believe he is now here in Meknes and held captive among the French prisoners from the galley.' Hector made the statement with as much certainty as he could muster.

'That, if I may say so, is hardly likely,' Maimaran replied. There was an edge of sarcasm in his voice. He was losing patience with his visitor. 'If the Order of St John knew that a leading member of their order was in the Emperor's custody, the grand council would already have opened negotiations with His Majesty for the knight's redemption.'

'That would be true if the Lion of La Religion were a knight of the Order of St John. But he is not. He belongs to the Order of St Stephen. The two orders are easily confused. They share the same symbol, the forked cross. I gather that the Order of St Stephen has almost abandoned the crusading zeal.'

'And now you tell me that this knight was aboard the French galley? That seems even more difficult to believe.' Maimaran remained incredulous.

'My informant is someone who knows the knight well, and has served under him.'

'And why has this informant not come forward before?'

'Until yesterday he was unaware that the Chevalier, as he is known, was among the prisoners.'

'And is he so sure that he is the right man that he can persuade others to believe him?' When Hector hesitated in his reply, Maimaran sensed that he had touched on a weakness in the young man's argument so he pressed his point. 'Your witness would have to give clear evidence about this so-called Chevalier's identity.'

Hector looked directly at Maimaran. 'That would be difficult,' he admitted. 'My witness is a mute. He lacks a tongue.'

Despite his usual self-restraint, Maimaran gave a derisive sniff. 'So your chief witness is dumb! How can you expect anyone to believe such a wild fiction.'

'There is evidence which supports his claim,' said Hector. He had expected that it would be difficult to convince Maimaran, and he knew his only hope of persuading him was to engage his curiosity. 'When your assistant visited the prisoners this morning, was he able to learn the name of the Frenchmen's galley?'

'Of course. Without knowing the vessel's identity, we could not begin to open negotiations with the French.'

'And that name?'

Maimaran failed to see what was the point of Hector's question. 'Surely you know yourself,' he said irritably. 'Were you not an oarsman on her crew?'

'Yes I was,' answered Hector. 'But it is important that these details come from an independent source.'

Maimaran sighed. 'The galley was named *St Gerassimus*. I thought it an unusual name when my assistant told me. But then I know little of these maritime traditions, except that the Christians often give saint's names to their ships, believing them to bring divine protection.'

'Are you familiar with the story of St Gerassimus?'

'I have not the least idea of who he was or what he did.'

'Then perhaps you will have heard of the story of Androcles and the Lion.'

'The fables of Aesop are known to me.'

'The tale of St Gerassimus is very similar. He was a Christian monk living in the desert. One day he removed a thorn from the paw of a lion, and thereafter the lion came to live with the saint, and protected him from his adversaries. Whenever anyone threatened St Gerassimus, his lion attacked his aggressors. You might say that the lion with the wounded paw became the saint's protector.'

'And now you are telling me that the Lion of La Religion is another St Gerassimus?'

'No. St Gerassimus represents the Faith, and the Chevalier sees himself as the Lion fighting to protect it.'

'And how would he have arrived at that strange vision of himself?'

'The Chevalier carries injuries on both feet. The injuries, now healed, were inflicted on him by the Muslims. According to my informant, the Chevalier was captured by Muslims early during his career. He was already known as a cruel and ruthless enemy of Islam, so they tortured him before releasing him in a prisoner exchange. Before letting him go, his captors branded the sign of the cross on the sole of each foot. It was their form of revenge for the Chevalier's fanaticism. They humiliated him by making sure that for the rest of his life, with each step that he took, he would tread on the symbol of his faith.'

Maimaran's mouth twisted in a grimace of distaste. 'And you

learned all this from your mute informant? He seems remarkably well informed.'

'He was there when the knight was tortured. He saw it for himself.'

'And why did he not suffer the same fate?'

'The Muslims took pity on him because already his tongue had been torn out.'

'And why was that?'

'He tried to explain to me but it was difficult to follow the details. But I did learn that it was the Chevalier who had ordered his mutilation.'

There was a long silence while Maimaran considered Hector's tale. The young man's claim seemed altogether too fanciful. 'Can anyone else testify to the supposed identity of this prisoner?'

Hector shook his head. 'I pulled an oar on the galley *St Gerassimus* but I never saw the Chevalier close enough to identify him now. As commander he joined the vessel shortly before we left harbour, and throughout the short voyage he stayed in his cabin or on the stern deck with the other officers. All but a handful of the other oarsmen are dead. They drowned, chained to their benches when the galley sank. Only the men on my oar bench got ashore, and one of those, a big Turk, never made it.'

'What about the other French prisoners, would they testify?'

'From what I have seen they are highly disciplined and loyal to the Chevalier. They would lie to protect him.'

'Is there anything else which makes you think this mute is telling the truth?'

Hector shook his head. 'The only other thing I can think of is the banner flown on our galley. It was the private flag of her commander. It showed the Five Wounds of Christ. Maybe that, too, referred to the injuries that the Chevalier had suffered at the hands of his enemies.'

Maimaran half-closed his eyes, and for a moment Hector thought that the elderly Jew was about to fall asleep. But the ransom broker was pondering his best course of action. If he went to Moulay with a tale that proved to be false, the Emperor was sure to fall into one of his murderous rages. Yet the young man seemed to be speaking in earnest, and there might yet be some slight substance to his extraordinary claim about the identity of one of the French prisoners. Maimaran opened his eyes and looked down at his hands. 'So what do you suggest?'

'We set a trap to unmask the Chevalier. The leader of the Frenchmen, a man named Piecourt, has twice asked for word of their capture to be sent to Jewish ransom brokers in Algiers. He tried to get a friend of mine to send this message soon after the Frenchmen were taken by the amazigh, and then yesterday Piecourt made exactly the same request to me. He mentioned the name Iphrahim Cohen. It seems that Cohen in Algiers would know who the prisoners are, and would be prepared to obtain their release.'

'And how do you set this trap?'

'The Frenchmen receive a note from Iphrahim Cohen, a note apparently smuggled in from Algiers. In the note Cohen writes that he has heard about the Chevalier's capture and has made arrangements for the Chevalier to regain his freedom before his identity is known. The note will contain details of an escape plan, the time and place.'

'And why would the Chevalier – if he is indeed in disguise among the prisoners – trust the note and not suspect a forgery?'

'Because the note will contain certain details known only to the Chevalier and the Cohens. I can supply those details.'

Maimaran reached up to readjust his black cap more comfortably before commenting quietly, 'For someone who has never met the Chevalier face to face, you seem very sure of what is in his mind.'

'If the trap fails, I will accept full responsibility for whatever goes wrong. There will be no mention of the Cohens or a forged letter. I will confess that I was paid by the Frenchmen to arrange their escape. But if the plan works, the Chevalier will have confirmed his identity.'

'I take it that you are proposing that I connive at the flight of one of his majesty's prisoners by helping forge this letter and then delivering it as if it came through the Jewish community?'

'Yes. It is the only way. Everything must be done properly. The French must not suspect anything, until they fall into the trap.'

Maimaran weighed up the young man's suggestion, then enquired, 'You realise, don't you, that even if your plan succeeds, you are asking me to compromise my relationship with my fellow Jews in Algiers? If word of this scheme gets out, the Cohens will regard me as someone who forges their correspondence for my own purposes.'

Hector's answer was sure and steady. 'The Emperor promised me that he would arrange the release of a member of my family if I served him well. If I deliver into his hands the Lion of La Religion, I will have sacrificed a Christian who is a hero to many of his own people. I will be doing this for the sake of my captured sister.'

Maimaran already knew of Hector's audacious request to Moulay Ismail for help in finding his captive sister. The young man's reckless bravado had been court gossip for several weeks. There was something about the strength and sincerity of Hector's resolve which made the old man say, 'Very well. I will prepare that forged letter if you supply the necessary details that make it seem authentic, and I will make sure that it reaches this man Piecourt. But if your scheme goes wrong, I will deny all knowledge of it . . .'

'I cannot thank you enough,' Hector began, but Maimaran held up a hand to stop him. 'Naturally I also expect some recompense for my cooperation. If the Chevalier is not a myth but a real person and is taken into custody, then I want you to give up any interest you may have in the negotiations for his full ransom which, as you say, should be very, very substantial. I alone will conduct those negotiations, and take the appropriate commission.'

'You have my word on it,' Hector assured him. 'All I want is to track down my sister and obtain her release.'

℃

AT MIDNIGHT immediately before the next new moon Hector found himself crouching with Dan at the foot of the rampart around the palace compound. He was breathing through his mouth and with shallow breaths. The ditch which ran along the outer face of the wall was used as a rubbish dump and the stench was appalling. The rotting carcasses of dead animals lay half-buried among pieces of broken pottery, discarded rags and all manner of unidentified nastiness. To make matters worse, the ditch was also a lavatory for the slave workers who by day had been repairing the wall above him. Hector feared that he had just rested his bare hand on a soft smear of recent human excrement. The advantage, he reminded himself, was that the ditch was so foul that it was avoided by the guards who occasionally patrolled the perimeter of the palace. Forty yards to his left Karp and Bourdon were also hidden. Diaz and his Spanish cavalry friend Roberto lay in wait in the opposite direction.

'We don't know exactly where Piecourt and the others will attempt to cross, so we need to cover as broad a section of the wall as possible,' he had told his companions that morning. 'I expect they will use the ladders which I saw in their cell to scale the inner face of the wall. Once on top of the wall, they will be able to dangle a rope on the far side and descend. The most likely place is where they themselves have been working during the day on their slave shift. They were repairing a section where the baked earth facing is crumbled away, and here the damaged wall offers a series of footholds. Once they are safely down, they only have to get across the ditch at the foot of the wall and then make their way to one of the villages in the valley. They will be expecting to meet a guide who will take them across country to the coast where a ship will be waiting to pick them up.'

'What makes you think that they will attempt their escape this evening?' Diaz had asked.

'Because there is no moon, and because tomorrow is the feast day of one of the local marabouts or holy men so the Muslim guards will be preparing their celebrations.'

'What happens if a whole gang of prisoners swarms down the ropes? There are not enough of us to deal with all of them.' It was Diaz's cavalry friend Roberto who spoke. He was checking over the pair of pistols that Hector had provided, weapons Hector had borrowed from the Arsenal without consulting Sean Allen.

'There should be only three men, perhaps four,' Hector had reassured the Spaniard. 'In the letter they have received, they have been told that the guide refuses to take more than three men at a time because a large group would be too noticeable as it made its way across country.'

'Let's hope the Frenchmen heed that advice,' the Spaniard had grunted. 'I don't fancy facing a whole lot of them with just a pistol in my hand and no back-up.'

'Try not to harm any of them,' Hector had reminded him. 'We want to take them alive.'

As the hours of darkness had dragged past, Hector was becoming aware of a flaw in his plan. He had failed to take into account the incessant howling and barking of the city's population of dogs. As one pack of dogs fell silent, another group started up, filling the night with their clamour of useless noise and evoking a counter chorus which slowly faded away, only for some lone animal to howl plaintively and start the whole process over again. The racket made it impossible to hear the sounds of anyone who might be scrambling down the wall across the ditch from him, and the face of the wall was so obscured in the gloom that his eyes played tricks on him. Several times he had imagined a shadowy movement, only to be disappointed when, after a long interval, all remained dark and still.

Beside him Dan seemed impervious to the long wait. The Miskito was squatting on his heels, not moving. Hector, by contrast, was obliged to shift his legs from one position to another whenever he felt the first warning twinge of cramp. And as the wait grew longer, Hector grew more and more fretful. He had expected something to have happened by now. He wondered if Piecourt and the others had become suspicious of the note they had received, or if they had decided it would be better to wait for the Franciscans to arrange their ransom. He looked up at the stars, trying to calculate how long he and his companions had been lying in ambush. It was a clear night with only a few shreds of high thin clouds, and he could easily identify the constellations he had studied on the star globe in Turgut Reis's library. It seemed so long ago that he and Dan had been held in the Algiers bagnio and discussed the possibility of their own escape. Now he was trying to prevent the escape of others. Everything seemed to have assumed a different shape. Back in Algiers he had told himself that he must survive the bagnio so that he would be free to track down his sister Elizabeth. Yet he had always known such an ambition was a fantasy. Now, however, he found that he was allowing himself to believe genuinely that he might locate her. He struggled to justify the reason for this new hope. Partly it was because he knew from Sean Allen that Hakim Reis's ship might put into port one day, and he would have the chance to interview her captain. Yet there was something else which was making him more optimistic: he sensed that at last he was gaining control of his own fate, albeit slowly, and that he was no longer at the mercy of others.

A light touch on his hand interrupted his thoughts. It was

Dan. The Miskito had not moved for so long that Hector had almost forgotten his presence. Now Dan was pointing upward. Hector looked towards the top of the rampart. For a second he glimpsed a shape, the outline of a man's head, dark against the starry sky. The town dogs had renewed their howling, so he could hear nothing except their uproar. He kept absolutely still, gazing up towards the parapet. Time passed, and he wondered if he had been mistaken. Then Dan tapped him again on the hand twice, then once more. A moment later Hector could make out two heads against the sky and, almost immediately the head and shoulders of a third man who was leaning out, looking downwards cautiously. Hector felt for the loaded pistol that he had placed beside him, slid his fingers around the butt of the weapon, and waited.

There was a faint sound, so close now that he heard it over the distant crying of the dogs, a gentle slap. Hector guessed that it must be the sound of a rope's end knocking against the wall as it dropped from above. He strained his eyes, trying to see the rope, but the outer face of the wall was in shadow from the starlight and he could see nothing. Looking upward he again detected movement, and this time he was certain. There was the dark outline of someone clambering out over the edge of the wall. The man, whoever it was, was starting his descent. Hector calculated that he would reach the ground about ten yards to the right of where he and Dan lay in wait. Still he did not move.

The figure passed into shadow and disappeared. Hector found that he was gripping the butt of the pistol so tightly that his fingers were numb. Gently he relaxed his grip. He no longer smelled the stench of the ditch. All his senses were concentrated on trying to gauge just how far down the rope the man had come, and to identify the spot where he would touch the ground. No more than half a minute later he heard a noise which he supposed was the sound of someone setting his feet carefully on the edge of the ditch. The base of the wall was so deep in shadow that Hector imagined, rather than saw, the dark shape of a man now standing and waiting there.

A scrabbling sound, and Hector realised that he had missed the start of the descent of a second man. He was already halfway down the rope and descending more swiftly than the first. The second man reached the ground even as Hector was coming to realise that he might have miscalculated badly, and had placed Diaz and his Spanish friend too far away to have noticed what was happening. He feared that they were too distant to help once the trap was sprung. Momentarily Hector dithered, his mind whirling. He did not know if he should act as soon as the next man reached the ground – he was now halfway down the wall – or wait to see if there were other escapees, more than the original three. He feared that if he delayed too long, those who were already on the ground would cross the ditch and escape into the darkness. And if they included the Chevalier, he might never be recaptured.

Hector came to a decision. He rose to his feet and called out, 'Stand where you are or you will be shot.' Hastily he climbed up the slope of the ditch, and ran to the point where he faced directly across to the three men. Dan was at his heels. The three fugitives remained in the deep black shadow at the foot of the wall and it was impossible to make them out distinctly. He hoped that there was enough starlight for them to see that he and Dan both held pistols.

There was silence from across the ditch.

'Now come across towards me, one by one,' Hector ordered.

The first shadow moved, stepped out into the starlight. Immediately Hector knew it was Yakup, the rowing master. The man's squat shape was unmistakable as he made his way down into the ditch, slipping slightly, then squelched his way across and clambered up until he stood in front of the young Irishman. Yakup exuded such a sense of raw physical power that a prickle of fear ran up Hector's spine, and he retreated a pace. 'Come no closer! Step over there and lie face down on the ground,' he ordered, motioning with his pistol. He heard movement over to his right, thankfully Diaz and the Spanish cavalryman were coming to his aid.

'And the next,' Hector called out. 'Move slowly. No tricks.'

A second dark figure detached itself from the shadows and began to make its way across the ditch. When the man climbed up level with him, Hector saw what he had expected: it was the tall stranger, the man with the speckled cheek, whom he had twice seen in Piecourt's company. 'Stand still, just where you are,' he commanded again. Then, speaking over his shoulder to Diaz who had joined them, he added, 'Keep your eye on this one and don't hesitate to shoot.'

He was certain that the third man in the shadow was Piecourt himself. There was a note of triumph in his voice as he called out, 'Now, comite, it's your turn,' and he watched as the third of the escapees made his way across the ditch and stood obediently in front of his captors. Hector felt the tension ebbing. His ambush had succeeded just as he had planned.

Piecourt was peering into his face and speaking. 'So my dogs have betrayed me,' he said. He must have recognised Dan and Bourdon as well, for he murmured, 'Bench three. I always suspected that you were trouble. What will you do with us now?'

'Hand you over to the guards,' said Hector.

'And then?'

'Tomorrow someone will decide your punishment for attempting to escape.' The words were hardly out of his mouth when he was roughly brushed aside. Someone had run up behind him and shoved him out of the way. His foot slipped on the edge of the ditch and for a moment he was off balance, sliding sideways. He half-turned and saw Karp. The expression on Karp's face in the half-light was frightening. His mouth was a dark hole from which emerged a yowling scream. For a ghastly moment Hector was reminded of a stray dog howling at the moon, though the sound that Karp made was more piteous. The Bulgar was moving with shocking speed. His hands reached out. A moment later he had seized the tall stranger by the throat. The force of the lunge knocked the man off his feet and he fell backward, Karp on top of him. In appalled astonishment Hector, Dan and the others stood gaping as the two men writhed on the ground while Karp tried to throttle his victim. Piecourt was the first to recover his senses. He lashed out at Hector, who was still off balance so that Hector fell back on one knee. Whirling round, Piecourt swung an arm at Dan standing guard with his pistol, and forced the Miskito to duck. Then Piecourt took to his heels, running directly away from the wall and heading towards the distant village. Dan straightened up, coolly raised his pistol and called out. 'Stop or I shoot!' When Piecourt failed to respond, Dan pulled the trigger. There was a bright flash, a spurt of red and yellow sparks, followed by the flat explosion of the shot. Thirty yards away the fleeing shadow tumbled forward.

Neither the pistol shot nor Bourdon's whoop of delight had any effect on Karp. He had succeeded in pinning his victim on his back, and was kneeling on his victim's chest with his hands still around the stranger's throat. His frenzied yelling had given way to low, fierce growls as he tried to kill his opponent with his bare hands. 'Karp! Karp! Leave him alone! Let him be!' Hector bellowed in Karp's ear. But the Bulgar was oblivious to Hector's shouts. He bore down with his full weight and was shaking his victim's head from side to side. Hector seized Karp by the shoulder and tried to restrain him. 'No, Karp! No!' he yelled. But it was useless. Karp was in a red mist of rage. In desperation Hector threw an arm round Karp and tried to drag him back, using all his strength. But Karp was berserk. 'Help me, Dan. Help me get Karp under control,' Hector gasped, and with Dan's assistance he wrestled the Bulgar away from his opponent who now lay choking and groaning on the ground.

'Control yourself Karp,' Hector begged. The Bulgar was

sobbing in distress. He was sucking in great gasps of air through his mangled mouth. Tears of rage were streaming down his cheeks, and he was still trembling. 'Everything's under control, Karp,' Hector reassured him. 'You will have your revenge.' Karp gave a gurgling choking sound, and turned his face away. To Hector's utter amazement, the Bulgar dropped to his knees and began to pray. He was weeping uncontrollably.

Hector helped the stranger up. The man was still in a state of shock, appalled by the naked ferocity of the assault. He was unsteady on his feet, coughing and wheezing as he massaged his bruised throat. 'Remember what you did to Karp, Chevalier. You could not have expected less,' Hector said. The stranger did not answer at once, but waited until he had regained his self-control. Then he raised his head and, looking straight at Hector, snapped, 'I should have strung up the villain when I had the chance. But such a death was too gentle for him.'

Dimly Hector became aware of Diaz's voice. The Spaniard was cursing steadily and fluently. 'He got clean away, the bastard,' Diaz was lamenting. He was rubbing his elbow. The rowing master was nowhere to be seen. 'We thought the pair of us had him under control, but the man has the strength of a bull. He took advantage of the commotion and jumped up off the ground and knocked both pistols out of my hands. When I tried to grab him, he twisted out of my grip as if I was a child. Then he dealt Roberto such a clout on the head that he was dizzy for minutes. By the time I recovered my guns, the brute had bolted. It was too late to take a shot at him and, besides, you had your hands full over here with Karp and his friend. I thought it better to come and help you secure the one bird that we had in the hand. There was no need to worry about that fellow Dan picked off. From the way he fell, I'd say he won't get up again.'

'Let's get away from here,' said Hector, suddenly feeling very weary. 'We've got the prisoner we were looking for, and the guard will arrive any minute. They must have heard Dan's shot and all the commotion. We can leave them to find Piecourt whether he's dead or only wounded. He never lifted a hand to help us, so now we'll repay him the compliment. Tomorrow I'll find out just what our captive is worth.'

ℂ

'TEN THOUSAND louis d'or, that's the ransom that I will be demanding for the Chevalier. I congratulate you,' said Maimaran. The Jew had sent word for Hector to meet him in the imperial treasury, and Hector was astounded by the contrast with the Jew's humble home. Maimaran was waiting for him in a reception chamber whose barbaric opulence was hidden deep in the palace compound. Sunlight poured in through the fine fretwork of arched windows and threw patterns across a tessellated floor of white, blue and red. The walls were hung with arrays of sabres, shields and muskets inlaid with gold and mother of pearl. Several iron chests, bolted and padlocked, stood against one wall. 'His true identity is Adrien Chabrillan, Knight Commander of the Order of St Stephen of Tuscany. He also holds various lesser titles of nobility and rank including the honorary rank of captain in the Galley Corps of France. As you rightly surmised, he is also known as the Lion of La Religion. The Emperor is away for a few days so I have not yet informed him of his captive's identity, but I know that he will be very pleased. It will enhance his reputation as a champion of Islam as well as make a very significant contribution to his treasury.' Maimaran nodded towards the iron-bound chests. 'The Emperor always needs money. His expenses are voracious, and his revenues unpredictable. The ransom of Chevalier Chabrillan will ensure a steady stream of income for quite some time.'

'I had no idea that the Chevalier could be worth so much.'

Maimaran gave a tight smile. 'His Majesty leaves it to me to act as the unofficial comptroller of his finances, and to maintain a balance between income and expenditure. The sum of ten thousand louis d'or is so enormous that it will take several years to raise. Doubtless Chevalier Chabrillan has friends and family who will advance what they can, and their contributions can be added to the sale of the more valuable possessions that he either inherited or accumulated over years of cruising against the Muslims. But that preliminary effort will raise no more than a down payment and will have to be followed by annual payments – perhaps for as much as another ten years. His supporters and family might even have to borrow additional funds from financiers, such as the Cohens in Algiers.' There was a hint of satisfaction to his voice as he added, 'If the Cohens charge their usual ten per cent interest, it will lessen any resentment should they ever discover that their name was used to trap the Chevalier.'

'And what will happen to him while all this ransom is being collected?'

'As long as the payments keep arriving, he will be kept closely confined and well treated. No one wants to see him perish. But should the flow of payments cease or slow to a trickle, then his conditions of imprisonment will worsen, and he will be given the opportunity to inform his family of his suffering. That should help loosen the purse strings once again.'

'And what about the other men who tried to escape with him? Do you know what happened to them?'

Maimaran glanced meaningfully at one of the muskets displayed on the wall. 'Your companion, the one with the dark skin, is an excellent shot. The man he brought down with his pistol died this morning. The pistol ball broke his spine.'

'And what about the other one? There was a third man who ran away. Has he been caught?'

'Not yet, as far as I know. But he won't get far. He is on his own and in a strange country. The commander of the palace guard has sent word to all the surrounding villages that a watch is to be kept for him. The commander wants him caught before the Emperor returns to Meknes, because it will look bad for him if a slave has been allowed to escape.' Maimaran broke off for a moment as he reached out to readjust a pile of ledgers on an elegant table inlaid with mother of pearl. 'But I did not ask you to come here to talk about the fate of the runaways. You told me earlier that you were trying to trace your sister who, you believe, might be captive in Morocco, and for this reason you wished to render a great service to the Emperor. Now that you have succeeded in the first part of that ambition, I was wondering what you planned to do next, and if there is any way in which I might help. You've made my task as comptroller of royal finances much easier, and I feel that I am in your debt.'

Hector looked around the strange disorder of valuables on display. There were enormous ostrich feather fans, heaps of costly rugs, beautifully worked saddles, an intricate-looking clock lying on its back on the floor, several looking glasses in gilded frames, a leopard skin. He guessed they were items of tribute rendered to the Emperor or seized by Moulay from his hapless subjects, and he remembered that Sean Allen had mentioned how Hakim Reis occasionally brought gunpowder as tribute to the Emperor.

'Do you know a ship captain by the name of Hakim Reis?' he asked.

'Another seafarer with piratical habits,' commented Maimaran softly. 'You seem to have a broad knowledge of such people.'

'I was wondering if you knew how I could contact him.'

To his disappointment, the comptroller replied, 'I've never met him myself. He usually stays with his ship down on the coast, at Sallee, and is tactful enough to send his Majesty some little curiosity by way of a gift. You see that clock over there, not the one on the floor, but on that far table. That is one of his presents which he sent to Meknes. It was made in London, and taken out of an English merchant ship that Hakim and his fellow corsairs waylaid off the coast of Spain. Naturally I keep a record of all such gifts. His Majesty has a habit of suddenly enquiring what happened to particular items. He has a remarkable memory.'

'Sean Allen said the same about the weapons he has to preserve in the armoury, even if they are so old that they are useless. He told me that he gets them also from Hakim Reis who in turn is supplied by someone called Tisonne or Tison. Do those names mean anything to you?'

There was a pause, and Hector's hopes rose very slightly as Maimaran said slowly, 'A name like that is vaguely familiar. I seem to remember hearing it in relation to the emperor's finances, but I cannot remember exactly where. However . . .' Then he reached towards his pile of ledgers and selecting a volume began to turn the pages, before he continued, 'This should tell me.'

Hector watched the old man fastidiously read down the columns until Maimaran gave a little satisfied grunt and said, 'I thought so. Here it is. A substantial payment in the name of Tison. The money was paid two years ago.'

'Was it for weapons? For gunpowder?' Hector asked eagerly. 'Sean Allen said that Hakim Reis obtained these materials from Tison or Tisonne. Does the ledger give any details who he is or where he might be found?'

'I'm sorry to disappoint you, young man,' said Maimaran, looking up from the page, 'but this entry is nothing to do with guns or smuggling. It relates to a horse, and if you want to find out more about it you need to go to the royal stables.'

NINETEEN

'A HORSE!' Diaz wiped his mouth with the back of his hand as he set down his drink. Hector had waited for the Spanish cavalryman's next visit to Sean Allen's office to ask his help in solving the mystery of the entry for Tison in Maimaran's account books. 'I wonder what the old Jew was referring to. I can't think what he meant.'

'You've never heard of Tison or Tisonne yourself?' Hector enquired.

'Yes, of course. Every Spaniard has,' Diaz replied cheerfully and, reaching down, picked up his sword and slapped it on the table. 'This is a *tison*, though in Castile we pronounce it *tizon*. It's a word for a sword, and celebrates one of the most famous weapons in our history. Our greatest hero, El Cid, possessed two swords; one was called Tizon, the other Colada. Every schoolboy is made to learn the poem of El Cid by heart. Even now I can still remember the line,' and he flung out an arm dramatically as he recited. 'Well worth a thousand golden marks was the great sword Tizon.'

'What did El Cid do with his sword?'

Diaz looked at Hector in astonishment. 'You don't know the story of El Cid?'

'No.'

'Six hundred years ago he helped drive back the Moors and used Tizon and Colada to do the job. According to legend, each sword was half as long again as the span of a man's arms, and its blade so broad and heavy that only El Cid could wield it in battle.'

'Then it seems strange to find a "tizon" in the stables of a devout Muslim prince. You would have thought it more likely that the great sword was kept here in the armoury or on display somewhere in Moulay's palace. Only yesterday Maimaran showed me various trophies that Moulay has put on show to celebrate his victories over the Christians.'

Diaz grimaced. 'Probably looted them from Spanish towns he captured in the north. Still, the only way to solve the puzzle is by going to the stables themselves. If Sean can spare you, we can set out right now. Just as soon as I finish this drink.'

DOZENS OF GROOMS and ostlers were busy bedding down the horses for the night when Diaz and Hector arrived at the stables. The air was heavy with pungent stable smells, squads of slaves were spreading fresh straw and carrying buckets of water to replenish drinking troughs, and Hector could hear the stamping of hooves and the snuffling of the animals as they waited hopefully for an evening feed. Diaz led him straight to meet the stable master, a small wizened Moor who must have been at least seventy years old and walked with a heavy limp which was the result, according to Diaz, of a riding accident. 'Haddu is from one of the desert tribes who are great horse handlers and breeders. He has been here since the first day Moulay began building his stables. Recently Moulay wanted to make him a kaid, a nobleman, as a reward for his services. But Haddu refused. He told the Emperor that he didn't want to be a kaid. Moulay was about to get very angry at being snubbed – you could see his eyes going red – but then Haddu added that he preferred horses to men and, as you know, Moulay likes his cats better than his servants, so he merely laughed and turned away.'

Unfortunately for Hector and Diaz, the stable master found it difficult to understand exactly what his visitors wanted. Hector and Diaz took it in turns to try to explain, but they had no success. Haddu looked from one to the other, increasingly puzzled. 'Tison? Tizon? Tisonne?' Hector repeated, trying every pronunciation he could think of. 'The Emperor's treasurer told me that he found the word Tison written in his ledgers, and it was something to do with a horse.'

'I know nothing about any Tison,' said the stable master, 'but everything to do with the royal horses will be found in the section of the stables reserved for the Emperor's animals. If we look there, perhaps you will discover your answer.'

The three men walked across to the imperial stable block that Hector remembered from his previous visit. There Haddu led them between the long lines of open stalls. The animals peered at them curiously, their ears pricked forward, heads turning to follow the progress of their visitors. Haddu stopped often to stroke a nose or scratch between a horse's ears. He knew the name and breeding of every animal, and all the while he delivered a running commentary about the creature's history and character. This horse came from the amazigh, the next was a present from the Caliph in Egypt, another was very elderly and stiff in the joints now but had been to Mecca and was sacred. Eventually they came to the last section of the stalls which, Haddu explained, was where the Emperor's own riding animals were stabled. These horses were kept exercised and fit, ready for Moulay to ride in procession and state occasions. Hector and Diaz looked at each one and complimented the stable master on the good condition of the animals. It was when they had reached the very last animal in the line that Diaz stopped dead, and then slapped his forehead and gave a cry of triumph. 'What an idiot I am,' he exclaimed. 'This is what

Maimaran must have meant.' Turning to the stable master, he asked, 'How long have you had this horse here?'

'Some two years. It is a most unusual animal, one of the Emperor's particular favourites. He would have had to pay a great deal of money for it because such horses occur very infrequently. This one has proved not only beautiful but easy to train. It is truly a gem.'

Diaz looked across at Hector. 'All that talk of El Cid's great sword distracted me. The clerk who wrote up that ledger Maimaran showed you didn't know very much about horses. He put down "tison" when, more correctly, he should have written "tiznado". The two words are both to do with the ashes or embers in a fire. Do you remember that evening when we watched the fantasia? Moulay himself was riding the three lead horses in the main squadron. He put on a great display, and I remember one of my colleagues, another cavalryman, spoke admiringly of the tiznado. I didn't know what he was talking about, and he explained that it was a word used in the Spanish colonies to describe a horse of a particular colour. This is just such a horse, a rarity, come and see for yourself.'

Hector went up to the stall. He found himself face to face with a handsome stallion who looked back at him, head held high, an intelligent gleam in its eye. The creature was strongly built with a powerful chest and a short back, clean legs and neat small hooves. Every line of its body told of speed and stamina. But what was truly eye-catching was the creature's coat. It had been brushed until it shone. The background colour was a pale grey, and scattered over it were dozens and dozens of small black spots. It was the horse that Moulay Ismail had been riding at the fantasia.

ℂ

'I COULD HAVE saved you the trip,' commented Bourdon when they got back to Sean Allen's office in the Armoury and reported on their visit to the stables. 'A spotted horse is called a tisonne in French. I know that because I once worked at an inn on the outskirts of Paris. I was only a youngster and the lowest of the low, so I was given the job of cleaning out the grates and fireplaces. Sometimes I had to climb halfway up the chimneys to get them swept. One of the local aristocrats, a vicomte, had a dog of that same speckled colour which had been trained to run along beside his carriage when he went driving out from the chateau. It was just showing off because the dog was a real eye-catcher with its black and white coat. Sometimes the vicomte stopped at the inn to take refreshment, and I remember one of the other inn servants took a great liking to the dog. He would pet the animal and feed it titbits. He had his own name for it. He called it Tisonne, and said his master really should have a tisonne horse to match. For a joke he sometimes even called me a tisonne saying that I had the white and pasty skin of a city dweller and was covered with specks of smut and soot from the fire.'

At that moment the door to the gun founder's office swung open and Diaz's friend Roberto burst into the room. There was a triumphant expression on his face. 'They got him!' he exulted. 'They got that apelike bruiser who escaped us. I just heard.'

'Yakup, the rowing master, may he rot in hell,' said Bourdon after Hector translated the Spaniard's announcement. 'Let's have a celebration. But speak slowly so that Hector can tell me the details as you go along.'

Roberto sat down on the bench and launched into his tale with relish. 'Apparently he managed to hide himself away in the countryside until by chance he was glimpsed by some locals when he came into a village to steal food. He beat up one of the villagers very badly, almost killed him. But he got himself lost and started wandering in circles. As luck would have it, he blundered into the path of Moulay Ismail's cavalcade as it was returning to the city. The Black Guards managed to overpower him and bring him before Moulay. It seems that the Emperor was in a foul mood. When the prisoner was brought before him, he flew into an even more vile temper. Moulay was so enraged by the sign of the cross on the rowing master's forehead that he ordered the Black Guard to toss the rowing master into the bottom of a nearby ravine, and if he tried to scramble out, they were to push him back with their spears. Moulay then turned to his son, that brat Ahmad who is called "the golden one", and told him that he needed to improve his shooting skills and that it was time he tried out his new muskets.'

'I know all about those,' interjected the gun founder. 'I adapted a pair of guns specially for the lad. He's only about ten years old though tall and lanky for his age. Dan here trimmed down the stocks to size, and fitted the latest locks.'

'Dan did a good job because the guns never misfired. Young Ahmad stood on the edge of the ravine and took one pot shot after another at the rowing master as he scrambled among the rocks and bushes trying to dodge. You could hear the bullets skipping off the rocks. Moulay himself stood watching, shouting advice and encouragement. When one of the Black Guards whose job was to reload the muskets was too slow, Moulay whipped out his sword and chopped off the man's fingers. Eventually young Ahmad succeeded in knocking over the rowing master with a lucky shot, but his target managed to get back on his feet. It took another three musket balls to bring him down for good. Moulay then gave orders that the corpse was to be flayed, and the skin nailed up on the city gates to discourage other runaways.'

'A fitting end for the bastard,' observed Bourdon. 'Let's drink to the eternal damnation of all rowing masters. When they arrive in Hell, may they be chained to red-hot oar handles, lashed with whips made from bulls' pizzles pickled in brine, and suffer from swollen piles whenever they fall back on the rowing bench.'

Hector noticed that Karp had been listening, his eyes flicking from one speaker to the next. With Piecourt and the rowing master both dead, the Chevalier seemed to have got off lightly, and Hector recalled the Chabrillan's sour remark that hanging would have been too gentle a death for the Bulgar. 'Karp, there are some questions I have to ask the Chevalier,' he said. 'I'm going to try to get permission to visit him in his cell. Do you want to come along?'

Karp gave a gagging sound and shook his head vehemently. Hector thought it strange that he looked not angry, but ashamed.

℃

CHEVALIER ADRIEN CHABRILLAN'S prison was close to the imperial menagerie. Hector could hear the coughing roars of the lions and a strange high-pitched whooping which he took to be the call of some exotic bird as he approached. The low featureless building looked from the outside like a servants' dormitory, and the sprawling imperial compound was such a maze of pavilions, mosques, guardhouses, stores, walkways and courtyards that, without the help of a guide provided by Joseph Maimaran, Hector would never have arrived at the Chevalier's cell on the ground floor. Only when he went inside and was brought to a heavy wooden door guarded by a suspicious goaler did Hector appreciate that Chevalier Chabrillan was, in effect, hidden away from the rest of the world.

The guard unlocked the door with a heavy iron key, and stood back to allow Hector to enter the cell alone. The room was simply furnished with a mattress on a low bed frame, a wooden table and two chairs, and a chamber pot. A blanket lay neatly folded on the mattress, and the only light entered through a small, barred window high up in the wall opposite the door. Hector noted that the wall itself was two feet thick. The room reminded him of a monk's cell, an impression strengthened by the fact that its lone occupant was kneeling in prayer, facing a simple wooden cross nailed to the wall.

The turnkey closed the door behind Hector, but the kneeling figure did not stir. The man was dressed in a loose cotton gown, and once again Hector found himself staring in fascination at the cross-shaped scars on the soles of his naked feet. Finally, after several minutes, the prisoner rose and turned to face his visitor. For the first time Hector saw the Chevalier close up in daylight and he was taken aback by the contemptuous stare. 'I gave orders that I would receive visitors only if they were here to discuss the conditions of my incarceration,' said Chabrillan. 'If I am not mistaken, you are an associate of that tongueless heretic. You will be disappointed if you came here to gloat. I have nothing to discuss with you.'

'I want only a few moments of your time,' said Hector civilly, marvelling at the unshakeable self-confidence of the Chevalier. He did not harbour any hatred for the man, now that he knew Chabrillan was very likely to be held prisoner for many years. 'I did not come to take pleasure from seeing your captivity. I only hope to understand why this has come about.'

'I would have thought that was obvious,' Chabrillan snapped. 'The schismatic wanted revenge. But it will make no difference in the eyes of God. I may remain here for many years, but he will spend all eternity in the fires of Hell.'

'He seemed so harmless until—' Hector began, but he was cut off in mid sentence by a snort of disdain.

'Harmless! That viper! He is no more harmless than the Satan whose path he follows, and whose poison he was injecting into others until I had his tongue removed.'

'But Karp could never have been a threat to someone as powerful and well connected as yourself.'

Chabrillan regarded Hector scornfully. 'What do you know about these things?' Belatedly Hector realised that he had come with the intention of questioning Chabrillan, but was already deferring to the aristocrat's arrogance. He resolved to stand his ground.

'Karp told me that you had his tongue torn out when you were both in Kandia.'

'Told? How could he have told you anything? He lacks

the means to do so.' This time there was a note of cruelty in Chabrillan's tone.

'He did so by dumb show. He also drew a map and tried to make me understand that you have the sign of the cross marked on the soles of your feet. At the time it made no sense.'

'And did he also tell you that he is a traitor to Christendom, a festering contagion eating away at the True Faith?'

Abruptly Chabrillan turned away. For several moments there was silence as if he was considering whether to put an end to the interview. Then he swung round to face his visitor, and in a flinty voice said, 'Kandia was where we took our stand against the Turk. There were thousands of us who believed that it was our sacred duty to hold the bastion. The rest of the island had already fallen, but the city itself held out month after month, year after year. Venice sent us supplies and reinforcements, and her fleet kept the sea-lanes open. I and other knights came with our galleys to try to stiffen the resistance shortly before the end. Doubtless that was when Karp wormed his way in. He was among the volunteers who arrived from all over Europe to assist us.'

'Karp is from the Bulgar lands ruled by the Turks. He would have risked his life to get to Kandia,' agreed Hector. He had intended to encourage the flow of the Chevalier's narrative but his remark only brought an angry retort.

'And that should have made me beware! He is no more a Christian than that blackamoor who guards my cell door. His homeland is a wellspring of heresy. From there the pestilence oozes and threatens to infect all.'

'I don't follow your meaning,' Hector muttered.

Chabrillan's lip curled. 'How would you understand? Am I right in guessing that you have taken the turban and your manhood has been trimmed?'

'I did convert when I was in the bagnio of Algiers,' Hector acknowledged, 'but only in the hope that it would ease my captivity. My faith has lapsed since then, both in the teachings of Muhammad and in the religion I was taught as a child by monks. They were good men who knew their gospel.'

'What would those monks say if they knew you had lifted a forefinger and pronounced that there is no God but Allah, and that Muhammad is his prophet,' Chabrillan sneered. 'In that benighted corner perhaps your monks have not yet heard the serpent's hiss, those who preach that Satan is the creator and ruler of the visible world. They deny the Holy Cross and refuse to worship the Virgin Mary and the Saints. That is what Karp and his foul companions do. They claim that the Romish Church is not the Church of Jesus Christ but a Harlot, while only they themselves hold to the truth.'

'But if men like Karp came to fight at Kandia alongside you, what mattered was their hatred of the Turk.'

'Karp did not come to Kandia to fight. He came to convert. He persuaded others in our garrison that atonement and redemption were meaningless, that the sacrament of unction was to be spurned because it is reserved for the rich, that every good layman is himself a priest. His blasphemy was endless.'

Hector felt he was getting nowhere. The Chevalier was clearly a fanatic, but that did not seem sufficient reason for him to have mutilated Karp, a fellow Christian, in the midst of a gruelling and prolonged siege. 'What reason did you give when you ordered Karp's tongue to be removed?' he asked.

'I needed no authority. Karp had attached himself to my troops in the guise of a cook, and he was under my command. It was enough that he was preaching disobedience, not only to Mother Church but to military authority and to natural order. He would have my men lay down their arms and renounce all violence. They were to call themselves "dear to God", and trust to prayer. That was sedition. So I stopped his mouth. I made an example of him so that others should take warning.'

'And how did he come to lose his nose and ears as well?'

Chabrillan gave a shrug as if Hector's question was

superfluous. 'When Kandia fell, the Turks allowed us to leave unmolested. I took Karp with me as a slave, intending to keep him as an oarsman on my galley. I felt that his punishment was not yet served out. Later he tried to run away. He lost his ears and nose for that. My comite carried out the sentence.'

'Piecourt is dead,' said Hector flatly.

'Then he will have his just reward,' replied Chabrillan. 'He always followed the true doctrine of the Christ, of the Gospel, and the Apostles.'

'And the scars on your feet? How did you suffer them?'

'In Christ's service,' answered the Chevalier grimly. Deliberately and rudely, he looked at the wall over Hector's head. 'The Venetians had agreed secretly that I alone of all the defenders of Kandia was to be handed over to the Turks. The infidels wished to take revenge for an earlier incident in my struggle against them. They mistook Karp for my personal slave and arranged that he dress my wounds after they had finished with me.'

'Is that when you first met Hakim Reis?'

Hector's question had a remarkable effect. Chabrillan dropped his gaze and stared hard at Hector. The Chevalier's supercilious manner had been replaced by a long, calculating appraisal of his visitor. After a lengthy pause he said softly, 'I thought that it was the Cohens in Algiers who had betrayed me.'

'The Cohens had nothing to do with it. They probably do not even know that you were taken prisoner from the *St Gerassimus* or where you are now.'

'Then who wrote that letter promising our escape?'

'It was prepared here in Meknes.'

Chabrillan's eyes searched Hector's face. Hector could tell that the Chevalier was struggling to work out the events of the past few days. 'Then Karp was the mischief-maker. But I don't remember that he ever laid eyes on Hakim Reis. And it is strange that he knew Hakim is expected soon in Sallee. From

Kandia onwards Karp has been nothing more than a mute beast, pulling an oar.'

'It was not Karp who prepared the letter,' Hector assured him. 'He recognised you by the scars on your feet, and identified you as the Lion of La Religion, but nothing more. As for Hakim Reis, no one knows when he will next visit Sallee.'

'Yet the message said that Hakim Reis would be waiting to pick me up.'

Hector decided that this was his moment to press forward. The Chevalier was off guard and might be shocked into a confession. He watched for his reaction as he said, 'I needed to confirm that you had dealt with Hakim Reis in the past and that you would expect him to connive at your escape. I had to be sure of my evidence.'

Chabrillan did not move a muscle. His eyes never left Hector's face as he asked, 'And what evidence was that?'

'First, the gunpowder in the magazine. It is a special pistol powder, impossible to manufacture in Barbary. It was not damaged or damp as if it had been captured at sea. The powder was in a keg, in perfect condition, fresh from the makers. I had seen similar kegs aboard the *St Gerassimus*. The gun founder Sean Allen said that the gunpowder had come from Hakim Reis, who in turn may have got it from a smuggler called Tisonne. That was when I first heard the name. Later a friend of mine, working in Moulay's armoury, came across some shoddy muskets made for the export market. Again the gun founder said that he had obtained the weapons from Hakim Reis.' Hector waited for several seconds before adding, 'I presume you got those marks on your cheek when a faulty musket barrel exploded in your face. Were you giving a demonstration of the weapon, and did Hakim accept the shipment?'

For a moment Hector thought he had broken through Chabrillan's calm detachment. The Chevalier moved a hand as if to touch the scatter of blue specks on his cheek, but then changed his mind.

TIM SEVERIN

'I shared an oar bench with a man with exactly that colour of mark on his cheek,' Hector added. 'He is marked with the letters GAL for galerien. He had told me that when the brand was first scorched into his flesh, it was made permanent by rubbing gunpowder in the fresh burn.'

'You seem to have an abundance of low-life friends,' Chabrillan remarked witheringly.

'Someone else said that to me recently,' Hector acknowledged, but then moved on. 'It was not until I learned that tisonne is a word for a horse with a spotted skin that I made the connection. My guess is that Hakim Reis gave you that cover name, and that you enjoyed the coincidence that tizon is also the name for a weapon which the heroic El Cid wielded against Muslims.'

'You have a very vivid imagination,' said Chabrillan. It was evident that he had regained his composure fully. 'Why should it matter to you that I am this Tisonne. I am held in this cell because I am a knight of the Order of St Stephen of Tuscany, not because weapons and gunpowder reached Meknes.'

'I will come to that in a moment,' Hector answered him. 'But there is something else which must come first, something more important than arms smuggling.'

'Please continue.' Chabrillan's voice dripped with sarcasm.

'Hakim Reis has the reputation of a lucky man. He always seems to be at the right place and at the right time. His galley intercepts merchant shipping with uncanny accuracy, and he is first on the scene when a peace treaty breaks down and a Barbary state reverts to piracy. It is as if someone highly placed in the councils of his victims is supplying him with vital information. I believe that informant was you.'

'And why should I do that?'

'That is what I did not understand until you told me why you had Karp's tongue removed: you nurse a violent hatred for those who you see as enemies of your Church, whoever they are, whether Muslims or dissenters. You would damage them in whatever way you can.'

Hector could feel Chabrillan's arrogance returning. It was like a physical force radiating from the aristocrat, his absolute certainty that his cause was correct, and that his breeding and privilege placed him above others.

'As a turncoat you would not understand,' Chabrillan said, his voice contemptuous. 'Christendom will prevail. But first it must cure itself of the heresies within. That is where the real and present danger lies. Schismatics and agnostics gnaw at the heart of Mother Church. Men like Karp must be rooted out. Nations who would question the authority of Rome must be put to flight. Only then should we turn our full attention to the Eternal War.'

'And is that why you allied yourself with Hakim Reis?' Hector spoke quietly. He knew now that Chabrillan's self-belief was his weakness.

'Consider where Hakim Reis operates – in the Atlantic, where he encounters ships from the trading nations of the north, from protestant nations. His activities and the attacks of corsairs like him weaken these nations and distract them from rivalry with the Holy Mother Church. The arms and gunpowder he brings to Moulay are used to drive the English from Tangier. A share of the money he receives, from the slaves and cargoes he captures and the arms he provides, goes to good purpose. Through me it has built galleys for La Religion, strengthened fortifications, and holds back the Turk.'

'Then why did you join the Galley Corps of France?'

Chabrillan gave a cynical smile. 'Did you not notice how many of the Reformed, as they like to call themselves, sat alongside you on the benches of *St Gerassimus*? Increasingly France condemns them to the oar. One day, I predict, King Louis will recognise the Reformed openly for the pestilence they are, and then the galleys of France will join in our crusade, rowed by unbelievers.'

'What about the innocent victims of your alliance with Hakim?' Hector asked. This was the moment he had waited for.

'Eighteen months ago Hakim Reis with two ships raided a small and undefended village on the coast of Ireland. He carried off slaves, both men and women. The villagers were taken by surprise because the authorities believed there was a peace treaty between Barbary and the English king. They did not know that the treaty had been torn up. Yet Hakim knew, and he profited from his knowledge. If Tisonne was his source — and you are Tisonne — then you are responsible for both Catholics and Protestants having been sold into slavery.'

'I care not for the Catholics of Ireland,' snapped Chabrillan. 'They failed us. When Ireland fell to the protestant English, she no longer sent her noblemen to Malta despite the requests of the Grand Master. Yet at home they continued to enjoy the Order's lands and estates. Your countrymen were too craven.' He looked at Hector with a sudden flash of understanding. 'Hakim Reis matters to you because you were taken in that raid?'

'Yes, I was a victim, along with my sister. She was carried away aboard another ship. I have not seen her since.'

A vindictive smile appeared on Chabrillan's face. 'Your sister?' he said slowly.

'Yes.'

The Chevalier considered for a short while before he declared, 'I had not intended to admit that I am Tisonne, but now I shall do so for the satisfaction it gives me when I address a weak renegade. Yes, I did work together with Hakim Reis. I supplied him intelligence and I provided him with weapons and gunpowder sold corruptly by the administrators of the Galley Arsenal and by other venal merchants. In return, whenever Hakim Reis sold prize goods, he paid me a share through the Cohens in Algiers, and in turn they placed credit for me with the Crespinos in Livorno. No one could trace the money, not even the Jews. Sometimes I met with Hakim at an arranged rendezvous at sea when I handed over guns and powder, and he provided me with his captives for me to sell in Valletta or Livorno.'

Chabrillan's manner was utterly self-assured. It occurred to

Hector that the Chevalier was pleased to have an audience to whom he could explain himself.

'For all his faults, Hakim Reis had scruples. Unlike you he believed sincerely that he should help his fellow Muslims. He would exchange his Christian captives for Muslims which I had taken. Hakim would then set his people free, and many of them went on to serve as crew aboard his ship. The men and women I received, if they were protestant, I sold in Valletta or Livorno, or kept them at the oar. I remember his raid on Ireland and you are right: I had sent him word that the treaty with England was soon to be repudiated. He took advantage, as I had expected. We had agreed to meet at sea afterward – to conduct our usual exchange of prisoners. But our rendezvous was disturbed. A foreign warship appeared and Hakim Reis wisely fled. He made for safe harbour. There he sold his captives – yourself included.'

'What of the other vessel? When Hakim raided Ireland, he came with two ships. What happened to the second vessel? Where did it go?' Hector was finding it impossible to keep the tension out of his voice.

'Some time later Hakim Reis sent me my share of the sale of the prisoners from that vessel. They were women. His colleague had got an excellent price for them. I was delighted by the sum. Your sister was no doubt among the wares.' He paused, coughed to clear his throat. A spiteful gleam had appeared in his eyes. 'Do you wish to know more?'

Hector's mouth was dry, and though he already knew the answer, he murmured, 'Of course.'

'Your sister and the other women from the Irish raid were landed in Sallee. If she was young and desirable, she would have been sold into Moulay's harem.' Chabrillan dropped his voice and spoke slowly and distinctly, relishing every word as he added, 'The thought that your sister is likely confined not so far from this cell is my consolation for the harm that you have done me. You would do well to reflect that once Moulay breeds on a woman, he casts her off like a used brood mare.'

TWENTY

HECTOR'S MOOD OF appalled dismay stayed with him all the way back to the armoury. His meeting with Chabrillan had shocked him into acknowledging that he had avoided facing the reality of what might have happened to Elizabeth. Chabrillan's malice had brought him face to face with the sordid possibilities.

Once again, it took Dan's calm advice to produce a glimpse of hope. 'You don't know for sure that Elizabeth is in Moulay's harem. She could have been sold to one of the kaids in Sallee and kept in his household. And don't forget that Moulay promised to set your sister free if he got his castle smasher from us. We could yet think up another way of pleasing him.'

Sean Allen was more cautious. 'Moulay may not honour that promise if it turns out that Hector's sister is in his own harem. The Emperor is not known for being open-handed with his possessions.' But the gun founder realised that he had been tactless, and quickly added, 'Hector, your best course is to try to find out whether Elizabeth really is in Meknes, and that's going to be difficult enough. The imperial harem is jealously protected. Every one of Moulay's wives is accompanied at all times by a eunuch guard as well as a serving woman who reports back to Lala Zidana.'

'Who's Lala Zidana?' Dan asked, for Hector was still sunk in dejected silence.

'Moulay's first wife and his most important one,' the gun founder answered, 'though the Lord knows why. She's an enormous woman, black as night and big as a hippo according to report. Moulay bought her for sixty ducats when she was a domestic slave and she seems to have established some sort of hold over him. There are rumours that she practises witchcraft. Certainly she rules the harem, and she keeps Moulay sweet by supplying him with the choicest girls. That nasty young pup Ahmad for whom we adapted the guns, is Zidana's son. His mother wants him to be Moulay's heir and she always keeps the lad in the forefront so that he is under Moulay's eye. That's her real influence: as long as Ahmad is the Emperor's favourite, the mother has direct contact with the throne.'

'Then we should use her to find our way into the harem,' suggested Dan. He earned a look of astonishment from the gun founder by asking, 'Could you arrange for me to meet young Ahmad? You could send word that his two new muskets need to be checked over to see if they require adjustment or have new flints fitted. You could flatter the youngster by saying that you had heard of his brilliant marksmanship when he shot down the rowing master.'

Sean Allen shook his head in wonder. 'Dan, you should be a full-time courtier. You're devious enough. I'll do as you suggest, although I don't have the slightest idea of what you have in mind.'

ⓒ

ONLY A FEW DAYS later Dan casually announced to his friends that he had been commanded by Lala Zidana to call on her. The cries of astonishment which greeted this announcement were followed immediately by questions as to how he had achieved his invitation. 'It wasn't difficult,' he said with a knowing grin. 'I went to Ahmad's quarters to work on the two muskets, just as Sean had arranged. Naturally the lad keeps the muskets close by him. They are his latest toys. He's very proud of what he did to the rowing master and boasts about it constantly, and likes to show off the guns. For sheer cruelty he really is his father's son. Sometimes he loads the guns and fires out of the window at passers-by. Luckily no one has been killed yet. When I arrived, he even grumbled that the guns no longer shoot straight, and complained that I should have come sooner to mend them.'

'But how did you turn that into an invitation to meet Zidana?' Diaz demanded.

'There were several serving women hovering in the background in Ahmad's rooms. I guessed that they were part of his mother's household and keeping an eye on the youngster. Of course they were curious about what I was doing. They came over to look at the guns and I showed them the inlay work. It's very ornate, you'll remember, with lots of curls and curves done in mother of pearl, and there's scroll work picked out in gold. I pretended that I had set the inlays myself and then, as if to prove it, I showed them this,' and he slid back the sleeve of his shirt. On his forearm was an intricate pattern of leaves and flowers, painted in reddish brown and indigo, with here and there a touch of yellow. Dan glanced across at Hector. 'My friend, maybe you've forgotten that I know how to do skin painting. At one time you were clever enough to put it to good use, and get me appointed to help colour Turgut Reis's maps. This time I've been able to assist you.'

He slid his sleeve back down so the skin paintings disappeared before continuing, 'Women who have little to do, love to primp and paint themselves. They'll spend hours at it, and run after anything that's new. Can you imagine the boredom in Moulay's harem – dozens, if not hundreds, of women all cooped up together. One thing I was certain of when I left young Ahmad's rooms was that those same servant women would carry word back to their mistress that there was someone newly arrived in Meknes who could beautify a woman's skin. It's taken less than twenty-four hours for my summons from Zidana to arrive. Hector can accompany me as my helper. When we meet the hippo, maybe I can put her into a good enough mood so that she'll let Hector try to seek out his sister. From what Sean has said, I'll have a broad enough surface for my paints.'

℃

FIRST WIFE Zidana proved as daunting as her reputation. When Dan and Hector were ushered into her presence, she was sprawled on a vast yellow satin couch fringed with tassels and heaped with cushions. Nearby was a clutter of low tables, stools, more cushions, and several large trays laden with bowls of fruit and sweetmeats. Behind the couch stood two elderly eunuchs, and half a dozen female attendants busied themselves in various corners of the room. The female attendants, Hector noted, wore veils or kept a fold of cloth across their faces, but their hands and arms were bare and decorated with intricate dyed patterns. Zidana herself wore no veil. She had slightly bulging eyes in a broad, pudgy and heavy-set face, and her massive bulk was swathed in layer upon layer of a shimmery green gauze-like material. On her head she wore a strange cap made of flexible sheets of gold and silver which had been cut through so that they resembled lace. The fringes of this headgear swung and tinkled as she heaved herself into a more comfortable sitting position and regarded her visitors. Her bare feet, which now touched the thick carpet, were surprisingly small and delicate. Hector thought that her eyes glittered dangerously.

'Which of you paints?' she asked in a harsh voice. She spoke Turkish with a strong accent.

Dan inclined his head politely. Zidana focused her attention on him and demanded, 'What country do you come from?'

'From across the western ocean. My people are called Miskito.'

Zidana frowned. 'Why is your skin dark? You look like the southern people from near the desert.'

'All my people are this colour. It is said that some of our ancestors came from Ifriqya and they mixed with the native peoples whose skin is the colour of copper. So our skin is halfway between the two.'

'Do your women guard their skin against the sun?' The question was blunt.

'No.'

Zidana turned towards one of her serving women and said, 'You! Come over here. Show him your hands.'

The woman did as she was ordered, and Zidana demanded of Dan, 'Can you do better?'

Dan looked at the patterns drawn on the servant's skin and murmured, 'They are well drawn but could be more striking and colourful.'

Zidana waved the servant aside and heaved her bulk closer to the edge of the couch. She extended her right arm and pulled back the silk sleeve. The arm was very fat. 'Could you make good colours on my skin?'

'I believe so.'

'Then proceed.'

'First I must tell you that what I will paint is not permanent,' Dan said. 'The colours will last only a few days.'

'That is not important. If I like your work, I will summon you again when the colours fade. You can paint them again or make different pictures for me. You will paint no one else.' It was clear that Zidana was used to giving orders.

Dan opened the cloth satchel he had given Hector to carry, and took out several small clay pots and jars. Hector knew that his friend had found the necessary ingredients for his skin paints in the Meknes marketplace which sold all manner of brightly coloured spices and powders. He had mixed them with coloured minerals that Sean Allen used in his foundry work.

Carefully licking the end of a brush, Dan dipped it into one of the jars, advanced on the plump arm and began to draw on it carefully. Zidana looked on in critical fascination.

'My assistant here,' said Dan casually as if making light conversation, 'believes he has a sister among the Emperor's women. He has not seen her in a long time and, with your permission, would like to speak with her.' He had drawn the outline of a flower on the pudgy arm, and was beginning to colour in the first of the petals.

'What is the name of his sister?' Zidana was so intrigued with the pictures appearing on her skin, that she hardly seemed to listen for the answer.

'His sister is called Elizabeth, but she may have another name here.'

Zidana withdrew her fat arm and held it up in the air, turning it this way and that to admire the first pictures that Dan had drawn. The images gleamed brightly, the paints still wet. Abruptly Zidana called across to one of the eunuchs. She spoke rapidly in a dialect that Hector could not understand, and the man beckoned to him to follow. Leaving Dan to continue with his drawing and painting, Hector followed his guide through a door concealed behind a heavy velvet curtain, and down several empty corridors until he was brought into a plain unfurnished room with bare walls. The room had two windows, both screened with a fine lattice of stucco. The window facing him was already blank, shuttered from the far side. His escort crossed to the open window where the sunlight entered the room and closed its shutters. 'Stay here,' he said and left the room, leaving Hector in near-darkness.

Hector did not know how long he would have to wait. His heart was pounding in his ears, and the dense gloom and stifling airlessness of the room made him feel adrift from the real world. As the minutes dragged past, he slowly became aware that the shutter facing him had swung open. He heard a soft footfall behind him and he sensed that the eunuch had returned. A moment later he felt a hand guide him forward so that he stood with his face close to the lattice of the window in front of him. His eyes had grown used to the dim light, yet he could see nothing except the pattern of the stucco a few inches away. He shifted sideways, trying to squint through the gaps. As far as he could make out, the room on the far side was similar to the one where he now stood. It, too, was in darkness except for a small glimmer of light seeping under a door to one side. He could just distinguish a dark figure standing in the middle of the floor.

'Elizabeth?' he blurted out. 'Is that you?' His mouth was dry with excitement and anticipation, and the fear of imminent disappointment.

There was no reply. 'Elizabeth. It's me, Hector.' What he had thought was a single figure, was in fact two people standing close together. One of them moved aside, and the shadowy outline came a little closer.

'Elizabeth,' he repeated. 'If it's you, please say something.'

There was a long silence and he could hear the wheezing breath of the eunuch standing somewhere behind him. Again the figure moved slightly. Hector's nostrils detected a slight musky perfume. He did not remember his sister ever smelling that way.

Finally, a woman's voice, barely audible, said, 'Are you well?'

Fighting down his anxiety Hector tried desperately to remember his sister's voice. It had been so long since he had seen her that he had forgotten what her voice sounded like.

'It's me, Hector,' he said again. 'Is that really you, Elizabeth?'

The answer was so soft that he had to strain to hear. 'Yes.'

Hector sagged against the latticework, his head pressed against the stucco. He felt dizzy.

'Are you keeping well?' he asked, trying to keep his voice gentle though his head was in a whirl.

'I am . . .' there was a pause. 'I am healthy.'

Hector swallowed hard. Suddenly his throat was unnaturally tight. He wanted to speak in a normal voice but somehow it seemed that if he did, it would break the spell and destroy his fragile link with his sister.

'How long have you been here?' he croaked.

But he was answered with a question. 'What happened to you? And the others?'

'We were sold as slaves in Algiers. I don't know what happened to the others afterwards, but I worked for a Turkish sea captain for a time, then was aboard a French galley. Now I'm here in Meknes.'

'Are you still a slave?'

'No. I'm not. I'm here with friends, and one day we may be allowed to leave. I want to take you with us, to bring you away.'

There was a long silence as the dark figure stood silent. Then Elizabeth's voice said,

'That's not possible.'

'Yes, it is,' said Hector fiercely. He was feeling better now, more sure of himself. 'The Emperor has promised to give you your freedom if I and my friends serve him well.'

Elizabeth seemed not to grasp the importance of what he had just said. She ignored his answer and instead enquired, 'Have you news of our mother?'

'I have heard nothing from home, nothing at all since we were taken. I'm hoping that she went back to Spain to live with her own people. You and I will go to find her as soon as you are released.'

Again, a long pause followed by a low whisper, 'I told you, Hector. That's not possible.'

'Elizabeth, listen to me,' Hector pleaded. 'I'm sure that I can get you set free. My friends will help me. We can get Moulay to agree. You must not give up hope.'

'You don't understand. That is not how it can be. Please don't ask again.'

'But what of our mother? You want to see her again, don't you?'

'Of course.'

Hector could tell that his sister was very close to tears. He could hear the tremor in her voice. But he knew that he had to insist.

'Please, Elizabeth, please. You must not give up hope. You will not be here forever.'

He heard a stifled sob, and then Elizabeth's voice said, 'It is not so bad here. We look after one another. I've learned to speak languages, and we try to keep ourselves busy. Our servants look after us so there's no drudgery. We gossip and amuse ourselves.'

'Elizabeth, I made myself a promise long ago, when I was first a slave in Algiers. I told myself that I would find you and bring you home.'

When Elizabeth spoke next, her voice was firm, and her response came like a blow. 'Hector, please go away.'

Hector felt his stomach turn hollow. For a moment he could not believe his sister's words. He was stunned at the rebuff.

'Are you frightened of Zidana?' he hissed, angry now. He was exasperated by his sister's obstinacy, and had to struggle to keep his voice level. 'Please don't be fearful of that old harridan. She can be got round. I can arrange that Moulay remembers who you are, that he treats you as special.'

There was a sudden note of alarm in Elizabeth's immediate reply. 'No, don't do that, Hector, I beg you. Don't do anything to attract Zidana's attention to me. She is dangerous. She is jealous of anything that may threaten her own position or her son as the Emperor's favourite. Zidana will destroy anyone who could be a rival to Ahmad. I told you, the women and mothers in the harem all gossip. They scheme and they plot. It's how they pass the time. No one is safe.'

'But you need not be involved . . .' Hector began, and then the meaning of her words sank in. 'Elizabeth,' he said slowly, 'are you telling me that you have a child?'

Her silence gave him his answer. He felt mortified, but he had to know.

'Is it a boy? And the father is Moulay?'

'I have called him Mihail. It sounds almost the same whether spoken here or back at home. He has our mother's eyes.'

'You could take Mihail with you when you leave,' Hector beseeched in desperation.

'You know that is not true. Moulay would not permit it, and what sort of life would the boy have, the son of a concubine from Barbary.'

'Then let Mihail grow up here. He's also the son of an emperor and can make his own way.'

'I cannot abandon him. I know what happens to Moulay's offspring. If they are not his favourites, they must fend for themselves. They have no one to help them except their mothers. I am not alone, there's an Englishwoman here who has had a son by Moulay, and several Spanish women. We have promised to help one another and our children, as best we can.'

'What am I to tell our mother?' Hector asked, his voice a hoarse whisper.

'Tell her nothing. Don't even tell her that you found me. Say that I have disappeared.'

Hector pressed his head against the surface of the lattice, the stucco hard against his forehead, feeling the pain. He felt completely empty, striving for words that would change his sister's mind. But he knew that it was useless. She had reached her decision much earlier, and nothing would change that. He gave a small groan of anguish.

'Hector, please try to understand,' his sister begged him. She had stepped closer to the grille now so that her words were very clear. 'I love my Mihail. He is my life now. I will watch over him, raise him as best I can. Moulay will not touch me again. He rarely returns to any of his women. I can forget him but I cannot forget my child. Through Mihail I will find happiness.'

Hector was drained of all emotion. He was numb, at a loss what he should do.

Elizabeth must have sensed his despair for she said gently, 'Hector, I did not mean to hurt you. I had never expected to see you again, and I am grateful that you did manage to find me. That was truly noble of you, and I'm desperately sorry that it has come to nothing. I know that it is a difficult thing to ask, but it would be best if you did not think of me again, except to recall your memories of our childhood together. I am a woman now, and a mother. My life has taken me down one path, and your future will be very different. I know that when you've had time to think about all this, you will be able to come to terms with our separate lives.'

Hector's eyes filled with tears. A great sadness was tearing at his inside. He leaned forward in the near-darkness, his eyes squeezed tight shut to hold back the tears, and reached up to cling to the lattice to stop himself from sliding down the wall, his legs weak. He reached with his fingers through the lattice and gripped tightly, feeling the pain as the sharp corners of the stone cut into his flesh. He was whirling in a misery of black despair. Out of that pit of desperation, he felt — or perhaps he thought he felt — a light touch on the fingers of his right hand where they gripped the lattice. It was as if someone on the far side had stroked them gently. But when he lifted his head and opened his eyes, the tears wet on his cheeks, he saw that there was no one standing in the far room.

TWENTY-ONE

❨

WITH THE BACK OF his hand Hector brushed the moisture from his cheek. The gesture reminded him of his parting from Elizabeth. She had urged him to forget her, yet the pain of her rejection was ever present. For several days after his meeting with her he had considered returning to Ireland to find out what might have happened to his mother, to learn whether she had stayed there or gone, as he had suspected, back to her own people in Galicia. But in the end he abandoned the idea, as he felt too bruised to embark on another search. And, he asked himself, what was he to tell his mother when he found her? He was unsure that he would be able to sustain the deception that Elizabeth wanted, to tell their mother the lie that he had never found his sister. He decided that if he was to find his mother, it would only be when there was something positive to say, something to make her proud, something that he had achieved. He was very concious that, at eighteen years of age, with his father dead and his only sister vanished into a Barbary harem, he was left to make his own life. Now, a month later, they were not tears which were running down his face. They were beads of sweat.

The day was as hot as he had ever known, hotter even than when he was working in the quarry at Algiers. He turned to look back at his companions. Dan, Bourdon and Karp were riding in single file behind him, Karp leading their packhorse on a halter. They had all wanted to take the chance of leaving Meknes. Dan, always level-headed, had made the initial suggestion. Perhaps his friend had wanted to jolt him out of his despondency by pointing out that staying so close to Elizabeth was only adding to his distress. There was no future in lingering in Meknes, Dan had said. There was nothing Hector could do to save his sister, and the day would come when Moulay demanded to see his castle smasher, and when it failed to materialise, Moulay's disappointment would have dangerous consequences. Better to slip away quietly, the Miskito had advised, provided that Sean Allen did not suffer as a result. The gun founder had assured him that there was no need to worry on that score because the Emperor always valued a man who would make and mend his cannon. Go south, Allen had urged, for that will give you several days' start on any pursuit. Moulay's people will search for you as soon as it is known that you have left without his permission, and they will presume you are heading west or north, directly for the coast. No one will imagine that you've gone towards the Great Desert. Then the gun founder had insisted that they accept his gifts of money and weapons – the latest muskets, pistols and powder – because their flight would surely lead them into wild lands.

Hector glanced up at the sun. It was well past the zenith but still blazing down, its heat reflecting from the rocky ground. He could feel his horse tiring beneath him. From time to time the exhausted animal tripped on a loose rock, the stone clattering away down the slope of the barren hillside across which the little column was moving. He reached inside his shirt for the qibla that he had bought in the market at Meknes. No one had thought it strange that a renegade should want to buy a little prayer compass. He checked the direction they were travelling in, for the land was featureless, a succession of rocky slopes with scrubby vegetation and dry water courses. From the outset the little group had avoided main roads. For the past week since leaving Meknes they had travelled by compass, using tracks and byways wherever possible, skirting around the towns and cities, visiting villages only to obtain fodder for the animals and some basic supplies for themselves. Diaz's cavalry friend Roberto had provided the essential directions. He had campaigned with the imperial army in this region, and Hector had written down the Spaniard's recollection of the towns, passes and days marched with the army, then transferred it all to a rough sketch which summarised the terrain. He hoped that the Spaniard's memory had been accurate. He dreaded wandering in a circle, like the dead rowing master, and perhaps stumbling on a detachment of Moulay's troops. But the others, riding behind, had confidence in him, insisting that he should be their leader. 'You're best qualified,' Bourdon had assured him. 'You're thoughtful as well as educated. It's more than just making a map of our route. You are good at making plans, and at taking everything into consideration. That's what a leader's for.' Hector had tried to dissuade the others, but they were adamant. They had resolved on trying to reach Negritia, the Land of the Blacks. From there they would find a ship far beyond the reach of Moulay Ismail.

Hector had fallen in with their plans because, in truth, he was uncertain where his own future lay. He had only his friendship to sustain him, his friendship with Bourdon and Karp, but above all with Dan. So when the three of them spoke of trying to reach the coast beyond Negritia, he had drawn a map, recalling details from the great map of Piri Reis. He had marked as many of the countries as he could remember and added the conjectured course of a substantial river curving through the interior. This river was reputed to join in one direction to the Nile of Egypt, he told his companions, while in the other direction it was known to empty into the sea at a place where the ships of many trading nations came to do business with the natives, carrying away gold, spices, elephants' teeth and slaves. 'Where do those ships return?' Bourdon had asked. 'From wherever they came – from England, France, Portugal, Spain, Brandenburg. We could take passage aboard them. You could go home to France,' Hector had replied. 'Do any of them sail onwards?' the pickpocket had asked, his finger tracing a course directly out into the ocean. 'That would take them towards the Americas,' Hector answered, and his words had decided their mutual fate. With a grimace Bourdon had touched his galerien's brand and murmured he would never be welcome back in France. Dan announced that he too would prefer to head westward and return to his own people. Finally Hector had looked across at Karp, who had been staring at the map and listening to their discussion. Karp had nodded his agreement without being asked. And so the decision was made.

Hector wiped his face again. He hoped that the ridge ahead of them would be the final one before they came in sight of Oued Noun. That was the name of the oasis which lay on the edge of the desert, according to Roberto. It was the last place where they would see real houses built of brick and stone. Everything beyond was nomad territory where people sheltered under tents. 'Whatever you do, don't try to cross the Great Desert on your own,' the Spaniard had warned. 'You wouldn't stand a chance. You have to know the exact direction and distance of each waterhole, and whether you will find water at that particular season and in that year. Sometimes the waterholes fail. If they do, then you perish. Your best chance is to join a coffle, a caravan, which is properly equipped and has a reliable guide. Just hope you find one when you reach Oued Noun.'

Cresting the ridge, Hector found that the land sloped away as a barren, stony, dun-coloured plain dotted with clumps of thorn bushes and an occasional acacia tree. Among the thorn bushes were the ungainly shapes of camels, at least a hundred of them, foraging on the prickly vegetation. Even as he reined in his horse to take in the view, there was a startled shout. A small boy, evidently a camel herd, had been dozing in the shade of an acacia. He sprang to his feet and went running away towards the low roofs of a small settlement in the distance to carry a warning.

Taking care to stay in view they rode forward. At the outskirts of the cluster of flat-roofed mud-brick houses, they dismounted and walked, leading their horses. A reception committee of about a dozen men, traders by the look of them, was already waiting. They were heavily armed and unfriendly looking. Hector noted more armed men lurking in the alleyways behind them. 'Salaam aleikom,' he called out, and when he had received the stock response, he added, 'If you are going south, we would like to join you.'

'Where are your trade goods?' demanded the group's spokesman suspiciously. He was dressed in a faded red burnous, and eyeing the solitary packhorse and the array of weapons that Hector and his companions carried.

'We have none. We ask only to accompany you,' Hector replied politely.

'And for what reason? We have prepared our coffle these past three months, fattened our camels, and shared our expenses. All our arrangements are made. We have no place for extra travellers.'

'We would be willing to pay our share of any expenses,' Hector offered. 'We ask only to be able to ride with you.'

'On those horses?' The spokesman gave a sarcastic laugh.

Hector was about to ask whether the coffle would accept an additional payment when there was a stir among the merchants. Several reached hurriedly for their muskets. Out of the corner of his eye Hector detected a movement. He turned to see that Dan had brought his musket to his shoulder, and for a moment he thought the Miskito was about to shoot down the man in the red burnous. Then he saw that Dan was aiming high and to the left. He pulled the trigger. There was a report of the gun, a puff of black smoke, and a vulture which had settled on a nearby roof was thrown bodily backward by the force of the bullet, and fluttered untidily to the ground.

'Tell them,' said Dan quietly, 'that we can protect the coffle from the desert marauders.'

There was a shocked silence from the merchants. Hector repeated Dan's offer, and they conferred in low voices until their spokesman announced reluctantly, 'Very well. You may join us, but on condition that you place yourselves wherever you may best protect the coffle, both by day and by night. As for the camels you will need, we have none to spare. You must arrange that with our guide. You will find him over there, by the village well.'

℃

'ASSHEADS! I don't trust them for a moment. They'd sell their own grandmothers, given half a chance,' Bourdon muttered angrily as he and the others led their horses in the direction of a herd of camels clustering around a watering trough. Amid the camel dung and smells and the continual bawling, groaning and grunting of the animals, a black slave was hauling a leather bucket up from the well. Hector asked where he might find the coffle's guide, and the slave nodded towards a nearby thorn bush. Spread across its branches was a tattered scrap of cloth. In front a young man sat cross-legged on the dusty ground. He was bent forward, braiding a new girth to a camel saddle.

As Hector approached, he saw that the young man could not have been more than sixteen years old. He was barefoot and dressed only in a long and ragged gown. His unkempt black hair was so long and stiff and wiry so that it stood out from his head in a great bush. 'Are you the guide for the coffle?' Hector asked uncertainly. He spoke in simple Arabic, and the youth raised his head to reveal a cheerfully intelligent face and a ready smile. 'No, that's my grandfather. I am only his assistant. My name is Ibrahim.' Without turning round he called out something in a language that Hector did not recognise. In answer something stirred in the patch of shade under the thorn bush. What Hector had taken to be a bundle of rags proved to be a

302

very old man, who climbed very slowly to his feet and came forward. Great age had so shrunk his frame that he could not have been little more than four feet tall, and he walked with the aid of a stick. Most astonishingly of all, when he came close enough for Hector to look into the lined and weather-beaten face, he saw that both the old man's eyes were filmed over with a milky glaze. The guide was stone blind.

Hector was about to speak up when, to his surprise, Dan greeted the old man politely. The response was a cluck of pleasure, and for several moments the two men talked together. Then Dan turned to his friend and said, 'He also is amazigh. He speaks the same language I learned when working in the gardens of Algiers. His accent is difficult but I have been able to explain that we will be joining the coffle as guards.'

'What was his answer?'

'He says that he is pleased. We will be acting as an armed escort. There has been much difficulty this year with a people he calls the Tooarick. They live by banditry. He knows we have good muskets for he heard my musket shot. He says it was the sound of a good weapon.'

'And can he provide camels?'

'He offers to trade our horses for camels. They can be left behind here, and he has cousins who will come to collect them later. In exchange he will provide us with camels from Talifat – apparently they are famous for their stamina – and supply saddles and teach us how to ride them. Also he will arrange that we have proper clothing for the desert. We must wear loose cotton gowns and cover our heads with cloths to keep off the sun. He says it would also be wise to leave behind our boots and shoes, and wear sandals.'

'I'm not giving up my boots,' interrupted Bourdon. 'Everyone knows that the desert is full of poisonous insects and serpents. I don't want to get bitten or stung.'

Hector hesitated. 'Ask him if we can't keep our horses. We might need them again on the far side of the desert.'

Dan translated his request to the old man and relayed his reply. 'He agrees that a horse is capable of crossing the desert, but only if accompanied by a camel carrying water. That means six water skins for every horse, plus another camel to carry dried grass, grain and blocks of dried dates as horse feed. Even so, the horse will die if it goes lame, or if the camel falls sick. He recommends we take only camels.'

'Tell him that we will follow his advice.'

ℂ

A WEEK LATER, with Oued Noun far behind them, Hector was regretting that he had accepted the old man's counsel. Riding a camel was uncomfortable. The creature's loose-limbed gait meant that he spent most of each day swaying back and forth awkwardly in an lurching rhythm. If he dismounted to walk beside the animal, he had to beware of the creature's foul breath and moody temperament. Before leaving the village Ibrahim, the guide's grandson, had shown them how to make the camels kneel, how to hobble them loosely so they could graze when there was any vegetation, and to tie them more closely by the knee when they camped for the night. 'Place your trust in Allah, but tie up your camel,' the young man had joked. But Hector still found the camels to be fractious and awkward to control. He would much have preferred to be mounted on a horse as he tried to ride at the flanks and rear of the coffle in case there was an attack from the mysterious Tooarick of whom the merchants were so fearful. He had expected the caravan to march as a long single column. Instead it advanced on a broad front, walking slowly across the bleak, flat landscape, each merchant and his slaves and servants attending to their own band of camels. Out in front rode Abdullah, the old guide, accompanied by his grandson. Each night when the caravan halted at a waterhole, Hector and the others would join the two amazigh at their campfire. The merchants completely ignored them.

'My horse could have come this far without any difficulty,'

Hector confided to Ibrahim one evening. It had been natural to strike up a friendship with the cheerful and enthusiastic young man. 'Each night we have arrived at a waterhole where the animals could drink. My arms are aching from trying to steer my camel in the right direction.'

'There's a saying that "the camel driver has his plans — and the camel has his",' was the light-hearted reply, 'and this is only the early stage of our crossing. Later we will find water only every three days, or less often. And there are places where the surface of the desert is dangerous. The ground seems firm and hard, but it is only a thin crust. It gives way suddenly. A horse would break its leg in the hole, but a camel is more flexible. It can be pulled out with ropes, and continue on the journey.' The young man tossed another dry branch from a thorn bush on to the fire and watched the sparks fly up into the night air. 'Besides, my grandfather tells me that tomorrow we will have the irifi, the desert wind. He predicts that it will only last a few hours but it will make life difficult for our beasts. You should warn your companions that they will need their sheshs, their turbans.'

The sky dawned an ominous reddish grey. The caravan had barely begun its march when the first puffs of a gentle breeze began to lift the dust and sand into little spirals that skittered and twisted across the ground before collapsing and disappearing. By mid-morning the wind had increased until sand particles were blowing painfully into the men's faces, making them sneeze and their eyes water. They were obliged to dismount from their camels, wrap cloths about their heads, and plod onward, heads bent low. Beside them the camels walked on, their nostrils narrowed and their eyes half-closed behind their long eyelashes. Until evening the irifi swirled around them, rising in strength to a full gale. Visibility fell to less than twenty paces, and the coffle huddled in a dense mass, fearful of losing touch with one another. A horse in such hostile conditions, Hector reflected, would have refused to advance and turned to stand miserably with its tail against the scouring wind.

'Now I know why Abdullah doesn't need good eyesight to lead the caravan,' Hector commented to Ibrahim as they rested by the campfire. 'I could scarcely raise my head against the sand blast. When I did, it was impossible to see anything.'

'It could have been much worse. The irifi sometimes blows for five or six days, and much more strongly. Entire caravans have been known to perish, unable to move forward or backward until buried by the sand. That was what happened to my father. He was leading a coffle which the wind destroyed. We never found his body. I expect he is lying somewhere beneath the surface of the desert, a dried corpse along with his camels and the merchants he was guiding. Sometimes, years later, the wind blows away the sand again. So maybe he will be found, and we can give him a proper burial.'

Picking up two metal bowls, Ibrahim rose to his feet and said, 'You and Dan can give me a hand. In less than a week we begin the most difficult stage of our journey. There will be no water for ten days and not a blade of grass nor a single leaf for our camels to eat. There's an old jmel among our beasts which will not survive the ordeal. It is better we put it to good use now.'

He led the way to where the camels were hobbled. Singling out the animal he wanted, he led it a little distance away. There he made the beast kneel, and showed Dan how to pull the halter so that the camel turned its head to one side, stretching its neck in a curve. While Hector held the bowl beneath the artery, Ibrahim expertly cut the animal's neck so that the blood splashed into the receptacle. 'Put the bowl on the embers of the campfire,' he told Hector. 'In a few minutes the blood will thicken to a good soup. Dan and I will start to deal with the carcass. Tonight we feast on the entrails. Tomorrow we'll begin to dry the meat in the sun, and we'll save the hide for when it's needed.' He slid his knife blade into the dead camel's gut, exposing a globular paunch which he carefully cut open. Inside was a thick green gruel, foul smelling with lumps. Taking the second bowl he scooped out the contents. 'This too can be cooked for our supper,' he said. 'It has already been eaten by the jmel. But we can enjoy it too. In the desert nothing goes to waste.'

A week later the camel hide was put to use when Bourdon reluctantly agreed to abandon his battered footwear despite his fear of snakes and biting insects. By then his boots had been cut to shreds on flinty gravel. Ibrahim expertly cut double-soled sandals for him using the skin of the dead jmel whose meat already hung in strips from their pack saddles, drying in the sun. They were now in the most difficult sector of the desert crossing, a desiccated brown expanse of sand and rocky outcrops which, in the simmering heat haze, could be mistaken for the roofs of distant towns. At its worst the heat was so intense that the coffle had to travel by night. The men spent the days sheltering from the sun under strips of cloth or in the shadow of piles of camel packs. The sand became so hot that it was painful to stand barefoot, and their precious water skins daily grew more flabby as their contents dwindled through evaporation. Finally, when it seemed that the ordeal would never end, Abdullah declared that they had passed the halfway mark. Hector, who had long since given up using the qibla to trace the direction of travel, was amazed by the blind man's certainty.

'How can your grandfather be so sure?' he asked Ibrahim. 'I have not the least idea how far we have travelled.'

'My grandfather has crossed the desert at least thirty times,' Ibrahim answered proudly. 'In his head he keeps a count of the days and hours on this journey, even the number of paces. He listens to the sounds of the desert, and he says that every part has its own feeling which tells him where he is. When in doubt, he smells the sand.'

Hector had indeed noticed how, from time to time, the old guide took up a fistful of sand and held it to his face. Now he was too tactful to question Ibrahim's assertion. Bourdon, however, was more dubious. He quietly scooped up some sand and wrapped it in a cloth. The following day he placed the sample in the old guide's hand and asked Ibrahim to enquire from his grandfather how many days were left until the coffle reached the next watering place. The old man sniffed the sample and, with an angry outburst, flung it down in disgust. 'What did he say?' Bourdon asked. Ibrahim looked hurt as he translated, 'My grandfather says that he is being taken for a fool. Either that, or the caravan has gone in a circle and we are back where we were yesterday.'

Bourdon was crestfallen. 'Please apologise to him from me. I meant no harm. All my life I have lived among rogues and charlatans so I always suspect some sort of cheat.'

Yet even Hector had reason to doubt the old man when the caravan crossed a low range of rocky hills and Ibrahim rode up to him to say that his grandfather had announced that they should be in sight of the longed-for watering hole. Hector strained his eyes, but could see nothing. The desert stretched out as usual, bare, monotonous, and utterly devoid of life. There was not even the false glimmer of a distant mirage which so often duped him into thinking that a lake lay ahead. Suddenly his camel lurched off at a trot, and within a dozen strides was plunging along at a mad gallop. All around, the other camels were similarly stampeding. They surged forward in a roaring, incoherent mass. Ahead, Ibrahim was goading his camel even faster, kicking up a cloud of dust. After some three miles of this mad careering gallop, Ibrahim drew to a halt, jumped down and began to scrabble at the ground, peeling back a cover made of camel and goatskins. Beneath the cover the ground was a water soak which had been protected from the sun. Ibrahim and the camel drivers dug troughs which filled with a few inches of water, and the thirsty camels shoved and jostled, biting and kicking one another as they fought to suck up the water that they craved. Ibrahim's face beneath his great bush of hair broke into a broad grin. 'My grandfather has succeeded again,' he exulted. 'The worst is over.'

When the camels had slaked their thirst, he asked Dan,

Hector and the others to go on ahead with him. 'There's a second, better, waterhole about an hour away. I will show you how we can harvest the desert's bounty. It's time to celebrate with a feast.'

'Please, no more camel's intestines,' groaned Bourdon.

'No. This time we'll have roast ostrich.'

Sure enough, as they approached the next waterhole, a flock of about twenty ostrich ran off. The giant birds paced away across the desert, their wings outspread. Hector had come across ostriches in the Emperor's menagerie. But this was the first time he had seen the birds in the wild.

'We'll never get close enough to shoot them. They run as fast as a galloping horse,' he said to Ibrahim.

'That's not how we'll do it,' the young man replied. 'This waterhole is where the birds prefer to drink. All we have to do is dig some holes in the sand where you and the others can lie hidden with your muskets. The birds are suspicious of camels so I'll take them back to the coffle, and bring the caravan here at dusk. Good hunting!'

The ambush was easier than Hector had anticipated. He and his three companions prepared their hiding places. Less than an hour after Ibrahim had ridden away, the flock of ostriches came walking back across the desert, unaware of any danger. The hidden musketeers waited until the great birds made easy targets. Their first volley brought down three ostriches. When the flock foolishly came back a second time, they killed another four. That evening the entire caravan fed better than it had done for many weeks, and Hector fell asleep on a patch of soft sand. He was gorged on roast ostrich meat.

A cry of pain awoke him. He sat up, feeling slightly groggy, and looked around. His eyes had to adjust to the half-darkness. It was still several hours before dawn but the moon had risen and was shedding enough light to see that the camp was in uproar. Dan was already on his feet, a pistol in his hand. Their camels, which had been hobbled kneeling, were straining at their bonds as they tried to rise to their feet. They were roaring and moaning in fright. In the distance there were shouts of alarm. Suddenly a figure flitted between Hector and the last embers of the campfire. For a heart-stopping moment he thought it was a djinn, one of the spectres which Ibrahim had spoken about, evil spirits which wander the desert in the form of men or animals or dust devils. This one had assumed the shape of a human. It was pale grey from head to foot, gaunt and stark naked. It held a spear in each hand, and the hair on its head was long and filthy. As the figure glanced towards him, the creature's eyes glittered for a moment in the moonlight. It took Hector a few seconds to realise that what he was looking at was a desert thief.

The attack was over before anyone could react. Ibrahim lit a brand from the fire and went to check their losses. Two camel saddles were missing, and several strips of dried camel meat. One of their animals was bleeding from a deep gash where a thief had stabbed it in the shoulder with his spear. 'The bandit probably hoped to cripple the creature so we had to leave it behind,' he commented glumly. He called out for his grandfather to come to look, and when there was no reply, went to where the old man had lain down to sleep beside a thorn bush. He found him sitting, dazed from a blow to the head. With his acute hearing Abdullah had been the first to detect the presence of the thieves as they crept into camp, and had tried to intercept them. They had struck him down without mercy. 'They must have been watching the waterhole, waiting for a coffle to show up,' said the old man after he had recovered enough to speak, and various merchants arrived with similar tales of thefts and losses. 'This time we were lucky. They were only sneak thieves. If there had been more of them, we might have been murdered as we slept.'

'Will they attack again?' demanded the merchant's spokesman angrily. He was wearing the same faded red burnous as the day Hector first saw him, and was in a foul mood. He had lost several packs of trade goods.

'They are Tooarick of the Labdessah tribe. They live by plunder,' answered the guide. 'It is best that the caravan moves on tomorrow before the word gets out that we are here, and the Labdessah summon their fellows.'

The spokesman rounded on Hector. 'You are meant to be our guards! Instead you were snoring by the fire.' He was spitting with rage. 'When we march, you will be sure to protect us. Otherwise it will be the worse for you!'

'There is no point in quarrelling,' the old man intervened. 'Save your strength for the journey. Now that the Tooarick have found us, they will not give up. They will follow us like jackals.'

His prediction was painfully accurate. The coffle moved on the next morning but the thieves struck again during the following night. Hector and his companions stayed on guard with their muskets but failed again to detect the intruders and did not fire a shot. The Labdessah were expert thieves. Stripped naked, their bodies smeared with ashes, they crept their way into the encampment and made off with more trade goods. They cut the hobbles of a dozen camels and drove them off into the darkness. A merchant who tried to stop them was stabbed in the stomach and died four hours later. The merchants swore and raged. They shouted at Hector and his companions, and blamed Abdullah for their troubles. But there was no remedy. On the third night the caravan was robbed yet again, and however urgently the travellers marched onward, they knew they were failing to shake off their tormentors. They embarked on a sand sea where a succession of tall dunes extended in every direction like waves on the surface of an ocean. If they looked behind them from the summits of the taller dunes, they could see in the far distance a Labdessah outrider mounted on his camel. He was tracking them, waiting for them to make camp so that his fellows could plan their next attack.

Hector grew more and more frustrated. 'We can't go on like this,' he confessed to Ibrahim on the fourth day of their ordeal.

The young man, who normally rode beside his grandfather in advance, had dropped back to join the rear guard. 'The caravan is being bled to death.'

Ibrahim shook his head. 'My grandfather tells me that it is impossible to shake off the Labdessah once they have attached themselves to a coffle. They are like the parasites that feed on the camels. Once they fasten on to their victim they do not let go.'

'Then I suggest we give the Labdessah a nasty surprise.'

Ibrahim cocked his head on one side as he looked at Hector with sudden interest. 'You have a plan?'

'The Tooarick don't yet know that we have good muskets,' Hector said.

Ibrahim thought for a moment before replying. 'Not unless they witnessed you shooting the ostriches. Otherwise you have not yet used your guns in their presence. The Labdessah have always attacked in the dark, and they are armed with spears or knives.'

'Then I propose we deal with them as we dealt with the ostriches. When we come to a suitable place – a dip between the sand dunes where we are out of sight of the pursuit – Dan, Jacques, Karp and I will get down off our camels and prepare an ambush. We will scrape out shallow holes where we can lie in wait with our muskets. You ride on, taking our camels with you, and rejoin the coffle. With luck the Labdessah will blunder straight into the trap, and we will give them a bloody nose. Later you can come back and collect us.'

Ibrahim's face lit up. 'We could set the ambush right now, over the next sand ridge. I'll tell my grandfather about it later. But please be careful. The thieves have the eyes of falcons and would immediately notice anything unusual. We must work quickly.'

The next hollow between the dunes proved an ideal site for the ambush. There was a patch of soft level sand on which grew a few withered bushes, no more than two feet high. Here Hector and his companions slid down from their camels and hastily scraped out shallow trenches for themselves. Placing their muskets before them, they lay down, and Ibrahim quickly threw sand over them to cover them. Then he remounted and led the camels off in the direction of the marching caravan. 'I'll be back before nightfall,' he called. 'In the name of Allah, shoot straight!'

Hector lay on his belly, feeling the heat of the sand spreading up through his thin cotton garments. To his right, about twenty paces away, Karp was similarly buried. Away to his left lay Bourdon and Dan. Each man had picked a location where a low leafless bush gave additional cover but did not interfere with his sight line. They lay in a shallow arc, facing the way they had come. Before them the dune sloped upward quite steeply, then came to a crest some fifty yards away. That was were they expected the Labdessah to show.

Gently Hector checked that the lock of his musket was in working order. Unwinding the end of his head cloth, he draped it loosely around the delicate mechanism to protect it from the sand. Then he lowered his face down to the sand, blew gently to clear a few loose grains from his nose and mouth, and closed his eyes. He settled down to wait.

After some time he became aware of a tickling sensation on his forehead. A small creature was burrowing up through the sand towards his face. He raised his head slightly to ease the pressure on the sand and give the creature an easier passage. The tickling became more of a scratching. He lifted his head higher still, allowing an inch or so of free space, and felt a slight rasping sensation just below his hairline. The creature was almost clear. He opened his eyes to see what it was. Less than an inch away stood a scorpion as long as his middle finger, and as fat. The insect must have detected the flicker of his eyelid, for suddenly it stopped and raised its sting, curling its body ready to strike. Hector held his breath. The green sea-pale transparency of the scorpion's shiny body was the colour of the tiny crabs which had crawled across the rock pools when he was a boy. Its armoured body was like a miniature lobster, only curled in reverse. He was almost cross-eyed with the strain of keeping the deadly creature in focus, yet holding completely still. The muscles of his neck complained as he arched his head even farther backwards. Ibrahim had warned them of the Saharan scorpion. The sting would kill a dog within six or seven minutes. A man would die in as many hours, from convulsions.

For what seemed like an age the black tip of the venom sting wavered in his face. Then the scorpion relaxed. The body slowly uncurled, and the insect crawled off on its crooked legs.

The next time he raised his head, Hector was shocked to see two camel riders had already started down the slope of the sand dune before him. They were Labdessah. Both men were swathed in loose blue garments, and their heads and faces were wrapped in folds of black cloth leaving only a narrow slit for their eyes. They were halfway down the slope, the feet of their camels plunging into the soft sand, when another half-dozen Tooarick appeared on the skyline behind them. Hector reached forward gently. His arm was numb where he had been lying on it, and he could feel a tingling as the blood began to flow again. Very gently he peeled aside the cloth protecting the musket lock. He took slow deep breaths. His eyes never left the two Labdessah as they rode closer.

A single low bush stood in isolation some thirty paces in front of him. It had been agreed with the others that this bush would mark the point where they would spring their ambush. The two cameleers were only a few paces away from it now. He raised his musket and took aim at the leading rider. The target came level with the bush, and he fired even as he heard the sound of Bourdon's musket to his left, and then a shot from Dan. Through the small cloud of black smoke Hector saw the lead rider crash from his saddle, hitting the ground so heavily that Hector knew he must be dead. The second man lurched sideways. He managed to stay on his camel, which gave a great swerve and began a panic-stricken run across the face of the sand dune. Farther up the dune were sudden shouts of dismay and alarm. The six Labdessah wrenched their camels around, and applied their goads as they forced their beasts into an urgent retreat. Within moments they had fled over the crest of the dune, closely followed by their wounded colleague and the runaway camel of his dead companion.

Bourdon gave a whoop of triumph. 'That should have stopped them in their tracks,' he exulted as he sprang up from his hiding place, and began to reload his musket. Hector and Dan waited for Karp to join them before they approached the downed Labdessah. The man had been killed outright. He lay on his back, one leg bent under him, an arm flung out.

'Did you get a good look at the ones who got away?' Hector asked Dan.

'Yes,' the Miskito replied. 'I'd say they learned their lesson. Only two of them were carrying muskets, and both weapons were obsolete and near useless. They know now that we can bite back.'

'Let's hope they leave the caravan alone in future,' Bourdon intervened. He was still jubilant. 'Maybe those bastard merchants in the coffle will treat us with a little more respect now they know what we can do.'

'We should not wait down here,' said Hector. 'If the Labdessah decide to come back, we're dangerously exposed. We'd better climb back to the crest of the dune. From there we can keep a lookout, and wait for Ibrahim.'

Feet sinking deep in the loose sand, they scrambled to the top of the dune. There was no shade anywhere, and the sun beat down on them out of a clear sky as they sat and waited for Ibrahim to bring their camels. The hours passed, and they became more and more thirsty. From time to time Jacques, the most impatient, stood up and scanned the horizon. There was no sign of the Labdessah, nor of Ibrahim. There was not a living creature in view except the distant black speck of a circling bird of prey. Finally, as the sun began to set, the

Frenchman voiced what all of them had been thinking. 'What do you think is delaying Ibrahim? He should have been here long before now. The coffle will have moved on so far that it will be impossible for us to catch up with it on foot.'

Hector rose and shook the sand from his clothing. 'Wait here and keep a good lookout. I'm going down to check the body of the Labdessah. Maybe he had some food on him, and a waterskin.'

But when he reached the corpse, he found that the man had carried only a dagger strapped to his forearm, and a small leather purse on a cord around his neck. The purse contained a handful of worn copper coins. Nearby lay two spears which had fallen to the ground when he was shot. His food and waterskin must have been on his camel, which had bolted. The effort of plodding back up the dune made Hector realise just how weak and thirsty he had become. He felt slightly dizzy by the time he rejoined the others, and was glad to drop down on the sand and rest. 'Nothing,' he reported. 'We'll have to spend the night here, and hope that Ibrahim shows up in the morning. It's sensible to stay where he knows to find us.'

After sunset the temperature began to fall rapidly. The four men shivered in their light clothing, huddling together trying to share their warmth. They took it in turns to keep watch, though none of them slept for more than a few moments. They heard scuffling noises from below, and guessed that a sort of scavenger was investigating the corpse of the Labdessah. Fearful that the dead man's companions might return, they jumped at shadows. Bourdon caught a glimpse of a flitting movement in the darkness. He raised his musket and was about to take a shot when the shadow revealed itself as a tiny fox-like animal with huge ears which gazed at them for a second, then turned and vanished.

Hector was on watch when the red-orange glow of another fiery sunrise began to light up the horizon. Below him was a remarkable sight. A blanket of white mist, no more than a few feet deep, had silently occupied the sand valley in the night. He marvelled that the vapour could form in such an arid land, and licked his cracked lips at the thought of the moisture, so close yet unobtainable. His gaze travelled down the length of the valley and there, some distance away, were the heads and shoulders of five men coming towards him. They must have been on camels for they swayed back and forth with the characteristic movement of their mounts. Yet the animals themselves were invisible, submerged within the layer of white mist. Briefly he was reminded of the day when Turgut Reis's galley had glided through the sea fret of Sardinia, and the sailor Dunton had told him that the lookouts at the masthead could be in clear sunshine above the fog. Now, even as he watched, the mist began to ebb. It shrank down, thinner and thinner, and the corpse of the dead Labdessah appeared like a dark rock when the tide receded. Hector came to his senses. He had been so cold that his thoughts were sluggish. He nudged Dan with his foot. 'Riders,' he said softly. 'Coming our way. Stay low. I'll let you know what's happening.'

As he watched, the camel riders continued their approach. They were in single file, with one man some distance in front. Presumably he was their scout. Something about the way they rode told Hector that they were keeping a watchful lookout. 'Slide back over the edge of the dune, and keep out of sight,' he warned the others. 'They look like Labdessah, five of them. Maybe they've not seen us and will ride by.' All five riders were dressed in the loose blue garments of Tooarick, and the black cloths wrapped around their heads gave them a sinister appearance. The only difference among them that Hector could see was that their leader rode a particularly fine-looking camel. Its bridle and trappings were hung with red and blue decorations.

'They'll be within musket range very soon,' he said softly. 'Get your guns ready. I'll give the word if we need to fire on them. They're still in single file. Karp, you take the second man in line. Jacques, the third. Dan, your target is the same as mine. The leader.'

'Why let them pass?' hissed Bourdon. 'They'll be carrying water, and without water we will die out here.'

'Let's wait and see,' Hector answered.

The main group of riders had halted. They were still out of musket range. Only their leader had continued forward. He was heading directly for the corpse of the Labdessah, clearly visible among the last wisps of mist. When he reached the corpse, he reined in his camel and looked down. Then he dismounted and walked across to the body. Leaning over, he began to search through the dead man's clothes. He was plundering the corpse. Turning about, he tied a hobble to his camel, hitched up the hem of his gown with one hand, and began to climb the dune. He was heading straight for where Hector lay.

'What's going on?' It was Bourdon. He had crawled up beside Hector and was peering down. When he saw the advancing Tooarick he pushed forward his musket, cocked the weapon, and began to take aim. 'Don't shoot,' warned Hector. 'He knows we are here. He wants something.' He had noticed that the man had left his musket strapped to his camel.

Thirty paces below them the man stopped. Reaching up, he unwound the black cloth which covered his lower face and called out to them. 'Peace be with you. I am Sidi Hasem of the Wadelim.'

'Greetings,' Hector called back. 'We are travellers.'

'You killed this dog of a Labdessah?'

'We did.'

'Then I welcome you. The enemy of my enemy is my friend.'

Hector rose to his feet.

'What are you doing? He's Tooarick!' blurted Jacques anxiously.

'Keep me covered. He wants to talk. He's our best chance of getting food and water.'

Hector slithered down the slope until he was a few paces from the stranger. The man who called himself Sidi Hasem had a sharp, narrow face. His skin was the dark olive of the desert dwellers, and Hector guessed he was about forty years old. His eyes were deep-set, almost black, and they regarded the Irishman calmly.

'You are from the coffle that passed this way two days ago?' he asked.

'Yes. We are waiting for our friends to come back to collect us.'

'Let me show you something,' said the Tooarick. 'Your companions up there can come down if they want. They will not be harmed. Or they can stay where they are, if they wish. We know that you can defend yourselves.' He glanced meaningfully at the musket that Hector carried. 'It will be easier if you left that here. We need to travel only a short distance and will be back very quickly.'

Sidi Hasem's self-assurance was persuasive. Hector found himself trusting the man. Turning towards Dan and the others, he shouted to them that he would be back shortly. Then he followed the Tooarick to where his camel was kneeeling. The camel saddle, Hector noted, was different from the plain pack-saddles he had ridden with the coffle. It had two elegant horns which curved upward like the wings of a butterfly. Hasem unhobbled the animal and gestured for Hector to climb up behind the saddle and hold on. The Tooarick then settled himself in his seat and prodded the camel with his goad so that it rose to its feet with a great belch. A moment later Hector found himself clinging on tightly as the animal moved off at a rapid trot.

Hector could see little beyond Hasem's blue-clad back as he guided his beast in the direction that the coffle had gone. There was a smell of camel and human sweat, and the occasional bubbling complaint of the animal as it was urged to climb the steep slopes of one dune after another. His owner remained silent. After about four miles the Tooarick slowed his camel to a walk, and Hector, peering over his shoulder, knew that no words were necessary. Even from a distance he could recognise Ibrahim's great shock of wiry hair.

A short distance ahead was an area of flat ground where the gravel showed through the layer of sand. Here a few stunted thorn bushes had taken root. Lying among the bushes was a body.

Hasem brought his camel to a halt. Dismounting, he led Hector to where the young man lay face down. The killers had stripped him bare. Blood had crusted black where there was a spear wound in his back. 'Is this the man you were expecting?' asked Hasem. 'Yes,' answered Hector. He felt sick to the stomach that his plan for the ambush had provoked such a disaster. 'We came across the body by accident when we were tracking the Labdessah,' said the Tooarick. 'They caught him, and then will have taken his camels.'

'What should we do now?' asked Hector. There was a lump in his throat, and he was at a loss.

'We bury him. Then we leave without delay.' He saw that Hector was dazed.

'Later you can grieve. Allah has relieved your friend of his burden.'

TWENTY-TWO

☾

'Sidi Hasem says that his group are already dangerously far out of their own territory. They were on a tribal raid and must withdraw before the Labdessah learn they are here,' Hector informed his friends after he had rejoined them and told them of Ibrahim's murder.

'Can they help us rejoin the coffle?' asked Bourdon. He was looking hopefully at the Tooaricks' camels.

Hector shook his head.

'We'll never catch up. The caravan's three days ahead of us. Old Abdullah won't know what has happened, and the merchants certainly won't turn back. They will presume that we were all killed by the Tooarick. That will make them travel away from us even faster, to save their own skins.'

'So what do you suggest?'

'Sidi Hasem is the denim, the leader of the raid,' Hector answered. 'He offered to carry us back to the Wadelim camp.'

'And what do we do when we get there?'

'He knows about the great river where the foreign men come with their ships. Every year the Wadelim send someone to a native market near the river to trade ostrich feathers and tree gum for blue cloth. This man could bring us there if we gave him a suitable present. Hasem didn't mention the price or whom he had in mind as our guide, but I suspect he means he himself would take us if we gave him one of our muskets.'

'Sounds like a bargain to me.' Bourdon had experienced more than enough of the desert.

'Saying that, Hasem and his men are carrying only enough water for themselves. With four more men, double-mounted on the camels, he warns it will not be comfortable as we have to travel fast.'

'Can't be much worse than what we've endured on the galleys,' Bourdon declared confidently.

He was much less complacent six hours later when the Wadelim made a brief halt to roast strips of dried meat over a tiny campfire made from pellets of camel dung. The Frenchman lay on the ground, complaining bitterly that a camel's bony rump had worn holes in the skin of his thighs and buttocks. The Wadelim had ridden at a fast trot, and Hector and his companions had clung on as best they could, using makeshift stirrups the desert people had fashioned for them from strips of cloth. But it had been an agonising experience, splay-legged, jolted on the camel's spine and rattled against the wood and leather backrest of the Tooarick saddle.

'Ask them what we will do when the water runs out,' Bourdon asked with a groan. Hector relayed the answer with a mischievous grin. 'Sidi Hasem says that when we are really thirsty, we drink camel's urine.'

Fortunately the water ration held up long enough for the party to reach the Wadelim camp three painful days later. As they rode to the cluster of skin and wool tents hidden in a fold in the ground, Hasem warned Hector and his companions not to be seen staring at the flocks of long-legged goats grazing among the rocks and scrub nearby. The Wadelim believed that strangers brought the evil eye.

'We don't have to stay for long,' Hector reassured Karp when the clan's children ran away screaming from poor Karp with his ravaged face. They were convinced that he was a yenun, one of the grotesque evil spirits who emerged from the desert in human form to harm them.

'Something has been puzzling me ever since we ambushed the Labdessah,' Hector continued. 'I never heard your gun go off, even though you were close by. And afterwards you did not need to reload. You never fired a shot at the camel rider, even though he was a mortal enemy. Yet when we hunted the ostrich, you hit your mark every time.'

Karp looked back at him. His face was strained.

Hector went on, 'You have no need to worry, Karp. I also remembered the time we trapped Chabrillan, the man who had caused you so much pain and grief. You attacked him under the city wall and nearly strangled him. Yet afterwards you cried. Was it because you were ashamed of your violence?'

Karp nodded. Now his expression was one of release. It was as though he was being relieved of a burden.

'You don't believe in violence, do you? It is part of your religion, something that you believe in profoundly. That is what you preached in Kandia when you joined Chabrillan's men when they fought the Turks. That is why you suffered all that time on the galley, and you never tried to expose the Chevalier. You did not want revenge. You believe in peace and forgiveness.'

Tears had filled Karp's eyes.

Hector felt a surge of admiration. 'Karp,' he said, 'you are a good man. It is my duty to tell the others that we cannot expect you to help us if we must fight our way to get clear of Moulay Ismail. But as long as I lead our little band, you will continue to be one of us.'

Sidi Hasem was so eager to earn his payment of a musket that the travellers stayed only long enough for him to assemble a consignment of trade goods. Then he led them southward, at a more sedate pace this time and with one man to a camel. They crossed a dreary flat countryside where the sun had baked the reddish brown soil as hard as marble. At night they camped under the sky or they stayed with other small groups of nomads friendly to the Wadelim who greeted them with bowls of zrig, camel milk mixed with water. Gradually the countryside became less austere. There were low hills and the occasional dry riverbed where, by digging in the gravel, they found a seep of water for their camels. Later they came across small wells. The shafts were dug so deep that they had to climb down wooden ladders to clear away a surface layer of blown dust and camel dung before they could fill their leather buckets. Finally they began to arrive at settlements, no more than a dozen or so mud huts which marked the outer fringes of the desert. Instead of zrig, they were given bowls of porridge made from millet. They had reached the land of cultivators. There, at a village known to Hasem, they left behind their camels and rode forward on donkeys, always heading towards the great river which now had a name. The local people called it the Wadnil.

The countryside continued to grow more luxuriant. They began to pass fields of grain guarded by old men and small boys who chased away flocks of thieving birds. There was pasture and woodland and herds of cattle. The people changed too. They were many more, living in village after village of round straw-thatched huts, and their appearance was very different from the sinewy, olive-skinned desert people. They were taller, loose-limbed and wore their wiry hair piled up on the top of their head in the shape of a pointed cap. Instead of flowing loose robes, the common folk dressed in no more than a small loincloth, and their women went bare-breasted, often with a baby slung on their back – a sight Hector had never seen before. As the travellers came closer to the river, more and more of the people they encountered were a deep midnight black, and their skins glistened for they loved to wash, then oil their bodies.

On the twentieth day of their journey their guide claimed his payment. 'Tomorrow,' he told them, 'we reach the market where I will sell the ostrich feathers and gum. You continue south, and by mid afternoon you will arrive on the banks of the river you have been seeking. But you must hurry. The local people say that soon the Wadnil will shrink within its banks. Then the river traffic ceases. They also tell me that there is a foreign ship anchored, even now, in the river.'

'That's good news,' said Hector. 'I had thought we would have to go down to the coast to find a foreign ship.'

'The local people also tell me that there are powerful merchants who resent the presence of this vessel. They see it as a trespasser, a danger to their trade. I think you know who I mean.'

'Are you talking about traders from Moulay Ismail's kingdom?'

'Yes. To them this territory is their own. They come here to take away the elephants' teeth, the gold, the slaves. They are like jealous hunters who believe that all the animals in a forest belong to them.'

'It's strange to think of merchants as hunters.'

Hasem frowned. 'The merchants, as you call them, bully the people into handing over their possessions, and if they resist, they hurt them. If they want them as slaves, they simply seize them and carry them away. I am told that is what their lord Moulay Ismail does to them. So they do it to others.'

Suddenly Hector felt despondent. After so many days' travel he had thought that he had heard the last of Moulay. Now, it seemed, the Emperor's malign influence extended even to the banks of the great river.

The Tooarick was watching him closely. 'There is more to tell you.'

'What is that?'

'The ship anchored in the river is a small vessel and has been in the same place for nearly two weeks. My informants don't know why it does not leave, because soon the falling river level will trap the vessel. No one comes ashore seeking to trade. It just stays there. Perhaps you can join the ship. I think that is good news.'

'And there is bad news as well?'

'The local people also say that the traders from the north have heard about the ship. They are sending some people to drive it away, or maybe to capture it and seize its cargo. My advice is that you hurry. Try to reach the ship before they do.'

The following morning, after thanking Sidi Hasem and leaving him with Karp's musket and most of their remaining stock of gunpowder, Hector and his three companions set out on foot. The road towards the river was well trodden, and they found themselves walking between thick, green plantations of palm trees and banana plants. The air was hot and oppressive so they were amazed at the costume of a local chieftain who was proceeding to the river ahead of them. The man was wearing what looked like a nightshirt of thick, stiff, striped cotton laced at the neck and extending to his ankles. He had a heavy felt cap, and his voluminous robe was hung with dozens of pieces of red coral, clusters of small seashells, amulets and charms which clattered and jangled with each step. The costume was so stifling and cumbersome that the chieftain was obliged to march along very slowly, accompanied by his squad of sword-bearing body-guards. Hector decided it would be prudent to turn aside and use a footpath through the trees which after a little distance brought him and his companions out on a bluff overlooking the river itself.

The Wadnil was more than a quarter of a mile wide, its turbid brown flood moving steadily towards their right. On its surface floated large branches and the occasional fallen tree, its great bulk circling slowly in the current. It was obvious that the river level was already dropping. Mud banks were beginning to show in the centre of the river, and nearer at hand the shoreline was a broad expanse of rich, black mud, already cracking in the sun. A few canoes were drawn up on the bank, stranded by the receding water.

Lying at anchor in the middle of the river was a small ship. To Hector's eye she was not much larger than the fishing boats he had known in his childhood. She had a single mast, from which flew a plain red flag, and a neglected air. A ship's boat was attached by a rope to her stern. Her deck appeared deserted.

'What do you make of her?' he asked Dan.

The Miskito squinted against the glare of the sunlight. 'She looks like the trading sloops that come to the Miskito Coast. At a guess I'd say she has a crew of no more than half a dozen. They must have had hard work getting her up here against the current.' He dropped his gaze towards the riverbank below them. 'Look who's here!' he said softly. 'We should keep out of sight.'

The chieftain and his bodyguard had reached the landing place where the road came to the riverbank. With him was a Moor who wore a faded red burnous. He was the same man who had been spokesman for the coffle.

'I wonder where the others are?' Hector said.

'There, about thirty paces farther along the foreshore,' said Dan who had the sharpest eyes. 'You see that big, grey tree trunk lying stranded? Men are crouched behind it. They've got muskets with them. I'd say that they're the rest of the merchants from the caravan.'

There were shouts from below them. The group standing on the landing place was calling and waving towards the anchored boat. The chief was trying to attract the attention of whoever was on board.

'The landing place is in easy range of the hidden guns,' said Dan. 'Whoever comes ashore from that boat, the minute they set foot on land, they'll be shot down. The Moors can then use the ship's boat to row out and capture the vessel.'

Hector glanced up and down the shoreline. 'We must warn whoever is on the ship. This may be our only chance of getting downriver.'

'We could fire a musket,' suggested Bourdon. 'That would warn them.'

'No. It would also alert the Moors. They would not treat us

kindly for interfering. Besides, if the crew of the vessel know they are in danger, they will raise anchor and sail away.'

'Then what are we to do?'

'We must get out to the vessel ourselves. Dan, what are our chances of using one of those canoes to reach the ship?' Hector pointed to the canoes drawn up on the bank.

The Miskito looked at the craft, then said, 'They're dugouts, hollowed from a single log. Even the smallest will be too heavy to be shifted by the four of us. We'll have to think of something else, and quickly. Someone on the boat is getting ready to come ashore.'

A figure had appeared on the deck of the anchored vessel. He was hauling in the ship's boat. A second man was getting ready to assist him. In a few moments they would be starting out for the shore.

'We'll have to risk the musketeers,' Hector said. 'They are on the far side of the landing place from us, and may not be good shots. We wait until the ship's boat is halfway across, then we leave our hiding place and run down to the shoreline. We'll have the slope in our favour so we should be able to move fast, and we'll have the element of surprise to help us. We should have covered most of the distance before the Moors even notice us. So we keep silent, just run like the devil.'

'And what then?' asked Bourdon.

'We run right into the water, heading for the boat. We get to the boat before it's in range of the musketeers, scramble aboard, and have the crew take us out to the ship.'

'You've forgotten one thing,' said Jacques quietly. 'Neither Karp nor I can swim well. This time we don't have empty barrels to float us.'

'I hadn't forgotten,' said Hector. 'If you look closely, you will see that the foreshore slopes very gently. Almost certainly it stays shallow for a long way out, far enough for you to wade out to the rowboat. It's our only chance. We must reach the boat before it falls into the trap.'

He looked around at his companions. 'No point in keeping your muskets now. Get rid of them. Strip off any clothing that may hinder you as you run. When I give the word, make a dash for it. As you run, spread out. That will make us a harder target for the musketeers. If anyone trips and falls, he must look after himself as best he can. The musketeers are bound to get off at least one shot, probably two. Any more will depend on how quickly they reload.'

He laid his own musket on the ground and unbuckled the belt that held his powder horn and stock of bullets. He removed his heavy sandals. Young Ibrahim had made them and he had planned to keep them as a memento of the young man. But running in bare feet was more important now. He pulled over his head the long loose shirt that he had worn in the desert. Now he was wearing only a pair of loose cotton drawers. The others followed his example, and when they were ready, he waved them forward. They crouched on the edge of the bluff, watching the ship's boat moving closer. There were two men in her. They were rowing steadily, taking a slanting course to counteract the pull of the river current. They were nearly halfway to the shore.

'Get ready!' said Hector quietly. 'See you aboard . . . let's go!'

He stood up and launched himself over the edge of the bank. The face of the bluff fell away in a steep slope, part sand, part gravel. The surface was loose and crumbly, and he felt his bare feet slipping and slithering. He plunged onward, concentrating on keeping his balance. It was impossible to control his speed. The angle of the slope made him set one foot after the other just to keep himself upright. He could hear the sound of his companions as they too pelted down the hill. Belatedly he realised that he should have told them to swerve a little from side to side as they ran, to put the musketeers off their mark. But there was no sound of a shot. As yet they had not been seen.

He was almost at the bottom of the slope when he heard the

shouts. Hector took another dozen strides before the explosion of the first musket shot. A moment later, there came the sound of a volley. He thought there was the sound of a musket ball whizzing past, but his breath was coming in great gasps so he could not be sure. He glanced around to see if anyone had been hit. To his shock he realised that he was the slowest runner of the four. Dan was several yards ahead of him to his left, and Bourdon was close behind him. Karp was level with him, a little distance away and running steadily.

Now they were on the level ground of the shoreline itself. The hardened mud of the beach was beneath the soles of his feet. It was easier to run without the fear of tripping or losing balance. The baked river mud stretched out before him, and he found himself wondering at the regular surface of plate-like cracks. He ran on.

He glanced to his left towards the rowing boat. The two men in it had heard the shots, and turned to see what was happening. They were resting on their oars. The boat had come to a standstill. In a few moments the current would catch it and it would begin to drift downstream. Hector hoped that the current would not take it out of reach.

His legs were tiring now and he could feel the air harsh in his throat. He forced himself to concentrate on taking steady strides. Soon he would be at the water's edge, and then in the shallows.

Without warning his right foot broke through the crusted mud. In a shocking plunge his right leg dropped straight down into the slime beneath. It was as if he had stepped into thin air. He was thrown forward and sideways and slammed face down, the breath knocked out of him. As he fell, he felt an agonising pain in his ankle. He twisted to one side, desperately trying to free his leg, grimacing at the fierce, lancing pain, and he remembered what the coffle's blind guide had said: a camel was uninjured when its foot broke through a crusted salt pan, but a horse would break its leg.

He looked up to see what had happened to his companions. Both Dan and Bourdon had turned back. They had seen him collapse. Now, to his mingled dismay and relief, they were hurrying towards him.

'Here, let me get you back on your feet,' offered Dan. He bent down and seized him by an arm. A moment later the Frenchman was on his other side, and had grasped him around the waist. Together they began to tug him clear. 'Leave me,' Hector gasped. His leg was buried up to mid thigh. 'Run for yourselves. I'll be able to manage.'

They ignored him.

'Here, put an arm over my shoulder,' Dan ordered. Working with Jacques, he wrenched Hector bodily upward. The trapped leg came out of the mud like a rotten tooth from its socket.

Several more muskets shots. Hector was amazed that no one had been hit. He tried to put his right foot on the ground, and gasped in agony. He almost fell again. Together his two friends began to carry him towards the water's edge, Hector's right leg trailing uselessly behind him.

'I said, leave me! I'll manage.' He spoke through clenched teeth.

Again they ignored him.

'Leave me, please!' he insisted fiercely. 'Three of us together make an easy target.'

Now he became aware of Karp. The Bulgar also had abandoned his headlong dash for the river, and had come to join them. He was hovering nearby, anxious to assist. Another musket shot rang out. It could not be long before one of them was struck down.

'Karp! Run on,' Hector pleaded. 'Get to the boat. There's nothing you can do.'

To his astonishment, Karp raised his hand in some sort of salute. Then he turned and began to run. But he did not run towards the shore. He ran directly towards the red-robed Moor still waiting at the landing place. As he ran he let out a great raw screech and began to flail his arms. He was like a madman, half-naked and howling with rage. There was a single musket shot, then a brief lull in the firing as the hidden musketeers decided what they should do.

In that pause Dan and Bourdon reached the shallows, with Hector hanging between them. The rowing boat was forty yards away, still motionless. As Hector felt the splash of water, he turned his head to see what was happening to Karp. The Bulgar was less than twenty paces from the man in the red burnous. Several of the other Moors had jumped up from behind the tree trunk and were running forward. The chieftain's bodyguards had panicked at the terrifying sight. They were fleeing. Karp screeched again, a long piercing howl which could be heard clearly, and bounded forward like a wild beast. The remaining musketeers had gathered their wits and took him as their target. There came a ragged volley. Karp was impossible to miss. Several musket balls must have struck him for he sank down on one knee.

As Bourdon and Dan lifted Hector farther into the river, the boldest of the Moors ran forward, sword in hand. Hector had a last glimpse of Karp as the scimitar swung up in the air and came slicing down towards the Bulgar's head.

Hector turned back towards the rowing boat. It was much closer. The two oarsmen were blacks. 'Help us!' Hector shouted.

His companions dragged him to where the water was up to their chests. Bourdon the non-swimmer could go no farther.

There was a peculiar whirring noise, closely matched by a gunshot. Hector realised that he was hearing the sound of a musket ball skipping off the water. The musketeers had turned their attention back to the fugitives now they had dealt with Karp. The range was too great for accuracy, but they were taking random shots, hoping to make a lucky hit. For a moment Hector felt like ducking out of sight beneath the surface of the river, but he knew it was futile. The gunmen would simply wait until he reappeared, then shoot. It was better to try to swim out of range. But he could not abandon Bourdon. Despite the excruciating pain in his leg, he and Dan would have to pull the Frenchman along with them as they swam.

Hector clenched his teeth. Every time he moved his injured leg, he felt a stab of pain from his ankle. Bourdon was reluctant to move out of his depth. 'Come on, Jacques,' Hector snapped angrily. 'Dan and I will hold you up. Trust us.' The Frenchman took a deep breath and floundered forward. He had the clumsy movements of a man who had never learned to swim properly. Hector reached out to hold his head out of water, and he was aware that Dan was supporting Jacques on the other side.

They made little progress. Bourdon was too frightened to relax. His frantic struggles only hindered them. Another musket ball struck the water just beside them – Hector saw the splash – and then went whirring onward.

Suddenly he felt Bourdon begin to sink. For a second he thought that the Frenchman had been hit. Then he knew that Dan had let go. Dan was swimming away.

Hector felt a brief surge of anger and disappointment. He had never expected Dan to abandon them. Then he looked up and saw that Dan was swimming strongly out into the river. He was heading towards the ship's boat. It had stopped. One rower had dropped his oar in fright. The other rower was shouting at him.

Dan reached the rowboat. He gripped the gunwale and in one smooth wriggling movement had hauled himself aboard. He pushed the frightened oarsman aside and took his place. He barked an order at the man beside him, and began to spin the little craft. The musket fire from the beach had slackened. Hector wondered if perhaps the Moors were running out of powder and bullets. He concentrated on keeping Bourdon's head above water until Dan had brought the little rowing boat close enough for him to grab on. He let go of Bourdon, who seized the boat so desperately that he nearly capsized it. With Hector pushing from below and Dan hauling him up, they hoisted Jacques into the boat, and a moment later the Frenchman was flopping on the floor boards like a landed fish. Then Hector pulled himself aboard.

The boat was over-loaded and sluggish in the water. Looking back towards the shore, Hector thought he could make out Karp's body lying on the strand. There was the puff of smoke from a musket, but the bullet flew wide. A group of Moors was clustering around one of the dugout canoes. With the help of some blacks, they were beginning to shift it down the beach. Dan had been right. The dugout was an awkward burden, and they were making slow progress. There was still time to reach the anchored vessel.

Bourdon had recovered from his fright. He began to search for something to help the oarsmen. There was a wooden paddle lying half hidden in the bottom of the boat. The Frenchman tugged out the paddle and began to take great scoops at the water. The speed of the little boat increased. They were almost out of musket range.

Moments later they had reached the anchored vessel. Her side was low enough for them to scramble aboard without difficulty. On deck there were the usual heaps of rope, some sacks, wooden buckets. But no sign of life.

A musket shot, and this time the musket ball slapped into the side of the ship. The Moors had succeeded in launching their dugout, and it was now being paddled out from the beach. There was a single marksman in the bow. He had fired the shot. There must have been a dozen men in the leading dugout, and a second canoe was being launched.

Dan sprang into action. He ran forward to the bow, and began to throw off the coils of the anchor line. But the knots had jammed. He turned towards one of the two black men who had come aboard with them, and mimed a cutting gesture. The negro understood him at once. He groped under a piece of sacking. A moment later he produced a long-bladed knife and running up to the bows began to saw through the anchor line. The first strands sprang up as they were severed. The river current was so strong that the anchor line was taut as an iron bar. Half a dozen more strokes of the blade, and the anchor cable parted. Hector felt the vessel fall back as the current took hold of her.

'Come on,' Dan was standing at the foot of the mast beckoning. He had a rope in his hand. 'Here haul on this! Jacques, you help him.' Hector limped over and took the rope. Dan and the two blacks had begun to unfasten the bands which held the sail along the boom. Then he and Bourdon heaved on their rope and the upper spar rose, the sail opening beneath it. The blacks and Dan joined them and added their weight. There was no one at the helm so the boat was spinning slowly in the current. The riverbank was sliding past and above their heads the sail flapped three or four times. The gap between the vessel and the pursuing dugout was widening. 'Almost there now,' called Dan. 'Make fast!'

The vessel began to gather pace. Looking aft, Hector saw the paddlers in the dugout had given up the chase. They were turning back to shore.

℃

'THERE WAS MUCH sickness on the ship,' said a deep, husky voice. Hector swung round in surprise. The speaker was one of the blacks who had rescued them. The man noted his astonishment. 'My name is Benjamin. I speak French and Portuguese also as I work with the foreign ships on the coast. When you ran down the hill, I thought you are runaway slaves so I wanted to help. I too was a slave once. Now I have been given my freedom. The foreign sailors call me a Laptot.'

'We were slaves too, at one time.'

Now it was Benjamin's turn to be taken aback. 'Your dark-skinned friend here was a slave, that I understand. But I have never met white slaves before.'

'We have reason to be grateful to you. Thank you for picking us up.'

Benjamin regarded him hopefully. 'You are a ship's captain?'

'No. The most I've ever been is a captain's secretary, or a galley slave. I've never been in charge of any ship.'

'This ship needs a captain. The old one is dead, and so are the first and second mates. All died from the sickness. That is why we were anchored. We did not know what to do. Maybe it is your turn to help us.'

Benjamin went on to explain that he and his companion, another Laptot, had been hired when the sloop called at the Residence of St Louis, the French trading station at the river mouth. The two of them had helped bring the vessel upriver until, two weeks into their journey, a fever had broken out aboard. The hard-driving captain had refused to turn back. He insisted on proceeding until finally the crew were so short-handed that they had been forced to anchor and wait for the sickness to abate. But the fever had raged all the more fiercely. One by one the foreign crew had died until only the two Laptots were left alive. Unable to handle the vessel by themselves, they had been marooned.

'What about the cargo?' Hector asked.

'We have touched nothing,' Benjamin answered. 'I will show you.'

Hector hobbled behind him as the Laptot led the way to a hatch, opened it, and disappeared below. As Hector's eyes got accustomed to the gloom in the hold, he had a vivid recollection of the interior of the ship in which he had been carried away by Hakim Reis. But what he saw now was different. Along each side of the hull were built rows of shelves as if in a trading post. On them were stacked what looked like trade goods. There were bundles of chintz cloth, axe heads, knives, and iron agricultural tools, trays of brass medals. But many of the shelves were bare. They also seemed unnecessarily wide and the gap between them was barely eighteen inches.

'Our captain had planned to go far upriver where there had been a native war. He was sure he would fill the shelves. He had already laid in stocks of food and water for the captives.'

Hector realised that he was looking at the interior of a slave ship. The wooden shelves were where the slaves would lie during the long passage to the Americas.

'Where did the captain keep his papers?'

Benjamin showed him into a small cabin in the stern of the vessel. A quick search of the dead captain's documents revealed that the vessel was the *L'Arc-de-Ciel* from La Rochelle. There were maps and charts of the west coast of Africa, of the mid-Atlantic, and the Caribees. There was no doubt that *L'Arc-de-Ciel* was a slaver.

Benjamin and Hector returned on deck. It was growing dark. Soon there would be the short tropical dusk, then nightfall. 'Should we anchor for the night?' Hector asked Dan. The Miskito seemed confident in his ship handling.

Dan shook his head. 'Our remaining anchor is not heavy enough to hold us in this current. With a little moonlight we should be able to avoid the mudbanks. We had best keep going.'

Hector turned to the Laptot. 'How far to the mouth of the river? When we get to St Louis, we can put you and your companion ashore. But we cannot visit the place there ourselves. One of us,' he nodded towards Bourdon, 'is a rowing slave who has run away. His former masters were French and would seize him.'

Benjamin looked doubtful. 'What will happen to the ship?'

'I don't know,' said Hector. 'My friends and I are hoping to go to the Americas.'

Bourdon spoke up. 'Then why don't we try to sail this boat all the way?'

Hector looked at Dan. 'Is that possible?'

Dan thought for a long time before replying. 'It could be,' he said cautiously. 'We'll need good weather. And our greatest difficulty is that we are so few aboard. Jacques, Hector and myself – that's not enough to manage the ship.'

'Then take us with you,' said Benjamin suddenly. Hector

337

blinked in surprise. Benjamin spoke urgently to his companion in their own language, then turned back to face the others.

'If we return to St Louis, the governor will want to know what has happened to the ship. We will be accused of failing in our duty to the captain, or even of killing him and the foreign crew. We may be hung and certainly we will lose our freedom and be sold again as slaves.'

'Can't you go ashore somewhere else, not at the Residence?'

Again Benjamin shook his head. 'We are Laptots. We were brought to St Louis as slaves, and our own homelands are far away. The local people would not accept us. Besides, without us you will never cross the bar.'

'What do you mean?'

'There are many sandbanks and mud shoals where the river runs into the sea. Ships can come in and out when the river is in flood, but now it is almost too late. This is the season when the sea breaks heavily on the bar, and it is very dangerous. It needs local knowledge to find a way through the obstacles and a travado to help us.'

'A travado?'

'A great gale of wind from the north-east, from the desert. The wind blows opposite to the sea, and drives back the waves. Also the ship is pressed forward and crosses the bar quickly.'

'Then we must all hope for a travado.'

Benjamin appeared to hesitate, then asked, 'Once we are out to sea, who will show us the way, who will navigate the ship? You said you were not a ship's captain, but now you are sounding like one.'

Hector found himself saying nervously, 'I've never navigated a ship before. But I think I can learn.'

ℂ

WITH THE RIVER CURRENT sweeping her along, *L'Arc-de-Ciel* took less than a week to reach the bar at St Louis. Hector spent much of the time studying the dead captain's sea charts and trying to understand his navigation instruments. The main item was a mystifying device as long as his arm and carefully stored in a cherrywood box. Its open frame supported two wooden arcs engraved with degrees of angle. Three small vanes were attached to each of the arcs, and he found he could slide the vanes back and forth. One of them was fitted with a lens. Puzzled, he took the instrument on deck and tried to use it. But it defied logic. He held the instrument up to his eye and tried looking through the lens. Then he slid the vanes to different positions. The angles they recorded made no sense. He turned the device around, and tried looking through it the other way. Still nothing worked. Bourdon strolled over to see what he was doing, and commented that he had seen an architect using something similar when he had visited the building work at Versailles. 'It's for measuring angles,' he commented. 'I know that already,' snapped Hector, increasingly frustrated. 'If I could use it to find the angle of the sun or of the north star, then it would be better than the astrolabe I learned to use among the Turks. There's a book of tables among the captain's possessions which gives the height of the sun or the star at different locations at different times of the year. With that knowledge I might even be able to take us to the Caribees.'

The Frenchman tactfully withdrew, leaving Hector to wrestle with his problem. Unexpectedly Benjamin provided the solution. He had seen the captain of a visiting ship use a similar gadget. Benjamin had thought the captain was touched in the head, for he had held the instrument to his eye in broad daylight and when facing out to the open sea. There was nothing on the horizon to look at. 'You must be wrong, I'm sure he was measuring the angle of the sun,' Hector growled. He was really irritated now.

'No,' the Laptot insisted. 'He was looking out to sea. The sun was behind him.'

To save his dignity, Hector waited until Benjamin had walked away before, still doubtful, he turned his back to the sun, peered through the lens, and fiddled with the vanes. By chance he saw the shadow of a vane pass into vision and across a graded arc. He lifted the instrument until it was level with the horizon and adjusted the vanes again. He placed the vane's shadow steadily on the arc, then brought the instrument down and took the reading. It was in the range of numbers in the captain's book of tables. He had discovered how to bring the ship to her destination.

They stopped only once on the river voyage, a brief halt at a friendly village to take fresh supplies and top up their water barrels. Then they dropped downriver until they began to feel the rise and fall of the tide, and Benjamin warned that the Residence of St Louis lay just ahead. 'We must stay close to the left-hand shore. The guns of the Residence do not reach that far. A few ships will be anchored in the roadstead, maybe a man of war also, but we can slip past them if the wind favours us.' He pointed to the north. A small dark cloud could be seen, far in the distance. 'I think we are lucky with the weather.'

As the day wore on, banks of thick, dark cloud formed on the horizon and began to coalesce into a solid black mass. From the underbelly of the clouds flickered distant flashes of lightning. Along the river there was an atmosphere of foreboding. The breeze dropped away and was replaced by an oppressive calm. The air seemed to thicken and become slightly opaque. It was difficult to breathe. The sloop glided on, her sails slack, carried only by the current. Hector listened carefully. There was a faint roaring sound far away. 'What's that noise?' he asked Benjamin. 'That's the sound of the waves breaking on the bar. Let us hope that the travado reaches us before we are in the overfalls, and that the ship survives the wind.'

Half an hour later the storm broke. There was a tremendous thunderclap and a great gust of wind swept across the river, driving spray from the surface. The squall struck the sloop like a fist. With a loud clap of canvas, the mainsail bellied out, and the sloop heeled over. Hector heard the groan of the stays under the sudden strain. *L'Arc-de-Ciel* surged forward as Dan and Benjamin struggled to control her helm.

A peal of thunder close at hand, and suddenly the horizon was blotted out by torrential rain which reduced visibility to a few paces. Hector's clothes were saturated in an instant. He remembered the long parched days in the desert and tilted back his head in sheer delight. He opened his mouth and let the rain pour in. When he swallowed, he could taste the faint grains of dust which the travado had brought from the interior. Benjamin appeared at his side, gripping him by the elbow. 'Go help Dan at the helm,' he shouted. 'I will show which way to steer.'

When Hector reached the wheel, Benjamin was already standing in the bow, peering into the murk. He raised his arm and pointed away to starboard. Obediently they steered to his instructions. Now the rain was hissing down, ochre rain on a brown river, and it was impossible to tell where the air and water met. More thunder, a massive growl which seemed to shake the sloop. A tremendous crack of lightning split the gloom.

Moments later the sloop was bucking and lurching as she was caught in the overfalls. Out of the murk raced a continuous onslaught of breaking waves. A lightning flash close at hand lit their foaming crests and turned them blinding white. *L'Arc-de-Ciel* surged on, the wind driving her forward. Benjamin gestured again, urgently this time, and Dan and Hector spun the wheel to bring the ship on her new course. There was no pattern to the waves breaking on the bar. They came from different directions, now smashing into her bow so she was tossed backwards, now heaving up along her sides so that she slewed sideways.

They never glimpsed St Louis. For two hours they battled with the overfalls, trusting to Benjamin's directions, ploughing onward until they were sure that the turbulence was easing.

Then the little ship ceased her wild gyrations and, though she still pitched and rolled uncomfortably, there was no mistaking that she was sailing on smoother water.

By nightfall the rain had ceased. The sky was still overcast so it was impossible to tell when the sun set, but the wind had eased to a moderate breeze and the air felt washed and clean. Benjamin came back from his lookout in the bow, and announced that they had cleared the bar and passed through the anchorage as well. They were in open water. Hector went down to the cabin and brought up the ship's compass and set it down beside the helm. 'Steer west,' he said to Dan. 'Tomorrow I will check the charts and set course for the Americas.' He looked up at the sky. As swiftly as it had arrived, the travado had swept onward and out to sea. The first stars were showing through rents in the clouds. He thought he recognised the constellation of Orion. Now he would use its stars to find his way across the ocean. He gave a slight shiver of apprehension. There was so much to learn, and it was so easy to make mistakes. He thought back to Ibrahim, his corpse lying on the sand and the crusted blood of the wounds where the Labdessah had speared him to death, because he had followed Hector's plan to ambush the Tooarick. And he recalled his last glimpse of Karp, the glint of the scimitar as it descended in a killing stroke. Poor mutilated Karp had believed in peace and forgiveness to the end, refusing to resort to violence even as he found a way to save his friends. Despondently Hector wondered if Dan and Jacques had been wise to place their trust in him. Too often he seemed to bring death and suffering upon his comrades.

His sense of gloom deepened as he allowed himself to recall his final meeting with Elizabeth, only to find that the details of that heart-rending encounter were already blurred. It seemed that the ordeal of the long trek across the desert had not only separated him from her physically, but was part of a great void that was growing wider and wider. In a moment of unhappy clarity he knew that, although he might return one day to trace what had happened to his mother, he would never see or hear from Elizabeth again.

Then he heard someone singing under his breath. It was Bourdon somewhere in the shadows. Hector could not distinguish the words of the song but it sounded like a Paris street ballad. Clearly Jacques was in good spirits and looking forward to reaching the Americas. At the helm there was a slight movement as Dan adjusted the wheel to hold the little sloop on her westward course. The Miskito appeared untroubled by the violent and sudden changes of fortune of recent days. Hector found himself taking comfort from his friend's composure. 'What's it like there, out in the Caribees?' he asked quietly. There followed such a long silence that Hector thought Dan had not heard his question. Then the Miskito's voice answered, 'There are places more beautiful than anything you could dream, sea as clear as glass, sand so fine and white that it looks and feels like flour, wreaths of mist hanging over jungle-covered hills.' There was another long pause. 'The people who live there are no different from those we have already known. Some are honest. Others are rogues and cheats. A number are men who have known hardship and are seeking a fresh beginning. They are like ourselves. When you have brought us across the ocean and I have visited my people, maybe we should try to join them.'

HISTORICAL NOTE

In 1631 a particularly brazen Barbary corsair was operating from Sallee on the Atlantic coast of Morocco. A sea captain from Flanders, he had 'turned Turk' and taken the name Murat Reis. That year, with two ships, he made a surprise raid on the Irish coastal village of Baltimore and successfully kidnapped almost the entire population: 107 men, women and children. He then took them back to North Africa to sell. A French missionary priest working in Algiers saw several of Murat's Irish victims put up for auction. After that, very little more was heard of them.

Slavery in various guises was flourishing on all sides of the Mediterranean throughout the seventeenth century. The Regencies of Tunis, Algiers and Tripoli were infamous in the Christian world as places where the unfortunate captives were either set to work or held for ransom. Yet there were also thriving slave markets in Malta and Livorno where Muslims – and sometimes non-Muslim as well – were bought and sold. The Knights of St John of Malta were at the forefront of the trade in much the same way that the corsair guilds in the Regencies, the taifas, were the chief providers of human merchandise in North Africa. By the same token, it was virtual slavery to be condemned to the oar in France's Royal Galley fleet, one of Louis XIV's pet projects. On the Sun King's galleys, French convicts sat alongside Turkish prisoners of war as well as Iroquois Indians captured in North America. The Turks could hope to be freed in a prisoner exchange, but many of the French galeriens died in chains while the unfortunate Indians mostly perished from fevers and malnutrition.

The turbulence of politics in the Mediterranean encouraged this state of affairs to continue. Against the general background of the

Eternal War between Cross and Crescent, the various European nations were competing with one another for commercial and territorial advantage. France was suspicious of Spain; the Spaniards mistrusted the Portuguese; the English, Dutch and other Protestant nations jostled with one another even as they warily dealt with the Catholic powers. Everyone was nervous of the Turkish Sultan in Constantinople. Amid such disarray the Barbary corsairs thrived. A shipping list for the period between 1677 and 1680 (roughly the time of Hector's and Dan's fictional adventures) shows that the Algerines captured no less than 160 British ships. This would have provided approximately 8,000 British captives for the slave pens of that Regency.

This was also a time when the nature of naval warfare in the Mediterranean was altering. Oared vessels, the preferred warships since the days of ancient Greece, were obsolete. Too expensive to build, their huge crews were too costly to maintain, and their hulls and rig insufficiently seaworthy. Above all, they could not carry the numbers of heavy cannon which gave their rivals, the sailing ships, such devastating firepower. Nevertheless the flamboyant galley with its colourful pennants and massed ranks of half-naked oarsmen remained a potent symbol, much loved by contemporary painters and illustrators, many of them Dutch. They often depicted imaginary battle scenes between galleys and sailing ships. These same artists also found the Barbary city states, particularly Algiers, to be a worthy subject, basing their images on the reports of the embassies to the Regencies as well as the harrowing tales told by returned captives. There were many such memoirs by the 'white slaves' from Barbary though, by contrast, hardly any of the galley slaves of Christendom wrote about their experiences. An exception is the account written by a Frenchman, Jean Marteilhe, a Protestant condemned to the oar in 1701. He joined his first galley at Dunkirk on the Channel coast and describes the extraordinary pantomime – hiding under the oar benches, kicking their legs in the air, holding up their hands, coughing, bowing, and so forth – which he and his shipmates had to perform for the amusement of their captain's guests on board.

Unlikely though they may seem, several of the characters mentioned in the preceding pages were real: the reverend Devereux

Historical Note

Spratt, Rector of Mitchelstown in North Cork, had been a slave in Algiers. Samuel Martin was the English consul in Algiers between the years 1673 and 1679, while Jean Baptiste Brodart, the Intendant of the Royal Galley base at Marseilles, was renowned for his venality. Joseph Maimaran, a Moroccan Jew, acted as chief financial adviser to the megalomaniac Emperor Moulay Ismail and served for many years as virtually his first minister as well as chief money lender. Unwisely Maimaran asked for repayment of a loan, and paid for his lese-majesty with his life. He was knocked down and trampled to death in the street by a loose horse belonging to a member of the Black Guard. The death looked like an accident but contemporary opinion held it was an assassination ordered by Moulay. The Emperor himself ruled until 1727, dying in his eighty-first year, and he did have an Irish gun founder who was overfond of the bottle. What happened to his monstrous favourite wife, Zidana, is not known. Famously, Moulay is reputed to have sired 888 children — 548 sons and 340 daughters — during his lifetime.

Buccaneer

C

Read on for an exclusive extract from Hector Lynch's
next adventure . . .

Published by Macmillan in March 2008

ONE

℃

HECTOR LYNCH leaned back and braced himself against the
sloop's mast. It was hard to hold the little telescope steady
against the rhythmic rolling of the Caribbean swells, and the
image in the lens was blurred and wavering. He was trying to
identify the flag at the stern of a vessel which had appeared on
the horizon at first light and was now some three miles to windward. But the wind was blowing the stranger's flag sideways,
directly towards him, so that it was difficult to see against the
bright sunshine sparkling off the waves on a late-December
morning. Hector thought he saw a flicker of blue and white and
some sort of cross, but he could not be sure.

'What do you make of her?' he asked Dan, offering the
spyglass to his companion. He had first met Dan on the Barbary
coast two years earlier when both had been incarcerated in the
slave barracks of Algiers, and Hector had developed a profound
respect for Dan's common sense. The two men were much the
same age – Hector was a few months short of his twentieth
birthday – and they had formed a close friendship.

'No way of telling.' said Dan, ignoring the telescope. A
Miskito Indian from the coast of Central America, like many
of his countrymen he had remarkably keen eyesight. 'She has
the legs of us. She could be French or English, or maybe from

the English colonies to the north. We're too far from the Main for her to be a Spaniard. Perhaps Benjamin can say.'

Hector turned to the third member of their small crew. Benjamin was a Laptot, a freed black slave who had worked in the ports of the West African coast before volunteering to join their vessel for the voyage across the Atlantic and into the Caribbean.

'Any suggestions?' he asked.

Benjamin only shook his head. Hector was unsure what to do. His companions had chosen him to command their little vessel, but this was his first major ocean voyage. Two months ago they had acquired their ship when they had found her stranded halfway up a West African river, her captain and officers dead of fever, and manned only by Benjamin and another Laptot. According to the ship's papers she was *L'Arc-de-Ciel*, registered in La Rochelle, and the broad empty shelves lining her hold indicated that she was a small slave ship which had not yet taken on her human cargo.

Hector wiped the telescope's lens with a strip of clean cotton rag torn from his shirt, and was about to take another look at the stranger's flag when there was the sound of a cannon shot. The noise carried clearly downwind, and he saw a black puff of gun smoke from the sloop's deck.

'That's to attract our attention. They want to talk with us,' said Benjamin.

Hector stared again at the sloop. It was obvious that she was closing rapidly, and he could see some sort of activity on her stern deck. A small group of men had clustered there.

'We should show them a flag,' Benjamin suggested.

Hector hurried down to the dead captain's cabin. He knew there was a canvas bag tucked away discreetly in a locker behind the bunk. Hector pulled open the bag and tipped out its contents on the cabin floor. There were some items of dirty linen and, beneath them, several large rectangles of coloured cloth. One had a red cross stitched on a white ground which he recognised as the flag flown by the English ships that had occasionally visited the little Irish fishing port where he had spent his summers as a child. Another was a blue flag with a white cross. In the centre of the cross was a shield bearing three golden fleur-de-lys. That flag too he recognised. It had flown on the merchant ships of France when he and Dan had been prisoner-oarsmen at the royal galley base in Marseilles. The third flag he did not know. It also displayed a red cross on a white background, but this time the arms of the cross ran diagonally to each corner of the flag, and the edges of the arms of the cross were deliberately ragged. They looked like branches cut from a shrub after the shoots had been trimmed away. It seemed that the deceased captain of *L'Arc-de-Ciel* had been prepared to fly whichever nation's flag suited the occasion.

Hector returned on deck, all three flags under his arm in an untidy bundle. 'Well, which one is it to be?' he asked. Again he glanced across at the unknown vessel. In the short interval he had been below decks it had come much closer. Well within cannon shot.

'Why not try King Louis's rag?' proposed Jacques Bourdon. In his mid-thirties Jacques was an ex-galerien, a thief condemned to the oar for life by a French court and he had GAL branded on his cheek to prove it. He, together with the second Laptot, completed their five-man crew. 'That way our colours will agree with our ship's papers,' he added, shading his eyes to scrutinise the approaching sloop. 'Besides . . . if you look there, she's flying the French flag as well.'

Hector and his companions waited for the stranger to come closer. They could see someone at her rail waving his arms. He was pointing at their sails and gesturing that they should be lowered. Too late, Hector felt a prickle of suspicion.

'Dan,' he asked quietly, 'any chance that we can get away from her?'

353

'No chance at all,' Dan answered without hesitation. 'She's a ketch and carries more sail than us. Best heave to and see what they want.'

A moment later Bourdon was helping the two Laptots loose the sheets and lower the sails so that *L'Arc-de-Ciel* gradually slowed to a halt, and lay gently rocking on the sea.

The approaching ketch altered course to come alongside. There were eight cannon on her single deck. Then, without warning, the little group on her stern deck parted to reveal someone hauling briskly on a halyard. A ball of cloth was being pulled aloft. A puff of wind caught it and the folds of cloth shook out, revealing a new flag. It carried no marks, but was a plain red sheet.

Jacques Bourdon swore. 'Shit! The *jolie rouge*. We should have guessed.'

Startled, Hector looked at him. 'The *jolie rouge*,' Bourdon grunted. 'The flag of the *flibustiers*, how do you call them – privateers? It's their mark. I shared a Paris prison cell with one of them, and a right stinking bastard he was. Smelled worse than the rest of us gaolbirds put together. When I complained, he told me that in the Caribbees he had once gone two years without a proper wash. Claimed to have dressed in a suit of untreated cattle skins.'

'You mean he was a buccaneer,' Dan corrected him. The Miskito seemed unworried by the sight of the red flag.

'Are they dangerous?' Hector wanted to know.

'Depends what sort of mood they're in,' replied Dan quietly. 'They'll be interested in our cargo, if there's anything they can steal and sell. They'll not harm us if we cooperate.'

There was a clatter and slap of canvas as the strangers' vessel came up into the wind. Her helmsman must have carried out the manoeuvre many times and was obviously an expert, for he deftly laid the ketch alongside the smaller *L'Arc-de-Ciel*. Hector counted at least forty men aboard, a uncouth assembly of all ages and shapes, most of them heavily bearded and deeply tanned. Many were bare chested and wore only loose cotton drawers. But others had chosen a ragbag of clothes ranging from soiled lawn shirts and canvas breeches to seamen's smocks and broadcloth coats with wide skirts and braided cuffs. A few, like Jacques's former cellmate, were dressed in jerkins and leggings of untanned cattle skin. Those who were not bareheaded displayed an equally wide range of hats. There were brightly coloured head cloths, sailors' bonnets, tricornes, leather skull caps, and broad-brimmed hats of a vaguely military style. One man was even sporting a fur hat, despite the blazing heat. A few hefted long muskets which, Hector was relieved to observe, were not being pointed at *L'Arc-de-Ciel*, nor were the deck guns manned. Dan had been right: the buccaneers were not unduly aggressive towards a ship's crew that obeyed their instructions. For the present the mob of ill-assorted strangers were doing no more than lining the rail of their vessel and appraising *L'Arc-de-Ciel*.

The slightest thump as the hulls of the two vessels touched, and a moment later half a dozen of the buccaneers dropped down on *L'Arc-de-Ciel*'s deck. Two of them carried wide-mouthed blunderbusses. The last man to come aboard seemed to be their leader. Of middle age, he was short and plump, his close-cropped reddish hair turning grey, and he was dressed more formally than the others in buff-coloured breeches and stockings, with a purple waistcoat worn over a grubby white shirt. Unlike his fellows, who preferred knives and cutlasses, he had a rapier hanging from a shabby baldrick. He was also the only boarder wearing shoes. The heels clumped on the wooden deck as he strode purposefully to where Dan and Hector were standing. 'Summon your captain,' he announced. 'Tell him that Captain John Coxon wishes to speak with him.'

Closer up, Captain Coxon's face, which at first sight had seemed chubby and genial, had a hard set to it. He bit off his words when he spoke and the corners of his mouth turned down, producing a slight sneer. Hector judged that Captain Coxon was not a man to be trifled with.

'I am acting as the captain,' he replied.

Coxon glanced at the young man in surprise. 'What happened to your predecessor?' he demanded bluntly.

'I believe he died of fever.'

'When and where was that?'

'About three months ago, maybe more. On the River Wadnil, in West Africa.'

'I know where the Wadnil is,' Coxon snapped irritably. 'Have you any proof, and who brought this ship across? Who's your navigator?'

'I did the navigating,' Hector answered quietly.

Again the look of surprise, followed by a disbelieving twist of the mouth.

'I need to see your ship's papers.'

'They're in the captain's cabin.'

Coxon nodded to one of his men, who promptly disappeared below deck. As he waited, the captain slipped his hand inside his shirt front and scratched at his chest. He seemed to be suffering from some sort of skin irritation. Hector noticed several angry red blotches on the buccanneer captain's neck, just above the shirt collar. Coxon gazed around at *L'Arc-de-Ciel* and her depleted crew. 'Is this all your men?' he demanded. 'What happened to the others?'

'There are no others,' Hector replied. 'We had to sail shorthanded, just the five of us. It was enough. The weather was kind.'

Coxon's man came out from the cabin door. He has holding a sheaf of documents and the roll of charts that Hector had found aboard when he, Dan and Bourdon had first set foot on *L'Arc-de-Ciel*. Coxon took the papers and stood silently for a few moments as he read through them while absent-mindedly he scratched the back of his neck. Abruptly he looked up at

Hector, then thrust one of the charts towards him. 'If you're a navigator, then tell me where we are.'

Hector looked down at the chart. It was poorly drawn, and its scale was inadequate. The entire Caribbean was shown on a single sheet and there were several gaps or smudges on the surrounding coastline. He placed his finger about two-thirds across the parchment, and said, 'About here. At noon yesterday I calculated our latitude by backstaff, but I am unsure of our westing. Twelve days ago we saw a high island to the north of us, which I took to be one of the windward Caribbees. Since then we could have run perhaps a thousand miles.'

Coxon stared at him bleakly. 'And why would you want to go due west?'

'To try to reach the Miskito coast. That is where we are headed. Dan here is from that country, and wishes to get home.'

The buccaneer captain, after a brief glance towards Dan, looked thoughtful. 'What about your cargo?'

'There is no cargo. We came aboard the ship before she had loaded.'

Coxon gave another jerk of his head, and two of his crew opened up a hatch and clambered down into the hold. Moments later they reappeared and one of them said, 'Nothing. She's empty.'

Hector sensed the captain's disappointment. Coxon's mood was changing. He was becoming annoyed. Abruptly he took a step towards Jacques Bourdon, who was loitering near the mast. 'You there with the brand on your cheek!' Coxon snapped. 'You've been in the king's galleys, haven't you? What was your crime?'

'Being caught,' Jacques replied sourly.

'You're French, aren't you?' A ghost of a smile passed across Coxon's face.

'From Paris.'

Coxon turned back towards Hector and Dan. He still had the sheaf of papers in his hand.

'I'm seizing this ship,' he announced. 'On suspicion that the vessel has been stolen from her rightful owners, and that the crew has murdered her captain and officers.'

'That's absurd,' Hector burst out. 'The captain and his officers were all dead by the time we came aboard.'

'You have nothing to prove it. No certificate of death, no documents for transfer of ownership.' It was evident that Coxon was grimly satisfied with himself.

'How could we have obtained such papers?' Hector was getting more angry by the minute. 'The bodies would have been put overboard to try to stop the contagion, and there were no authorities to go to. As I said, the vessel was half way up an African river, and there were only native chiefs in the region.'

'Then you should have stopped at the first trading post on the coast, sought out the authorities and registered the events,' countered Coxon. 'Instead you set sail directly across to the Caribbees. It is my duty to regularise the matter.'

'You have no authority to take this ship,' Hector insisted.

Coxon treated him to a thin smile. 'Yes, I do. I have the authority of the Governor of Petit Guave, whose commission I carry on behalf of the kingdom of France. This vessel is French. There is a branded convict aboard, a subject of the French king. The ship's papers are not in order, and there is no proof of how the captain died. He could have been killed and the cargo sold off.'

'So what do you intend to do?' Hector asked, choking down his anger. He should have realised from the start that Coxon had been trying to find an excuse to seize the vessel. Coxon and his men were nothing more than licensed sea brigands.

'This vessel and those found on her will be taken to Petit Guave by a prize crew. There the vessel will be sold and you and your crew will be tried for murder and piracy. If found guilty the court will decide your punishment.'

Unexpectedly, Dan spoke up, his voice grave. 'If you or

your court mistreat us, you will have to answer to my people. My father is one of the old men's council of the Miskito.'

Dan's words seemed to have carried some weight because Coxon paused for a moment before replying. 'If it is true that your father is of the Miskito council then the court will take that into account. The authorities in Petit Guave would not wish to anger the Miskito. As for the rest of you, you will stand trial.'

Coxon again slipped his hand inside his shirt front and scratched at his chest. Hector wondered if the itching was what made the man so irritable. 'I need to know your name,' the buccaneer said to Hector.

'My name is Hector Lynch.' The hand stopped scratching. Then Coxon said slowly, 'Any relation to Sir Thomas Lynch?'

There was a wariness in the man's tone. His question hung in the air. Hector had no idea who Sir Thomas Lynch was, but clearly he was someone well known to Coxon. Hector also had the distinct impression that Sir Thomas Lynch was a person whom the captain respected, perhaps even feared. Alert to the subtle change in the buccaneer's manner, Hector seized the opportunity.

'Sir Thomas Lynch is my uncle,' he said unblushingly. Then, to increase the effect of the lie he added, 'It was why I agreed with my companions that we sail for the Caribbean without delay. After we had brought Dan to the Miskito coast, I intended to find Sir Thomas.'

For an alarming moment Hector thought that he had gone too far, that he should have kept the lie simple. Coxon was eyeing him narrowly. 'Sir Thomas is not in the Caribbees at this time. His estates are being managed by his family. You didn't know?'

Hector recovered himself. 'I was in Africa for some months and out of touch. I received little news from home.'

Coxon pursed his lips as he thought over Hector's statement. Whatever Sir Thomas Lynch meant to the buccaneer, the young man could see that it was enough to make their captor reconsider his plans.

'Then I will make sure that you are united with your family,' the buccaneer said at last. 'Your companions will stay aboard this ship while she is taken to Petit Guave, and I will send a note to the authorities there that they are associates of Sir Thomas's nephew. It may stand in their favour. Meanwhile you can accompany me to Jamaica – I was already on my way there.'

Hector's mind raced as he searched Coxon's statement for clues as to the identity of his supposed uncle. Sir Thomas Lynch had estates on Jamaica, therefore he must be a man of substance. It was reasonable to guess that he was a wealthy planter, a man who had friends in government. The opulence and political power of the West Indian plantation owners was well known. Yet at the same time Hector sensed something disquieting in Coxon's manner. There was a hint that whatever the buccaneer captain was proposing was not entirely to Hector's advantage.

Belatedly it occurred to Hector that he should put in a good word for the Laptots, who had proved their worth on the trans-Atlantic voyage.

'If anyone is to be put on trial in Petit Guave, Captain,' he told Coxon, 'it should not be either Benjamin here, nor his companion. They stayed with the ship even when their previous captain had died of fever. They are loyal men.'

Coxon had resumed his scratching. He was raking the back of his neck with his nails. 'Mr Lynch, you need have no worries on that score,' he said. 'They will never be put on trial.'

'What will happen to them?'

Coxon brought his hand away from his collar, inspected the fingernails for traces of whatever had been causing the irritation, and wriggled his shoulder slightly to relieve the pressure of the shirt on his skin.

'As soon as they are brought to Petit Guave, they will be sold. You say they are loyal. That should make them excellent slaves.'

He looked straight at Hector as if to challenge the young man into raising an objection. 'I believe your uncle employs more than sixty Africans on his own Jamaican plantations. I am sure he would approve.'

At a loss for words, Hector could only stare back, trying to gauge the buccaneer's temper. What he saw discouraged hope. Captain Coxon's eyes reminded him of a reptile. They protruded slightly and the expression in them was utterly pitiless. Despite the balmy sunshine, Hector felt a chill seeping deep within him. He must not allow himself to be deceived by the pleasantness of his surroundings, with the warm tropical breeze ruffling the brilliant sea and the soft murmuring sound of the two ships gently moving against one another, hull to hull. He and his companions had arrived where self-interest was sustained by cruelty and violence.

Visit **www.panmacmillan.com** to read more about all our books and to buy them. You will also find features, author interviews and news of any author events, and you can sign up for e-newsletters so that you're always first to hear about our new releases.

www.panmacmillan.com

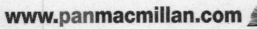

GIFT SELECTOR
YOUR ACCOUNT
WISH LIST
WAITING LIST

| HOME | ABOUT US | IMPRINTS | TRADE/MEDIA | CONTACT US | ADVANCED SEARCH | SEARCH | GO |

| BOOK CATEGORIES | WHAT'S NEW | AUTHORS/ILLUSTRATORS | BESTSELLERS | READING GROUPS |

Coming Soon...

Reading Groups

Competitions
Feeling Lucky?

Extracts
Sneak Previews

Interviews

Events
Meet Our Stars

Reviews
What The Critics Say

News & Awards

Editor's Choice
What We're Reading